Universe of One,
A Love Story

Universe of One,
A Love Story

J. R. Johnson

For my true love:
Carla

CHAPTER 1

Book of Revelations

*"Sometimes truth is stranger than fiction.
And that's a fact! I'm not being facetious!"*

ROBERT CLARENCE HENRY

I can't breathe!" she screamed.

With my wife as copilot, I'd just taken off in a private plane from Miami, Florida. The sun turned black. Darkness was on the face of the deep. A tempestuous beast raged across a dark and stormy sky. I accelerated quickly to avoid the mass of demonic thunderclouds. But the clouds' gaping jaws swallowed the sleek craft completely. Wind screeched, rain pelted, lightning half-blinded me. I climbed upward, hoping to exit into clear sky. My compass whirled counterclockwise. Navigation equipment stopped working! Bitter black smoke assaulted my nostrils. I remember squirming, choking, then blackness. I woke up in a Nassau, Bahamas hospital. They said, "Your wife is dead!"

I skipped breakfast and set out on a much-needed Roman holiday, wanting desperately to forget the horror of that nightmarish series of events. Unfortunately, I couldn't wash the obscenity off

1

myself. The scent of shame over killing my wife lingered like a musky cologne.

It was a spring sunrise at its most superb; budding twigs delightfully attempted to catch the breezy air. Portions of the street I strolled were still veiled in dawn's semidarkness. Suddenly, out of the early morning shadows, a child emerged without warning, like some spirit of the dark. As I walked toward Vatican City, he came running after me, shouting in Italian-accented English.

"Hey, mister! Wanna know the Secret of the Ages? It's right here in this black book. Probably worth millions! But what's the use of pretending? Money—I need it like a drowning man needs air! So Matteo will let you have it for just ten American dollars."

My immediate response was one of mild annoyance at the intrusion. The boy had startled me—he had broken in abruptly upon soothing therapeutic solitude. The truth is, my grieving heart hungered intensely for the nourishment of that mind-liberating silence.

At first I turned stiffly to frown at him. Dressed in navy-blue shorts of old, threadbare cloth, he might've been around nine, although he could've been younger. He seemed bright, brash, and full of the illusions of ignorance and youth. His hair was raven black, had an abundance of dust caked in it, and his skin was ashy for need of a bath. His features seemed tough, almost distorted by hunger and by the draining effects of having to care for himself vastly too early in life.

"Sorry, Matteo. Don't have ten dollars. All I have are these three American twenty-dollar bills."

Matteo's eyes looked puzzled.

"Take it—it's yours!" I said.

Matteo grabbed the money and enthusiastically handed me a black leather-bound book. He quickly placed the three bills into his right rear pants pocket and patted his pocket profusely.

"Thank you! Thank you! It's a gift I'll never forget. You must be super rich."

"Simply enchanted by the incredible little entrepreneur who sold me the book."

"What's your name, mister?"

"Dr. Jekyll."

"Wow! Like the one who turns into a wolf? Bites people when the moon is full?"

"That Dr. Jekyll's fictional. I'm Benjamin Franklin Jekyll, a psychiatrist who helps sad people become happy."

"You any good at it?"

"Never discuss myself."

"Why?"

"Think of it: you're bound to lose. If you belittle yourself, you're believed; if you praise yourself, you're not."

"I'm not gonna discuss myself either! Well, thanks for the money Doctor J. And don't bite anybody while you're here in Rome. Just kidding!" Matteo turned and sped off as fast as he'd appeared— leaping joyously and yelling, "Strawberry gelato!"

In one of those moments that seems eternal, my tiny endowment to the frail, vulnerable child caused me to feel a warm glow and strangely peaceful.

Gazing off at bare-breasted marble nymphs relaxing in a sunlit fountain, I continued along the picturesque boulevard. I stopped in at a charming eatery full of women with lonely eyes and faces like lost battles; I sat in a cozy booth. I entered a timeless realm of dark mahogany, richly upholstered booths, and engaging paintings amid flickering candlelight. Suave waiters with handsome accents described entrées with unforgettable flair. After a few sips of espresso, I ordered a humble risotto that they masterfully elevated into a dish of depth and distinction.

I glanced over at a lovely smiling woman sitting in the booth adjacent to mine; I returned her smile. Her smile widened.

She got up from her booth and seated herself next to me. I gave her a half-startled look. As we exchanged pleasantries, she slightly parted her legs, took my hand, and slid it between her soft, warm thighs. "Look what I have for you," she said in a low, breathless voice. A slow sly smile started to build as her tongue darted out, licking her lips.

I looked at her, stunned. What was happening to me seemed impossible, but it was happening. Within seconds my mouth became moist, I developed rushed breathing, and I experienced a tantalizing stir and tingle that brought shivering pleasure. Stammering in a weakened voice, I said, "I—I'm sorry. I can't do this! My wife just…she just passed away…recently."

My tantalizing companion turned to me and smirked. "Sure, handsome." She pushed away my previously stiff, turgid—now limp—member and said, "It's dead anyway." *Ms. Tantalizing* picked up her stylish handbag, marched over to the restaurant's entrance, looked back at me a moment in silence before storming out.

Filled with an enormous amount of self-conscious discomfort, I slumped down in my booth. Hiding my intense embarrassment behind the book and a fake smile, I placed my newly acquired treasure on the table under a petite chandelier that threw bubbles of white light on the pages, and I began to read.

Barely more than five minutes later, the flush that crept across my cheeks dissipated, and I became totally mesmerized. I felt a sense of exhilarating release as if I'd been let out of a dark cave I hadn't known I was in. I started to feel again the sense of belonging and purpose I thought I'd forfeited. This book penetrated my being and spoke to me, giving me instructions for living.

I used to marvel at things like humpback whales composing ever-changing songs. But this! This enthralling black gem made me realize humankind is not at the pinnacle of knowledge. We're just experiencing the tip of a boundless iceberg.

I got back here to New York as quickly as possible. I just couldn't wait to share the astonishing mysteries embedded within my captivating black prize with my precious little girl.

Sweetheart, I know your career hasn't progressed as you'd hoped. You've just been dumped by another one of those philandering sleazebags. Now you're being forced to contend with the aftermath of the plane crash. Your mother, with whom you'd just had that explosive dispute about your choice in men—killed. Just keep in mind, princess, that in spite of any spats, your mother loved you intensely.

Your mother and I would've given anything to restore the gift of sight that Leber's disease robbed you of at birth. I can't imagine what it must be like to live in constant darkness. I so wish you could see what a beautiful young woman you've developed into. Actually, you should take some time off from that unpleasant job you're stuck in; go away to someplace warm. Give yourself a chance to rethink your career, find true love—turn your life around!

I'm going to reveal something I might regret! I went through your mother's closet, looking for a tasteful dress to bury her in. There was a jet-black box hidden under a load of stuff. What I discovered inside left a bruise so deep I feel it in my soul. Maybe someday I'll tell you more about it; maybe I won't. Truth is, the pain's now too great—too raw. That's where this book fits in. Its secrets will unburden your spirit, stretch your mind, unlock your potential. In short, it will open the way to infinite possibilities.

I want you to pay close attention to every word of this extraordinary tale. For this love story is no story but truth, translucent as an insightful thought suddenly whispered aloud. Hiding in plain sight among the events are secrets capable of unlocking the door to all you've ever dreamed about. Sounds incredible? You be the judge. Decide for yourself! You need only possess the will to re-member who you genuinely are in order to live your dreams and see the brightness of a new page of your life where everything yet can happen.

But forgive my *faux pas*. I've gotten ahead of myself; even un-conventional love tales that are peppered with life-altering truths have a beginning. So let us start there.

CHAPTER 2

Thirteen Coins and Lillies

Father Jason Xavier Roberts, an ordained priest, was one of those rare individuals who had just about everything—or so it seemed to all who knew him. He was thirty-nine, six feet three, sturdy, broad shouldered, and athletically built. His hair was rich, dark, somewhat wavy. His sinewy, muscular back, covered with scars. His square-jawed face, just shy of being classically handsome. His eyes, blue, confident, cheery—a paradox for someone who'd witnessed and experienced countless horrors.

Father Roberts was also brilliant and fluent-thinking—a legal shark whose razor-sharp mind had earned the respect of both adversaries and colleagues. Most mornings Father Roberts stuffed one pocket with dollar bills for any of the homeless who crossed his path, especially the two war-wounded ex-marines who stood in the gutters selling bottled water; one had multiple medals pinned to his ragged olive coat.

Another pocket bulged with a plastic bag of old bagels. Those he fed to a host of strutting pigeons nesting in the small urban park a brief distance from his fashionable Foggy Bottom office in Washington, DC.

Logic isn't very helpful when you're trying to solve the riddle of a rugged, strong-willed male like Jason Xavier Roberts. It was whispered that this man of God seemed much too chummy with notorious womanizer, club owner "Smooth Bobby" O'Brian, and the grandmother of small-time hood, suspected murderer "Sukie" Tyler Jones.

Rumor even had it that Father Roberts had purchased Mrs. Jones a spectacular home in exclusive Chevy Chase, Maryland. Other morsels the gossip mill ground unrelentingly were that he exhibited a bit of rudeness, a tendency toward salty language, and great fondness for the opposite sex.

In his pre-priesthood days, Jason had been known to have an exceptionally powerful effect on women. His self-assured air, rugged good looks, and captivating charm had drawn women to him like a magnet. Many had eagerly extended him the friendship of their inner thighs. Jason's sensual nature made him a gentle, protective lover who was vulnerable to fragrant perfumes, silky hair, and the warm touch of feminine skin. Soothing, haunting music stirred his soul and set the mood for a wondrous journey of breathless, torrid…well, you know.

During the holidays, he came calling loaded down with magnificent mysterious packages. He'd suggest moonlit swims, picnics in alpine meadows, romantic getaways featuring pounding tropical surf. He liked to see his fiancé in chic attire. He loved to dine with her in fine restaurants where great chefs enchanted patrons with lusty but elegant cuisine and spoke of their bistro's mission in mystical terms. Jason also exhibited calm, sentimental, easygoing ways and kept up a rigorous fitness regimen.

He said, "I intend to forget the past—to live all my remaining days without regret. I like to dwell in the sunlight, swim in the Potomac, and drink the wild air of Rock Creek Park. What's more, I want to find the best darn peanut butter and jelly sandwich ever."

Jason respected women with fire, flair, intelligence. He was the ultimate man's man whose love was simple, plain, and honest. He'd do anything for the woman he loved, except allow her to wear the pants in the relationship.

Life with Jason Xavier Roberts was a warm experience packed with love, except for those rare occasions when greatly provoked. During such times, this sinewy ex-marine exploded in stupendous anger.

Terrorists killed medical missionary Doctor Natalie Roberts, Jason's adoring favorite sibling. Her home and its first-floor clinic had been set ablaze then leveled with dynamite. Doctor Roberts dispensed free medical aid to the needy in Southeast Asia before a campaign of terror ended her life. Her body had been found hanging upside down from the branches of a nearby flowering yellow mai tree. She'd been saturated with a flammable liquid and set on fire.

When he learned of his sister's fate, some force stronger than him compelled Jason to fall to his knees. He was so filled with sorrow he could barely breathe. "What the hell is this world coming to?" He grimaced in pain. Shortly after the shocking incident, Jason abruptly left his thriving law practice to serve in the war.

While stationed in Vietnam, he received a tattered copy of a Washington, DC, police report from his eldest sister, Liz. The attorney general for the District of Columbia, in her impeccable black pants suit, had delivered the report to Liz personally. Liz was a television morning news coanchor, who emerged as a surrogate mother figure to her younger sister and older brother.

Multiple men had proposed to Liz. But jerking away from contact, or even the suggestion of contact, she'd say to them with eyes that appeared cold, dead, flat, "It's complicated! Just want to stay single!" Haunting, overpowering childhood memories left her feeling tainted.

Liz worked as a reporter for various wire services and eventually as a Pentagon correspondent before coming to television. Her station broke the highly disturbing story regarding Jason's beautiful young fiancé.

The police report read in part: "At or about six thirty-five in the morning on Saturday, August 28, local restaurant owner Giuseppe 'Poppa' Martinelli was walking his dog along the Southwest Waterfront. Through the thick morning fog, he saw the body of a young Caucasian female lying near a host of sizable thorny shrubs.

"Mr. Martinelli said, 'I recognized her right away! Seen her plenty of times—once on TV, a couple of times in the newspaper. Numerous times in my own restaurant. She was even there Tuesday. I think she had the eggplant parmigiana with a salad. She told me being a federal prosecutor was her dream job. That she was engaged to be married to a great guy. Also a lawyer, I think. She did seem a bit jittery about their upcoming spring wedding. But I think that's normal. Then she was lying there. Stone still. Gray sweatpants down to her ankles. What a real shame!

"'Seeing something like that knocks your socks off! I reached down—touched her cheek. It was cold. I pulled up her pants to make her decent. Hiked nearly ten blocks before I spotted a police car. You know, Sergeant, had to keep wiping tears from my eyes the entire time I was walking, looking for one of you guys.'

"DC homicide detectives identified the victim as Samantha Brownrigg, an assistant US attorney for the District of Columbia.

"The chief city medical examiner stated, 'The victim's stomach was cut open with a jagged incision running from the bottom of her ribs to her pelvis. Some of the intestines were pulled out. The cause of death was a deep gash in the throat that exposed the vertebrae. The killer placed the victim's one-and-a-half-carat diamond engagement ring and thirteen silver coins at her feet; a torn envelope and a bouquet of thirteen white lilies were found near her head. My autopsy also revealed the slayer removed the uterus and the upper part of the vagina.'

"City detectives arrested, questioned, and are holding in custody gynecologist Doctor Mark de Sade. He said:

"'Sam had a fake little-girl innocence about her that men just ate up. But the bitch was a viper with a slit! She was smart, sexy, ambitious, and probably fucking half of DC.

"'I'm unmarried. Been impotent for years. This damn job! I'm sure a macho guy like you, Detective, probably thinks I've got a great job. Perhaps you may even consider it sexy to be a gynecologist. It's true; I'm in between countless women's legs all day long, every day. Oh, it was a pleasure feast when I was a young intern. But over the years, the job has taken its toll.

"'Well, even though she was engaged, Sam was banging somebody in the DA's office. Got knocked up. She also had huge political ambitions, so she wanted an abortion off the books—one that absolutely couldn't be traced. I accommodated her. In payment, we had this sort of *arrangement*. She had a stupendous appetite for all things sexual. We engaged in vile, disgusting acts both of us immensely enjoyed. These sessions were the only times I could get *relief*. She was one of those rare sick freaks you encounter only a few times during your life.

"'We were a match made in heaven; she just refused to recognize it. Ultimately she decided to end our secret rendezvous and marry her fiancé—some hotshot lawyer turned "soldier boy." I didn't want 'em to end. She mocked me—poured scorn on my attempts at lovemaking!

"'That crackbrain cunt was too damn contemptuous for her own good! Something snapped. I was driven to a frenzy of anger, rage, madness. I knew she liked to run along the river early in the morning. So one day before sunrise, I dressed in old shabby clothes, went down to the Southwest Waterfront...I'm sorry! I—I just can't go on any longer. The problem, put simply, is pastrami. I'm *dying* for a hot pastrami sandwich on rye bread and a pickle!

"'You're glaring at me mighty intensely, Detective! You upset about something?'"

CHAPTER 3

———— ❧ ————

It Was Bloody

At 9:00 a.m. on a radiant autumn morning, a troop plane carrying Jason Roberts roared off the runway in Okinawa en route to Da Nang Air Base in the Republic of Vietnam. When the plane arrived over Da Nang, artillery fire lit up the night. The base was under attack. Barely more than thirty minutes later, the pilot's voice came over the intercom. He sounded frantic. "We're running low on fuel! Don't have enough to get back to Okinawa. I've circled Da Nang as long as I can. I'll try to land this crate in the dark and pray we don't get hit by a shell. Brace yourself—it's gonna be a rough ride!"

Without warning, the massive airliner bucked wildly. It then dropped steeply and suddenly downward, its running lights off. The landing strip was virtually dark. The huge jet bounced several times. Tires screeched. The plane skidded sideways; one of its wings slammed into the control tower. The tower crew watched in shock as the aircraft spun violently off of the runway into the reddish dirt. A terrified young private cried out to Jason, "I've never been in a war before! What should I do, sir?"

"Follow me, hit the chute, and run like hell!"

The emergency exit exploded open. Anxious leathernecks slid down an inflated rubber chute. The rumble of rockets, artillery thundered everywhere! The marines ran in a zigzag pattern over long grass, slick rocks toward what they *hoped* were friendly forces.

Afterward, shivering uncontrollably on the inside but seemingly calm on the outside, Jason turned to the pilot, who had a black patch over one eye. "What's that terrible smell?"

Arms crossed, clenching his jaw the pilot said, "Either it's supper or the toilet."

A few weeks following his fiancé's sadistic murder, Jason Roberts found himself deep in bloody no-holds-barred combat. Lieutenant Roberts stood at the front lines with his platoon. The thermometer sizzled. Flies and mosquitoes bit his face. In front of him, ants scurried about the remains of a guerilla lying, bleeding in the dirt—one he'd killed the day before. A colony of ants also crawled up a hillside over his food rations. Jason brushed them off and ate it anyway—along with some of the stragglers. He washed it down with water he'd retrieved from a nearby spring. It tasted of rock, root, earth, and rain.

The heat and sun glinting off the front sight of his rifle during the day made him heavy eyed. Plus, some jarhead had pissed in the tall grass about a yard behind him. The smell of stale piss, gunpowder, and rotting flesh permeated the stifling air. The comingled stench seemed so thick he could almost taste it.

For endless days there was the ghastly glimmering of guns, the thundering clamor of mortar rounds, the hollow crashing of shells. Noise! Noise! Noise!—till nerves shrieked with pain; eardrums throbbed in agony; despair did violence to the soul. Amazingly, the staggering intensity of the battle never let up.

The air was dense with steaming sweat. Jason stood under a towering shady tree on the outer edge of the sun baked battlefield, absorbed by the rustle of lizards and wolf snakes in the dry grass and thorns.

Suddenly, the scenery erupted into an ambush of merciless fury. The marines were mightily overpowered by a barrage of rockets, grenades, and machine-gun fire. They fought under the shadow of certain death.

A private spotted a Vietcong guerrilla, fired, and wounded him. The guerrilla, mad with pain, rushed at the teenager; he gored him repeatedly with a bayonet! Lieutenant Roberts heard the sickening groans; he shot the guerrilla in the face with a 45 automatic. The gun blast blew off the back of his head, causing it to explode like a balloon full of blood. Jason scrambled to the fallen marine's side. When he arrived, the youth was softly breathing his life away. There was dark blood flowing down his skin as his eyes grew heavy and dim.

Seconds later, blood gushed forth from another youthful marine. Deathly pale, he fell to the ground. "I'm scared, sir. My wife's mighty sick, really needs me. Please don't let me die!" he said in pain and misery. Jason had no power to utter a word—he'd turned pale himself. He caught the young marine up in his arms and tried to stop his wound's gory flow. But blood glittered in the youngling's frightened eyes. While Jason held him, the young warrior's head fell back as a flower does when its stem is broken.

The Earth trembled with the shock of the fighting. A nearby river ran red with blood; bodies could be found rotting up and down its banks. Buzzards could be seen picking at who knew what. Down the rushing river, wild with foam and glitter, floated a dead marine with his guts exposed, half an arm missing. A ghastly torrent of similarly mutilated, decomposing, fish-eaten corpses followed.

Jason turned to his gunnery sergeant, Ian "Iron Mike" Michaels. Iron Mike was late thirties, scarred, gigantic, yet not unattractive.

He had the patience of a firecracker, but through the tough demeanor of this relic radiated an extraordinary human warmth.

"Gunny, I gotta do something about this damn mess, or we're screwed! So you've got the stick."

"Maybe I should be going instead of you, Lieutenant."

"I'll accept death if it comes. Look, Mike. I've got eighteen months experience as a marine. You've got eighteen years. Believe me; these hardheads need you more than they need me. If I don't make it back, you make sure they all get home to their mamas."

"Aye, Aye, sir!

"What the hell are we doin' here in the worst place on Earth, fightin' a war nobody understands, possibly spending our last night alive? Bet you wish you were back in your plush law office right now, Lieutenant, shuffling legal papers and eyeballing the pretty girls."

"That sure sounds good right about now."

"Fucked up, didn't ya?"

Jason gave Mike an annoyed glare, said in a sharp tone, "Wipe your wise-ass mouth, Sergeant! Too much bullshit on your lips."

"I'm a grunt. My job's to hurt people—bust up shit. No disrespect intended, sir. My social graces are still a work in progress," Mike said in a gravelly voice.

Mike turned to his platoon of weary marines. His big eyes darted about. "Listen up, ladies. Lieutenant's got something to say. I know it's difficult to focus tonight. Your minds are probably hazy, your eyes, tired. But pay close attention anyway. I don't want this operation turning into a damn cluster-fuck."

The exhausted young lieutenant's blue eyes grew stern. "Vietcong have their mission. We have ours. He who hits hardest wins. It's how you play this shitty game.

"We're vastly outnumbered. Need to do something to change those odds. So I'm gonna attempt to get inside their stronghold under the cover of darkness. Try a little razzle-dazzle I think just might work. Gunny will babysit till I get back. Now, don't worry about me. I'll be all right. God looks out for infants and idiots.

"In this platoon, when the wolf's at the door, we invite 'em in. Eat him for dinner! Marines hammered—shaped in blood like us—don't give up, don't back down, never fail a mission. And we aren't gonna start tonight!"

"What do I shoot at?" asked a tan, freckled, baby-faced private lying prone in the grass. His hands were bloody from some unknown cause. He lifted them, held them in the wind to dry.

"Any damn thing that moves. If you spot any son of a bitch at all, light 'em up! Blast 'em a new asshole!"

Jason turned to a cocky black lance corporal who was all muscle, sinew, and living gristle. "Let me borrow your firearm, Corporal." He swaggered up beside Jason; his thick-veined ebony hands presented him the superfast automatic rifle.

"She's a good girl, sir. Don't keep her out all night!"

"I'll bring her home soon as the party's over," Jason said, flipping his hair back.

In a choked voice, Iron Mike said, "Take this hunting knife too. Its blade's as sharp as a razor! It was my father's. Gave it to me when I joined the corps."

"Thanks, Mike!"

"Give 'em hell, Lieutenant!" they all shouted, still battle fatigued but laughing and grinning again.

Jason ran, panting hard, his chest heaving like a bellows. Sweating and miserable, his pace slowed; he then jogged endless hot and treacherous miles toward the enemy's camp. His shirt ripped on the branches, green barbs stabbed at his eyes, brambles scratched his ankles. Still, he set one foot in front of another and kept trudging through the vast tangles of thick jungle brush. As a further inconvenience, a profusion of rockets whizzed overhead. The whishing rush arrival of enemy shells burst startlingly behind him, ahead, and in the deep, tangled forest.

Jason ultimately fought his way to the enemy's right flank, along a rain-rutted trail surrounded by trees covered with heavy green moss. Exploding shells thundered all around him in the dense, dark jungle. One came within inches of his right ear. He heard its final rush of splitting air before it hit a massive, deformed plant just yards away. Splintered wood, sap, steel fragments shattered outward and covered Jason from head to toe. "Damn close!" he grumbled; then reached down and gripped hold of the helmet that'd been blown off his head.

Minutes later, Jason turned the corner of a dense grove of trees, and there it stood.

The Vietcong stronghold was scarred by moonlight. The pale, cool rays of the full moon shone down upon trampled mud-and corpse-filled trenches. In the shadowy distance, a young marine was hanging by the neck from a gnarled branch. He was nearly dead when cut down, disemboweled, and his entrails burned in front of him. The sounds of this staggering horror were enough to make the stars weep.

Sick, revolted, Jason took the razor-edged hunting knife from its sheath. His ruggedly handsome face was hard, and a vein pulsed in his forehead. All around lay guerrillas, exhausted, sleeping in the heavy heat. Lieutenant Roberts plunged his blade into a guerilla—saw his tongue extend and his eyes go shocked and vacant.

He proceeded to slit the throat of man after man so skillfully that not one uttered a groan as he died. Their blood spouted and splashed his camouflage fatigues, hands, and face with dark spray.

Suppressing wild anxiety, he stole from one end of the camp to the other, leaving gory dead bodies everywhere.

When he arrived in Vietnam, Jason felt compassion. He was very human. On this distant battlefield, however, Jason was no longer a man but had instead transformed into something strange—something frightening. "It's just"—Jason said, quietly shuddering—"just evil. Horrible! Wars are never moral or uplifting. They're purely sagas of complete obscenity, wickedness. In order to survive 'em, you gotta get a little blood on your hands, and that's the truth!"

Dawn's light streamed through shadowless willowy branches. A sentry detected a glint from Jason's rifle and challenged him. In one quick motion, he hurled his knife into the lookout's neck. The guard tried to scream, but all that came out was a loud gurgle. Red fluid gushed out of his neck as he slumped to the ground, firing wildly. Multiple bullets found their mark!

Lieutenant Roberts woke up in a Vietcong prisoner-of-war compound. In a letter to his sister Liz, he wrote in part:

During the day, intolerable closeness; at night, unendurable itchy moistness. All the floors are rotten. Filth on the floor so thick, we easily slip and fall. The tiny windows are so covered with muck that it's almost impossible to read at any time of the day. An inch of slime on the panes. Drips from the ceiling; foul-smelling drafts everywhere. We are packed like sardines in a can. There's no room to even turn around. The torture is unrelenting. From sunrise to sunset, it's impossible not to behave like animals. There are moments when I hate everybody I come across and look at them as thieves who are robbing me of my sanity with impunity. The most unbearable thing for me is when I myself be-come unjust, vicious, vile; I realize it, I even criticize myself—but I just can't help it.

At sunrise, the first shell resonated thunderously. Endless bullets then streaked across the devastated area separating the battle-hardened leathernecks and the POW complex. The indomitable marines fought with bold, stirring, hair-raising courage.

Jason's platoon attacked with raw power to rescue their wound-ed leader, and Vietcong began falling like blood in a slaugh-terhouse. When the shouting and wailing of the battle ended, countless dead guerrillas lay heaped and scattered amid blood and mud-filled ditches.

Startlingly, a rampaging battle tank came thundering across the field; its treads grabbed savagely into the Earth and threw clods of red dirt and mud into the air behind it. A roaring cannon pointed from its turret like a gigantic steel penis. Terrified guerril-las fled in six directions at once.

At about the same time, a jeep came bouncing around a bend, its mounted machine gun blazing! The driver, Charley "Clam Chowder" Smith, kicked up a small cloud of russet dust as he skid-ded to a stop. Sergeant Smith and his machine gunner scrambled toward the injured lieutenant with their rifles raised, placed him in their muddy four-by-four's rear seat, then sped rapidly back down the reddish-brown dirt road.

They came to a wooded area with trees crowded to the road's edge. Suddenly the marines felt a powerful jolt. The fast-moving vehicle began to bounce dangerously up and down and side to side. There was the sound of screeching tires. Then there was a vio-lent jerk as the sergeant slammed on the brakes. And just in time.

No more than sixty yards ahead, a startling noise ripped through the air: a huge rocket obliterated the road where the trio of warriors would've been.

The jeep had hit a colossal tree branch in the road, which kept the three marines from being killed by the rocket's staggering explosion and murderous hail of hot metal chunks. Staring at the whopping blackened crater that could have been his grave, Clam Chowder looked up to heaven, said, "And thank you very much!"

After his heart quieted from the near miss, the sergeant delivered Jason to a crude improvised hospital staffed by worn-out, blood-splattered doctors. The scene inside shocking, primitive, horrifying. Part of the ceiling had fallen; splinters, dust, blood, vomit—everywhere. Amid the dust specks drifting on ambering light were agonizing cries of "Doctor! Help me!"

A sinewy young marine who'd lost an ear in a firefight was dripping and hot with salty sweat. He wore a bloodstained apron that stank of gangrene. What's more, he was engaged in the exhausting, gruesome work of carrying away the corpses. One body consisted of only seven bone fragments and portions of a camouflage jungle hat that'd been placed in a tiny plastic bag.

In a shadowy corner stood a heap of amputated feet, legs, arms, hands. Human fragments—cut, bloody, black and blue, swelled, and sickening, along with the wounded and dying—lay everywhere. The hospital's still, stifling atmosphere reeked with the sickly sweet smell of death.

Fortunately, by then the explosive encounter was over. A strategic military location had been captured; a POW compound liberated; a multitude of enemy soldiers, killed. Jason, his platoon, and the tank-led reinforcements had wreaked carnage and destruction beyond imagination.

Lieutenant Roberts suffered critical wounds to his right thigh and lower-left back. A military transport flew him from the gunpowder and rubble of the war-torn countryside to a naval hospital in southern California. Having the world snatched from us makes us grateful even for small wonders. Upon exiting the aircraft, Jason felt moved by a rich harvest of California clouds tinted pink with the setting sun—a view too vast and lovely for words.

Following Jason's recovery, the president stated during a medals award ceremony in the White House Rose Garden: "Throughout its proud history, the Marine Corps has had in its ranks the finest of young American manhood. These marines have proven themselves to be the masters of our enemies whether on land, sea, or in the air. Today, we pause to salute one such marine and all who serve in this horrific war so well yet receive no parades, no flags, and so little thanks.

"A proud and grateful nation hereby awards Marine First Lieutenant Jason Xavier Roberts the Navy Cross and Purple Heart for extraordinary military leadership and courageous action while under fire."

Jason's acceptance speech concluded with the words, "The war trumpet's an instrument that awakens those demons sleeping in the human heart. These demonic forces ride on the tones of that trumpeting horn. The demons hover over battlefields, gorging themselves on blood dripping from the wounds of the suffering and dead. They live on blood and the exhalations of slaughter. Their vampirish cousins feed on hatred. They suck hate spewing from the lips of old men who initiate wars then send young patriots to die. The raucous cry of war produces hate in the mind, hate in the soul, hate at the end of a rifle. Hate becomes an almost sensual luxury.

"Whenever the noise of the battle horn erupts, valiant marines, sailors, soldiers, airmen forfeit their lives that this nation might live. I've seen countless marines killed. I've seen 'em bear pain. I've seen what hope, fatigue, fear look like. I've seen bravery, fidelity, dark lines of despair etched on men's faces. I've seen faith shine in the eyes of marines who trusted in me. I've also seen courageous jarheads greet certain death with an ironic joke because they were too proud to let those about them see the terror in their souls. God bless all our brave warriors; we should treasure them. We should cherish our freedom—because freedom damn sure isn't free!"

In the Spartan comfort of his room at the Bachelor Officers' Quarters, Lieutenant Roberts rose from his cot at last admitting sleep had eluded him. War is a cauldron from which virtually no souls emerge unscathed. Jason was the victim of a staggering, unrelenting nightmare:

A bloody, bullet-riddled man tearing at a sweaty guerrilla who is raping his wife. A teary mother wringing her hands as her daughter is sodomized by brutes blind with lust, hate, and madness. A screaming woman shaking bloody hands, her fingers hacked off for the rings on them. The corpse of a naked pregnant woman floating in dirty water, face up in the pale light. The little girl staring in horror at her mother's unclothed, sodden corpse, crying. Burned, wailing babies, their parents bludgeoned into pulp. A marching column of guerrillas, their fixed bayonets gleaming. In tow, seminude women stumbling along in grief-torn bewilderment. Men kneeling, hands tied behind their backs, shot in the head. Teenage boys buried while still breathing. Children— hands cut off. Green fields stained with blood; the hum of crickets drowned out by cries of pain and rage.

Wrapping himself in an olive robe, he opened the single window his room boasted and stared across the lawn. He was recalling the bloodstained letter of the Marine Second Lieutenant who'd died leading a raid. Jason had promised he'd personally hand deliver it to the slain officer's wife.

Upon recuperation, he located a beautiful young woman in a bright, cozy home in a pleasant community—a cozy home that contained a tiny bed in a corner bedroom. In the bed was a child about five or six years old. The little boy could hear the voices of Jason and his mother as the two chatted. Looking up admiringly at the medals on Jason's dress-blue uniform, the boy asked his mother, "And when will Daddy come home?"

She nervously pulled at her hair. "I—I don't know, sweetheart."

"Daddy will come home, won't he? You're sure he'll come home?"

"I pray every night for the war to end and for your father to come home soon," she said as her eyes rested lovingly on her husband's portrait on the mantle.

With moist eyes, Jason reached into the pocket of his uniform and pulled out the bloodstained envelope. As he stretched out his arm to the petite woman, the child cried. And his mother also knew and was very still...

Fog had crept in with the approach of dawn. Somewhere in that mist was battalion headquarters, where Jason Roberts would receive a medical discharge from the Marine Corps. Sighing dejectedly, staring off, he reflected on the tidal wave of hero's blood he saw spilled in Vietnam; and contemplated the return to his prominent law practice.

Less than nine months later, Jason sold his respected, flourishing Washington law firm that specialized in corporate litigation. His ex-partners—bullies, bastards, sharks—came off aloof and emotionless. They seldom smiled and wore conservative suits, preppy ties.

The new managing partner resembled a bespectacled tortoise in a pinstriped suit. His speaking style was precise, penetrating, intelligent; each elegant word seemed like it knew what it was doing. Secretly, "the tortoise" hated Jason enormously; and felt elated that Jason was leaving the Washington powerhouse he'd single-handedly created.

The tortoise was married to a striking woman and had two beautiful children. He was also involved in a long-running affair with a bright young associate. They were working late one evening, as usual. While deep in the throes of passionate "research" on the sweat-laden conference table, the alluring attorney, in the midst of a high-voltage orgasm, screamed, "Don't stop, Jason! Don't stop!"

Embarrassed, perspiring, shaken, she then said, "I don't know why, but I find Jason Roberts irresistibly attractive. Just can't stop thinking about him! I feel—I don't know—weak, wet, wild eyed whenever he comes near me." This revelation did not sit well with the tortoise. Red faced with humiliation, boxer shorts around his fat ankles, he glared at her menacingly in stunned silence…

Jason pulled open the distinctive, towering glass doors of J. X. Roberts & Associates. He marched down the majestic hallway toward the executive wing. Sighing dejectedly, he stepped across the threshold of his old office, paused, took one long last look around the opulent premises. Every picture, every piece of furniture held memories.

After soul-searching of epic proportions, Jason Xavier Roberts joined the priesthood, seeking a refuge from the brutishness of the world.

I'm going to now quote from Jason Roberts's haunting memoir verbatim, sweetheart. Frankly, the delivery of Father Roberts's personal narrative is the most uncomplicated method of sharing his extraordinary odyssey with you.

CHAPTER 4

Small Corner of Hell

One night last year in London, I was strongly impelled to take up a pen and write, though what I was to write about, I had no idea. Yielding to the impulse, my hand was seized as if by some external force, and the following seemed to sail into my mind on a river of crystal light:

Whether humankind's knowledge is almost complete or not, we actually know very little about ourselves. I suspect countless persons have been put away in insane asylums simply because they were gifted with uncommon insights or suffered unprecedented experiences. There may well be stories that have been told by alleged lunatics that, if listened to or investigated, might lead to extraordinary disclosures.

What to me, Jason Xavier Roberts, are genuine truths can produce only beliefs in you at best, unless you've had experiences similar to my own. I'll share my truth, allowing you to form your own beliefs, which experience may, in time, convert to unequivocal truth for you.

My maternal grandfather, Robert Clarence Henry, was a hospitable, unassuming man. He appeared exceptionally proud and boastful, however, of two things: that he was head chef of a major Washington landmark and that I was his grandson.

He also seemed to be much wiser than most people without making a point of it. As if trying to prepare me for some great truth, he would endlessly say:

"Sometimes truth is stranger than fiction. And that's a fact! I'm not being facetious!"

I was too young, however, to completely understand the meaning of *facetious* and equally too young to comprehend his profusely repeated point about truth. I doubt if even he could've spoken any words into my youthful ears that would have prepared me for the true nature of being.

No one ever genuinely knew me, though they thought they did. Few would've suspected that I, an ordained man of faith, was troubled by inner conflicts. Facing myself in the bathroom mirror each morning filled me with immense revulsion. Even as I shaved, the ugly feelings festering and clawing within me rose dark and bitter.

My mother was a pregnant fifteen-year-old bride who'd dropped out of eighth grade and worked as a hotel maid. On a cold, bleak wintry day, she ushered me into life—a life that was like a wonderful gift, but one that arrived broken. Every child born into this world has a lot of suffering ahead; mine just started earlier than most. So it shouldn't have come as any great surprise that I spent my babyhood blanketed in a bloodstained shawl in a dresser drawer that served as my crib.

It's terrible not to be loved. It makes you hard, violent, mean. Cruelty, madness, and death were the black angels hovering about my cradle as I began life in the Roberts clan—a Baltimore,

Maryland family plagued by demons that must've lurked in dark crooks of a loveless family tree for generations.

By any measure, my childhood was a relentless horror. I was disliked by my emotionally unstable mother, Harriet, who lost her dignity at the bottom of a liquor bottle. I was also ignored by my tyrannical father, "Big Richard," who made me and my younger sisters the targets of his screaming rages. He was an ex-fighter who worked at a local steel mill; a battered hulk of what had once been an enormous, muscular man. His speech was slow, halting, inarticulate. Big Richard would take off his belt and lash my quivering back with little or no provocation.

Once, my oldest sister, Liz, came to me crying hysterically. She was having her period; had no sanitary napkins, and there was no money to buy any. So I went into Big Richard's bedroom and found an old faded green sheet he'd swiped from a motel. I cut it into numerous pieces and said, "Here, Liz, use this!" She did. I was beaten with that thick, scarred brown belt until I nearly passed out for cutting up the stolen sheet. What's more, Big Richard and Liz seemed to have a very strange relationship— one she felt too ashamed to talk about—and everyone else pretended not to notice.

We lived on a repulsive street in an ugly house in a small corner of hell. Candy wrappers, condoms lined its fringe. The houses in my neighborhood, Hustler Hill, were dark, overcrowded, austere; often overrun with mice, rats, and roaches. Patched and broken windows scowled dimly like eyes that'd been hurt in drunken fights. Water had to be carried from an outdoor pump that often froze in the winter.

The Hill was also notorious for gambling dens, street gangs, and prostitution. Plus countless stray dogs roamed the Hill's littered alleys. Everything appeared loathsome, drooping, and decayed. Our house always felt damp and drafty; its age-old wool carpeting housed living things and sometimes sprouted mysterious vegetation.

Intense dark moods had been my mother's rhythmic lover for as long as I can remember. She was a shameless, foul-tongued woman of easy virtue who disappeared for numerous days at a time. Her clothing always seemed to reek of cigarette smoke laced with the stale fumes of spilled whiskey. The truth is, there was always a bottle of liquor around but never enough food.

Dreary days started with bacon spitting in a greasy pan. For most meals all we had was coffee and bread. Big Richard once said, "Look, stupid—coffee and bread is a balanced meal! How do I know? 'Cause it contains a liquid and a solid."

With a hollowness in my chest, I stared at the fuzzy, greenish mold growing on the bread.

Alone in my dingy room, sickened by yellow light, night would offer itself to me. I'd watch ragged shadows flowing against the sweating walls in pure despair. Now and then, the noise of a mouse in the wall would keep me awake past midnight. Other nights, I'd watch by the amber light of a dirty bulb, peeling turquoise paint flurrying down from the ceiling.

Harriet and Big Richard's room stood next to mine. Several times a week, their loud angry voices thunder through the wall, she screaming over and over, "I didn't do anything!" and he pounding her, yelling, "Shut the fuck up, you no-good lying bitch!" Unable to sleep, I'd toss and turn in my steel bed, its coiled springs squeaking with every subtle move.

One sweltering summer night, electrifying screams pierced the silence. I ran to the doorway of the adjoining bedroom; saw Big Richard pick up a metal shoe tree and hit my mother on the side of her head with raw power. It slammed into her head and face so hard she crashed into a wall, making an explosive racket, then staggered onto the bed. Blood spurted out, splattering him, her, and their bed. He ripped off her white dress with pearl buttons, shoved her nude, bloody body onto the gory sheets, and said, "I want some of what you've been givin' those low-life bastards you fuck behind my back."

Big Richard spied me at the door, bellowed, "You lil' son of a bitch, stop sneaking around where you don't belong! Get back to your damn room. Your mother and me want some privacy while we're makin' love."

The shocking spectacle broke my small heart open like a shotgun blast. I turned, trudged back through the dim, grotesque space called my room, and stumbled over to the window. With my hands cupped over my ears, I gazed up at the night sky and stared at the faraway moon's pale, lonely light. I tried to think of love, peace, joy—images remote from screaming, fighting, drunkenness. There I stood, a tingling in my chest, my thoughts scrambling to understand.

In those dark hours, I sometimes felt like a weeping willow tree rustling over a gravesite called my life. I wondered who would hear me if I cried out, who would even care. I remember kneeling on the musty carpet, half choking in my room's thin brown air, praying, "Forgive me, God, for interruptin'. I know you're busy. Do you hear 'em? They're at it again!

"For me, Liz, and Natalie, nights' are like a haunted house where doors torn open by our tiny hands lead into endless dark corridors. And there's no way out! Why can't ya find us? Natalie keeps vigil with a holy candle she found behind the little church on the corner. But she's still afraid! Her stuttering even seems to be gettin' worse."

But there would only be an outcry of silence.

When I was seven, my mother was pregnant with Natalie. She and Big Richard were on the front porch, each with beer can in hand—got into one of their usual arguments. He knocked several teeth from her bloody jaw and ended up kicking her in her swollen belly. She screamed, "Please! Pleeeeease—don't kick me again!" Liz and I cried. The neighbors all closed their doors.

When I was fifteen, Big Richard beat me unconscious with a wooden hairbrush. My head was bloody but unbowed. Later, I discovered him on the dining room floor stark naked and dead drunk. I stole out of the house, sped along the dark alley, hid in the shed of a friendly neighbor who lived down the street. I sat in the darkness on a rat-infested mattress, shivering as the hard, cold north wind slipped under the doorsill.

The neighbor's dog began barking explosively. She ran out to investigate, invited me into her house, and tended to the gory gash on my head. I told her what had happened and that I'd decided to run away. She said I could rest on her living room sofa overnight, get a fresh start at dawn. I thanked her profusely.

About 2:00 a.m., I awoke with my super friendly neighbor hovering over me in a slinky, black nightie. Her long raven-black hair hung loosely to her shoulders; and her face was adorned with a petite, black-feathered mask. What's more, the lovely lady's daring outfit barely contained her shapely, nude, sensuousness. My sexy fairy godmother whispered softly, "Accept this *special going-away gift* to remember me by."

She surrendered her gift with breathless passion. I seized it with great vigor!

Simply stated, I remember my extraordinary neighbor warmly to this day.

I heard a despondent whistle blowing on a distant track. Within minutes, the quietude of unpeopled streets was broken by the slow, heavy meter of freight trains clankin' by. I wished I was on one. I had a shoe box of peanut butter and jelly sandwiches my neighbor made but ate everything amazingly quick. Homeless and hungry, hanging around streetwalkers and vagrants, I took any job I could find. I slept in dark alleys, public restrooms, once on top of a tombstone.

I cleaned my clothes at the Laundromat next to Wee-Wee's Liquor Store. I'd pile the wet wash in plastic trash bags, take it to the alley behind Wee-Wee's, dry it on the store's rusty fence. My laundry route took me past backyards you weren't supposed to see. They enclosed brown lawns, moldy wooden porches, and grubby clothes hung from old clotheslines. Garbage cans encrusted with lumpish goop and overloaded with snot, vomit, filth guarded the entry to every yard.

The alley behind Wee-Wee's was the daytime abode of strange men—drunks lying in piss, addicts doing drugs, weirdos moving about in the shadows. The alley's frightful stench caused the sunlight to reek!

One calm afternoon, an extraordinarily dapper man parked in that stinking alley; he'd just stepped out of his car with a gorgeous birthday cake when a tan car with two men came barreling down the alleyway. The passenger had a machine gun; he shot the guy in the chest and face countless times as they raced by. Terrified, I screamed, "Holy shit!" I ran past the blood-soaked body, swarms of flies, pickpockets, and prostitutes vigorously plying their trade.

Wee-Wee was a compact guy, three feet six inches tall, described by one jerk as "no bigger than half a bar of soap." Nonetheless, he was smart, charming, a self-made man. Truth is, he was educated on the streets by bums, con men—and "connected." He was also

married to a long-legged redhead who drove the finest black se-
dan you could own. I washed it every other day. The sixty cents he
paid was good money back then. I told him all about my parents'
brutality and my running away.

Wee-Wee said, "I'm sure the sun, the moon, shed tears from
their eyes for you, kid. I do!" His expression changed. He pulled a
gun out of his leather shoulder holster and screwed on a silencer.
While wiping the gun down with a gray silicone cloth, he looked
me in the eye and whispered, "If you want, I could make a call—
have your old man castrated, his bloody balls stuffed down his
throat till he chokes, and his body packed in a crate and shipped
to your boozer mother. Or if you'd like, give the matter my personal attention—make 'em both *disappear!*"

Moving back a bit, I looked at Wee-Wee in alarm. "I, er..." My
voice trailed off.

He said, "Listen, kid, clearly you've been dealt a bad hand.
Know what your top job is right now?"

"I—I'm not sure."

"Figure out what you wanna be. Then work your skinny ass off
to bring it about like I did."

The truth is, I was just a mild-mannered Sunday-school boy, but
life on the streets turned me into an explosive, snarling wolf. That's
why I sharpened an old steel spike and used it to cut anyone I
didn't trust who came near. I was so mad when a local grocer tried
to cheat me that I punched him, stabbed him, and then wounded
his clerk when he intervened. What's more, I once slashed a drunk-
en vagrant suspiciously eyeing my wet laundry; almost killed him.

At one point, all I had was seven dollars, one dime, and a stray
cat who befriended me. On a hot Saturday afternoon, the sun's

rays beamed down from the cloudless sky and singed my skin as if under a magnifying glass. I walked down a dingy street past a tiny ramshackle store. Sitting in front of the place was a wooden basket full of enormous, delicious red tomatoes. Hunger ravaging my belly, I bought one for three cents and shared it with my cat. It provided a moment of happiness—pure happiness—simple as the satiating juice that ran down my chin.

The next morning, I woke up in the ugly shelter on Bleeker Street. Discovered my seven dollars and steel spike had been stolen from my pants pocket. I complained to the hunchback man on duty who walked with a limp. His voice was hoarse and raspy, his eyes, the coldest I'd ever seen. Personal hygiene was not one of his priorities. Inexplicably, the guy jumped me, dragged me to a side exit, and shoved me out into an alley. I stumbled, fell, scraped my palms and knees on the hard concrete.

He noticed the shy tread of my half-starved cat circling a grimy trash can; kicked in her protruding ribs. Then he beat her with an old nearby ax handle, transforming her coat of soft grays and browns into a shocking, bloody mess. "Hate cats! There're creepy—sneaky. Just like kids," he said under his breath, brandishing the gory weapon and glaring at me.

"Didn't have to kill her! You're just plain crazy!" I yelled, crying, bleeding, running as fast as I could down Bleeker Street toward the railroad tracks. I intended to hop on the first boxcar heading out of Baltimore. I ran for what seemed like an infinity, slowed to a jog, then a painstaking walk. Each step seemed more difficult than the one preceding it. My breathing came in small gasps as I plodded toward the train tracks and began tromping along its side.

"Feel mighty tired! Need to sit down!" I groaned in agony. My feet seemed heavier with each step as I moved shakily along the wooded railroad track banks. Spying a moss-covered log lying under an inviting shady oak, I decided to rest—maybe even take a brief nap.

There was a rocky ditch separating the train tracks from the oak tree. I ran toward the chasm, took a flying leap across it. But I came up short. I landed in the ditch instead on a pillowy sort of something and felt a burst of agony as if my leg had exploded. In horror, I realized a king-sized copperhead was hanging onto my lower leg—and it wouldn't let go! The fiery pain flared up in strong waves. I'd never felt pain so intense.

What's more, the huge snake's fangs seemed to be stuck in my calf muscle! After a terrifying eternity of frenzied leg kicks, it released its grip, slithered away. I groaned in relief, staggered unsteadily, dropped to the ground between the rails of the track. I tried again and again to get up but was unable to move.

I was fighting a surge of overpowering fear—had trouble breathing. Turning blue in the face, struggling for breath, I realized my strength was ebbing quickly. Shocked and in a panic because of my deteriorating condition, I wept quietly with exasperation, exhaustion. Through a haze of sharp throbbing and apprehension, I cried out, "Help! Help! Help me, please!" My heart was racing, nearly exploding as I spotted a colossal black man in bib overalls running toward me.

"What's wrong, kid?"

"Been snake bit! Think it was a copperhead."

"What color was it?"

"Reddish brown, hourglass markings down its back."

"That's a copperhead all right. They're deadly! You're in great danger here."

"Sure am, mister. I'm feeling real sick from the snake bite."

"Didn't mean just the bite. There's a train due along here in 'bout a minute or so. Gonna have to move you quickly. Might hurt a bit."

I'd forgotten that at that time of day, commuter trains thundered through the area at frequent intervals. The overall-clad giant lifted and carried me to his burnished, blue pickup parked by the side of the road. As soon as we reached the truck, a speeding passenger train roared past! Stunned, I stared at the fast moving train. The hot metal-and-oil smell lingering over the rails filled my nostrils, causing me to shudder. I realized that without the immense man's help—I would've been killed!

"Close call, son! Lucky I was drivin' by. We better git ya to a hospital quick!"

The huge stranger eased me into the passenger's seat of his pickup truck and rushed to the hospital. He barged into the emergency room, carrying me in his arms.

"Need help here—and fast! Boy's been snake bit. He's swelling up—he can barely breathe!"

A thin blond doctor sprinted to my side. My towering Good Samaritan vanished.

"Who was that enormous black guy, young man?"

"Have no idea."

"You've got a nasty bite here! He probably saved your life."

"Yeah! At least twice!"

I felt trembly, exhausted. I closed my eyes and fell into a deeply satisfying sleep.

After treatment, hospital staff phoned Harriet and Richard. Upon arrival, Big Richard stared angrily at me; then he turned toward my mother. With a grim twist to his mouth, he said, "We were better off before those damn brats were born, and we'd be better off without 'em now!"

Suddenly, the gut-wrenching wail of a newborn baby echoed like a frightened, wounded dove. Lost in thought, my eyes watering, I glared at a glittering glob of blood oozing down a wall. The attending nurse's eyes narrowed in concentration as her gaze darted between me and the bleak, unsmiling Harriet and Richard. She broke into a cold sweat. With an ache in her throat, she smoothed my hair. Then the moist-eyed nurse pulled me into an endless, parting side hug.

Our house's atmosphere felt as tight and constricting as the collar on our pit bull, who howled on his chain all night long. What got me up mornings was the thought that someday, I'd be as far away from that hellhole as I could get. There are fathers, mothers, and there're animals who spurt out offspring. Fate chose to provide me the latter.

Sukie Jones, my black football teammate, was passionate, intense, and dominating. We talked about everything—all our dreams, thoughts. Got to be close. Big Richard often mumbled, "That ugly, greasy nigga's at the door again," whenever Sukie showed up.

I met Sukie shortly after starting high school. About a week into the school year, I was harassed by Bug-Eye George and two other brutes. They came down on me in a vicious attack: one hit me hard in the face, another punched me mercilessly in the gut, a third's booted foot kicked me brutally in the ass. I was slapped, punched, kicked—"beat the fuck up"—and it hurt like hell! Sukie intervened with a wild fierceness. The battered, bloody punks looked at each other, panicky; then hobbled around the corner at breakneck speed. Sukie's right hand and blackjack were drenched in their blood.

Sukie was a pool shark, gambler, and thug who had grown up in the rough-and-tumble Baltimore City housing projects. He also packed a pearl-handled .44 in an ankle holster and could shoot the head off a rat with his eyes closed. Just did it from the sound he heard.

"Thanks! Name's Jason!" I said, red liquid oozing from my nose, dripping from my lip. Sukie glared at me. "You owe me no thanks! Look, I don't give a shit bout you one way or another, white boy.

Bug-Eye's crew was creeping round here on the West Side uninvited; just wanted 'em to suffer a lil' for their damn impertinence." Then with a fiery stare and a clenched jaw, he walked off.

Despite our unpromising introduction, Sukie and I subsequently hit it off and became great friends.

There was something in Sukie's eyes and demeanor that caused others to treat him with enormous respect. It was even rumored that Sukie had killed a man in a street fight. Baltimore police discovered the victim lying in an alley in a huge pool of blood. He'd been beaten, slashed and kicked to death.

Everyone in the neighborhood looked upon Sukie Jones as "somebody you don't fuck with!"

CHAPTER 5

Childhood Secrets

One Friday after school, Liz stood in heavy silence. The pale-blue skies restructured into the flash and roar of a thunderstorm that echoed outside the classroom windows of her high school teacher, Grace Featherstone. With wet eyes, a blank look, she said to Mrs. Featherstone, "My father...he did things that were...unforgiveable! I'm completely gripped by fear of him. Beats me virtually every day with his leather belt—a practice his mother, Zelda, had encouraged. Other times he locks me in a closet totally naked.

"Fragments of horror from those times litter my mind. One of the most terrifying is a game he enjoyed when I was little. He'd pick me up, hold me firmly atop his shoulders. With an orgy of belly laughs, he'd dance around the room. Then he'd saunter through a doorway, smashing my head into the wall above the door."

Trembling, Liz pulled and tugged at her clothes, then said tearfully, "I was only six when I was awakened one night by my father. Dropped his dingy, stained underpants, got into my bed poached in sweat, smelling like a fermenting pig. His—it was stiff and swollen. I felt my pretty pink nightgown being lifted. 'No, I don't want to!' I screamed.

"He put his grimy hand over my mouth; forcefully spread my legs...squeezed my thighs so hard I could feel the blood draining out. I was filled with overwhelming terror. I can still recall his huge hands stained with dark streams flowing from the blood of my ripped hymen. I can still see in my mind's eye the sight of the two of us reflected in the mirror. I shuddered…cried. Time dragged, doubling itself in passing during these horrendous ordeals. I was in tears, weeping in pain. All my prayers—cries of 'Father, Father, don't!'—meant nothing.

"He'd pitilessly shove his — inside me, deeper and deeper, rubbing my skin intensely sore. Every once in a while, I could actually feel my warm blood gushing out. But, he'd rage on!

"I was usually raw and lacerated afterward. The pain and misery were excruciating. In a guttural whisper, he'd always warn me: 'Listen, you little bitch, I'm leaving now. If you ever tell anybody about us I'll…'" Liz's body froze in place, grimacing, visibly sweating, she said, "The threat is truly too horrible to describe. I'm sorry, Mrs. Featherstone."

Squirming, clearing her throat, Liz continued: "Er, after threatening me he'd stagger out the door into the blackness. I would lay there in the dark, my heart pounding, replaying in my mind the chilling nightmare I'd just experienced. I have virtually no clotting ability. So numerous times, huge amounts of dark blood oozed out of me. Deep pools of unclotted blood filled my bed and continued to flow from my…

"Eventually, I would get up, my legs trembling, go into the bathroom, and stuff endless wads of toilet paper inside myself to stop the bleeding."

Liz pressed her palm over her lips to hold back a cry. "In addition to rape, the other perverted acts I've been forced to perform over the years are truly, truly unspeakable! One time I was so sickened I clawed at the walls until my hands were bloody. Nobody'll ever really understand, Mrs. Featherstone—understand the isolation and pain of losin' your virginity in the disgusting way I did. I don't know how I've physically survived.

"My father's stench stains my mind!"

"Don't worry, Liz, I won't let him hurt you again."

Liz smiled and cried at the same time. The visibly shaken teacher put her arms around Liz in a motherly embrace. They both wept uncontrollably.

"I want you to go find your sister, Natalie. Bring her here. You girls are coming home with me tonight. While you're gone, I want to call my husband. Then I'm going to contact the police and child protective services. Trust me, everything will be all right."

"I'm scared, Mrs. Featherstone!"

"I promise you, Liz, things will be immensely better from now on."

The vile, brutal, repeated rape of Big Richard's daughter shocked the City of Baltimore, and he was given a high-profile trial. The courtroom was packed with TV cameras, reporters, spectators. At the defendant's table, he sat slouched back in his chair, looking like a pale, oversized hog.

He swiveled his fat head around and glared ominously at my sister, Liz, as she took the witness stand. In a towering rage, he screamed at the jury, "Never did any of that stuff, I swear! That little whore is a damn liar, just like her fuckin' slutty mother!" Unsurprisingly, Big Richard received a substantial jail term for multiple counts of child abuse and rape. In short, during his first night in prison, correctional officers found Big Richard dead. He suffered eleven broken ribs, a punctured lung, a broken neck, bruised internal organs, and he'd been sodomized unrelentingly with a wooden plunger handle.

During the trial, my mother went to live with Big Richard's mother, Zelda, who'd mercilessly beaten him as a child. Believe it or not, stern and self-righteous Zelda Roberts was viewed as a community and church leader.

The day following Big Richard's death turned out drizzly and bitter cold. Just after 8:00 a.m., the telephone rang at Zelda's house. It was the police. They gave my mother the staggering details. Hysterical with grief, she started screaming at the top of her lungs. Zelda tried to console her. But she suddenly bolted toward the front door.

"Where are you going, Harriet?"

"I gotta have something to steady my nerves!"

"Richard was my son—I feel horrible too! But what we need now is to pray for strength—to pray for his soul. Besides, it's too early in the morning to be drinking cheap whiskey. That stuff'll rot your guts! You're drinking yourself to a slow death, Harriet."

"They broke his damn neck! Forced a wooden stake up his ass, for God's sake! I need somethin' strong to get me through this! I need somethin' a helluva lot stronger than all that praying shit!"

During the night, the cement front porch became glazed with ice, and as my mother stepped onto it, both feet slipped out from under her. She plummeted face-first down the cold hard icy steps. Her head split wide open like a smashed ripe watermelon on the frozen concrete sidewalk. She died instantly.

Due to a paper work mix-up, my mother's body was cremated by the city, along with the unclaimed bodies of derelicts. Zelda buried Big Richard in an obscure graveyard. After the mourners departed, I pulled out my penis—pissed on his grave. A nearby cemetery laborer who was leaning on a shovel shook his head as if to acknowledge how I felt. He stated matter-of-factly, "Don't mind me, mister. Know *exactly* how you feel! I was raised by one myself!"

I thought I'd feel ashamed for doing it. Now I'm ashamed because doing it actually made me feel better. But I'm mostly ashamed because I should've killed the bastard myself!

Mrs. Featherstone took my two sisters home to her college-professor husband, who was as gracious as she. They had no children; cared for Liz and Natalie as if they were their own. The girls enjoyed a host of delightful years with the Featherstones.

Best of all, thanks to the vigorous effort of Grace Featherstone, Liz and Natalie both received full academic scholarships to a respected, major university.

Maybelline "Mama" Jones was Sukie's grandmother. Her husband had been robbed and stabbed to death. Young, frightened Maybelline had gone to work as a maid to support her two toddlers. While being served breakfast in bed, her illustrious employer forced his clammy hand between Maybelline's trembling thighs, tore off her brand-new ivory panties…

Within days of the incident, he developed a mysterious illness doctors could not identify. The result? He died in overwhelming agony, screaming incoherently.

One day Mama whipped up an extraordinary mixture of roots, herbs, other pungent ingredients. She poured the strange amalgam into two five-gallon kosher-pickle jars; etched my name on the brass lid of one, Sukie's on the other. She instructed Sukie to stir fingernail clippings and a pinprick of blood from his right hand into one of the jars. I did the same to the other. The purplish potion was left to ripen in a dark, dusty corner of Mama's broom closet.

About three weeks later, the concoction turned smoky gray. The brew swirled eerily around the insides of the jars as if it were somehow alive. Mama told us, "Dis a special old family recipe.

Made it the way my mama used to make it down home. Now take just a teensy tiny sip and you'll have a gold mine of future success in alls you do."

I took a whopping gulp.

Mama Jones loved to cook. What's more, I was usually hungry when I showed up, and she could always sense it. "Thought I'd warm us up a few leftovers," she said one late summer afternoon. Over a mouth-watering meal of lemonade, fried chicken, cornbread, macaroni and cheese, collard greens, sweet potato pie, Mama good-naturedly teased Sukie.

"When Sukie was born, I thought, 'Ain't he a praiseful thing.' But he was also a lil' chubby, bald-headed, bow-legged disturber of da peace. He comes into dis old worl' frownin' mad, fists all balled up, hongry as a hound. Had to drop all ma biznis and tends to 'em then and there when he piss his britches, or else I heers from 'em loud and often. He always been powerful tough with an explosive-hot temper. But oh laud, honey, ah loves dat boy—strong tempers and all!"

"Know what I wants most? It's for both you boys to git to college. I mean a high-society one. The Ivy League kind. I want you to make somethin' grand of yourselves."

Staring down at my feet, I said somberly, "Takes a great deal of money, super grades. You know neither me nor Sukie has either."

Mama began pacing her hands moving in jerks, which caused a kitchen chair to tip over. "Gotta keep any devilish lack of faith way down in a hole—that's what I know! I'm gonna git you boys to one of them fancy Ivy League Schools usin' pure faith! With the help of the laud and Mama's 'pickle-jar magic,' I know it can be done. You'll see!

"Now, Jason, I wants you to eat up. Baby, you needs to put some meat on dem skinny bones!"

Two years prior to my sisters Liz and Natalie moving in with Grace Featherstone, Sukie and I both had won full athletic scholarships to "one of them fancy Ivy League Schools," just as Mama said. I arrived on campus with a change of socks, a thin coat, and a snub-nosed revolver courtesy of Sukie.

We were roommates. Our opposing teams' players used to rough him up a bit, which comes with the territory when you're a star player. I used to wonder, though, if he got a little *extra* because he was black. But Sukie never complained about any "special" treatment. Perhaps it was because he was ruggedly built, strong as a stallion, tough as buffalo hide.

One evening during our senior year, Sukie called me totally excited. He'd just been offered a multimillion-dollar professional football contract by the team of his dreams. He said explosively, "Told you, Jason, I'd make it to the pros!"

"Always knew you would, Sukie; it was me I was worried about. I'm still not sure what to do with my life."

"My first game, I'm gonna send you some tickets. Best seats in the house! I'm flying you down here first class. After the game we're going to the finest restaurant in town, have the choicest steak dinner on the menu; you can even bring your new girlfriend too. The sexy one!"

"Suk, I'm really looking forward to that. But let's be honest— my girlfriends were *all* sexy! Cream of the crop!"

"You're an arrogant SOB, Jason."

"SOB, yes! But it's hardly arrogant when you're tellin' the truth. You probably mean Samantha?"

"Yeah, Sam! Bring her too. By the way, how did a poor, ignorant white boy like you end up with a gorgeous, classy girl like Sam anyhow? Pure pity?"

"It's my irresistible charm and winning personality."

"You're about as charming as a pig in shit, and you've got the personality of a fence post. You're just lucky girls here can't resist the quarterback. Even a sorry-ass one like you."

"If my *sorry ass* didn't get the ball to you as often as I did, you wouldn't be—"

"Shut the hell up, Jason! I'm losing my train of thought. Oh yeah! What I was gonna say is we go way back. We been through a lotta crazy shit together. I'm rich now! What's more, I'm gonna be the greatest player in the history of the game. So I'll be needin' a good lawyer. Might even pay for your law-school classes."

"How 'bout throwing in a yacht?"

"How 'bout kissing my ass!"

About a week later, I drove Sukie to the airport to catch a 9:00 a.m. flight to his team's headquarters. He was totally unsuccessful in containing his excitement. The truth is we both seemed to be walking on air. In barely more than an hour, with the stroke of a pen, Sukie Jones would be a famous young sports celebrity— and a multimillionaire!

About 6:00 p.m. on the same day, my football coach knocked at the door. He was a beguiling, witty man with an artificial leg and a habit of sleeping with other faculty members' wives. The coach had an intense expression on his face. He looked into my eyes. "Jason, there's been an accident. It's Sukie…"

"Sukie! What happened?"

"The plane he was on crashed."

"How bad is he hurt?"

"He didn't make it. Jason—he's dead! The airliner exploded; fragments of metal, garbage, body parts—hurled into the sky."

There was an overpowering sinking sensation in my throat and stomach. Tears fell uncontrollably from my eyes. My insides cramped, twisted, squirmed.

Staring down at my hands, I muttered, "The touch of love can be physical—a kiss, a caress. Or love can be something subtle like someone's grandma sharing her food when she saw you were hungry. Someone who talked you out of doing something stupid when your thinking was clearly insane. Someone who kept the bullies of the world off your ass when you needed it most. He was black. I'm white. What color is friendship? What color is love? No one ever knows how much another hurts. Why you hurt, friends guess they know. How much—never!

"But all that happened a long, long time ago."

CHAPTER 6

─ ❦ ─

Mr. J's

My occupations of priest, lawyer, lobbyist led me from city to city. I was assigned to the nation's capital when I first encountered Jacqueline O'Sullivan. We met at a jazz club on Capitol Hill called Mr. J's. Behind its unmarked crimson door lay an intimately lit jazz lover's paradise. For jazz junkies, being at J's was like being in heaven without going to all the bother and expense of dying. J's was as tough a jazz club reservation as you could find. Its proximity to the White House made it a perfect power-dining spot.

This effortlessly cool joint for serious jazz lovers boasted exposed brick walls and polished wood tables flanked by cushiony red-leather seating. Its chalkboard menus heralded dishes of genuine mastery. The softly lit wood-paneled backroom, called the "VIP Lounge," played host to private meetings—and numerous love affairs.

The handsome wooden bar was a magnet for the nation's most distinguished and influential. Its drinks—a mix of old classics and new inventions—were among the best in town. The walls were packed with caricatures of politicos past; the chairs were often filled with politicos present. Bustling bow-tied waiters laughed and joked with customers and went about their tasks as though pleasing you was the only thing on their minds.

Frankie, the club's most popular waiter, was square jawed, jet black, and built like a heavyweight boxer. Yet his manner was unequivocally feminine. What's more, it wasn't unusual to see Frankie show up a little tipsy on his day off wearing a superb wig, an exquisite gown, and stiletto heels. Frankie always wanted to look his best.

The owner, Smooth Bobby, schmoozed with the city's movers and shakers from behind the bar. A crowd of elites jockeyed for barstools on most weekday evenings. Bobby exuded a warm storyteller's charm and was a prodigious teller of Washington-insider tales. In addition to his intriguing—oftentimes scandalous—gossip, he also offered Washington sophisticates an opportunity to sip, savor, indulge in some of the world's best collectible wines.

Bobby capably assisted his blond scarlet-vested bartender, Olivia "Sunny" Day, a gorgeous ex-congressional aide. Sunny raced her red Italian sports car at a suburban racetrack on weekends; dated a tall, muscular, black jazz-saxophone player who went by the name Bo Peep.

This attractive, effervescent woman carried around an overwhelming secret torment. Sunny and her twin sister were born with long, sensuously beautiful blond hair. One night in their late twenties, both went to sleep and awoke completely bald. Their hair had fallen out and lay in huge clumps on their pillows. They were the victims of acute androgenetic alopecia—their heads were as smooth as eggs. Both twins were unceremoniously dumped by their significant others once the men learned about their respective girlfriends' heartbreaking misfortune.

Sunny's twin swallowed a colossal dose of rat poison. It resulted in intense dizziness, difficulty breathing, a coma with seizures; her skin turned cherry red. She died in incredibly torturous pain.

The Monday following her gut-wrenching, soul-crushing breakup, Sunny drove from her Arlington, Virginia, apartment to Southeast DC. Uneasily twisting the magnificent glittering

ring on her finger, she entered the elegantly appointed Cannon House Office Building to see her ex-fiancé, a Congressman. As she entered his posh, Oriental-rugged, wood-paneled office, the Congressman appeared shocked, stunned; his mouth fell open. Sunny took a seat in front of his huge mahogany desk; sat on the finely crafted chair's edge, her spine straight as an iron rod, glaring at his sweating face.

Seven adoring, passionate years she'd given him. Now he wouldn't even look at her moist eyes and trembling chin; he just kept staring into the fireplace and fidgeting with the elegant ornaments on his desk. Clearly, he was tremendously uncomfortable, but Sunny wasn't in the mood to make it easy for him.

"Sunny, er...Forgive me! I—I know I've behaved very badly." The air suddenly felt suffocatingly warm to the Congressman, which made it hard for him to breathe. He cleared his throat numerous times. "It's perfectly understandable if you feel a little upset at the moment. But I hope we can still be friends. I also trust we can continue to work together without feelings of bitterness, resentment, or anger getting in the way."

Sunny smiled sweetly. "Of course! And to show there're no hard feelings, I bought you a big cup of that superb coffee you love."

"Thanks! You're second to none."

"At last! You noticed."

Sunny bent over kissed him tenderly on the forehead—still smiling—she dumped the steaming hot coffee into his crotch. She could still hear his electrifying screams as she kicked over a petite antique table, which skidded across the room, and stormed out the office shouting, "I saved the best news for last. I quit!"

After resigning from her job as a congressional aide, Sunny embarked on a drinking binge of epic proportion. Eventually she concluded her self-destructive pity party and nearly tripled her previous income by going to work for Bobby. In no time at all, she also acquired a finely crafted blond wig with the help of Frankie's capable assistance.

Sunny greatly wanted to protect the secret that was so extremely destructive to her self-respect and dignity. She said of her sensational, sassy hairpiece, "It makes me feel good all over—makes me brand-new again."

Bobby was a congenial man with a scruffy beard, ponytail, and engaging blue eyes. He drove an age-old black pickup truck. Bobby and I grew up on the same block in Baltimore. His house was just a dash less ugly than mine. Bobby was a buck-toothed, big-eared street urchin who always wore baggy, worn-out clothes. His head was perfectly bald—shaved to get rid of lice.

Bobby's entrepreneurial mother supplemented her public assistance checks by dabbling in the world's oldest profession. While jogging along the Tidal Basin, he once said in an emotionless voice, "I was a remarkably naïve youngster. I knew my mother was exceptionally popular with men. They also seemed to spend a great deal of time in her bedroom, but I didn't know why. Unfortunately, one day I peeped.

"My mother did what she did. My mother was what she was. That's why I've got nine half-siblings, each fathered by a different john. When the O'Brian kids romped in our tiny, grassless backyard, it was easy to mistake the darn place for a day care center. Cold hard fact is none of us look even remotely similar to one another.

"What's more, all my siblings seem constantly located right in the heart of adultery, unwanted pregnancies, jail time, or alcoholism."

Bobby worked his way through dental school by satisfying the carnal needs of a host of older married women. These immensely grateful ladies provided tuition assistance in the form of tasty meals, flashy clothes, and ample cash. On one occasion, a passionate husband came home for a taste of afternoon delight. The result? He discovered Bobby masterfully delighting his yearning, burning wife. What happened next was anything but delightful.

Bobby's ensuing dental practice was…a total flop. That's why I co-signed the loan that launched Bobby's incomparable jazz club, Mr. J's.

One hot, weary dead-September sunset, Bobby and I sat together over a bottle of vodka until past midnight. Bobby leaned forward, hesitated briefly, assumed a grave expression, and said, "As a kid my bed was packed with platoons of cockroaches that invaded the night. I had rags for blankets, stolen potatoes for supper. I lived in fear every day—and that's the truth!

"I was trained through terror and trembled whenever 'dear Ol' Mom' called me. She was completely merciless, even to her children. I frequently stole away from home in hunger, searching for somethin' to eat. I was kept cold and starvin' and made incredibly vicious by my old lady, who allowed me to eat only what I stole and shared with her. In my savage search for food, warm clothes, money, I'd pounce on any livin' thing I laid eyes on weaker than myself.

"I was unrelentingly frantic with the pain of fear and would evade my mother's sadistic punishment by beating, cutting, robbing anyone I found walking alone in the neighborhood. I'd drag them screaming into the shadows, take anything of value…"

A raw stillness suddenly echoed about the trendy bar like an unfinished sound.

Bobby looked down, started fiddling with his gold cuff links. Then he cleared his throat and continued in a weakened voice. "That gut-wrenchin' fear instilled in me an intense hunger and high-powered ambition. Think of it: this is where that fear has brought me—beautiful mansion among the city's elite, loads of sizzling sex, and at least one true best friend, you."

I sort of half smiled. "No doubt about it, Bobby. We've clearly been to hell and back together."

"You've probably noticed this place's endlessly packed with people who're silly, pretentious, shallow. But they're always chock-full of my food, liquor; and rollin' in the aisles over Frankie's hilarious antics. Their great love of booze and jazz guarantees this once-poor Baltimore boy all the money I'll ever need!"

"You've got a goldmine here, all right. What's Frankie's story?"

"A handsome, young boxing sensation. His goal? To qualify for the Olympic boxing team then turn pro. The nitty-gritty: father went to the store, never returned. Worst of all, one hot summer night his mother called out from her bedroom in a stammering voice, 'Frankie!'"

"Stop—heard enough, Bobby!"

"Gladly, Reverend!

"Let's switch to something to cheer about: white-hot sex with an unfamiliar woman! Aren't you intrigued by that scrumptious, dark-haired beauty sittin' over there all alone? Her body has just the right touch of sensuousness. Bet she's velvety soft, smooth as silk in all the vital locations. Wouldn't you like to liberate little Miss Gorgeous from any sexy lingerie and fill her furry furnace with an all-powerful joy?

"Gimme a quick bless, padre. I'm goin' over, and I wanna be at my super charmin' best."

I grunted. "That's a dumb-ass idea, you horny bastard. You clearly possess an unending stream of lewd thoughts."

"Untrue! I only have 'em about once every six seconds."

"Bobby, leave that lovely young creature in peace! What's more, despite what you may've heard, I don't play games with my priestly authority. So go to hell! And be very quiet about it! I've got a jumbo headache, and I'm certain you played a major role in its formation."

"I remember Sukie Jones, the meanest motherfucker ever to wear shoes, havin' a mighty foul mouth. Your language's worse than his! You're in great need of an exorcism, *Holy Man.*"

"I'm touched. I'm greatly honored that you would consider me superior in some manner, Bobby. One thing's for sure: you're not half as stupid as you appear."

"Remind me to complain to the bishop about your being such an absolute wise ass, Holy Joe."

Cocking my head, I said with a smirk, "I'm sorry I hurt your feelings when I called you stupid. I truly thought you already knew!"

"Look, Mr. O'Brian, if you're serious about complaining, outline your concerns on a single sheet of your finest bond paper. Place it in a premium-quality white business envelope. Fold it carefully lengthwise—then shove it up your ass!"

"Sounds mildly uncomfortable."

"I'm going home, Bobby, to sleep off the pain in my head. Put all of those watered-down drinks you served me on my tab."

"Tab! You, preacher man, *have never paid for anything since the place opened!*"

"That's because I don't believe in starting bad habits."

I still recall the first time I went to a private party at Bobby's posh Virginia estate. I rang the doorbell. A stunning-looking blonde who was completely naked except for a pair of expensive designer shoes answered the door. As she approached me in the elegant spiked heels, her lovely breasts responded with a titillating buoyant movement. It was Sunny, flaunting the kind of sizzling body most men have only dreamed about. She smiled and casually took my hand.

"Father Roberts, so glad you decided to attend. Your utmost enjoyment is my foremost desire." Sunny moved closer, her tantalizing breasts lightly touched my chest. "See anything you want?" Sunny said, moistening her lips.

"Er...nice shoes!" I said, touching my throat in shocked disbelief. "Ms. Day, you're not wearing your lovely red vest; I almost didn't recognize you."

"Friends call me Sunny."

"You can count on me being friendly," I said in a stammering, weakened voice.

"I'll go slip on my vest if you'd like, Father."

I pulled at my collar. "Actually, what you're wearing, Sunny, is, is absolutely unforgettable!"

"Why, Father, you're so sweet. Bobby never seems to notice anything I wear. Thanks for noticing," Sunny said, grinning and kissing me lightly on the cheek.

"My pleasure," I said visibly sweating.

I followed my alluring greeter into an immense, luxuriously appointed room. "Oh!" I said. My face became a mask of amazement. The guests included a fascinating montage of some of the foremost male dignitaries in Washington and a sea of gorgeous, naked female bodies all moaning, undulating, and squirming about on the plush carpet, chairs, and couches.

My voluptuous escort touched me on the arm, looked me in the eye, and said in a staggeringly sexy voice, "Excuse me, Father, but I've got a *naughty little dessert* I'd love to give you. Interested?"

I glanced at her sensuous nude neckline then quickly cast my eyes toward the floor before attempting to give a priestly answer. Swallowing hard, I said weakly, "Sunny, I..."

Before I could finish responding, she handed me an off-white, gilt-edged plate elegantly framing the sublimeness of strawberries and angel food.

I went to J's regularly to lobby and be entertained by members of both chambers of Congress. The atmosphere was cozy; the jazz, first rate. My friends and I dressed casually when going to this refreshingly different power spot in order to relax, blend in, avoid recognition.

It was during intermission; the featured quartet was taking a well-earned break. Jackie got up from her table in a secluded corner of the club. Her three friends ran jeweled fingers over crystal champagne glasses. They looked at each other quizzically as she walked over and sat at the piano. The noisy club full of Saturday-night revelers settled back in their red-leather chairs; became completely absorbed. We all intuitively knew we were about to share something special.

Jackie touched the piano; I knew from the response that years of practice and love had preceded that touch. Every gesture, every movement was perfectly synchronized with the pulse of the music. As the melody crescendoed, magic began to envelop the softly lit room. Then another instrument joined in; we all knew at once that there was a young woman who had loved much—been hurt much. She sang a captivatingly beautiful love song—and she made our hearts sing.

Her evocative music opened an ache, an emptiness, a sorrow deep in our souls that none of us understood. I wept. I looked around: all the others were crying in their beer or shot glasses too.

Sometime during the piano's first crescendo and final decrescendo, I found my eyes riveted on the beautiful woman sitting at the magnificent piano. I love beauty, whether in pianos or in women; I seemed mesmerized by both.

The lovelier of the two looked up and smiled in my direction. She was so ripe, so mouthwatering I could've drowned in her sweetness. As her haunting eyes caressed mine, a spell was cast. I was bewitched!

I gave my waiter, Frankie, who was full of funny stories as usual, an exceptionally generous tip; I was virtually walking on air. That night I'd only gone for the music, but left with an invitation to the charm and grandeur of one of Jackie O'Sullivan's exclusive Georgetown parties.

CHAPTER 7

— ⊗ —

Love-Starved Beauty

hree weeks went by. The light changed from white to amber to the pale violet of an autumn Saturday's twilight. It was the night of Jackie's party; I wasn't sure if I should even attend. But my curiosity got the best of me. So I drove over to Georgetown's West Village. The street's cobblestones appeared mystically luminous. Lights had come on in the lane's row of houses, and glowed from their windows onto the dew-covered street. I arrived at her stunning *crown jewel of the neighborhood*, with its beautifully manicured lawn, a little after eight. There was a misty tingling in the evening air.

Elegant guests stepped out of shiny limousines and made grand entrances amid the vibrant glitter of street lamps at sunset. I strolled alongside women in mink, men in tuxedoes up a vintage brick walkway. A dapper servant greeted me at a raven-black door. He escorted me into a majestic salon teeming with smiling faces. The women were all bright and beautiful; the men were all witty and charming. I was the only thing in the room that didn't reek of old money.

Servers in formal attire offered cocktails from silver trays. Appetizing cuisines arrived via a splendid buffet. A string quartet set a lively, sophisticated mood. The attention to detail was scrupulous. There was a subtle quiver in my stomach; I lifted my chin in an attempt to look dashingly confident. The truth is my tough, disadvantaged early life caused me to feel ill at ease around people with great wealth.

When the music paused, Jackie appeared at the top of a magnificent mahogany staircase dressed in a soft, trailing gown. Slowly, with liquid grace, our smiling hostess began floating sensuously down the stairway. Her superlative diamond accessories sparkled dazzlingly. Her luxuriant hair caressed bare shoulders, accentuating slim arms and gloved hands. She was a symphony of undulating colors, beauty, and style. The effect was mesmerizing. All over the spectacular room, men gazed upon her with wonder and breathless adoration.

Every woman is mystifying—an enthralling puzzle to be solved. After a sip or two of a dry vodka martini, I began pondering what I'd discovered about my captivating hostess with the impish cheeks and delicate chin.

The truth is this dazzling picture had its dark spots. I realized that with all of her bright beauty, there was something very sad and wistful about Jacqueline Sophia O'Sullivan. She was tall and slender; her perfectly balanced neck, shoulders, and nose could've been drawn at a school of fine art. She had long, dark hair swept into a chignon at the nape of her neck and flaunted a sleeveless, trailing champagne-hued gown.

Moving gracefully through the living room of her impeccable Georgetown home, she seated herself before an ebony concert grand piano and began to exquisitely play Chopin's piano *Études*.

Beneath the delicate assurance of her piano playing, affluent background and charm, underneath her popularity and ravishing good looks, Jackie—like me—seemed afflicted by deep psychological scars. She had every material thing a young woman could wish for; but Jackie's childhood, like mine, completely lacked affection.

Teased as a little girl for being chubby, Jackie became an avid lifelong runner and took up yoga. Those practices greatly improved both her body and her low self-esteem. Due to inadequate pigment to cover blood vessels in her irises, Jackie's eyes appeared an exotically beautiful shade of violet. At age eighteen, Jackie moved to New York to study piano at the finest music school in the city. She possessed a genius for the instrument; she had hoped to become a world-renowned pianist.

Jackie's dedication, however, shortly began to fade. She was distracted by the appeal of her socialite lifestyle. A profusion of buying sprees and parties took up more and more of her time. What's more, Jackie distracted herself by engaging in multiple casual affairs to stave off the boredom of her empty, meaningless existence. A New York gossip columnist wrote, "She has in her brief life, perhaps, had more men really, truly 'dead in love' with her than almost any other girl in New York."

Jackie eventually returned to DC. Shortly thereafter, the twenty-seven-year-old beauty married twice-divorced sixty-six-year-old real estate mogul Patrick O'Sullivan. Patrick had a bulbous nose, pronounced chin, was stupendously rich and magnificently ugly. Yet despite being remarkably hefty and unattractive, in his vast ugliness resided a most powerful "something" that, within moments of meeting him, stole forth and charmed one's mind.

After her piano performance ended, I started to wander somewhat uneasily among the black ties and elegant gowns until I reached a wall of bay windows. The immense windows were hung with gracefully contoured baskets of gorgeous colorful blossoms. I retrieved a sumptuous miniature chocolate from an ornate dish. I placed it between my lips. Delicious!

Turning to face the crowded room, I knew I had to speak to the dark-haired woman who'd so thoroughly intrigued me. I scanned the guests; she appeared on the far side of the swarm near the dazzling buffet table. Her lovely, black-lashed violet eyes seemed to be looking my way as she chatted with a woman gowned in basic black whose white hair was arranged with panache. Nervous, I rubbed the back of my neck and endlessly cleared my throat.

Finally I strode into the crowd, weaving past elbows, wine glasses, savory trays of hors d'oeuvres until I was by her side. Although self-confident by nature, sweat ran into my shirt sleeves. I felt uncommonly awkward as I approached.

Lightly gripping Jacqueline's delicate hand, I said with a lingering touch, "These are the hands of a world-class pianist. You're simply amazing!"

She appeared to not even recognize me. A bit humiliated, I reminded her, "Ah—I'm Jason Roberts. We met on Capitol Hill at Mr. J's three weeks ago."

Out of sheer nervousness, I also mentioned I was an attorney as well as a priest. The latter confession being totally unnecessary and absurd given the fact that I was wearing a black suit and clerical collar at the time. Her response struck me as rather formal, distant, aloof.

A few minutes of politics-oriented conversation later, she said, "Would you be interested in seeing a rare, historical journal my husband acquired? It once belonged to Abraham Lincoln. It's a journal Lincoln kept from the time he was a young lawyer up until his presidency."

"You bet! Love to see it!"

She motioned to me. I followed. She moved with self-assurance, her ripe, sexy butt hardly swaying. Her purposeful stride seemed to be holding in pent-up passion—passion that might otherwise fall from her tantalizingly sculpted body and be wasted.

After twisting and turning in bright art-embellished hallways, we arrived at two handsome carved doors. They opened into an immense moonlit library situated in a secluded rear corner of the mansion. With a false smile, accelerated breathing, I strolled into the room and leaned against a convenient wall. Jackie moved closer; handed me the rare, hand-tooled leather journal.

"Want this?" she said, brushing her voluptuousness up against my tense muscular form.

I swallowed excessively, smoothed my hair. "Journal's, er, truly incredible!"

There was the scent of roses coming from a jade vase. Just outside the library's enormous bay window, tips of willow branches waved in the moonlight. A great stone fireplace completely covered one wall. On the mantle above the fireplace sat an intricately detailed crystal sculpture of Jesus in a superbly etched robe.

Astonishingly, I seemed to sense an aura of desire. Surprised and confused, I stared at one of the loveliest women I'd ever seen, dumbfounded. I looked back at the journal. My heart began pounding wildly. But were the vibrations emanating from this beautiful, out-of-reach female fantasy being misinterpreted? I felt a sudden rush of absolute uncertainness.

The stirrings of the north wind were chiming in the trees outside the window. The dancing flames of the crackling fire created a cozy ambiance. The crystal sculpture of Christ glittered on the mantle. The brown-leather binding of the Lincoln journal appeared well worn. But the leather craftsmanship was exquisite.

When I looked up from the journal, Jackie was sashaying toward me, wrenching off her designer clothing as she came. She walked out of her long champagne-hued gown like an ivory nymph, revealing a sleek, shapely body. Bra, slip, panties dropped to the floor. I stared at her legs: the calves were beautiful, ankles long and slim, thighs—utterly graceful in form and movement. She was mind-blowingly more stunning disrobed than with her fashionable clothing on. Wonder at her beauty took hold of me.

She ambled across her elegant fallen wardrobe, past the roaring fireplace, arching her chest so she could project as much of herself as possible into the refined room's sumptuousness. She sauntered whisper soft—like a tigress—so that no single sound should fall to ripple the clear surface of her anticipated joy.

Jackie slithered provocatively to the floor. She lay on her stomach, trembling with readiness. She was stark naked, her skin glowing in the firelight. She began to rotate her sculpted, tantalizing derriere slowly, sensually. Smoldering heat raced through her body. A subtle moan echoed across the room. Jackie rolled over, spread her shapely legs, and began to rock from side to side.

I frantically searched my mind for suitable words with which to diffuse the situation and to extinguish the monumental torrid lust rapidly building up inside me. But before I could think clearly, my black suit and clerical collar lay crumpled in a pile. Worst of all, I was kneeling between Jackie's warm, welcoming thighs, caught up in a kind of surreal enchantment by the sight of her luscious lips, succulent breasts, and all of the pleasures below.

"Think this is a bad idea, Mrs. O'Sullivan," I said with a rapidly racing heartbeat.

"I completely agree," she whispered in an alluring, honey-dipped voice. "Unfortunately, the doors are all locked, the only thing I'm wearing is diamond earrings, and a handsome, muscular brute is looming over me. What's a poor, helpless girl to do?" she said while pulling me down into her glorious naked wonderfulness.

Jackie gave me a long, passionate kiss. Our hands began exploring titillating places. Breathlessly, fervently, shamelessly, we embraced each other in an amazement of raw, primal lust. The burning desire devouring my soul blazed up even more fiercely. Eager fingers plunged into her garden of delight's smooth softness.

I began stroking her body like one playing a rare musical instrument. My tongue played a sensuous melody over Jackie's masterpiece of beautiful curving lines. I touched her in places that'd not been touched before—in ways that should not be spoken of. It unchained her passion. I'd discovered fire down below. The fire exploded out of her in a quivering ball of fierce, unrelenting, primitive passion. It lit up my face so it glittered brighter than the flames of the fireplace behind me.

My strong, rugged, willing masculinity captivated her soft, rounded, eager femininity. Our white-hot desire to merge as one all came together in a brilliant flash. We rocked, writhed, gyrated like two wild animals on a soft, thick Oriental rug once gracing the lobby of a remote British embassy, nearly driving each other mad with ecstasy. A mystical waterfall of pure rapturous delight cascaded throughout Jackie's suppressed womanliness. Her tongue—like a red fire—sent my neglected maleness on a euphorically wondrous journey.

Heaven rolled. The crystal Messiah looked down on us. The sky's purple shadows grew ominously dark. Thoughts of shame flashed across my mind. But Jackie was an absolute volcano—one who'd passionately erupted for the very first time. My shame became quickly overpowered by sensuous elation that penetrated through my body and reached my soul.

Suddenly there was a shriek followed by a moan. I arched myself against her softness, and what was within me entered her at last. Our fires subsided, smoldered, went out. It left a pool like wild honey on the handsome silk carpet. Jackie and I then lay without moving in each other's arms, skin wet, glistening, our bodies moistened, bedewed by forbidden pleasures. The rain came, the wind howled, the thunder rumbled, and nearby trees began to toss off their autumn leaves. Jackie slept spontaneously; her whisper-soft breathing permeated my ears.

I'd made love to every inch of her body, from her sweat-soaked silky hair down to her beautiful feet. The dark groans of suffering were then absent from her face. She seemed blissfully annihilated, as if I'd given her the intense joy she wanted, needed, craved. As I casually fondled her breast's supple, swollen form—like a soft, hot melon in my hand—I noticed a scar resulting from a cancerous lump's removal.

I kissed it tenderly.

Then, for the first time, I looked at her intently. There, curved close and warm against my body, lay love, joy, bliss in the shape of a woman—but far more lovely than any mere mortal is supposed to be. In the radiant glow streaming in from an enthralling midnight moon, she opened her eyes and ran her fingers over the edges of the jagged battle scar on my right thigh. She whispered, "Tonight! It's what I've been waiting for. I'm awake—alive—for the very first time."

Plainly, we both possessed hidden scars, some physical, the ugliest, emotional.

Jackie rose to her feet, wandered over to the fireplace, gazed into its flames. She closed her eyes and swayed to soundless tunes; entered an intimate, timeless realm. The glowing firelight shifted into iridescence upon her alluring bareness. The ashes gave off a subtle aroma. The wind whistling through the willows produced a sound unlike any other. This captivating, mystical melody brought Jackie hastily back from those enchanted places she'd been visiting.

There was nervous laughter as we picked up our clothes from the floor, quickly dressed, and rejoined the party. We apparently weren't missed. Nothing in the immense festive room appeared to have changed. But Jackie and I had changed. Neither one of us would ever be quite the same again.

Subsequently we laughed, spoke at length, secretly made plans to meet at Point of Rocks. This serene section of the Potomac River features calm water perfect for the compact powerboat I'd rented. The river wound blissfully past shoreline cliffs, a pristine forest, and abundant wildlife. Midday we stopped at a secluded island to enjoy a boxed lunch we'd purchased earlier. Our sun-and-surf date ended at a quaint waterside winery with an evening outdoor concert at the vineyard.

Jackie stared intensely into her crystal flute of chilled champagne while biting at her lips. "I was never free from the oppressive sense that I had two enormously baffling beings to please—God and my mother; and my mother was the most baffling of the two. What's more, within days of my nineteenth birthday, I found myself orphaned by the rude calling card of death. My parents and sister all died in a horrible ski mishap while vacationing in the Swiss Alps.

"When the authorities notified me, I probably wasn't as devastated as I suppose I should've been," Jackie confided with moist eyes. Fidgeting, clearing her throat, she continued: "When I was small, the only thing I wanted to be was a woman because I was a huge failure as a little girl. I was precocious, full of hellish energy, and had a hard time finding a boyfriend. Still, I kept trying.

"My older sister was beautiful, popular, and my mother's favorite. My mother used to look at me as if I were a side dish of brussels sprouts she hadn't ordered. In a family of beautiful women, I was not a beautiful girl. My sister snickered 'jumbo,' 'fat ass,' 'little miss fugly'—her shorthand for fat and ugly. Her words hurt deeply. I was the unpretty one—the awkward ugly duckling of the litter. But through some mini miracle, I did eventually manage to get a handsome beau.

"One evening my piano teacher had an emergency, dismissed class early. I arrived home and stopped short at my sister's room. 'Someone's coming!' she whispered. I gave her an incredulous stare. My mouth fell open as I saw my new boyfriend face-deep in my giggling, wriggling, breathless sister.

"I preferred putting my overwhelming world in order with a diary. I wrote about the hurt, shame, quiet lonely moments of a childhood marred by great mental suffering. Our house was a vast museum of magnificence and misery; no one spoke of love, except me. 'I love you,' I muttered painfully to just about any boy who smiled at me, my words crying for a tenderness I'd never known. But I was usually laughed at. I'd run to my room; hide under the covers, weeping until the pain and humiliation subsided.

"I sat sad and solitary most weekends, biting my nails—hugging my cuddly taupe teddy bear, Mr. Max—desperately wanting to be loved. At sixteen, I went to the library and picked up a book at random. It was a volume of poetry entitled *Unloved*. The last stanza read, 'Warning: This woman is not mad, answers to any name/ Responds to love, don't call her or she will come.' It expressed exactly how I felt at the time: unloved."

Jackie wet her lips, gave a hard, obvious swallow. "Want to know my biggest, most embarrassing secret? I—I liked to run naked in the rain, through flowery meadows when no one was around. The way I looked at it, why be given a beautiful body if you have to keep it shut up in a case like a rare antique violin?

"One brutally hot day I was hiking a serene trail alongside Rock Creek. I came upon a crystal-clear stream that widened into a pool deeply shaded by silvery willows. I let my trendy garments fall at the water's edge. Slipped my sweet, young nakedness into the cool, delicious water. I swam idly to and fro in utter peace.

"Suddenly, I sensed someone watching me. Frightened, I sprang to the bank. As I did so, I heard footsteps, heavy breathing coming closer and closer. Without looking back, I fled from the stream to the woods. I was hotly pursued. My one thought—to escape! I heard the 'heavy breather' trip, stumble, and fall. But I continued to run with all the speed the terror flooding my heart gave me. The chase left me panting, exhausted, with my virginity still intact—though barely. I made myself a solemn vow never to go nude in the wilds again."

"How old were you?" I said my eyes widening as I moved closer.

Jackie didn't answer. Just smiled and added this postscript: "I've been running away from that awkward, unpretty, unloved little girl all my life. Unfortunately, the long shadow of my ugly childhood still follows me every day. For a substantial time, I couldn't transform my pain, so I transmitted it."

As joy replaced unease, my uncomfortableness around the super rich inexplicably disappeared. Jackie's expensive trinkets, servants, posh mansion receded in my awareness. I saw beyond appearances; my heart opened to love.

We often sail to distant shores, seeking what lies hidden right in front of us. I required no such journey. The gifts of love overflowed before me. Adrift on the tide of our passion, joy sparkled in Jackie's eyes; love's flame illumed me. Jackie's love nourished my passion-deprived body, my love-hungry soul.

Simply stated, into my life she fell: a love-starved beauty sure to plunge us both into hell. Our affair proved to be intense, sensual, and passionate.

CHAPTER 8

A Flagrantly Expensive Knife

Several Saturday evenings later, a twilight hush fell over Georgetown. The wind stilled; the quiet shadows grew deep. The streetlamps twinkled with a special radiance. I remember Jackie and me wandering brick-paved sidewalks at sunset. We walked in the rain, where the air is fragrant with love. We walked hand in hand in the moonlight. Our walks were punctuated with sweet glances, tender touches, warm hugs: her soft kisses and giggles echoing in the still night air.

Spring rain sounds like silver music. It's a superb mirror for moonlight. I remember the reflections of moonbeams and Jackie's outline mingling magically in rounded puddles. I also remember sharing Georgetown's quiet, colorful afternoons of sheer beauty—the pale soft sky, so clear and tender. We'd amble along the riverbank, arms around each other's waist. We'd ooh and aah at blossoming cherry trees resembling pale-pink clouds and sailboats skipping over the water, the swift, silent river slipping by. I adored Jackie, and my face showed it.

Our love was like a delicate rose. We nurtured it. It flourished, bringing beauty to us both. But most of all, I remember making love to Jackie by candlelight on an unforgettable autumn evening. Thereafter, I hungered for her affection so obsessively that I could taste it as I breathed.

Our favorite hangouts were owned by friends—people we trusted, who we dared to be ourselves with, like Smooth Bobby. Still, from time to time, I'd bump into lawyers, lobbyists, politicians who recognized me. Mostly they would be with someone other than their spouse. We'd greet each other politely; masterfully pretend not to notice the other's attractive companion.

What's the point in being virtuous when you're starving for human affection? We all have one foot in heaven and the other on the banana peel of self-denial. Jackie had ushered into my life a spine-tingling existence of delirious sex and intense happiness I just couldn't deny myself. Torrid feelings coupled with a radiant bliss consumed me day and night. Caught in that sensual music called love, I didn't care what people thought or what they would say.

Truthfully, Jacqueline Sophia O'Sullivan seemed like a glittering whirlwind to me, all contradiction and enticing mystery. She possessed an alluring elfin beauty men found irresistible. What's more, she had immense charm and an unbearably delicious smile. She looked as delicate as a butterfly; could whisper with gentle persuasion. Her hair customarily smelled of an unforgettable fragrance. But there was a superb mind behind those soft dimples. Her intellect, logic, sparkling wit were dazzling. Plus, her opinions were presented on a silver platter of graciousness.

I also soon discovered she had a hidden drive as strong as any alpha male's. At the same time, she was incredibly sentimental and as affectionate as a woman has any right to be.

Gradually the radiant picture-perfect Annapolis, Maryland sky darkened until it revised into a moonlit summer night. The sounds of the shimmering bay, of the gulls grew pale and relaxing.

We'd spent the day under sail, gliding tranquilly past magnificent mansions, the State House, the Naval Academy. Jackie and I were lying on deck naked. Our nude bodies subtly touching periodically felt wonderful. I tenderly stroked her gorgeous derriere, sleek thighs, and other places of interest. Jackie's slender body quivered; moonlight filled her eyes. She began doing to me that titillating thing she did so amazingly. My excitement started to build. Suddenly, in a fever of impatience, Jackie wanted me desperately, needed me to fill her urgently. She made violently passionate love to me.

Afterward I turned to Jackie and looked at her in pure astonishment. "I..."

She placed her finger to my lips and whispered, "Shhh!"

When Jackie spoke again, her voice was choked, her eyes, moist. "I'm not certain about males, but females are lonesome animals. We spend all of our lives trying to be less lonesome. The majority of women are like me, Jason. We have to truly like a man a great deal to love him. Otherwise, you're simply unbearable.

"I realize I'm a female who desperately needs a man's companionship. I need to love and need to be loved, to be happy. So I made a vow within my soul that I'd do whatever it took to meet someone I really loved and who truly loved me." I watched Jackie's full lips part and smile as she reached out, touched my face. "I've now fulfilled that promise to myself!"

"Wow! Probably stay awake all night thinking about that revelation, babe." Lowering my head and swallowing hard, I then said, "I've seen people in relationships with everything but love; I've seen those whose only true joy in life was love. I know absolutely which is better. So I attempted to find a special girl, the one and only, to share my love. I knew the rest of life's bullshit, even if served in an exquisite silver bowl, was still simply a bowl of shit. I thought I found the perfect woman. Unfortunately, I later discovered my dainty-fingered sweetheart was humping everything in DC except the Washington Monument."

"That's a gut-wrenching story, Jason." Jackie said sniffing, wiping at her nose.

"I can see clearly now, Jackie; I was looking for love—looking for you—but in all the wrong places."

"For many, Jason, heartache falls upon us like the rain. Incompatible lovers, finding nothing, leave the failure of each other's arms every sunset. When two who loathe each other must share the same bed, things seem strange and out of place. Lying there in the twilight hours they hold their breath in shame. Unfortunately, I know all of this from personal experience. Let's not relive our pain!"

"No problem! Get back to what you were saying, babe."

Jackie looked at me with a thoughtful expression. "I feel a woman's nature is like a magnificent mansion loaded with rooms. But beyond the numerous rooms we wander about daily are other rooms, the handles of whose doors are never turned. In the innermost room, our intimate, special place, our souls sit alone and wait for footsteps that never come.

"I want us to live in a beautiful, serene place, Jason. Our living spaces shape us; ugliness only brings out evil. Frankly, a tremendous sadness hovers about me. Feels nearest when I'm alone! That's why I want a home loaded with giggling children. Honestly, outside of our family and a few close friends, no one on Earth cares that much about you. Life seems packed with loneliness, misery, unhappiness, and it's all over much too quickly."

Jackie's desire for true love constituted her deepest need. She hid her splendid mind behind utter femininity. Yet Jackie turned out to be anything but a gentle moon maiden from some misty garden. She wore slinky silk during our private moments; looked like a princess when attending a ball. She laced her boots, zipped her hooded sweatshirt, and often helped me saw logs for the fireplace. The dust, grime, sweat did nothing but strangely enhance her beauty.

At times, fate is a cruel taskmaster. It appeared to relish the notion of forcing me to choose between serving the church and loving a woman whom my very soul boundlessly cherished. I found myself at a crossroad, uncertain as to the right path to follow. So I chose to do nothing. I sat by the side of decision road, waiting for fate to make the next move. I failed to realize that to live is to be uncertain: certainty comes only at the end of the journey.

A rich harvest of joy-filled, magical, shameless months slipped quickly by. It was a calm, clear evening just before the death of day. The view from the dining room was stunning. Jackie said, "You've probably noticed that I've put on a little bit of weight."

I gave a too-quick smile. Glanced around uneasily. "Well, er, yes. I—I didn't want to say anything to…Look, it's OK!"

Jackie responded with rapid, high-pitched laughter. "Try this on for size: inside me our love took on a beautiful form—and I've decided to call him Ethan."

With a dazed look, my mouth falling open I stared at the half-eaten pizza's melted cheese hardening on the plate.

A week later, Jackie entered the handsome ebony door of her prestigious Georgetown mansion. Within minutes, she was in the midst of a high-voltage confession of infidelity. Her husband, Patrick, boiling with violent wrath, snatched Jackie's treasured antique vase from a nearby glass shelf.

"This is a going-away present for you. I'll save you the trouble of wrapping it!"

He threw the rare vase violently against a wall: it shattered explosively. Patrick reached out a huge, exasperated hand. Jackie gave him a scathing look. "Don't!" she hissed, drawing away with loathing.

"I could break you in half!" Patrick shouted, trembling with rage. "You must be out of your mind leaving me! I've been damn good to you! Ask anybody!"

"How can a bird born for love, intimacy, joy sit in a gilded cage and sing?"

"What the hell does that mean? You're a rotten, shameless bitch—know that? Just—just get your skinny ass outta here! Go back to whoever you've been sleeping around with. It's probably some spoiled snob born with a silver spoon stuck up his ass who's never had to work for a livin' like me.

"I know what it really is! I didn't want to adopt a damn kid—is that what this is all about?"

"No, it's not that."

"I'm too old for you now, is that it?"

"It's not your age, Patrick. You're violent, vulgar, self-absorbed. Simply looking for another trophy to impress your friends. You wear me on your arm around Washington like some lovely accessory. I'm just tired of playing that role. I need a man with passion. One who loves me for me, in spite of my faults. One who can satisfy me emotionally, intellectually. In ways you couldn't possibly understand. I feel no physical attraction to you! When you kissed me yesterday, I felt no more than I would have if I had been kissing a cold, wet rock."

Clenching his fists, Patrick bellowed, "OK! I love you! There—I said it!"

"You've also said numerous times, 'You are beautiful.' But that's not love! Your so-called *love* disgusts me—sickens and horrifies me." Jackie then glared at him with steely eyed revulsion. "I know about you and the senator! No wonder you've contributed a whale of a bundle to his endless campaign fundraisers."

Patrick looked startled. There was instant panic. "Lies! Those vicious rumors are barefaced lies spread by the opposition party. It's just a sleazy attempt to damage his fine name. They want to ruin mine too because I'm his biggest contributor. Those lowlifes want his damn Senate seat, that's all. Besides, he's—he's married."

"So are you, Patrick! Frankly, a wife *can feel* when something's not right. I hired a detective months ago! In a confidential report loaded with vile, shocking pictures, she confirmed the ugly rumors that've been circulating about you and that political *lightweight*.

"Love without trust is a river without water. Simply stated, you're a first-class asshole who absolutely cannot be trusted! For all the wrong reasons, I've hesitated leaving this strange, dead marriage. The truth is that our marriage has all the warmth and sentiment of an obscenity scribbled on a prison-toilet door. My parting gift is my great pity for you!"

There was a venomous look on Patrick's reddening face. He began shuddering with fury. The silence that followed was broken by Jackie's hurrying footsteps.

Patrick stormed angrily after Jackie; he halted at the mansion's entrance, yelled out into the street, "You fucking whore!" and slammed the door behind her.

His third failed marriage and Jackie's discovery of his secret sex life left Patrick feeling dark, empty, hopeless. His despair proved suffocating in its intensity. Patrick began to nurture his bitterness like a rare prized orchid. A sense of deepening depression and self-pity set in. Shaking his head and crumpling onto a sofa, he muttered, "I curse myself night and day for stupidly allowing that prissy political hack to dominate my life." Pressing his hands against his cheeks and dropping his chin to his chest, Patrick let out an endless, deep, uncontrolled moan.

Unable to bear the darkness any longer, Patrick lumbered into his magnificent, upscale kitchen. His shivering hand grabbed a flagrantly expensive knife. As if in a slow-motion nightmare, he watched the long, glistening razor-edged blade being thrust into his side. He admired the craftsmanship of the superb German steel as it pierced his rib cage, sliced through his intestines. Blood spurted up over the walls, dying them a deep red.

Then there were screams—awful, guttural screams—in a cascading ecstasy of agony. The corpulent mound of flesh slumped to the burnished oak floor, dripping butcher knife clutched in his fist, eyes closed. Tears streamed down his podgy cheeks.

CHAPTER 9

Dark Storm

At 2:49 a.m., the ringing telephone jolted me awake. Frowning, blinking rapidly, I stuttered, "Hel—hello." It was my jazz club owner friend, Smooth Bobby. "Jason, know it's early. Sorry if I woke you. It's Pat O'Sullivan. Just saw a news flash on TV. Reporter said the fat bastard killed himself with a fancy German butcher knife. Sounds like this could be great news for you and..."

"Bobby!"

"What? I just call 'em like I see 'em."

"Not tonight, Bobby. Please!"

"I hear ya, Holy Man. No harm intended. Sometimes I forgit you hang around with Jesus and 'em."

"I forget sometimes myself, Bobby."

"Later!"

Bobby's shocking news packed a wallop. I felt awful, guilty. I had trouble getting back to sleep.

It was a warm June day several months following Patrick's death. A cooling afternoon shower had just started to let up. I glanced out the corner of my left eye and spotted a shaft of sunlight striking the lingering droplets of water in the air. The light refracted into a rainbow. I was driving Jackie's silver British convertible from a marina in St. Michaels on Maryland's magnificent Eastern Shore.

"Salt Spray" is a yacht club where excellence is a tradition. The membership requirements included a hefty initiation fee, a substantial net worth and ownership of a snazzy yacht. Each member's yacht colors were emblazoned on pennants that hung from the club's towering ceiling. The floor of the main saloon was filled with groupings of oversized, comfortable leather chairs.

I ordered a vodka on the rocks from the bar, and the two of us took a seat in a glass-walled restaurant overlooking the water. I ate *Maryland Caviar,* blue crab, lump crab cakes so sensuously, sinfully delicious that a spontaneous orgasm would not have been surprising. Jackie enjoyed delectable Chesapeake rockfish with mushrooms in a white-wine sauce. After eating, we strolled past the fishing boats, yachts, and skipjacks along the harbor. We crossed a footbridge into the heart of picturesque St. Michaels, picked up several bottles of locally made hot sauce renowned for its fiery spiciness.

We'd spent the morning aboard Jackie's incomparable Schooner, *Silver Girl,* a true Siren of the Sea. "Hoist the sail!" I yelled. Then I joined the crew as it raised the sails. The billowing wind filled them; the crew drew taut the sheets.

The Lady of the Harbor left port flying under full sail. Her sleek, brilliant whiteness sliced swiftly, soothingly, through softly heaving purple waves, affording spectacular views of rippling blue water, craggy rock sculptures, and towering green pines. Morning ocean, sunswept. Sky, crystal clear. Horizon, naked ring of nothingness snugly encircling the Eastern Shore and us.

Now I was speeding rapidly into the late afternoon sun after having enjoyed a bit too much of Salt Spray's superb vodka. We were tired, annoyed, our tempers flashing in lighting-like bursts over Patrick's death, my career, our unborn child.

Jackie shouted, "You're not cut out to be a priest! Just been hurt one time too many, that's all. Stop hiding from life! Go back to being an attorney. You're good at it. Or start some new and exciting business. Money's not an issue. I've got enough to last both of us a dozen lifetimes.

"We all suffer hurts; that's life. But you can't run away whenever life trips you up." Her hand gripped my arm. "I need you! You need me! You and I belong to each other. Love like ours must be held onto. I can barely imagine ever again playing the piano, eating, or even walking about Georgetown without you somehow a part of it."

Jackie's eyes welled up with tears. "Last night I had a dream, vision, or...Well, I saw him, Jason! Saw him!"

"Who?"

"Our son! Just as clear as I see you now."

"Jackie, you're not being reasonable!"

"Felt his tiny body, no bigger than my thumb, huddled, snug, and comfy against my insides. He said, 'I'm Ethan! I heard you whisper my name when you thought no one was listening. But I was listening. I hear everything you do, say, or think! My soul hovers near you even now. One special morning, heaven's light will descend to Earth, cuddling me within its radiance. I'll stretch out my hands unto you and pass into the soft, warm, cozy essence you're nourishing into creation. Most importantly, I'll look out the pure eyes of my new form—and see you. Are you ready?' I then fell into sublime unconsciousness."

Jackie moved closer and began stroking my arm. "First time I met you, I saw my baby's father in your eyes! I dashed out of Mr. J's and ran through traffic across the street. I turned and looked back with a quickening heartbeat, your irresistible attraction took my breath away. I rushed off because I didn't know how to speak to you. I wanted to pour out all I felt at once. I would've given you my soul if you had asked me. I fell in love with you instantaneously—madly, miserably in love. I'm ashamed to be so enthralled by a mere man. But I don't care. I'm utterly unable to change the way I feel.

"I've waited long enough. Time's running out! I wanna have our baby! Marry you! I don't give a damn about anything else!" Jackie covered her face with her hands. "I—I feel so emotionally naked, raw, humiliated. What do you want me to do—fall on my knees and beg?"

"No, damn it! Of course not. Just stop yelling! I need time to think this through!"

I was conflicted—torn between renouncing the priesthood and a life with Jackie. What's more, I wasn't sure what kind of father I would make given the role model I'd had and the life I'd led.

In my vodka-marinated anger, I ignored the danger of twisting River Road in the beautiful Maryland countryside. At one of the bends, I accelerated quickly to avoid hitting an enormous deer. Bewildered, the huge buck bolted toward the car. I swerved hard, barely missed colliding with it. But the vehicle seemed to pick up unnatural speed.

My heart raced; I felt sharp tingling in my hands! Sweat enveloped my forehead. The car crashed through a low steel barrier. Flew into the air. It bounced down the side of a steep ravine, uprooting small trees and bushes.

A thundering explosion ripped apart the sky! Its violent power rammed the silver convertible into a grove of trees. Jackie and I were hurled from the car—each in a different direction. Jackie lay helpless in pain, screaming, "Jason! Oh, God, Jason, please help me!"

Our eyes met; a frozen look of terror seized her face! She passed out. Then there was another earth-quaking explosion. I watched the wild flames roar up and engulf the full length of Jackie's left side! Her beige dress then her hair caught fire. Glowing, white-hot burning gas exploded forth and swallowed up the entire left side of her face!

Dazed but conscious, I became horror-struck, transfixed by the unrelenting nightmare unfolding before my eyes. I coughed, sputtered, my lungs scorched by the hot black smoke pouring from the car. It seemed like an eternity before the fire trucks arrived. The team of firefighters scurried down the steep incline; leaped fearlessly into the flames! They placed Jackie on a canvas stretcher with great care and quickly carried her to a flashing, blaring ambulance.

Amazingly, I sustained only superficial scrapes, bruises, cuts. After being treated by the paramedics, I got to Potomac Village Hospital as fast as I could. When I arrived Jackie lay unmoving on a cold steel operating table amid a forest of glistening monitors, machines, and wires. Her body was smeared with blood and marred with broad patches of seared flesh. I gasped in horror. I felt as though I'd been kicked in the gut.

A group of startled surgical-masked faces looked in my direction. All appeared disheartened. I slumped dispiritedly into a nearby chair; sat there, filled with dread. A pleasant, attractive Hispanic nurse approached me.

"Hi. I'm the admissions nurse. Are you the husband of the burn victim in OR3?"

With a glazed look, quaking voice, I said, "Er, yes. I—I'm her husband."

"You look exhausted."

Bringing a shaky hand to my forehead, I said, "I'm OK."

"Please be assured, Mr..."

"Roberts."

"Mr. Roberts, we're doing everything humanly possible for your wife. Our doctors are some of the best anywhere.

"I'm sorry, unfortunately, there're forms we need filled out. I can give you a few moments to compose yourself. Bring 'em over in about ten minutes if that's all right?"

I forced a smile. "Fine."

"Here. These are her things. Thought you might want to hold onto them."

The nurse handed me a plastic bag containing pieces of Jackie's scorched, blood and skin-embedded beige dress. As I opened the bag, I slumped to my knees—wept. I felt like my heart was dying inside me and slowly, progressively being destroyed from the inside out. I buried my face in the dress to muffle my sobs. The blood from the dress mingled with my own through the open cuts on my face. The warm tingling it generated caused me to bellow involuntarily in a long, piercing, primal scream of anguish.

The doctors glanced in my direction with moist-eyed sympathy but nonetheless continued nonstop with the work of soaking oversized gauze bandages and placing them over numerous parts of Jackie's red, blistered body. She moaned in pain! The entire left side of her body seemed badly charred. Her left eye appeared to have been burned out of its socket; the left eyebrow disappeared in swelling, oozing redness. The doctors and nurses kept applying sopping wet gauze, leaving it on briefly, then carefully lifting it off.

Pounding my fists against my thighs, I overheard a thin, spectacled, vinegar-faced doctor say, "The patient should receive all the morphine she needs. I feel there's little hope she'll survive another twenty-four hours." He also whispered to his surgical team that the child his patient had carried for twenty-one weeks—the one she'd already named Ethan—had died in overwhelming agony.

The operating room door flew open. A graying doctor with a stethoscope draped around his neck strode into the waiting area and introduced himself. "Mr. Roberts, I'm Dr. Everett. Your wife's in critical condition, but she's now resting comfortably. Your son, however, sustained massive injuries. We operated on him right away, but…"

Devastated, numb, I begged to see my son. The physician looked at me for a long time then agreed. I was ushered into the operating room. A nurse, Frances Carter, retrieved a petite bundle from a far corner of the operating room. She handed the baby to me, simultaneously rubbing my back with a soothing hand.

My world turned upside down as she handed me the tiny bundle wrapped in that pale, thin blue-flannel blanket. I held my son in my arms against my chest. He had no pulse, no heartbeat, and had turned cold. I felt a strange sensation, like a light going out in my soul. I shivered. Clutching my child's limp body, "Oh, Dear God!" was all I could find the strength to say. I stared into the distance with tired, overflowing eyes. The tears ran down my shirt; it became wet—soaking wet.

I suddenly felt powerless—vulnerable in the most sensitive part of my being. I couldn't shake the doctor's vivid description of how little Ethan had been crushed to death. I couldn't rid myself of the image of Jackie's fire-ravaged body amid piles of bloody gauze, harsh lights, shrieking monitors.

Since the accident, I have suffered endless nightmares, uncontrollable weeping. Worst of all, I've been forced to witness the descent of a beautiful, gifted woman to a grotesquely maimed cripple isolated from the elegant society that once adored her.

CHAPTER 10

Argotique

Summer surrendered to winter's frost. The world appeared reborn in beauty, all the starkness of midwinter hidden by glistening, cottony snowdrifts reminiscent of a wondrous, sumptuous dream. The delicate, wispy whiteness brought a hush over Washington's magnificent panorama. It seemed as though the entire region had taken a deep breath in anticipation of some poignant moment. Jackie sold her posh Georgetown property and retreated to her ancestral Maryland estate, Argotique.

The frozen wintry months found Jackie living with a private nurse, a maid, and her trusted butler, James. He was part servant, part bodyguard, part voodoo priest; and resembled a midnight black mountain more than he did a man. Jackie and gigantic James played together as children and grew up alongside each other at their beloved Argotique.

It was the pale dust of an expiring day. I sped along the Washington beltway, turned off at the Potomac exit. I went north on River Road and ultimately arrived at an imposing iron gate. I entered the manicured grounds via my key card and exited my car at the spectacular gushing fountain.

Argotique was the kind of place God would've bought if he'd had the money. It was an unparalleled limestone manor possessing a certain *je ne sais quoi* married to the primal beauty of secluded virgin acreage. Its peculiar witchery generated a spell of delight. Exquisite groves of shapely, graceful poplars contributed greatly to its beauty in every season. In the spring a maple bud would uncurl, begin life as a leaf. It would break out of its tight brown bud, take a deep breath, slowly stretch out. There'd be branches all around with hundreds of little leaves popping out just like it. On the ground below, delicate wildflowers ran along the road leading up to the estate; together with their maple-tree cousins, they further accented the surroundings.

The rear windows breaching Argotique's ivy-covered walls provided breathtaking views of the Potomac flowing gracefully through the hills. Lively hawks, eagles, and herons would soar nearly out of sight, swing back in graceful circles, dive, then float into easy glides along the silvery water's tree-lined banks.

Sometimes the sun appeared ethereal when there was mist upon the river. Radiant light would permeate the misty air, illuminating a river scape framed by old trees, wild roses, and random piles of mossy boulders. The full range of the Creator's glory was on display in this sylvan paradise. Argotique was truly a gem of botanic expression.

I paced Argotique's inviting gardens, swearing at myself for stopping by against Jackie's wishes. Not seeing or hearing from her was driving me mad. I mumbled, "My drinking, speeding's responsible for the host of shit Jackie's been through. What the hell am I doing here? I'm probably the last person on Earth she wants to see."

As I walked toward the mansion, I felt my stomach churning into a gigantic ball of knots. I was conscious of every sound—a nearby rushing brook, the wind in the trees, a winter fox chasing its mate pass a pile of broken logs. At every step, the sound of snow crunching underfoot seemed thunderous. An internal voice chided, *You're a former hand-to-hand combat instructor with multiple medals for valor. You've seen death in a hundred faces—and won. Surely you've got enough guts to make it to the front door.* Suddenly, a screech! I looked up and watched a red-tailed hawk rise from the Potomac's rocky banks.

It climbed steeply, silhouetted in the evening light against rolling hills of snowcapped forest green. I gazed at the hawk until it soared out of sight in the clear azure sky. Wood ducks quacking on the winter-glazed river interrupted my momentary escape.

I exhaled, realizing I'd been holding my breath. Strangely, my brief, spontaneous diversion caused me to feel a bit less nervous. I continued up the stone walkway. My knees were actually shaking. I hesitated anxiously at the rich mahogany doors before knocking. I started to perspire inelegantly in the snow, sweat dripping from my nose.

I knocked. Jackie's mixed Irish setter, Riley, began barking excitedly. Then there was a sluggish shuffle of soft-slippered feet. The door opened slowly. Jackie came out on the steps, appearing startled. She glanced at me, made eye contact, gave a questioning look. Her eyes were sad and tender. She nervously giggled, offered me an ill-at-ease smile, which I returned. Clearing my throat, I felt uncertain what to say. Fumbling for the right words, none would come. All my thoughts became throbbing purple blurs. I wanted to curl up into a tiny ball—disappear.

A long, cool stillness dangled between us. The thick, musky, suffocating layer of silence grew awkward. Finally, she motioned me to enter her sumptuous home; we ended up in the elegant living room. My gaze went to the floor, followed by hers. We both fixed our eyes on an exquisite Oriental rug—throwing self-conscience glances at each other.

What my eyes beheld, my heart didn't want to see. Stirring pain stabbed at my soul like a dagger. But I couldn't help myself. My gaze seemed irresistibly drawn to what my recklessness had done. What a gruesome spectacle! I glanced at Jackie, and like a landscape seen in lightning, I glimpsed a face scarred and distorted. Her left eye socket held an artificial eye. Mouth, pulled askew. Lips, shadowed by burns, a dead purplish red.

Jackie's expression now seemed empty, twisted by the fire into something akin to a demonic grimace. Her left hand was covered with blisters, puckered skin appearing useless. After staring at her in sudden anguish, I quickly looked away.

The concert grand piano she loved was in the crystal-chandeliered music room, but Jackie's playing days were over. The burn's aftermath ended her symbiotic partnership with the keys to her soul. But with her right hand, so pale, eerily unnatural, she unleashed her creativity via watercolors of delicate spring blossoms.

On an oak easel in front of a north-facing window sat a spectacular painting. It depicted a couple hugging under a canopy of blossoming cherry trees near the Potomac River. The blossoms danced a cherry-petal ballet around the happy couple.

"Ah...Well, please sit down. I'm just having a cup of coffee—want some?"

"No, thanks—I'm cutting down."

"Good idea—should myself." We both then sat quiet, each groping helplessly for something meaningful to say. Jackie's eyes widened. She said half-jokingly, "How about a peanut butter and jelly sandwich?"

"Actually I—I've got one in my pocket," I said, straightening my tie.

"You're kidding?"

"Brought it for Riley."

"Jason, you're incorrigible. You've turned Riley into a peanut butter addict."

"It's Riley's absolute favorite treat!"

Jackie chuckled as I pulled out a plastic bag containing the sandwich. Riley smelled the treat and rushed in a gallop to where we sat. He gulped it down and licked my hand enthusiastically, wagging his tail happily. Jackie smiled broadly and began lovingly stroking him.

I scraped a sweaty hand through my hair. Then I closed my eyes, took a calming breath, and cleared my throat. "I hate to be a fool, and I hate to do silly things. But I stood alone in the moonlight on a hillside in Rock Creek Park last night, thinking.

"You know that cozy, intimate feeling you get sometimes when we're in the same room, perhaps each reading or watching TV, not speaking, not even looking at one another? It's subtle, a fleeting thing—one we too often fail to savor and fully appreciate. Sometimes, it takes a few months of empty solitude to make us realize how significant and important it actually is.

"Know how people draw closer by doing stuff together? And still more so through talk and most of all, perhaps, in moments of passionate sex? When you stop to think of it, all these dealings are primarily aimed at one thing: that rare inner feeling of being truly loved.

"Truthfully, the absence of your love has completely overwhelmed my soul. It's echoed in my heart with a powerful intensity I previously had no conception of—a hundred, a thousand times more powerful.

"I'm filled with a pure despair I've never, ever experienced before!" Visibly sweating, I leaned forward and in a weakened voice, said, "I wish with every fiber of my heart I could right this wrong. Tell me straightforward: have I lost you, Jackie?"

Pulling back slightly, biting her bottom lip, Jackie said, "My, that's a wonderful new suit you're wearing."

Eyes glaring, tone deepening, I said, "You—you like my damn suit! Cut the shit, Jackie! Stop screwing with my mind!"

Jackie simply stared down at her empty hands.

Sliding down in the posh chair, wincing, I said, "You're going to leave me hanging here?"

Jackie continued petting Riley. Finally she looked up, her face clouded. Tears spilled down her cheeks. Jackie's voice was a painful shadow of a whisper.

"Countless nights, I suffer through restless sleep; wake up slick with sweat. I'm a fool to even rise at all. This damn depression sucks the world right from my senses. Last night I had a terrible nightmare: a gigantic black-winged creature was pressing down on my chest. I woke up gasping for breath!

"Men used to say I had the face of an angel. Now it's more like a pan of worms. And that's not all! At times, I drive down to Bethesda to visit my doctor. When people see me, they recoil like snakes startled by the beat of a tambourine. Some won't meet my eyes. Others peer, point, and wonder; their long gazes dropping, embarrassed, and quick. Suddenly I'm left all alone—alone in a body that causes whispering in dark streets.

"For years friends all thought my life was idyllic. Yet as I lay in bed at night, I secretly felt unfulfilled, unhappy, restless. Buried, unspoken was the silent question I was afraid to even ask myself— 'Is this all there is?' A nonspecific *something* was missing. And without it, my seemingly perfect life felt lifeless. I now realize the subtle, haunting longing I've had all my life was for you! Without you, I just feel like life'll never again be magical. I feel it's now impossible for me to reach 'happily ever after.'

"Daily survival is like licking honey off a thorn. Your love transformed my life's pain into honey, Jason, that you enthusiastically licked to my soul's great delight. What magic does your body's touch create, I crave it so. It made the flower of my womanhood blossom. Even the sound of your voice kindles a fire within me, causing my entire body to throb, tingle. Mornings I step from the shower, look into the mirror, thinking you'll never touch me again. Not hold me. Not caress the softness of my breasts, my eager thighs, the warm moistness waiting inside me.

"Frequently, I daydream about us. You passionately kissing my expressionless mouth into a smile. The great sailing by day and cozy anchorages at night. Our graceful dancing on deck under the stars. Me wearing my white jeans with intricate blue embroidery. You stepping on my toes. Lovers moving rhythmically to soft music is life lived as it should be lived.

"I still remember our strolling hand in hand in the rain. Georgetown's trees were in their autumn beauty. The night's starred and moonlit face transformed those tiny moist droplets into glittering diamond waterfalls. I remember how you softly kissed the raindrops from my lashes.

"I also think about the countless times you were inside me… in the dark…drifting across the blue and sudden stillness of the open sea. The soft heat of your breath. The urgency of your belly against mine. Your lips roaming my smoldering nakedness all through the night. These images churn my mind, swirl like a fitful storm, bringing suffering along with their delight. I usually fall to my knees; start to sob. Only weeping can bring me full release.

"I have trouble every night sleeping in my own bed without you in it. I don't want to sound dramatic. But I soak my pillows, yearning for you to put your arms around me, hold me. I want to lay my head on your shoulder. Want you to scratch my back. Put your hands on my skin. Feel me—squeeze my butt! Yet I find myself sitting here on the banks of the Potomac, twitching about like some oversized fish already rotting but still alive.

"Some nights I wake up crying, put my hands over my mouth. I feel like screaming, 'Fuck me, Jason—fuck me! I want your scent on me again! That's what men and women do! That's what they've always done—what they'll always do. It's nothing to be ashamed of—and I'm not! I've had to repress in myself everything that should've remained alive, flourishing!' But fear of waking my staff keeps me quiet. And, yes, the shame…That silences me too.

"As for Patrick—was it *the real me* or just my beauty, my body, my status-symbol value he was in love with? Would he want me now? Knowing him, I sincerely doubt it.

"When I married Patrick, I didn't dislike him, but I didn't love him. I settled for him. My heart had grown weary of trying to find the great love of my life. As our marriage progressed, I descended into a sort of scaled-down mental illness; feeling constantly nauseated and exhausted.

"A dark sorrow trickled unyieldingly throughout my soul! Instinctively, I put up a defensive shield in an attempt to block it. I hid behind shopping, food, friends, traveling, getting high—anything. Yet despite those *cures*, I still silently suffered. What's more, I didn't want to end up being alone. A woman no man wanted. An old maid living with a cat! If I ended my days a dried-up old spinster, what would my friends think of me, whisper about me? How would I feel about myself?

"That's the raw ugly truth! The real reason I got married when I did.

"Oh, don't be shocked! Numerous women end up marrying someone who wasn't their first choice—maybe not even their second. They get married for the same reasons I did." Leaning forward, in a soft voice that cracked with emotion, Jackie said, "But you came along! You had the thundering passion of a panther. The savage sweetness of your love kindled burning desires in me I didn't know existed. You made me feel like—like a woman! You're the first man who…but your being here…seeing me like this. It's killing me, Jason. Killing me! So please leave—and don't come back. Ever!"

There was a stunned silence. I looked at Jackie in astonishment. "Wow…'don't come back, ever.' I thought we had a love that was *for real*!"

"What'd I ever give you, Jason, except pure misery?"

"You saved my life!"

"Saved you? When?"

"The second I met you! Your love's the only thing real in my life, Jackie. The rest is a damn nightmare. How can a love once tender and warm turn so icy cold?"

"Jason, I know I'm going to sound heartless," Jackie said, watching my face carefully. "But life's cold. I'm sorry, you've gotta learn to stay warm in it now without me. Pain like ours was never meant for mere human beings. If you really care about me, you'll go. Please!"

"You can't hate me more for what happened than I hate myself. Can you ever forgive me?"

"We were two lonely people desperately seeking a taste of real love—and through some miracle, finding it in a loveless world. And that requires no forgiveness, Jason."

I got up, walked over to a mahogany tea table displaying framed photographs, a vase of dying roses, and Jackie's childhood teddy bear–confidant, Mr. Max. I picked up a vacation photo—she in a bikini, me in swim trunks. The pounding surf spray glittered in the air and cascaded over our wet, chiseled bodies.

Looking past the picture of us cuddling and smiling during happier times, I said, "I've spent time lately poking at parts of myself normal, sane people leave alone. When I came here today, I was half-afraid I wouldn't love you as much because of the accident. But I now know I don't love you less, but differently. I've realized that I don't give a shit about your looks! Every woman's beauty fades sooner or later, for one reason or another. Another fact is I'm in love with the spirit, the essence that is *you*, not your body!

"I hear what you're saying. I really do. I realize I must kill the memory of us once and for all. I must turn my soul to stone. I must learn to live again without you. But I can't! Unfortunately, I love you far too much, Jackie. But I couldn't love you a bit less, even if I tried."

Each saw our pain mirrored in the other's eyes. After a graceless silence, Jackie got up from her chair, walked over, and looked at me, confused. She closed her eyes, dropped her head into my chest; we exchanged a brief hug. Jackie gave me an exceptionally tender embrace. She took a deep breath, moved away. Sorrow sharper than the lash of a sadist's whip assaulted my heart. Tears traced their way down the side of my face, spilling onto the lapel of my new blue suit. I wiped the tears away with my sleeve.

"I—I know the temptations you must've been exposed to since my accident. I realize how weak men are…" Jackie stopped abruptly; a flush crept across her features. She stared at me briefly then slapped me hard across the face. "I can't do this! You're making me crazy, Jason! Now get out of here," Jackie snapped, tears running down her cheeks, her breathing accelerating rapidly.

Reflecting on Jackie's brutal words caused my soul to feel hollow, dark, lifeless. Completely crushed, I began to depart the suddenly claustrophobic room. Gazing back despondently, I said, "I don't know how to say good-bye. Just can't speak the words."

I could feel Jackie's eyes on me as I trudged out the front door. She timidly peered out from behind a tear-streaked, icy windowpane. Head down, I ambled into the pitch dark of night feeling like a complete idiot. My bumbling ineptitude throughout the evening made me sick to my stomach. Our painful reunion seemed like some sort of test. And I failed!

Stumbling blindly along the stone pavement, a low-hanging branch lashed my face. It produced a gash in my cheek; blood started flowing. I got into my car. Slammed the door. My car's high-powered engine broke the stillness of the night as I sped the length of the mansion's cobblestone drive. Teeth tightly clenched, I stared fiercely straight ahead down the long, dark road, teardrops falling sporadically. I glanced angrily into the rearview mirror at Argotique's rapidly receding image. A rosary entwining the mirror like a beaded black snake with silver cruciform fangs glared back.

Jackie had watched my steel-gray German sports car exit the driveway. She'd rushed out into the darkness, weeping bitterly. Jackie couldn't see me—she only heard the angry roar of the sleek roadster speeding rapidly into the night. Suddenly winter bared its teeth. The windswept iciness bit into her exposed flesh. Jackie retreated slowly back through the exquisite mahogany doors to the foyer and in sorrow fell against the walls, numb.

"Jason, forgive me...Please forgive me," she sobbed, beating at the wall. Jackie shut her eyes, listened to the mansion's vacant sounds, the gusty breathing of the wind. Her eyes opened; she felt forlorn, forsaken with only memories for company now they seemed sour, dingy, depressing. "I feel ashamed, ugly, all alone," she muttered tearfully.

Jackie staggered into her deserted living room. There as she wept and shivered, Riley ambled over, licked her trembling hand with a loving wet tongue, and lay down at her feet. She stooped down. Moist, happy kisses rained upon her face.

Jackie caressed Riley's cuddly, silky head, looked into his trusting eyes, and in a pained voice said, "Without him, it's like being the only survivor on an abandoned ship in the middle of an enormous dark sea. I live at the pitch that's near madness." Jackie's quivering fingers lightly stroked Riley's soft, velvety coat. "*Snuggle Love*, you were the starlight that shined down on me in my darkest hours. You've faithfully loved me even when I didn't know how to love myself."

Thirty minutes later, I arrived home; lay on my back in the dark—lonely, turbulent, sleepless. But my home seemed not to be home anymore. It now felt bleak, desolate, doleful. The stars were falling all around me. Even the moon shined like it didn't mean it. A quiet storm raged within my heart, tumultuous and wild.

CHAPTER 11

———— ✄ ————

Stone-Hearted Bitch

The morning following my disastrous encounter with Jackie found her wandering Argotique's vast grounds weeping and drinking profusely. She was haunted by overwhelming feelings of intense hopelessness, sadness, worthlessness.

On this gloomy Sunday, Jackie's icy loneliness was interrupted by a visit from Bernice, a fashionably overdressed friend from Washington, DC. She looked as if she must've come from some medieval royal court; she had a three-carat rock on her finger. Her clothing—the color of stale pigs' blood—was pearl-studded and deliciously, awe-inspiringly ugly.

Bernice and Jackie had been friends for years. From the first day they met, she had envied Jackie's wealth and beauty. She hated the fact that men seemed to prefer Jackie over her. Bernice even felt a bit pleased that her secret rival was no longer physically more appealing than she.

Bernice was no hunchbacked troll. Actually, she was a vain woman, arrogant, boastful, and fond of bragging she was more beautiful than women half her age. Bernice, however, had been self-conscious since puberty about the dimensions of her sizeable feet. To mitigate this cruel joke of nature, she converted a spare bedroom into a luxurious *shoe boudoir* housing, at last count, 327 pairs of astonishingly expensive, glamorous "monstrosity mitigators"; many had never been worn.

The most remarkable thing about this attractive, treacherous woman was not her feet, but her voice. It fell on the ear with a brutal monotony, irritating to the nerves like the pitiless drip of a leaky faucet. The cold hard fact is that I love Bernice best when she's not around.

Bernice sat on the stunning camelback sofa daintily sipping her tea. She tightened her lips then smiled with all the phony sweetness of an open coffin. "Jacqueline, darling, we all miss you, especially during our regular Thursday Girls Day Out." She handed Jackie a dozen pink roses. "Picked these from my garden. I know they're your favorites. Thought they might cheer you up a bit. How has it been going, really?"

Staring down at her hands in a monotone voice, Jackie said, "Frankly, when I saw him walking toward me at Mr. J's, my breathing seemed to stop, and I had an extraordinary feeling of excitement in the pit of my stomach. I managed an outward show of composure I didn't really feel. He had a sinewy, dark kind of allure. Power and self-confidence practically flowed from him. The aristocratic carriage of his head and shoulders, the natural, easy elegance of his tall, handsomely put-together body drew me irresistibly to him.

"There was no mistaking the invitation in his captivating eyes! Passion seemed to glow from him like the sunrise glittering off the Potomac. What's more, there was something dangerous about him; and yet I was helpless against his dashing manner and rugged good looks. I miss Jason enormously!"

"Well, on the bright side, no Jason, but at least you've still got oodles of money."

"Ever tried fucking a thousand-dollar bill, Bernice?"

"*Touché!* Just trying to be uplifting, darling."

"When I met Jason, an electrifying sensation possessed my breasts; it was pleasure…a potent delightfulness I had once thought could never pervade them, ever. But so it did. First time we made love, I felt like I was tossed and turned by the rush of a wild, sweet storm. He pulled me close. Then his hands, his tongue, his sizeable *magic wand*; my thrashing legs, my quivering thighs, my hot *goodie basket*—it was wonderful! Never knew love could feel so good. To say it was torrid, breathless, and perhaps even magical would be a colossal understatement."

"Really, Jackie—magical?"

"Yes, Bernice, astonishingly, incredibly magical!"

"Fine, darling! You know I don't pull punches. I'm just trying to keep it real. The truth is, I haven't had sex in nearly three years, and my sweet little pussycat is beginning to cause us both to hiss, claw, and bite."

"Tell me about it! Maybe we should form a club, Bernice."

"Yeah! Call it the Washington Horny Bitches Society. No doubt about it—Mary Margret would join in a snap. Her husband hasn't touched her in more than six months."

"Bernice, you're awful." Jackie fingered a tiny gold cross suspended from her neck. "The truth is, I've gotten cranky and old maid–like. I feel as if I'm lying in a grave while still alive. How lonely this world is growing. Something so desolate creeps over my spirit, and I don't know its name, and it won't go away. There's an icy emptiness in my chest. I—I feel an immense hollowness, the deepest misery I've ever known.

"I can't understand why this happened to me! It seems like a mistake. And mistakes ought to be rectified; only this one can't be. Frankly, Bernice, I'm slipping like sand slipping through a child's fingers. It's hard to breathe in a tight grave."

Baring her teeth slightly, Bernice leaned closer. "Simply everyone in Washington keeps talking about the tragedy that ruined your looks—your now frankly dreadful face, hands, and skin. Of course, whenever they say anything nasty about you, I tell them how wrong they are. But I don't think I could live if I were in your place. How can you stand it? I mean, how can you bear to even look at yourself?

"Oh! I'm sorry. Are those tears? Didn't mean to upset you. Please forgive—"

"Bernice, stop! Please stop it."

"What on Earth do you mean, darling?"

Adrenaline rushed through Jackie's body, and her nostrils flared. "This morning I gazed out my kitchen window, pining for the child I never got to see alive. This overwhelming moment of sadness was interrupted by these damn menstrual cramps that effectively turned a shitty morning into an immensely miserable day. As if that's not enough, you march into my home pretending to be my friend, all the while spewing your venom into my raw emotional wounds.

"In plain English, Bernice, I want you to point those enormous, hideous feet of yours toward the front door—and get the hell out of my house and my life!"

Nostrils flaring, mammoth James stomped into the room bearing his usual surly scowl, and boomed, "Best you leave by the door mighty-quick, or go headfirst through the window!" Cracking his knuckles he continued, "Don't matter much to me which!"

Bernice's hand flew to her chest and she let out a gasp, stunned. She stared at Jackie in great surprise, gawked at James in stupendous shock. Bernice felt suddenly faint. "I—I don't know…" Unable to speak, she staggered to her feet and stumbled out the front door with a bowed head, flushed face, and her mind churning.

Many say the ugliest sounds are created by nails on a blackboard, squealing brakes, or terrified screams. The way I look at it, the ugliest sounds come from the mouths of evil people. Bernice couldn't help herself. It seemed no matter how much she smiled, sooner or later, out flew the dagger like comments. Bernice was just one slimy, stone-hearted bitch. As she slithered away to resume her assault upon the remainder of humankind, Bernice took the last faint flicker of Jackie's hope.

Later the same evening, lost in despair, Jackie stared mindlessly out a rear window. A vein of naked lightning streaked across the sky. She felt suddenly drained. The light went out of her eyes. Jackie stood still, hushed, awe-bound as the great dark thunderclouds slid up from the far south. She had an inordinate fear of storms. She witnessed a full moon casting dramatic shadows; under its spell, carbon-black clouds had already devoured most of the world.

An enormous gusty wind tussled with gaping billows, slamming them against each other until they groaned. The rain poured! A black storm came in with a startling jolt, encompassing with shadows her imposing home. In the dark shapes of the swaying trees, she began to sense the prospect of a long, lonely winter ahead and a continuance of her friends' gossip, mockery, pity.

Jackie moved slowly over to her dearly loved piano and tenderly lowered its ebony cover. She stroked its glossy veneer as if reassuring a child troubled in sleep. Then she opened her patio door and walked out into a starless, howling winter's night.

The darkness of her soul matched the bitterness of the black-hooded evening.

The tempestuous north wind had been waiting outside the door to greet her. Her hair blew wildly. Jackie looked back for a second to get her breath. The dark sky fell to Earth in a torrent. Driving rain began beating against her face. Lightning streaked, thunder crashed, and blustery winds pushed hard behind her, almost knocking her flat. But with a straightened back and head held high, she sloshed through the puddles of the rain-drenched field—separating her elegant home from the shoreline—to where the wild waters roared and heaved.

Jackie proceeded slowly, painfully, past dark shadows of leafless oak trees to the banks of the wrathful river. She descended a trio of slippery wooden steps to a stormy beach of sand and slick pebbles soaked by the merciless showery dance. Slowly and deliberately, Jacqueline Sophia O'Sullivan walked into the frigid and turbulent water—and kept on walking...

Next morning I awoke as the sun was reddening. Compelled by some unknown force, I returned to Argotique. I marched directly to the banks of the Potomac, in the rear of the estate, to gather my courage, rehearse the words I intended to say.

As I gazed across the fog-shrouded river, far off on the water I saw something floating. The tide was coming in; the thing came nearer and nearer until I knew it was some poor wretch's dead body. I watched it with pity and horror in my heart as it drifted slowly toward me. It came closer, closer, and closer to the riverbank. Suddenly, I winced in gut-wrenching pain. Filled with a blinding panic, I screamed, "No! No!! Jackieeeee!!!" Wild red lightning struck my heart! My emotions all met in a mad hurricane! I ran and leaped into the icy water—overwhelmed with grief and terror!

With outstretched arms, I clasped her drowned, naked, dripping-wet body to mine. I kissed her cold lips. Tears streaming, in a voice broken with sobs, I begged, "Wake up, Jackie—wake up! For God's sake, please don't leave me! Pleazee! Pleeeeease!! Look at meeeee!!!"

Such were the thoughts passing through my mind as my eyes followed the fireplace's flickering flames in our *castle of love*. This charming old house by the water where the red ferns grow on the shores of a sickle-shaped bay abounded with stirring, haunting memories.

It'd been quite some time since Jackie's injury and subsequent suicide. But I could still smell the pungent stench of burning flesh. In waking nightmares, I could still see the flames subdue her screams. I still recall the painful note she left on her kitchen table. My hands shook, my heart raced, tears filled my eyes as I opened the note, read it, and read it again:

Dear Jason,

It is two minutes past ten. I must tell you how much I love you at two minutes past ten on this gloomy Sunday. My love for you tonight is so deep and tender that it feels like one of my life's most treasured moments. I love you—I love you—how wondrous it is to love you. Even now the tears rush to my eyes and sobs choke my throat as these thoughts fall heavy on the page. We're given but a dreamlike instant in which to sigh, grieve, cry. Then we die. What we put into those intervening moments is all we have. Thank you for each wonderful, magical moment you gave me. I've arranged with my attorney to leave you everything, including beautiful Argotique. Swear, my heart, you'll enjoy and delight in it as much as I did. Fate made it impossible to hold for long what I treasured most in this world. I knew I loved you far too much to live with you, Jason. I now also realize I cannot bear to live without you. I want to die—allow the great unknown terror to dismember me. Death is not the worst thing. Living without you is!

Jackie

Gone from me too was Jackie's dog, Riley. Before the car crash, we jogged together along the tranquil trails of Rock Creek Park daily. I hunted everywhere for him. He simply vanished into thin air the night of Jackie's death.

I took a snapshot of Jackie from my wallet and stared at it intently as though the next day I'd be stricken blind. I smiled. Somehow Jackie's picture grinning back at me slowly froze the smile off my face. My memories triggered a tearful eruption, like a painful abscess breaking.

Moments later, I again lovingly fondled Jackie's photo, and with a fluttering in my stomach said to it, "I often sit at our favorite spot amid the wild plums, roses under the Japanese maple tree on the banks behind Argotique. The spot where you first left me speechless, breathless, walking on rainbows.

"Last night I sat under our red maple, watched the moon wrap its radiant beams around the shivering Earth. Its light seemed mysteriously soft—soft as the first gleam of your love that penetrated my heart. I thought I spied a woman with long, dark hair admiring the maple. She looked exactly like you from a distance. I ran as fast as I could to the bank of the river, but when I reached it—no one was there."

There was a sinking feeling, a shudder in my chest. I felt choked as though I desperately wanted to breathe and could not. Took a sip from a half-empty shot glass of vodka. Finished it. Extracted the last remaining drop. Exhausted, I slumped down in the huge leather chair; inexplicably, I couldn't move my lower body. Trancelike, I stared deep into the fireplace's crackling flames.

Suddenly I felt a hand in mine, and though she was invisible to me, I knew that Jackie was there. She spoke, but I couldn't understand her. She spoke again, and I still didn't answer; yet I knew from the pressure of her hand she was present. Hand in hand, we lingered in the velvety silence, I, speechless and bewildered but still clinging to her hand. Seconds ticked by. I felt a stab of fear; my eyes grew wide and frightened. She attempted to retreat into the shadowed night. But as I took her hand and pressed it lightly to my lips, something mystical seemed to pass between us. Jackie addressed me again. Instantly, a soft storm whispered through my brain.

Cause my death to slip from your mind and thoughts, Jason. As the eagle freed from its cage soars to its natural heights, so too has my soul, freed from flesh, risen and returned unto its Natural Home, naked and unafraid.

My soul trembled; I was pale, shaken. I stared motionless at the logs in the hearth which stirred, gave off a few sparks, and then slumped together again.

CHAPTER 12

Inward Journey

The melodious sound of the doorbell stirred me from a fitful sleep. I peered out my bedroom window and was immensely surprised to see Sunny Day. She was wearing snazzy high heels and a stylish cashmere coat scarcely concealing a feast of smoldering, bare-naked beauty clearly intended for my pleasure. I groggily staggered toward the front door, but hesitated and went instead into the library. Within minutes, I heard Sunny's classy sports car speed away. Unable to get back to sleep, I started a relaxing fire in the hearth, plopped down in my favorite chair, stared intensely into the mesmerizing flames.

My eyes were drawn to the antique clock at the foot of the staircase. In a few seconds more, midnight. It would mark the anniversary of Jacqueline's death. I lit my pipe and still I sat, lost in a moment of eternity. I slouched in my chair, angry with God for having permitted Jackie to take her life, for not being allowed to even say good-bye. Nonetheless, my eyes misted; I stared out the window into the silent, empty-vaulted night and prayed:

"I can't believe Your boundless universe turns on an axis of suffering. Surely the extraordinary beauty of the world must somewhere rest on love. I live every day with agony just under the surface, like a wound not fully healed. Mornings I wander in a fog through Washington's streets to the other end of nowhere, pretending to be cheerful. Evenings I'm sprawled on my sofa submerged in the raw process of human grief. Nights I fall asleep on faded dreams, feeling weak as water. I seem to be reliving the journey of my life—a long night's trek to a miserable dawn.

"When I found Jackie, everything came alive. Without her, my heart feels exhausted, bled of purpose. I'm no different than anybody else. I want to live endlessly, savor happiness. The thought of my own dying is strange, depressing. But they lie, those who say death is worse than the loss of love." Grabbing fistfuls of hair, I said in a shaky voice, "Wherever Jackie's gone, I desperately need to find her. My soul feels like a dark pain-plowed field in the cold rain. I'm hanging by my fingertips on the edge of sanity."

Then a storm of high-voltage exasperation exploded into anger. I was so furious that I could hardly speak. Looking up toward heaven I shouted, "What the heck's wrong with You; can't You see I urgently need help—I need a miracle!"

I abruptly leaped to my feet, stomped about the room slamming doors. I turned on the radio. The music was whopping loud; the rich bass throbbed deep in my bones. Spontaneously, in a wild, thundering, unearthly voice, I yelled at the top of my lungs, "I've got pain that reaches down into my soul! I'd rather drink battery acid laced with broken glass than go on living like this. I'd be better off dead!"

Suddenly, a booming chime signaled the witching hour of night. The grandfather clock in the hall outside the mahogany-paneled library began tolling its twelve bold strokes. But before the last sounded, I felt a sharp twinge! It felt as if a jumbo fist had grabbed my heart, wouldn't stop squeezing. Pain radiated out from the middle of my chest to my jaw. I couldn't breathe. The radio was knocked to the floor, it shattered into a million bits. I grabbed for the phone to call for help, but before I could do so, there was a loud whooshing sound!

With heavy breaths, bulging eyes, I saw myself as a tiny dot on the outside of my body, which lay motionless below me. What's more, I found myself enveloped in oppressive darkness, experiencing feelings of overwhelming loneliness.

The bright stars were extinguished! I wandered in rayless space! The icy Earth swung blind and blackish in moonless air! I became conscious of a beam of brilliant white light. I felt myself being pulled quickly through a high, rounded, spine-tingling passageway toward the light.

As I was hurled, gasping, trembling, flinching through the dark cylinder, I became conscious of multiple levels upon which there seemed to be movement. On the first level, there emerged vague, horrible shapes—grotesque forms such as those you see in nightmares. As I passed on, there became visible on either side forms of seemingly misshapen human beings with some parts of their bodies oversized.

Again there was a change; I became aware of smoky gray-hooded forms moving downward. These forms became increasingly pale in color. Then the direction changed. The forms moved upward. The color of their robes grew rapidly lighter.

Next, there began to appear on each side vague outlines of buildings, trees, clouds. But initially, everything seemed motionless. It felt like being inside a magnificent oil painting. The clouds appeared immobile in the sky. The sun seemed stationary. There was no breeze.

As I wandered on, I observed dazzling light. This incandescence appeared to radiate from a brilliantly luminous, sublimely beautiful city of striking architectural design. Numerous Greco-Roman-styled marble buildings occupied the landscape. Each possessed immense marble steps leading to grand burnished doors, towering columns, their elegant dome-shaped tiaras soaring toward the upper heavens. Behind them arose three sets of twin towers that were gigantic, daring, distinctive.

All six towers possessed massive facades of pearl-white marble, ice-blue glass, glittering gold doors. Water flowed soothingly down their sleek outer walls. Becoming suddenly still, I observed that each stunning piece of architecture was situated flawlessly in the delightful setting of an exquisite garden.

In the beginning, the atmosphere felt a bit cool. But I quickly adapted to it. My heart seemed to freeze then pound as I became conscious of sounds—at first indistinct rumblings, then dainty melodies, laughter, and the singing of birds. There seemed to be sparkling light, overwhelming illumination everywhere. The incandescence grew lighter, brighter. The colors turned vivid, magnificent. Then, there appeared to be a blending of sound and color. All seemed so dazzling, so beautiful, so serene. It was as if I'd learned to see all over again.

With halting breaths, I found myself enveloped in a brilliant vault of light radiating sensations of joy, peace, harmony. I felt flooded with the most blissful feelings I've ever known. Absolute ecstasy engulfed me. The past and future seemed equally present in the moment. Amazingly, I could also see in all directions without turning my head. I felt utterly awed.

Then ahead of me an explosion of brilliant colors in tiny dots formed multiple erratic shapes. First, dazzling emerald. Then, lemon yellow. I seemed involuntarily drawn into one of vivid tangerine. I couldn't move. Suddenly a series of pulses throbbed into my awareness like a succession of mild electric shocks. They felt unyieldingly demanding—seemed like a sort of binary code.

Yet what appeared to be trying to communicate with me wasn't a computer but a living being. As my mind became accustomed to the pulsations, a picture began to form. It was a flaming sun with an arrow pointing into it. But that couldn't be. Or could it? The trio of color-dot beings seemed to imply they once lived inside a fiery, white-hot sun.

I found I could communicate without having to listen or speak. I'd judge the beings' reactions by observing their energy fluctuations. As I spoke, I'd see the colors change in their energy fields; I could see how they felt about what I said. When the energy fields became foggy, I knew the color-dot life forms hadn't understood my question or answer. Within minutes, the color-dot trio lost interest, released me from their grasp, and resumed their journey.

In the early stages of activity in this realm, I seemed to retain the form of my usual physical body: head, arms, legs. But after awhile, I became less humanoid in shape and finally seemed to disappear altogether. There existed no part of me that I could see. I became an observer surrounded by images. I didn't have a human body anymore. Instead, I had a translucent energy body, like a halo around a core of vibrating matter. This core possessed only geometric shapes made of hard vibrations of matter. I appeared to be a luminous ball of energy.

The experience of my becoming less human and disappearing seemed similar to that of an ice sculpture taken out of a mold on a hot summer day. The ice retains the form of the mold for brief seconds; then it begins to melt around the edges, ultimately becoming a liquid and evaporating. When that happened to my body, it took only a thought to go from invisible to ball of energy to totally human in appearance again, which generated in me spontaneous laughter.

On this plane you must start thinking in order to realize your individuality. Sounds incredible, yet it's true! I had no experience of existence without thought. Life here proceeds unconsciously;

only the act of thought allowed me to see the edges of my separate energy body within the limitless sea of energy existence. Yet no matter what shape I assumed, I remained me. I remember musing in wonder, "But I'm still me! I still feel like me!"

I seemed to walk but wasn't walking on anything. There appeared to be no ground, no sky, no boundaries of any kind. I had trouble initially adjusting to the amount of energy necessary for specific actions. It required little effort to move about. When I started to go a brief distance—say, three feet—I'd find myself almost a mile away. I had a great sense of freedom. I felt euphoric, as if I'd merged into the quintessence of existence and became at one with the universe, like a cloud within a boundless ocean of clouds that extends forever. Yet paradoxically, I felt more strongly self-aware than ever.

Ultimately I ended up in a gorgeous green valley with mountains on every side, everywhere I looked there was a breathtaking brilliance of light and color. Coming toward me from all sides were people I'd known in life and had thought of as dead. Everyone seemed delightedly intent upon mysterious errands. Amazingly, some I had known very well took no interest in me, while others I'd barely known seemed tremendously overjoyed to see me.

At one point I found myself in front of a court of incomparable beings. They had little interest in the usual misdeeds so frowned upon in Earthly society, but they were greatly concerned about my waste of valuable energy and about how I had wasted abundant opportunities to accomplish my primary goals.

At another juncture there was a spine-tingling sense of hurtling through space, and I awakened looking into the loving, radiant face of Natalie, my deceased younger sister. I was shown all the things she seemed to think I should see. My celestial tour was much like a friend from a foreign nation introducing me to her country's customs, and myriad points of interest.

I explained my plight: I was desperately seeking my friend Jackie O'Sullivan. Suddenly the light grew dim, colors faded. Through a haze I saw Natalie's body also began to fade away. I cried out to her, "Natalie!—what's happening?" and she seemed to hear me, but I could not hear her reply. Then total unconsciousness.

I awoke a bit staggered from yet another astonishing experience of floating dreamlike through space. Subsequently, with widening eyes, I came upon a myriad of glowing beings. They emitted intense light. I could describe this powerful luminescence as either light or love; it would mean exactly the same thing.

The biggest of these beings I remember clearly: There appeared at first a dazzle of light. Then I saw this light had come from the heart region of a gigantic figure with a body seemingly made of milky, translucent, shimmering air. Throughout the body ran a radiant electrical fire of which the heart appeared to be the center. Around the head of this being and through its waving, luminous hair, which was blown all about its body like living strands of gold, appeared flaming wing like auras. From the being itself, light streamed outward in every direction.

Its effects on me were feelings of extraordinary lightness, joyousness, ecstasy.

I stared at the remarkable glowing entity, the one who appeared to be the leader. I became mesmerized and was at a loss for words. Though strangely, I didn't feel afraid. The creature's radiation stunned me, however. It felt nearly overwhelming. One moment it seemed male, but then I felt certain it was female. I wondered, *Does it realize just how dazzling it is? Is it male? Female?*

With a thrust-out chest, the mighty being said, **You will become accustomed to the light. To us, you too emit the same luminosity. In this realm all life radiates vivid, glittering light.**

"Incredible! You actually know what I'm thinking!"

The titanic life form crossed its arms. **Here beings speak directly from their thoughts. We have audible thoughts. Therefore, I can read your mind. Just as you can read ours.**

"I can?"

You are doing it now.

"You're right. It's certainly not words and sounds. It's a language human tones can't master. I hear you—I hear you in my mind."

Your soul remembers the language of the realm of Light.

"You know, I am actually recalling the language."

The magnificent creature cocked its head. **It is good you remember. That you are not alarmed. Much can be accomplished when mortal fright is restrained.**

"I don't know why I'm not terrified at this moment! Right at this instant I'm here talking with you in a rational way. With you—someone who seems hospitable and congenial, a brilliantly glowing being many would interpret as God, an angel, or, at the very least, some saint. Yet we're here, talking just like two ordinary people. Except we're not speaking words. We're using our minds. But who are you actually? Or maybe I should be asking, what are you?"

In due season all shall be recalled. I too once dwelled in the outer world.

"You were an Earth dweller?"

Rocking back on its heels, the extraordinary figure said, **I chose to experience life as a sea creature. A type of man-fish. I believe you children call them dolphins.**

"You—a dolphin!"

It is the reason I felt attracted to you. I sensed you are fond of dolphins.

"Love dolphins! Even toyed with the idea of becoming a marine biologist."

The glorious life form assumed a wide stance. **Souls can elect to incarnate as anything on the tree of creation, provided an appropriate vessel is available. The life experience you chose, a human-animal being, is superb. Such lives are extraordinarily rare. Successful graduates of the earth-life system are tremendously respected on this plane.**

Spirit beings who encounter Earth graduates recognize them instantly. This is why my companions are staring at you so admiringly. Your experience with overcoming the trials of mortal existence will be a source of tremendous benefit to you in this dimension. Your tiny blue world of warring "civilized" apes is a superb teaching vehicle for the soul.

What I am? An answer, you still desire?

I nodded. "You bet!"

With a look that radiated superiority, the incomparable creature said, **In the beginning the Source issued forth one infinite soul. All beings throughout the countless dimensions of the Whole are cells of the one primordial soul. There are those who spend their entire lives together. They possess a strong desire yet cannot explain what they wish of one another. For the intense yearning that each of them has toward the other is not actually the desire of sexual intercourse. The truth is that both long for their original mate.**

Your soul has a twin. Initially the Divine Mother-Father created you, your twin flame out of a single white-fire body. It separated this fiery egg-shaped mass into two spheres of being: one with masculine polarity, one with feminine polarity. When souls descend to the numerous worlds throughout Creation, they are separated into male and female.

Love will restore you to your original state, make you complete again. But before that can happen, you and your twin flame must unequivocally fulfill your karmic obligations.

To answer your questions specifically, I am! Yet what I am, none knows. Although my countenance and mannerisms appear masculine, actually I am not male. I am not female. I am Aviar—an extension of the Divine, a balance of male and female energies, a being that is complete. This explanation satisfies?

"Genuinely! By the way, I'm Jason. Where am I?"

Squeezed between yesterday and tomorrow.

"I mean, is this heaven?"

Aviar crossed his powerful arms. There is a deep unconscious desire that drives every mortal soul; the nostalgia—the yearning to go home. You feel like an alien on Earth, one from someplace unknown. Somewhere in your mind, you know this is true. A persistent feeling, a tiny throb, a subtle memory of your real home keeps haunting you, calling you to return.

All mortals know whereof I speak. Yet some try to suppress their painful longing in games they play to occupy their time. Others lie to themselves, deny their sadness, or do not recognize their tears at all. They go about in an endless search, seeking in darkness what they cannot find, not even recognizing what it is they seek. They acquire multiple homes, yet none content their restless minds. They do not understand they build in vain. The home they seek cannot be made by Man. There is no substitute for heaven. All Man ever made was hell.

Many think it is their childhood home—the shelter they lived in, the town, the city, the nation in which they were raised—that calls them. In truth, this is the place that causes the great homesickness mortals can never shake off. Heaven was created as the natural dwelling place of God's children. You are not at home anywhere else.

Yet the habitation humans refer to as "heaven" is not a place with streets of gold and gates of pearl. Anyone can stretch out their arm and reach heaven, right where they are. Frankly, heaven is within you, envelops you. As a priest, you might recall the same thought is expressed in the proverb "the kingdom of heaven is within."

"Within what?"

Your mind! Heaven is simply a state of consciousness. Or, if you would prefer, a consciousness plane.

"Wait a second! Based on what you're saying, physical death is like stepping outside of your body and walking into the center of your mind."

True!

"I'm exceptionally open minded. But that's a bridge too far, even for me."

Let us travel across this extraordinary viaduct a bit further. I believe you will be astonished to see where it leads.

CHAPTER 13

—— ❧ ——

Raya

Absentmindedly, I looked about in wonder at my "home in eternity." Steep and lofty cliffs bathed in dramatic celestial light silhouetted the western sky. A spectacular forest provided a fiery awning of oranges, reds, yellows; its leaves shadowed a stone-strewn brook that merrily auditioned its music beneath the shade. The colorful, eloquent leaves spoke the dialect of pure being.

I stepped from a mossy bank into the rushing brook. A white turtle swam lazily by, the soothing liquid sliding over and under its belly. The water running through my toes felt light, bubbling, electrical. Inexplicably, when I stepped out an instant later, I found myself laughing. Silvery light weaving in and out of the graceful branches guided our every stride. The light's glittering radiance subtly conversed with the surrounding flora, wind, and water.

I gasped in delight at the sumptuous beauty snuggling up against my essence while God's peace serenely flowed into me as sunshine flows into trees. At last, drawing a long breath, I turned my eyes to Aviar and said, "Forgive me, Aviar. I was enraptured by the view. If I seem bewildered, it's because for a moment I wasn't sure whether we were walking through a picture-perfect forest or whether my mind had surrendered to a spell of enchantment. You were saying heaven's a state of consciousness."

Aviar looked at me in silence for a few seconds; then said, **In the 1950s, a distinguished psychiatrist conducted studies to determine if a specially formulated hallucinogen had therapeutic applications. To the doctor's astonishment, his patients' consciousnesses appeared to expand beyond their natural boundaries.**

Aviar's eyes suddenly turned dark; his demeanor, serious. **Incredibly, one woman gave an exhaustive description of what it felt like to be a female prehistoric reptile and noted that the colorful scales on the heads of males triggered within her feelings of strong sexual arousal.**

Patients also tapped into the consciousness of ancestors. Their descriptions contained little-known historical facts completely at odds with their education or exposure to the subject.

In fact, Jason, they seemed capable of knowing what it was like to be everything on the tree of evolution. They experienced what it was like to be a blood cell, an atom, a thermonuclear process inside the sun. Even the consciousness of your universe. What's more, they displayed the amazing ability to predict the future. Stranger still, some encountered beings without physical bodies, spirit guides, and superhuman beings from higher planes of consciousness.

As if that were not enough, subjects traveled to other levels of reality! In one exceptionally unnerving session, a young male found himself in what seemed to be another dimension. It had an eerie luminescence; although the male could not see anyone, he sensed it was packed with spirit beings.

Suddenly he felt a presence very close to him. To his surprise, it began to communicate telepathically with him. It asked him to contact a couple living in the Moravian city of Kromeriz and to let them know their son, "L.," was well taken care of. It then gave him the couple's name, address, and telephone number.

The doctor called the number in Kromeriz and asked if he could speak with "L." To his astonishment, the female on the

other side of the line started to cry. When she calmed down, she told him with a broken voice, "Our son is not with us anymore; he passed away. We lost him three weeks ago."

The researcher also studied the drug's effect on a sizable number of volunteers.

"The result?"

He found the episodes recurring unrelentingly!

All cultures in human history, except Western industrial civilization, have held such states of consciousness in great esteem. They induced them whenever they wanted to connect to their deities, forces of nature, or other dimensions of reality. They also used them for diagnosing, healing, artistic inspiration, and telepathy.

"Heaven, a state of consciousness! A bit difficult to get my mind around such a fantastic concept. But thanks for stretching my mind.

"Maybe you can help me with an unconventional issue. Need to find a friend. She died—or whatever you wanna call it—not long ago. I have no idea how or where to even start looking. Her name's Jacqueline O'Sullivan."

I proceeded to share with Aviar the story of who I was, why I'd come. When my saga ended, Aviar sat silent, entranced by the tale.

Interesting! Suicide—a tremendously overwhelmed soul. I know a perfect place to begin your search.

The commanding creature ascended skyward, beckoned me to follow him.

Are you ready?

Feeling a subtle weakness in my knees, I stammered, "I'm not a bird. I can't fly!"

Rolling his eyes, Aviar said, **You do know how to, as you put it, "fly." You have always had the ability to self-teleport. Even now, there are those on your world who do so. Simply use your mind, Jason! Think yourself to where you want to go!**

Aviar looked up at the sky and gave a heavy sigh. **Your river of recall is running shallow and muddy. Clearly, we must replenish its waters.**

Aviar touched my forehead with his finger. I blacked out.

I awoke on a strange, glittery, crystalline world. It seemed devoid of vegetation. I was surrounded by a huge, flat glassy plane bordered by a soaring, sparkling mountain range. It looked mysterious, daunting, beautiful. Everything everywhere seemed to be made of the same clear-crystal stuff that flashed, glowed, and glittered.

Be not alarmed, Jason! You are at The Royal Raya Academy, a university of the Spirit.

"Is this world made completely of pure crystal?" I said, lowering my voice.

The surface of Raya is not pure crystal. Raya is composed of an enormous single diamond.

Eyebrows rising, I said. "Diamond! A planet-sized diamond! Incredible!"

This type of planet-sized diamond, as you call Raya, is quite common throughout our realm. Such planets are simply former white dwarfs.

I gave Aviar a blank look.

A white dwarf is the dense, cooling ember of a star that has exhausted its nuclear fuel and has collapsed under the force of its own gravity. Raya no longer radiates heat. Its cold ashes have been removed, exposing its carbon core, which has morphed over time into a massive diamond. As you no doubt are aware, a diamond in its natural state is merely a chunk of colorless crystalline mineral consisting of pure carbon.

"How many gigantic diamonds like Raya are there floating in the skies of the universe I came from?"

I, my mate, watched in awe and wonder as your tiny, infant universe came into being. It seemed surreal. Somewhat frightening. Spectacular beyond words. But this happened only fourteen billion years ago. It takes about twenty-one billion earth-life years, however, for one of your white dwarfs to cool off like Raya.

Chief among the many splendors of Raya is The Royal Raya Academy's sprawling compound. Built on a low hill in the center of a village of surpassing splendor, multiple diamond edifices opened onto a courtyard containing the dazzling academy. Upon entering the court, a velvety carpet cushioned my steps. I glanced down; the magnificent square was covered with plush emerald-green grass. Also, artfully scattered throughout the immense enclosure stood gigantic, exotically unusual Japanese bonsai-type trees.

Under a gloriously beautiful tree several yards to my right sat a rich harvest of ravishing creatures glittering with angelic loveliness. I paused and crossed my arms, stealing looks every so often at twelve incredibly alluring, dark-haired, violet-crowned young women all dressed in flowing white garments. They were reclining on the sumptuous grass erotically waving about them with hair-fine green fronds.

The enthralling females appeared to be engaged in a class of some sort. If they were aware of my gawking, they gave no indication of it. Their instructor, who wore a violet sash around the waist of her slinky, brilliant-white vestment, seemed intent on trying to communicate some important topic. Her students appeared mesmerized as they looked up into her bewitching face framed by long flame-colored hair. The coeducational campus teemed with students whose skin tones ranged from exquisite hues of ebony, sienna, tan; yellow to alabaster.

Abruptly, my stunned eyes looked up. A powerful winged figure approached. He had big shoulders, bulging biceps, powerful chest, rippled rock-hard abs, and strong legs. His well-defined, impressively muscled body would've turned heads on any beach. He escorted Aviar and me past an elaborate entrance that breached a wall of clear, sparkling diamond. Within the embrace of this glittering barrier stood The Royal Raya's magnificent, solid-diamond Greco-Roman-styled building. Statues of angels glittered from every shadowed crevice.

The colossal Archangel Gabriel wore only a deep-violet loin-cloth-type garment and had the bearing of a military general. The luminous being also wore a mysterious gold hexagonal medallion around his neck. Gabriel and I gathered around the embers of a sunken rectangular pit of violet fire. Aviar was already seated, gazing intensely into the purplish-blue flames.

At Gabriel's request, I nervously donned an off-white linen garment. It was only at that moment that the strangeness of it struck me. I was wearing clothing—the same clothes I had on when I died. Why or how that was even possible, I couldn't grasp. In the process of changing clothes, I experienced another surprise: my spirit body was exactly the same as my human body, complete with genitalia. After dressing, I reported back to Gabriel. He instructed me on how to achieve an unyielding flow of inner silence.

Pay the price. Victory will be born! Settle down! Relax, Jason! I will refresh your memory.

Just follow my instructions. Breathe deeply, evenly…Silence you mind. Focus on what you want, the destination you want to reach…Then let go!

After a brief time, I became able to enter into a state of complete quietude.

You can "fly" anywhere, everywhere. But unless you revive your childlike wonder and imagination, you may never experience such things.

Gabriel was speaking of the trust, the innocent acceptance of things not provable. In short, he was speaking of faith. Gabriel's voice issued orders with calm authority and gentleness joined with wisdom. **Up! Pull up! Come down just a little. Down a little more...Not so fast. Easy, easy now,** he commanded.

Just when I was about to give up, I found myself, to my amazement, soaring the serene heavens effortlessly.

Initially, the view beneath me sent tremors of fear through my spine. Once, I tried to descend and hit the top limbs of a bonsai tree. However, I quickly learned to enjoy my bird's-eye view of the terrain. I beheld gorgeous vistas of rich, downy softness, a wealth of white fleecy "clouds" piled in waves as far as the eye could see. Above me, a clear deep-blue expanse that contained infinitely delicate and mellow tints.

These delightful aerial experiences left me with a sense of indescribable wonder. After a multitude of successful trial flights, Aviar thanked Gabriel warmly. We then retreated into the academy's sprawling courtyard.

Aviar stood shoulders back, with perfect posture. **Fortunately, there are two alternatives. We can have our destination come to get us, or we can utilize the slower method you call flying. Since it is picturesque, a pleasure feast for the senses, we shall use the latter. One thing's for sure: even after your refresher course with Gabriel, you might not fully comprehend how the mind accomplishes such feats. Few of us do, as the technique involves unprecedented ways—ways that cannot be totally known, just practiced. Some of life's lessons must be lived to be understood.**

Aviar gripped my forearm. Waves of cold electricity shot through me. My celestial companion's firm grasp soothed my nervous quivering as I gracefully ascended into the sky. The scenery of our location quickly dissolved into blackness.

CHAPTER 14

The Black Abyss

Our voyage took us into realms both stranger and more beautiful than I had ever imagined. As I rode on the back of the cool morning air, the most extraordinary astronomical views, the most spectacular images unfolded before my eyes. We navigated through dying stars that bloomed and faded, through dark, misty stardust afire with newly smelted, luminous celestial bodies.

I saw galaxies locked in gravitational combat, tearing each other apart or swallowing their companions completely. Then, out of the blackness, a mist-shrouded landscape emerged. We halted, motionless in midair. Aviar waved his hand. The blue-black mist parted to reveal a shockingly familiar-looking region.

Honest to goodness, it looked the same as Earth. So much so that at first glance, there seemed to be not a dash of difference. I saw mountains, valleys, plains. I beheld bodies of water and myriads of other things you'd find on Earth. Aviar lightly touched above the bridge of my nose with his forefinger. I experienced a warm sensation, like a hazy film being peeled from the corners of my eyes to the center of my nose. My inner-soul sight had been opened. Initially, my vision seemed dim, blurry, distorted. But as it cleared, I began to see with supersensitive vision.

I could see *under* the hills and valleys with surprising vividness. But to my horror, beneath the leaf-green landscape appeared a vast, empty midnight-black plane. The two of us descended to this underworld via a huge, deep, dark crater. We landed near a grouping of volcanic-like rocks immersed in a cold, white light that suggested illusions of the ruins of dead cities. As my eyes got accustomed to the dimness, I also encountered, like motionless phantoms, the tormented forms of disfigured trees. In the minds of most of us, such a place could not be. Yet there it stood.

We hiked through the desolate terrain without encountering a living soul. It had an endless series of long, narrow grooves etched into its pitch-black surface. Its dark, loamy sky was thick enough to scoop with a shovel. At the midpoint of the shadowy domain was a pyramid-shaped mountain that consisted of sleek, coal-black rock.

The titanic black pyramid possessed a vertical slit running from its base to its apex. We entered via a lightless corridor of stony pavement covered in a slime of mold. A stairway hewn out of the mountain led down into a sea of spiders. A gigantic ghoulish catacomb emerged from the misty darkness, a black abyss, a place every eye would shun.

This chamber of horrors consisted of a maze of murky passages with dripping crypts leading off of them. Each gruesome tomb had its own unique brand of revulsion being carried out. I heard despondent souls crying in the distance. Despairing shrieks! Such pitiful wails! Dismal, bitter moans assaulted my senses!

I placed my hands over my ears, attempting to block the tumultuous, pitiable barrage. With trembling lips, I yelled, "My God! Do you hear that? Where am I?"

Projecting his voice, Aviar said, **There are numerous "hells," and they are mostly of our own making. This is one of those clichés that is based upon simple fact. In this dimension, as with any other, kindred spirits congregate together. Like attracts like. Everything has a specific mental atmosphere of its own. This surrounding influence decides what is to be irresistibly drawn to it.**

There is also an infinite variety of evil that exists; each type has its own horrifying consequence, hence the limitless miniature hells within these corridors cloaked in darkness.

Looking about, lowering my voice to a whisper, I said, "What kind of sins did these poor souls commit to cause God to put them here?"

Souls plunge themselves into the black abyss. No God puts them here.

"How long do they remain in this shocking black pit—endlessly?"

Eternal damnation! Believing in such an absurd notion is straightforward ignorance. Each wretched soul remains only as long as necessary.

This Great Black Abyss is separated into regions. The scaled-down chambers in the western quarter are the worst, most terrifying of all, and become more frightful incrementally the farther they are from the east. The most horrifying are off to the side toward the northern quarter; the less horrifying are toward the southern quarter. This dark chasm also spirals downward countless levels, much like the multiple levels in an underground parking garage in your world.

The actual number of levels it coils down, I do not know. Some say it has no bottom! There is a narrow passage between the walls of the chambers on the top level in the northwestern region. It leads to The Garden of Evil, where wicked spirits roam like wild beasts. Let us start our search for your mate in the southeastern chambers.

With a churning stomach and darting gaze, I observed that some of the gelatinous-splattered chambers looked like the lairs of deranged animals. Other crypts resembled shadowy caves with caverns slanting downward into dark depths. Surrounding the mountain's base were numerous other entrances to it through moist clammy grottoes or beside deep black lakes.

Its major opening seemed colossal; others appeared tiny in comparison. But all were chilling, with illumination like you'd get from glowing embers. Vapor resembling smoky soot seeped out, steamed upward from multiple entries. The dark haze reeked with an incomparable stench so overwhelming that my eyes teared, my nostrils throbbed, and I gagged. What's more, the gruesome chasm's rutted walls appeared to perspire a thick, sticky, luminous slime.

The acts I witnessed in the repulsive dank crypts defy all belief. Some despairing souls seemed to be tortured more intensely than others. Spine-tingling screaming, crying, moaning echoed throughout the vast midnight blackness. There were profuse tongues, horrible language, outcries that wailed so sorely. Anger in diverse accents, deep and hoarse, made up a thunderous tumult that swirled and billowed, creating a hair-raising, gut-wrenching, unnatural tornado.

My stomach tightened; it was difficult to breathe. "Aviar! What is that?"

Scowling, Aviar said, **Speak not of them! All here have earned this fate. They were betrayed by the same power that lured them to their last temptation. Focus on your beloved. Pass them by!**

But through blackness thick as muck, I nonetheless witnessed merciless horrors that no words of any language could describe. They practiced unspeakable acts—so many that listing them would fill a book and defining them would take volumes. Most of these savage, bitter torments are unknown in our world. I won't attempt to recount many in detail for the simple fact that these torments wouldn't be understood; they're also utterly unspeakable. But most of all because you just wouldn't believe it; I barely do myself.

With the sound of my heartbeat thundering in my ears, I turned to Aviar. "Is there a Satan who—"

Belief in a supernatural Satan is clearly childish. When one listens to the voice of your abominable history, it becomes evident mortal beings are quite capable of any and all of the vilest evil. For the depths of human nature are gargantuan, black, and terrifying. The natural condition of Man is to be brutal and lawless. Thus early human society concluded that they could not urge the wicked to decency by common sense alone. There was also a need for an invisible watchman: Religious Fear.

Aviar adopted a grave expression. This type of fear cannot be aroused without devils, fires, taboos—"boogeymen"—to scare the simpleminded. Heavenly hopes, devils, Satans lend weight to morals and inspire the masses to put up with reasonable restraints.

Satan is not some red-suited demon with horns, tail, and pitchfork. This medieval image was derived from the mythical Greek god Pan. The frightening-looking Pan, born half-goat, half-man, possessed goat horns, beard, legs, and tail. His trident, or "pitchfork," was borrowed from the mythical sea god, Neptune.

Satan refers to a state of being rather than an actual being. It is a form of insanity. Those afflicted are true sociopaths: merciless, amoral, valuing no life but their own. They view others as pawns to be used, manipulated, destroyed in some fashion. Evil is simply an experience we are allowed to have until, through negative experiences—negative karma—we learn to use the Law of Cause and Effect positively. Consequently, any being, mortal, or spirit has within them the potential to become a "Satan."

Face turning ashen, I gazed in fearful wonder at the outcasts of heaven around me. Every single one seemed plainly Satanic, full of hatred, wickedness, spite. What's more, they utilized horrendous skill and brute violence in torturing one another. The sad and tortured *passed the time*—for such an existence can't be called living—harboring wild fear. Suffering was dished out in cruel and vicious form.

I saw torture-worn souls passionately praying for a second death in order to escape their incredible agony. All the pain and misery distressed my spirit. I closed my eyes; overwhelming pity flowed down my cheeks.

Suddenly in the twilight gloom, the region trembled as if it'd been shaken by a thundering quake. Pulse racing, leg muscles tightening—my body seemed ready to run. The eerie, dark domain gave forth an explosive blast like lightning that shot out of its depths with a fiery red flame. My jaw dropped. I shook, pale with fright. I glanced into Aviar's fearless eyes. Seeing my distress, he gripped the scarlet bolt and blocked its flame with his hand, diverting it back into the portal from which it sprang. Within seconds it fizzled then died out.

Veins standing out in my neck, I stared in disbelief. "That's impossible!"

Aviar deliberately raised his eyebrows. **Impossibilities are simply things you have not learned or you subconsciously do not wish to happen. Nothing is any more impossible than you believe it to be!**

"But how? How'd you do that?"

With a jutting chin Aviar said, **By intending to make it happen then doing it!**

Aviar was a riddle wrapped in a mystery inside an enigma. He was a fierce, mighty, masterful warrior who never backed down and never backed up. He was bold, confident, and intense with a fiery heart. He commanded firmly, was no nonsense, and seemed completely in control of every situation. He appeared to be a cross between an electrically charged dynamo, a flaming torch, and a high-powered explosion.

What's more, he was the most un-angelic spirit you could ever imagine. Aviar once said with a smirk, **I am always triumphant, ever a victor, never defeated, need no champion, and walk unafraid through life!** I have a feeling that lurking beneath this powerful spirit's persona lies an inferiority complex he'd rather die than have exposed. Nonetheless, I stood transfixed in astonishment at this spectacular being's power.

The two of us descended deep into the steamy subterranean recesses of the abyss. An aroma like decaying flesh greeted the nostril with every breath. At the six hundredth level, I saw an astonishing lake of blood. I witnessed souls tormented there with staggering brutishness. They resembled helpless lambs trapped in the grips of bloodlusting sadists. They passed me, speechless, trembling.

With a fearful expression, one by one, they immersed their naked selves into the squalid crimson filth, glazed teardrops distilled with bloody foam running down many chins. Numerous backs had been stripped of skin by incredible savagery, exposing raw flesh, their owners too anguished to drop a tear.

The tormentors were dark angels. All appeared in the form of twelve-foot-long blood-red serpents with pale eyes, forked black tongues. These monsters with skin transparent as glass moved about vertically, balanced on split tails. They could divide their tails at will, which allowed them to either stand or slither about.

Terrified souls choked, strangled, vomited reddish mucus in that bottomless chasm of putrid blood. Those drowned were quickly revived then immediately hurled in again. Unable to escape their misery, in foolish wrath, a multitude of them gnawed their limbs in blind rage, their blood then mixing with that of the scarlet sea.

One pale, gaunt soul had a dark angel's fangs slice deep into the nape of his neck and part of his brain. He was dragged to its strangely glowing edge and flung into the gory pool. Crying! Kicking! Screaming!

Like a shot out of hell, another red serpent sprang upon a female and fastened itself about her. The slimy viper entwined itself around her breasts, arms, belly; inserted its tail between her bare thighs, curled it along her right leg, sank its fangs deep into her face—pierced her left nostril and cheek. They stared fiercely—eye to eye—at each other. Thick warm vapors wafted from its rancid mouth up her nostrils while its dark tongue flicked periodically against her cheek. Writhing mightily, both fell into the bloody pit.

Such beastly acts of hate left me feeling neither dead nor living. Sorrow grips me even now whenever my thoughts reflect back on the hideous sights of that day.

Arm thy heart with strength, Jason. We must depart from evil so extreme before deeds more ugly arrive.

I bit through my distress. Uttering not a word, our heads down, we moved on.

On level 666, Aviar and I came upon a pit of unspeakable agony. A strange, sulfurous vapor, burning and sickening, assaulted us as we approached close enough to breathe it. We were confronted with arms, legs, the bubbling of faces. Fire, smoke, and a glowing, white-hot, gooey flow of naked beings met our gaze.

Bare bodies boiled into grotesque formations seemingly erupted from everywhere. Thick clouds of them bubbled into thin, foul-smelling vapors. All around me were the sounds of things I couldn't see. A staggering, gut-wrenching torrent of wails resonated to the sky. There were pleas to the saints, profanity. These horrible cries shattered into screams and prayers to God.

Suddenly, the hellish cavity exploded into steam, sparks, whips of smoke, zigzag streaks of fire. Showers of burning cinders engulfed the gloomy atmosphere. The intense darkness took on a lurid red gloom. As the scene of horrific crimes became increasingly more distressing, I spied a brooding, stupendously evil "thing." It was jet black with the wings of a gigantic bat.

The thing turned toward us; its eyes were livid, wild. As the beastly growls of the monster grew louder, a shivering horror swept over me. My heart pounded, my head reeled, my breath came in sobbing gasps. Shaking uncontrollably, I fell into a catatonic shock. Thereafter, I saw without seeing, heard without hearing.

Aviar, ever the bold, daring warrior, examined the remainder of the lower levels alone with me in tow. After concluding the search, he observed my heart region closely. **Believe it or not, sound can heal either mind or body,** Aviar said, giving me an easy nod**.** Then slowly, in lovely, soothing, mystical tones, he recited a rhythmic prayer, a magical formula in a language unknown to me. Within minutes I took a deep, shivering breath. I was myself again.

Aviar and I then soared quickly upward to The Garden of Evil.

CHAPTER 15

Garden of Evil

From the rear of the great dark chamber we emerged into an even more weird and spooky place—a boundless valley where the sun never shines and all appeared wrapped in shadows. The atmosphere was clammy. The terrain, enveloped by turbid mist, like the moon half-visible through clouds. Suddenly a sticky coal-black rain fell. It looked like ink had a fetid stench and bizarre taste.

I saw horrors piled upon horrors. We plodded ankle-deep across a forest floor alive with slithering, slimy olive-colored worms, slugs, toads, muck, and mire. I observed rough, knotted trees; foliage with blackened hues; deformed branches, matted and thick; bushes with poison-spitting thorns. The wind howled. No light appeared in the shadowy sky. But there were *things* wailing among the trees in that raven-black wood. The thick black rain ended as abruptly as it started.

We marched past ebony trees with snarled, pointy twigs upon which grew unprecedented fruit. They were bowl shaped; eight inches in girth; covered with brown, hairy, bumpy nap. I picked one of the fruits, lightly licked the skin; it blistered my mouth and made it sore. Upon removing the nap, a bright buff-colored, pulpy substance exuding an offensive, suffocating odor was revealed. Within seconds of exposure to the atmosphere, its buff color changed to a livid red resembling venous blood. "Good grief!" I said in disgust as it quickly became moist and liquefied in my hand.

Beyond dark, twisted branches that lashed and scraped at the air, I glimpsed a meadow of strange, pallid, ghostly flowers. A massive fire raged at its center. I made out the image of two long, lean, hungry-looking beings with the faces of gargoyles and the stomachs of unfed leeches. They were accompanied by a trio of wolf like creatures with baleful eyes. What's more, the pack of demons also included a nude raven-haired female of surpassing beauty with cloven hooves instead of feet.

All were stark naked, dancing riotously around roaring-hot flames, wildly waving ivy-wreathed wands. When the hideous sextet discovered Aviar and I watching, all rushed hastily through the woods and valleys, uttering high-pitched, penetrating sounds.

We trudged further down the mud-and-slime path. I spied something writhing frantically in an enormous black claw being borne up to a towering, somber branch. It breezed pass me. The victim's dripping blood splashed on my forehead and trickled down my face. As it did so, there rang out a heartrending, piercing scream of anguish, torture.

I heard hushed voices, breathing, and rustling coming from the thickets. But not a thing could be clearly seen.

Suddenly, there seemed to be crackling and crunching all around and then frightful, thunderous crashing sounds. I felt an overwhelming sense of dread—the coldest, most abject terror I'd ever experienced. I felt the hair on the nape of my neck rising. I could neither move nor speak.

From the outer darkness emerged a myriad of utterly hideous sights. My heart staggered. They appeared part human, part animal, part brute force and evil. All stood well over ten feet tall, sinewy, and powerfully built. Each one was covered with smooth, glossy-black hair like well-groomed black horse's hide. Their lean, skeletal faces possessed lips pierced by claw-like teeth, a hole where a nose should have been, plus soulless eyes flickering like intense red flames.

The savage creatures also had pointed heads, narrow slits for ears, and powerful shoulders with massive, long arms ending in clawed hands. They made sounds like the bark of a hoarse dog.

Hideous and huge, tall as mountain crags, the hellish army approached. I was terror-stricken; backed away in quick, jerky steps. What's more, an irritating odor akin to strangely scented urine secreted from their gargantuan bodies, which bore recent and old wounds. The pungent odor drifted around us in a thin fog.

The colossal leader was terrible to behold: he was a pitch-black Cyclops with an enormous red eye stained with the glitter of fresh blood that glistened like rubies. The creature's eye had no fatlike substance within it and glared with pure, high-voltage hate. In his left hand, he clutched the hair of a decapitated head oozing dangling skin, flesh, and entrails. His putrefying trophy gave off an intolerable stench.

As if that weren't enough, multiple others also held assorted stumps of bleeding, raw red flesh. A profusion of mouths were gorged full with things decayed and rotted. What's more, I saw one pounce on a living something or someone and carry it screaming into the shadows, tear it limb from limb, and devour bloody shreds of its soft tissue.

With an icy look of sheer contempt, their dark prince raised the severed head high. His savage temper escalated. He uttered something in a booming voice. Then he stretched out his mighty left arm, whirled the bloody head he clutched in his great hand, and dashed its brains out on the ground. A sea of giant fangs spat and drooled venom. All eyed us with pure naked malice. A looming hulk crept ever closer toward me. My stomach churned. The wind hushed.

The savage warriors, battle mad, appeared invincible. It seemed impossible for Aviar and me to either conquer them or escape. I turned toward him. My face was ghostly white; my heart, beating so fast that it felt as though it was going to leap from my chest.

Aviar stepped between the wicked legion and me.

Leaning forward, giving an arrogant laugh, Aviar thundered, **Fear no evil and no shadows in the night! The power of the God Force is ever with us. Nothing affects you except your own thoughts. Nothing can hurt you unless you give mental consent!**

Then, glaring at the great multitude of demons, Aviar roared, **Withdraw! Or you will wade through blood!**

Without warning, a half-eaten thigh bone was hurled toward me. I deflected it with my forearm. I felt both terror and anger. Some power from on high breathed a mad courage into me. The ensuing battle was gory but short. Aviar's fierce eyes flashed! They generated intense rays, a glaring fire that was like thunder with a breath of flame. This powerful stream of flaming light moved quickly along his line of sight, demolishing targets explosively.

That awful glory of burning light from his eyes caused a cataclysmic explosion in the atmosphere. It created a dazzling yellow, scarlet, green ball of fire in the heavens, igniting the gnarled forest. Countless twisted trees, bushes were knocked over in a pattern radiating out as far as the eye could see from where Aviar and I stood, their limbs, bark stripped away. Monsters lurking in the trees scattered in a panic.

The sky was split in two. High above the ebony woods, the entire northern part of the gloomy ether appeared to be covered with fire. Then there was a thunderous *Kaboom* in the heavens and a stupendous crash! The entire region shook, shuddered with a mammoth earthquake-like trembling as fine dust drifted over the area. The fiery forest fell, faded; towering, crackling trunks extinguished with a crash. And all was dark again.

Aviar drove a white-hot flame into the Cyclops's eye. The one-eyed giant clutched its charred eye socket, screaming with shock and pain. With a shriek, he sprang several feet up into the air. This way and that, he flung about, grasping blindly for his tormentor. He tore a hefty rock from the ground, threw it forcefully.

The massive stone came within a hair's breadth of crushing me! Adrenaline rushed through my body. I picked up the biggest pointed branch I could find, aimed it at his throat, and hurled the spear into his gullet with all of my might. The monster's knees buckled. He slumped to a seated position. His militia gaped at us with awe. Many stole frightened glances at each other, trembled, cowered, then shied away.

On fought Aviar, glorious as the sun when it rises. I battled with great vigor beside him. Aviar's mighty gaze blazed everywhere. When he struck, he struck like a thunderbolt. My belligerent companion shot a fiery spike through the left cheek, up behind the left eye, and out the top of the head of another gargantuan brute. The demon vomited explosively; the effort of vomiting pressed out a sizeable glob of its brain, which splattered upon the trail.

Bluish-black blood gushed far and wide. Fear seized the bizarre beings. They attempted to shield themselves with raised arms. As the ground turned bloodier before my eyes, the monsters' screeches, screams grew louder. Their squealing groans of agony echoed in the trees! Some gasped, snorted with wide-stretched nostrils: inwardly burning, outwardly smoking from stinging, bleeding wounds. Others wailed in a strange tongue. Threw themselves to the ground, twisting, churning into loops like half-crazed serpents.

Barely more than five minutes later, the fiery, fierce Aviar bellowed, **Be Gone!** with such a shockingly loud timbre that it made thunder seem feeble. At the earsplitting sound, trembling seized the entire savage band. The Cyclops—shapeless, huge, his eye put out, lying gasping on the ground—leaped up. He staggered, stumbled, and plunged recklessly back into the outer darkness. The other terror-stricken creatures bolted behind their stunned leader. Stragglers crawled frantically over furrows flowing with blue-black blood. A few left pieces of their raw flesh dangling from nearby wild thorns.

Aviar stood firm and strong, observing the monsters' hurried retreat, roaring and glaring terribly. His fierce, maddening rage passed, but very slowly. Fortunately, I suffered only tiny cuts.

Pity not the savage ones. They reap what they sowed.

Profusely sweating, in a hoarse, shaky voice, I said, "Just what were they?"

Illusions! Troubled primitive souls indulging in sharp-edged children's toys.

"Illusions? Toys?" I looked at Aviar curiously. "What the heck does that mean?"

Dwell not on the inmates of this evil realm. Dwell thou on finding your mate.

Far away, lightning flashed. I stood chest-high amid incomparably disgusting plant life, my feet sinking in absolutely sickening black muck. I stared at my repulsive surroundings in disbelief. What I was experiencing seemed impossible, but there I was, experiencing it.

"Where to now?"

Squinting and flashing a hard smile, Aviar said: **Mount Gehenna!**

"Sounds unpleasant."

It does not attract many tourists.

We journeyed until we reached a mountain that arose in the center of the mournful wood. It seemed deserted, like a forbidden thing. We ascended the peak by a steep, narrow trail. A powerful airstream thrust me off balance. I could hardly manage to keep from being blown off the path. High up the bleak mountain, on the stony surface of a windswept-plateau, loomed a ghostly circular cluster of immense stones. A dark haze hung over the cluster like the bridal veil of the goddess of death. A dirt lane emerged, teeming with tiny, black creepy-crawly things.

We arrived at a clearing in front of the stone cluster. Amazingly, the forceful, blustery winds howling in the treetops seemingly died. I felt nothing at all. Ahead, poised in isolated splendor, two rings of sixteen-foot-high ebony stones—some appeared to weigh as much as fifty tons—enclosed an ancient form. Towering ninety feet above the gusty, flat terrain, the enigmatic creature proved as fascinating as it was malevolently majestic. The creature's left side was made of the finest pure gold; its right, of pure silver. Close up, its evil grandeur felt overpowering.

At its base, there was a gray slab of stone. Black trees heavy with slime drooped on each side of the huge slab. Books made of antique gold and engraved with astonishing symbols rested upon the monumental piece of rock. I touched one of the gold volumes. A terrible power entered into me briefly.

Flowing in front of the stone altar, a murky stream opened to bottomless depths. The circle's ebony stones were capped by twelve-ton stone rafters that formed an unbroken ring of stone overhead. A fence of stacked rib and vertebra bones topped by skulls spewing tongues of fire completed the complex. The skulls cast a sinister glow across the thick, dark forest.

I was expecting to be blown nearly off my feet. But to my great surprise, I felt nothing. There didn't seem to be any air moving at all within the circumference of the mysterious stone complex. Puzzled, I looked up at the trees outside the circle of stones. Far from being motionless, they swayed wildly. I could actually hear the branches creak with the strain. But I felt nothing, not even a wispy breeze.

I took a few steps. Stopped in amazement again. Rushing past the complex's exterior in a whirlpool of motion were dead blackish leaves propelled by the worse gale I'd ever seen. Incredibly, a storm continued to rage outside, but it didn't touch us at all.

And that was only the beginning! A blizzard of gigantic vampire bats with white froth dripping from their bloody mouths scattered as Aviar and I ventured into a foul-smelling, dank, dark tunnel. My heart began to beat faster. I backed up a step then another. Warm, slimy dung made the dim, sloping passage treacherously slick. I swallowed my fear, forged through the thick, slippery brown muck toward a far-off opening.

There, high up, wraith-like in the waning mist, loomed an old stone castle atop a steep barren hill. Its moat was overflowing with disgusting dark blood. The castle seemed packed with guests.

Out of the blue appeared a dark-haired creature swimming rapidly upstream toward us. My face lit up. I shouted, "Jackie! Almost gave up hope of ever finding—"

Aviar grabbed my arm, snatching me back from the stream's edge. I felt my pulse both in my throat and under the grip of Aviar's hand crushing my forearm. My bathing beauty emerged from the water onto the craggy bank. Only it wasn't Jackie. This spine-tingling sea nymph had a thirty-foot-long, brown-and-black-spotted, snakelike body as thick as sixty entwining serpents.

The slithery sea witch came armed with hooked claws, eyes like globs of cold fire, a tail split into multiple spines. Its humanoid face and torso included a gaping mouth full of razor-sharp teeth and a three-foot-long leathery tongue. I shuddered violently! The scum-splattered she-devil reared up, burning with hate, and lunged forward with glistening fangs.

I stood there, filled with blind terror, fighting to keep my nerves steady. A strange loud rumbling sound stabbed the darkness. Aviar's

Herculean reverberations were staggering. His savage fierceness violently erupted. He seemed like a great white-hot volcano emitting thunderous detonations. The terrifying monster sprang wildly toward us! Aviar shoved me aside. With raw power, he broke apart the demon's jaw, showering the ground with gory falling teeth.

Death exploded from the mighty angel's glare. A fiery fist knuckled with pain burned a huge gash in the bizarre demon's chest. Aviar then ripped out its bloody beating heart in one quick motion. The serpent shot upward, reeled, and shook out torrents of scarlet blood. The shadowy stream became choked with floating red fluid. Quivering, the creature slithered backward into the dark of the green waves, disappeared in the mists of the deep.

Exhausted, relieved, I leaned upright, dripping with sweat against a massive boulder. I felt as if I was suffocating. I spied an enormous olive-gray toad stool, plopped down. Started to breathe again. For a time I sat speechless. The giant olive mushroom was surrounded by a patch of coal-black leafy plants. They felt fibrous, moist and smelled like rotten seaweed. A rush of cooling breeze chilled my soaking-wet skin and roused me from my stupor.

"Thanks!" I finally said, in a shaky voice. "Exactly what type of raw craziness—"

When you need to know, you will know! There are things better left unknown! Especially those so horrible they would haunt you for all eternity.

Our search of the horrifying forest proved fruitless, so we returned to the shadowy chasm. The abyss's inhabitants scattered in terror whenever Aviar approached. Each soul appeared in the form of its own evil, with glaring eyes like smoldering coals. These spirits manifested in forms of various shadings of hatred, vengefulness, cruelty. Though the atmosphere was blackened with shadows, I could still see that no two tortured souls looked exactly the same.

These creatures possessed appalling, lifeless faces—some like little torches, some encrusted with pimples and huge ulcerated sores. Some had no visible face at all, only something hairy, bony or "simply-teeth" in its place. Many seemed eager to speak; others shrank away.

Suddenly, sounds of struggling penetrated the darkness. There exploded ear-piercing screams, groaning, a noise like warring winds. "No more! I beg you! Pleeeeease—no more!"

I drew back with disgust and caught a glimpse of a tortured, trapped, anguished expression. Behind this tormented soul, taller than he and bending over him with its bloated, ghastly, glimmering face pressed close to his, was a gruesome beast. The thing's eyes were like those of a rat glowing in the dark. It appeared half-dead, half—I don't know what. The hands of the demon were clutching the distressed soul's form: one long naked arm was around his shoulders, the other, around his hips. It was forcefully sodomizing the life out of its inconsolable victim.

The creature mercilessly plunged its massive, veiny "rod" inside the terrified soul, farther, farther, and farther. The despairing wretch felt the cruel brute tearing the inside of his body. There was excruciating pain, violent screams; blood ran out of the wildly crying, gasping victim's rear end.

Dread was in the eyes of the miserable soul—dread of the future into which he feared to look. Filled with terror, pain, unspeakable horror, the frightened soul sought to escape. But the arms of the thing, then his master, clutched him tighter and tighter in a painful, viselike grip.

The creature's sodden, vaporous flesh pressed closer to its victim; the desire of the vampire creature, who was ever aroused, was seemingly unquenchable. At long last, the wretched soul stumbled blindly through the sweltering darkness, bald, naked, trembling, his cheeks moist with blood-mixed tears. Piled in a shivering bloody heap he laid, the adjacent ground flooded with crimson stain.

This despicable wretch was a sadistic rapist in mortal life. Every cause is accompanied by its own effect, which nothing can modify, not even deathbed repentance. If you recognize the fact you have harmed others, set up good actions more powerful than your harm; reap the reward for that!

In short, within that evil black domain, you could hear the screaming of women, the crying of adolescents, the wailing of men…Some prayed for help. Others wished for quick annihilation…But still more imagined that there was no God left to them—that their universe had descended into eternal darkness. Cruel, spine-chilling sights greeted me wherever I looked. Through the dim midnight air, I saw scores of grisly faces simply beyond my ability to depict. They were clothed in hideous bodies of flayed, worm-infested, rotting flesh.

I closed my eyes, gave a deep sigh of relief, murmured, "Thank God Jackie isn't here!" Then with a thick throat, I said, "She's not here! What do we do now?"

Aviar clenched his jaw. **Let us forsake this pit of agony.**

We retraced our steps along the path that would take us out of the blackness. The black gradually turned to blackish gray as we climbed upward. At length, we made our exodus through the towering slit opening of the dark pyramid. An eerie hum to my left caused me to freeze in my tracks. Aviar boomed, **Do not look back!**

Despite his warning, I sneaked a quick glimpse. At the summit of the great black mountain stood a mammoth tree. High up in its bent, twisty branches I spied an enormous, hideous figure with a serpent's tail armed with talons, huge belly, and wings.

Aviar fired a fierce glare in the direction of the frightening beast. Inexplicably, it shot past the monster, the immense tree, into the murky heavens. Without warning, ruby-red blood began trickling down the gnarled, bumpy trunk of that soot-black tree. Seconds later, the sky dripped a gelatinous substance similar to raw egg whites followed by more fresh, glowing deep purplish–red blood. The blood and gelatinous goo both had a strong sulfurous odor. Incredibly, the gooey blood hissed as it spattered on the ground.

I shook violently; terror crept into my voice. "The sky's raining blood!"

You shudder. You would tremble even more convulsively had you seen the sickening things that I have witnessed here.

With trembling lips and chin, I looked up into the sinister heavens. Utilizing my supersensitive vision, I saw dark rivers of blood that veined a raw egg–like sea, a gigantic embryonic reservoir within which this disgusting world sat floating. The entire revolting world appeared to be a vast living thing! Aviar's potent glare had hemorrhaged the embryonic reservoir, causing the shower of blood falling from the repulsive world's sky.

A strong wave of uneasiness washed over me. I turned to Aviar, still quivering. He shook his head, as if both annoyed and amused at the same time, roared, **Follow me!**

We took flight; moved through black-winged clouds oozing through a desolate, soulless sky. We soared upward, out of that mist of toxic stench into the pure ether at blinding speed, without a backward glance.

CHAPTER 16

A Stroll Through Paradise

I felt stung by grief to nearly the point of madness by all I set eyes on in the great abyss. But elation renewed my heavy spirit as soon as we escaped from that nightmarish black chasm. In no time at all, we found ourselves back in a world of radiant light directly over what appeared to be a charming little hamlet.

On its outskirts stood a huge, brilliant-white glass-and-marble structure resembling an airport right out of tomorrow with an extraordinary clamor coming from within. Dotting the perimeter of the complex was a series of long one-level buildings with flat white roofs. We drifted down alongside a grove of trees, just south of the conventional-looking town. I began to walk toward what appeared to be a main-street retail shopping district.

To my surprise, three normal-looking men in white shirts and business suits were standing around on a sidewalk engaged in casual conversation. Strolling along the other side of the street, chatting and gazing into store windows, were two equally normal-looking women.

One was probably in her late twenties, tall, slim, attractive, with long brown hair. She wore black slacks, a distinctive hip-length jacket. The other was dressed in a chic gray pantsuit; her silver-white hair framed a face that appeared tough, and worldly-wise, almost harsh in its vintage beauty. All the men and women seemed unusually serene and calm. One of the men spotted me. Looked perplexed. He came over, introduced himself.

My name is Daniel. We were not expecting you. Your name is not on the list.

"I'm here with Aviar."

Oh! That explains it. You do not look like the others.

"What's that mean?"

Your illumination is a little bit dim, and your silver cord is still intact.

Daniel then smiled, turned, walked back toward his friends, who stood staring in our direction. He shouted over his shoulder, **I am sure we will meet again when the time is right.**

I retreated back to the thicket of trees where Aviar sat resting on a huge flat rock.

Come sit with me. It is shady, just right for exhausted searchers.

I poked, prodded the massive rock with my foot. "Where are we?"

Village of Peaceful Crossing. Many mortals come here when they transition.

"Why would they come here?"

To lessen the trauma of the change of state humans label death. We try to ease the shock, to calm the panic by providing a comfortable, familiar environment during transition to this realm. Most new arrivals are processed at the Transition Reception Center complex just north of here.

I saw you talking with Daniel, a member of The League. Let him show you around. Peaceful Crossing's realistic earth-life structures truly delight the eye.

I tilted my head a bit. "Do all who arrive here come via a *tunnel* as I did?"

Breathing slowly and evenly, Aviar said thoughtfully, **Many seemingly cross over a bridge. Some arrive by seemingly crossing a body of water. Others seemingly stroll down a winding wooded** road until they reach this inner realm. It is generally based on one's culture.

Frankly, virtually all of Earth's spiritual traditions contain descriptions of this plane. Numerous trips to heaven described by prophets in your Holy Books have simply been journeys here. What you mortals have been viewing as quaint folklore and charming but naive mythology are actually sophisticated accounts of excursions to this Inner-verse.

Suddenly, there appeared an "Ah ha!" expression on Aviar's rugged face.

"What'd we forget?"

The Garden of Light! It too is a place to ease the trauma of transition from physical life to this energy system.

It is extraordinarily unlike me to not have thought of the Garden sooner, he said, grimacing and crossing his arms.

"Happens to the best of us! No harm done."

Simply hike east until you reach Emerald Spirit Trail. It will take you directly to the Garden.

"Been an honor to've searched by your side. You've been a great teacher, true friend. If I need help, may I call on you again?"

Just hold my image in your mind. I will come! I am never far from you. I dwell at the corner where the west wind crosses the north wind.

Wheresoever you go, whatever you do, go and do with all your heart. Stay in the Light!

My hand touched my lips. "Stay where?"

It is a timeless, good-bye phrase. Frankly, Jason, after all the places we have searched, all we have experienced, perhaps you are naïve to endure.

"I was born dirt poor—enduring is all I've ever known."

Aviar got up from the flat rock he was reclining upon, swaggered toward me. **Now, for the first time, I am truly amazed at the unyielding-persistence of a mortal. Jason Roberts, you have the tenacity of an enraged bull!**

"No, just the heart of a man in love."

With newfound hope, I headed off in the direction of the Garden. Three hundred paces later, I entered on a trail bathed in golden light. Meandering through the fertile woodland left me speechless. Socializing on a low branch was a trio of astonishingly white doves. They began to lead me along the path, flying a short way, then stopping to glance back in my direction, then flying again until I found myself deep in a forest of proud, towering trees like something out of a dream. Cuddly, beige teddy bear-like creatures on a high bough looked down chattering.

A narrow path covered with exotic grasses led through an opening. I followed it, enjoying the music of swishing grass struck by my foot. Although I felt eager to get to the Garden, I nonetheless chose to stroll at a leisurely pace. The feel of soothing, moist grass against my bare feet felt much too delightful.

I just couldn't get used to the fact that though *dead*, I still felt very much *alive*. I seemed just as full of life, just as human as ever. I was seeing, hearing, feeling, tasting, smelling in a physical manner. My new spirit body felt remarkably light, extraordinarily flexible, and inexplicably absorbed enormous amounts of water. Otherwise, nothing had changed!

I wiggled my toes and dug them into the cool, moist grass. I bent down, picked up several blades from the ground. I crushed, sniffed, chewed them; their smell, taste, texture were no different from grass found on Earth. It was totally mind-blowing.

As I roamed this unique yet glorious forest, a light breeze blew through my hair. The enchanting green wood overflowed with remarkable trees; fragrant, regal shrubs; and brilliant wildflowers, some resembling living rubies encased in gold.

A beautiful saber-tooth leopard the size of a small horse wandered gracefully onto the footpath. Sat down. Eyed me with an apathetic glance. I rambled past the big cat toward trees with blazing hues. One boasted golden pears—golden marvels—irresistibly beautiful with pert tops, plump bottoms, long-curved leaves, their golden sheen captivating. I took one, ate, and felt enlivened. Other trees possessed fan-shaped leaves, fernlike fronds, and brilliant red berries. The fusion of delicate scents teased me to euphoric distraction.

Birds of every color of the rainbow hopped, played, and warbled a blend of exquisite notes. This included nightingales that sang more beautifully than anywhere else in creation. Plus, there were mystical species trilling, flying from tree to tree, sweeping across my path.

A raven, pure white with striking snowy plumage, flew down from high in the towering trees. Dancing on my shoulder, the winter-white raven sang softly into my ear; then it whistled to a mate hidden in the swaying treetops. A few yards along the trail later, with a final peck on the cheek, it returned to the upper branches. Wonderful, brilliantly hued songbirds seemed everywhere I turned. A host of handsome peacocks stood aside and watched my passage curiously but without wariness.

I began to tread ever more slowly in absolute wonderment. My hand reached out, plucked spring-green needles from the branch of a pine tree. They felt moist, full of life and smelled just like the Christmas trees of my youth.

Gradually it dawned on me that somehow the birds and trees seemed more real, more vivid, and more alive than those I encountered on Earth. Without warning, a magnificent young elk with golden antlers trotted across the trail, paused, sniffed, licked, nuzzled my toes, then continued its journey. His antics took me by surprise, causing a rollicking chuckle.

There was a strange sense that everything felt amazingly perfect. I marched on, lost in astonishment at the flash of splendor greeting my every glance. Soon I arrived at a bend in the trail. It terminated at a cedar walkway spanning a miniature wetland that was bordered by a remarkable forest overflowing with unusual trees and flowering shrubs. The shady cedar path wandered through a fragrant meadow where violets peeped from the ground.

I paused, exhilarated by my immersion in so much splendor. A tiny, fascinating, creature landed on my hand, flaunting its stunning jeweled head. It enjoyed the back scratches I gave it with my finger as I strolled through this place of mystic beauty. The tree line ended abruptly. My feathered companion took flight. Individual rays of light pulsed into a clearing. Just past the clearing, a wealth of flaxen trees with indigo berries shimmered across a tranquil blue lake beyond which stood The Garden of Light.

CHAPTER 17

Garden of Light

The sight of the Garden through groves of golden blueberry trees caused an odd, glorious sensation to fill my entire being. I found my eyes in tears with emotion. The strange, wondrous beauty, the myriad of tantalizing aromas transported and ravished my soul. I felt total delight. Total beauty. Total bliss. I felt a rush deep inside me—a thrill, a joy at being alive. I began paying attention to every unforgettable detail.

An off-white marble promenade encircled the garden, extending as far as the eye could see. Sun-swept footpaths branched off from the walkway, ending at attractive satellite garden spots.

White-marble benches hidden in sacred privacy among canopies of graceful ferns and red-purple flowers appeared situated throughout the landscape. Trees with masses of cascading double-pink blossoms or colorful leaves stunned the senses. Rolling lawns of countless hues and majestic tree clusters delighted the eye. Sparkling streams and beguiling sculptures occupied this storybook world as well.

The Garden continued on, its gently rolling green terrain extending for some distance before ending at a deep ravine. The bench-lined, gloriously flowering expanse made me want to rest, lie down, relax. At the edge of the rugged canyon stood a Japanese-styled Tea House with a cedar-shake roof.

It was surrounded on three sides by rolling, grassy knolls. It was also enhanced by sculpted ponds that were home to swarms of glittering, diminutive fish. Its only access was a natural bridge of gray stepping stones. Its entrance was framed by gorgeous mahogany: two huge columns supported a massive curved beam with a straight crosspiece below it.

In front of the Tea House was a site for contemplation with built-in seating made of sleek granite, the color and details of which were picture-perfect. This striking veranda highlighted an inviting fountain. This gracious wellspring spouted a sparkling mist that danced in a magnificent reflecting pool encircling it. A fresh-scented breeze floated to my face subtle sprays of tantalizing dews. It felt cool, soothing, invigorating.

The Tea House terrace overlooked the deep, long purple gorge and soaring, majestic Crystal Fortress Mountain Range. These palaces of nature possessed rich vegetation. The tallest peak arose, bold in outline, withholding none of its majesty. It was capped by a pyramid adorned with an extraordinary gold emblem. A dazzling eruption of water hurtled down in opposite directions from this regal central peak, ending in the awesome grandeur of four thundering waterfalls that cascaded into the ravine, carrying the flow out to a peaceful sky-blue sea.

The structures there appeared simple yet most artistic. The breeze felt cool, soft; the luminosity, warm and fresh. Colorful, lazy-paced clouds drifted above through a clear, bright azure sky. Only they weren't really clouds. This light-as-air stuff flowed in shades of glowing color—in every color I'd ever thought of, plus many I only remember but can't express.

I stared in amazement; yet I wasn't only seeing, but also feeling—feeling the colors! In addition there was beautiful music—coming from where, I do not know—played by seemingly thousands of instruments. Melody weaving upon melody! The music was all around me, inside me, so relaxing, absorbing.

I sauntered down the grassy slope to the nearest bench past a brilliant-white pavilion. It stood covered with aromatic flowers and was flanked by gigantic trees laden with astonishing blossoms. A charming creature rose from the marble bench as I approached. She was tall and willowy with smooth, radiant skin. Her ideally proportioned feminine form and her ample, sculpted breasts were lush beyond compare. Her luminous, almond-shaped hazel eyes and the way her sleek dark hair fell straight to her slender waist made me gasp.

She wore a loose-fitting white garment. It was crafted of delicate, flowing stuff that came down to her perfectly formed bare feet. She was a flawless, long-haired beauty—a strange seraphic piece of life and loveliness.

When I first saw her, I could barely believe my eyes. Her captivating beauty was mesmerizing! I felt absolutely spellbound! Surprisingly, she seemed somehow familiar.

As I approached, I could detect an aura of white, gold, purple, green, yellow, and pink rays surrounding her. On her eyes, bright with happiness, light shone as on the surface of a crystal pool. She smiled effervescently.

Welcome back, Jonjaie!

Jonjaie? My soul's name? The sight of this being stopped me short. Wonder seized me. My name had been spoken by this bewitching creature in this enchantingly beautiful place!

She kissed me lightly on the cheek. It felt moist, warm, electrifying, and caused my entire body to tingle. What's more, when her soft, dainty form converged with mine, it produced delicate, wind chime–like tones. As she led me to the marble bench where she'd been reclining, my body's reaction to her contact initiated a state of delight I'll never forget. She gestured for me to be seated, but as we were about to sit, she hesitated.

On second thought, I think you might enjoy the Tea House setting better. It possesses a spectacular view—that is, if you do not mind a brief walk.

"Of course not. I'd enjoy a stroll." I said, striding quickly to erase the distance.

The promenade was packed with couples, all adults. Each appeared around thirty; they wore a variety of clothing. Surprisingly, some appeared to be from other planets.

My lovely companion and I wandered through flocks of elegant birdlike creatures with stunning plumage that were strutting throughout the landscape. Innumerous butterflies of every size and hue glittered over the vale, especially among the miniature gardens. One plot had fragrant herbs, vines, and bubbling fountains to stimulate the senses. Another offered exotic flowers and lush, shady arbors with open-latticework roofs. A third boasted an aquatic garden of remarkable water lilies. The Garden of Light was truly a poem of exquisite, perfected landscape glory.

After a relaxing hike, we arrived at the Tea House. As we were about to be seated, I said, "Are you a saint, an angel? Truth is, I'm an ordained priest; I read about these types of encounters in the literature on the miraculous endless times. But I never expected to experience anything like this myself.

"Which are you, saint or angel?"

Neither. I am a Master of Wisdom. I, along with the members of my order, The League, provide assistance in assessing future options to newly transitioned souls like you, Jonjaie. Or would you prefer I address you by Jason, your mortal name?

"Jason, please. And I'm still trying to recall your name."

Camr.

"Should I address you as Master?"

Call me Camr or Sister. I am simply an extension of the Whole, as you are.

"But this garden—this magnificent garden—who created it?"

A team of talented beings who had fulfilled their cycle of incarnations. It is not complete—still a work in progress. This Garden, all you observe in this realm, was created by the power of focused, externalized thought.

"Any laws?"

Love all; treat all as you would wish to be treated. This is the lone-note song of the Kingdom.

"Of course! What else could it be? Ever thought about incarnating on Earth?"

Camr pressed a fist against her chest. **In my last life on the water star, I wanted to be a ballerina. I trained hard but was clumsy. Ultimately I grew disgusted with the artificial glitter of the world of show business, got married. I wanted to be a mother more than anything. Intended to have oodles of babies! My congenial but incompetent doctor astonishingly burned a hole in my vaginal canal during a simple procedure. That brought a shocking end to my childbearing aspirations...felt like half a woman! I cried, cried, cried; shed endless gut-wrenching tears!**

I felt totally and completely destroyed, ravaged, ruined, but I attempted to show a jolly face to the world. I sought a tonic to renew my mental state—became a foster-mother to multiple at-risk youngsters. I like to believe my children adored me. I was their buddy and experienced supreme enjoyment playing with each one. I read them funny stories with happy endings and took them on sudden, impulsive picnics in the woods to look for fairies, elves, unicorns.

"Bet you're turned on by mild-mannered guys."

While I disliked being bossed around, I loathed spineless men. Honestly, I could have been the softest, most feminine woman an Earthly male had ever squeezed. I enjoyed being

protected, cried rivers at sad movies, read poetry with misty eyes. The truth is, I am a trusting child at heart. I wished on a rainbow for someone to share my love and to show me the way to the stars. Even though I prided myself on being intelligent, self-reliant, my heart was defenseless. It got knocked down, bruised quite often.

Camr was super friendly with her own distinctive brand of charm. She had a sunshine personality capable of melting even the hardest heart. Camr was also cheerfully optimistic. Gloom, pessimism actually made her ill. Before anyone could get discouraged about any issue, she'd look at them with guileless hazel eyes, say, **Things will get better!**

"Hope you don't mind my endless questions, Camr."

My purpose here is to make you comfortable, answer questions you may have. My work is a labor of love.

"Great! Tell me, why do we only get a tiny fraction of the things prayed for?"

Scores have been taught to beg an invisible old man who lives up in the sky who records your every act—one who gave you ten rules to pursue and whose upkeep you must pay for at least weekly. But no matter how much you give, He always needs "just a little bit more!"

If his children should fail to follow his wisdom, he purportedly becomes enraged. As a consequence, he banishes his naughty offspring to a nightmare of anguish and agony where they will burn and smoke, sizzle and char, scorch and scream every minute of every hour of every day—for all eternity. But you are assured "He loves you!"

Your prayers are unsuccessful, Jason, because you learned amiss. You beg an invisible old man up in the sky instead of calling on the Unlimited Power within you. Mortals too blind to see this fact are sadly children of a shockingly primitive god.

The truth is, you answer your own prayers! Whatever you sincerely believe, your unconscious simply brings forth. The magic wand is the energy of the mind. True prayer is an act of spiritual cocreatorship with God. Once your subconscious accepts an idea, it quickly opens the way to goals. The major causes of prayer failure are a lack of faith, too much effort. If you have faith as tiny as a mustard seed, nothing shall be impossible to you.

"Don't think we humans consider ourselves children of a primitive god! Our religion's a bit difficult for nonhumans to grasp. In order to better understand it, you'd have to read—"

Your Holy Books! We have. We noticed blood flowed more frequently than holy water in those volumes. Your entire history reveals a strange, sad, confusing tale of never-ending brutality and conflicts. Neighbor attacking neighbor. Each group of neighbors praying to "their god," asking for protection. Each group pleading with "their god" to provide assistance in slaughtering another group of the Creator's children. Each believing only their cause to be just. Then committing appalling horrors in the name of God. All in a never-ending story of violence, terror, and blood-drenched madness. Earth is a strange star.

"People in one group tend to distrust, even hate, those in another. Why?"

Camr's eyes grew wet, dull. Genetically controlled superficial physical characteristics like skin color, eye shape, and hair type are the major basis of racial intolerance. What's more, periodically, there develops increasingly pent-up aggression looking for an outlet. You become prisoners to the "Snarling Dogs of Hate and Aggression." The madness you mortals label war provides an outlet for those evil dogs on a grand scale.

In your foolish wars, numerous mortals are killed—then someone declares victory. A few seasons later, friends become enemies, enemies become friends; the entire stupid cycle starts all over again. Hate, destruction, brother killing brother only to be followed again by more hate, more destruction, more slaughter. Being a victor in war does not determine who was right—it only determines who is left. To realize your dreams, you mortals will need more than brutality. You will need to exercise discretion, a little mercy.

The Watchers who walk among you have observed humans with intense sadness and weep for you mortals, Jason. The "gods" whom you mortals believe condone such savage behavior? We know of no such gods. We here know only of the One Mother-Father who is no respecter of persons. Who cherishes none more than any other. Who adores each of Its children with equal love.

Someday, you mortals will look for your enemies within—will fight the evil in yourselves—then there will be no need to slay your brethren. Someday the children of Earth will return to the love that many have now long forgotten. Someday love will reestablish itself upon the throne of the human heart. The truth is, with so many weapons of mass destruction now at your disposal, you must either learn to love one another or die!

"Do unearthly beings exist? I saw two males dressed in silver jumpsuits during our walk. They appeared to be Caucasian with light-brown hair. One had a goatee. But I couldn't help noticing that both had piercing pink eyes without pupils or irises."

Souls from other worlds do tarry here. Truthfully, the lives of so-called aliens are not much different than your own. Vast numbers of your celestial cousins are flesh-and-blood biological creatures who are born; engage in child's play; are educated; fall in love; experience work, financial, stress, health issues; age; and "die" just as mortals do. Some are kindhearted; others, villains. Some, wise; others, foolish. Some, attractive; others, hideous by human standards. **Loads of your cousins possess more advanced civilizations; others possess civilizations less advanced than your ocean world.**

Plenty have even lived on the water star you hail from.

An icy chill trickled down my spine. "Actually, this knowledge makes me uncomfortable—enormously uncomfortable!" I said clutching my throat, horrified.

This I promise: Despite our numerous outward appearances, all intelligences—human and nonhuman—share one Divine Source. All are simply souls temporarily encased in a myriad of outer forms made of vibrating atoms.

"Tell me more about life here in the inner world."

Face beaming, Camr said, **Residents on this self-lighted, shadowless plane materialize in any body type they want, can see with any area of their body they wish. We experience an eternal day with illumination cycling from dusk-type light to early-morning-sunrise-type illumination. Plus, a single thought can materialize anything a citizen could desire. What's more, there are a bonanza of conventional "heavens," or Belief-System Territories, where like-minded souls reside.**

The Heaven Country's located east of the Crystal Fortress Mountains. Souls dwell there in a wealth of heavens, singing in white robes, harps in their hands.

"You're kidding, of course. White robes, harps?"

I have witnessed multitudes even wearing crowns.

"You say there's a Heaven Country. Aviar told me heaven's in the mind."

Both statements are factual.

"Robes! Harps! Crowns! Multiple heavens! It sounds too fantastic to be true."

Natives here have simply let the limitations they laid upon their minds while navigating the outer world be lifted.

"Honestly, Camr, I'm having difficulty believing it all."

Truth is beyond belief.

"Actually, I'd like to explore in another direction—miracles."

No problem!

CHAPTER 18

———— ❧ ————

Deep Interconnectedness

I gazed out over the Tea House terrace's elegantly contoured fountain. Sumptuous light permeated its misty spray, causing a rainbow to camouflage the sparkling, tranquil air. In the distant background a regal white lion drank from a sylvan pond. In the middle of the pool, I caught sight of a bloom more beautiful by far than any I'd ever seen—a strange glory of a flower, a marvel to behold. An enormous pink lotus broke through the pond's shallow water to breathe the upper atmosphere. Its blossoms, awe-inspiring. Its fragrance, extraordinarily sweet. Its beauty, so great that all who saw it longed for it to be theirs.

As if that weren't enough, silver drops of morning dew moistened magnificent, flowering pink shade trees. Wild white violets slumbered peacefully in the moss. A vision of Eden couldn't have been more enchanting. My gaze then fell back on Camr's charming attractiveness. I briefly pleasured my eyes by way of this radiant goddess then resumed our chat.

"Miracles—legitimate or pure fiction?"

Virtually all miracles performed by mystics of your world's great religions have been duplicated by psychics. This suggests "miracles" are produced by forces lying deep in the mind—forces unawakened in all mortal beings. The Creator gives no special favors. No individual has any power not available to all others.

Let us examine a rich harvest of the phenomena mortals call miracles. Fortunately, Jason, I recently received some fantastic new material from The League on this very topic. But rather than simply discuss the subject, the experience I will now share is what souls here refer to as a "Light Picture."

"You mentioned light pictures earlier. But honestly…"

Camr gave me an understanding nod. **A light picture is organized thought energy transmitted from one mind to another. It is like a mental book, complete with sensory and emotional sensations. Are you ready?**

"Hold on! What do I have to do?"

Simply still your thoughts. Make your mind blank, as if you were in meditation. I will then send the light picture from my mind to yours.

"OK. I'm ready." I said with quick, high-pitched laughter.

A soft beam of light began to stream out of the center of Camr's forehead, just above the bridge of the nose. It projected a three-dimensional, eerily convincing image of an open scarlet leather-covered book with gold-tipped corners. I could actually walk around the projection and view it from different angles as you would a real book. When I reached out and tried to touch the book, however, my hand wafted right through it. But I quickly discovered I could turn the pages with my mind. Mesmerized, I began committing to memory the following:

November 30, 1931, "J." died in his home in Youngstown, Ohio, United States of America. He was a "healer." "J." never studied medicine. The only instruction he ever received was from an aged healer in the mountains of Wales, when he was a boy. Doctors were incapable of explaining his art, satisfied themselves he

was not a charlatan, shrugged, and said simply that he had "divine power."

"J." made a fortune out of his practices. He was associated with no church. "J." was about thirty years old when he became aware of his talent. One day in 1887, a man in a mill fell from a ladder, was injured. It was a severe spinal sprain, according to a physician. "J." stooped down, ran his fingers up and down the man's back. The man smiled, and while the physician and other mill workers gaped in wonder, he rose to his feet. The mill worker announced he felt strong again with no trace of pain. He went back to work, and "J.'s" reputation as a healer spread abroad.

There were thousands of cases of successful treatments. A celebrated Major League baseball player was carried from the baseball field one day. Something in his back snapped. It seemed his career had ended. "J." treated him. Within a few days, the legendary player was back playing baseball. A well-known British politician visited the United States. He was suffering from twisted, cramped muscles in his hands. "J." shook hands with the statesman, pressed gently, then harder, and disengaged their hands with a wrench. The renowned politician's hand was strong again.

It was the morning of February 23, 1885. "JL," in his cell in the penitentiary in Exeter, England, was waiting to be hanged. "JL" was led into the prison yard past a group of motionless witnesses to the scaffold. There were newspaper reporters present. "JL" was a laborer who hadn't a friend and hadn't a dollar. Noose on his neck, up on the scaffold, they stood him on a trapdoor. The door was held in position by a bolt. When this bolt was drawn, the door would fall.

The sheriff waved his hand. The bolt was drawn. But the trapdoor did not fall. "JL" stood silent, the noose still around his neck. They tinkered with the bolt. There was no difficulty whatsoever with the bolt. But when it was drawn—with "JL" standing on the trapdoor—the door would not fall. The people in the prison yard fluttered. Hosts of them began talking it over. Wardens looked into the matter—except there was not anything to look into. Every time they drew back the bolt with "JL" out of the way, the door fell as it should have fallen. One of the wardens stood in "JL's" place, but instead of placing the noose around his neck, he clung to the rope. The bolt was drawn; the door fell as it should have fallen; down dropped the warden as he should have dropped.

"JL" was led back to the scaffold. The witnesses did not know whether to be in awe or not. After all, it was just one of those things nobody could explain. It certainly could not happen again. Could it?

The bolt was drawn. The trapdoor did not fall. Incredibly, "JL" stood there trembling, yet: "unhangable."

They had done everything imaginable. Somebody suggested rain might have swollen the wooden door, causing friction. But there had been numerous tests and no friction. What's more, just as a precaution, a warden had planed the edges of the door. They experimented countless times: each time the door fell as it should have fallen. They stood "JL" on the scaffold again. The door would not fall! Newspaper reporters dashed out into the streets. They ran, shouting through the city about "the man who could not be hanged." The matter was debated in the House of Commons. The result was that the execution was not attempted again. "JL's" sentence was commuted to life imprisonment. But he was released in December 1907.

In 1905, Iceland's leading scientists decided to investigate the supernatural. They chose "I." as one of their subjects. At the time "I.," a country bumpkin, could effortlessly move objects with his mind. But most bizarre of all, sometimes while deep in a trance, different parts of his body would completely disappear. As the astonished scientists watched, an arm or a hand would fade out of existence, only to reappear before he awakened.

In the 1920s, there was a performance of sorcery in the village of Doa, in the Ben-Hounien territory of the French West African Colony. In brief, there were two mortal males, each clutching a sharp, steel sword rigidly upward in his left hand. With his right hand each hurled a tiny startled child high into the air. They caught the terrified children on their blades' tip, impaling the little bodies through and through. The huge gathering screamed! Numerous covered their eyes, fell to their knees. Multiple females passed out. Incredibly, no blood flowed and the trembling children remained alive, without injury.

1923: In addition to her mystical crucifixion wounds, Therese Neumann displayed the fantastic ability to live without food. It began when she transferred the throat disease of a young priest to her own body; she subsisted solely on liquids for multiple years. What's more, in 1927 Neumann gave up both food and water entirely for the next thirty-five years.

Circa 1967: A host of famous surgeons, professors of medicine, and department heads of large medical institutions felt uneasy about their unique abilities to make accurate diagnoses by observing patients' energy fields. Most were unaware others existed who possessed similar gifts. They described what they were seeing as a moving web of frequency completely penetrating their patient's bodies. Some saw whirlpools of energy at certain points along the spine influencing the endocrine system. Their abilities were kept secret out of fear of damaging their professional reputations.

September 7, 1871, "NC," an elderly black male, blacksmith in Easton, Maryland, United States of America, demonstrated he could handle red-hot metal without being harmed. In the presence of a committee, he heated an iron shovel until it became glowing; held it against the soles of his feet until it cooled. He also licked the edge of the red-hot shovel; poured hot melted lead in his mouth, allowing it to run over his teeth and gums until it solidified. After each feat, doctors examined him yet found no trace of injury.

Circa 1727, Paris, France: A puritanical sect of Dutch-influenced Catholics known as the Jansenists displayed amazing abilities. This matter was caused by the death of Jansenist deacon François de Pâris.

Jansenist beliefs differed dramatically with Roman Catholic doctrine. However, they quickly gained followers among the French populace. Both the Church and the Catholic King Louis XV constantly undermined the movement's power. A huge obstacle to these maneuverings was that Jansenist leaders seemed skilled at miraculous healings. Nonetheless, the Church and monarchy persevered. On May 1, 1727, at the height of this power struggle, François de Pâris died and was buried in the cemetery of Saint-Mèdard, Paris.

Because of François's saintly reputation, worshipers began to gather at his tomb. From the beginning, a host of miraculous healings were reported. The ailments cured included cancerous tumors, paralysis, deafness, arthritis, rheumatism, blindness, ulcerous sores, persistent fevers, and prolonged hemorrhaging. But there was even more. The mourners also started to experience strange involuntary convulsions. The streets quickly filled with adult males, females, children all twisting and squirming.

While in this trancelike state, the "convulsionaires," as they came to be called, displayed incredible talents. A twenty-year-old convulsionaire named "JM" leaned against a wall while a very strong male delivered one hundred blows to her stomach with a thirty-pound hammer. Another convulsionaire, "MS," stretched herself on two chairs over a blazing fire: she remained there for half an hour. Neither she nor her clothing showed any ill effects. "MS" also once sat with her feet in a pan of white-hot burning coals. Her shoes and stockings were burned off, but her feet were unharmed.

Convulsionaire "GM" was impervious to blows, sword thrusts; she stuck her head into a roaring hearth fire and held it there without suffering any injury. Eyewitnesses reported afterward that her clothing felt so hot it could barely be touched; yet her hair, eyelashes, eyebrows were never even singed.

In still another instance, a convulsionaire bent back into an arc so her lower back was supported by the sharp point of a peg. A fifty-pound stone attached to a rope was hoisted to a towering height; it was allowed to fall with all its weight on her stomach. The stone was hoisted up and allowed to fall again and again. But the female walked away from the ordeal without even so much as a mark on the flesh of her back.

The convulsionaires could not be hurt by the blows of metal rods, chains, or wooden clubs. The strongest males could not choke them. Some were crucified. Afterward they showed no trace of wounds. They could not even be cut with swords or hatchets. The sharpened point of an iron drill was held against one convulsionaire's stomach. It was pounded mightily with a hammer. He maintained an expression of perfect rapture, said, "Courage, brother, strike twice as hard, if you can!"

During their seizures, some Jansenists could predict the future. Others could read with their eyes tightly bandaged. What's more, instances of levitation were reported. When witnesses tried to forcibly hold levitators down, they could not succeed in keeping them from rising upward.

Jansenist miracles were witnessed by thousands and were the most talked about events in Europe for nearly a century. The frenzied gatherings in the streets surrounding Abbé Pâris's tomb occurred day and night for years. Even two decades later, miracles were still being reported. The Jansenists became an international phenomenon.

When King Louis XV tried to stop the convulsionaires by closing the cemetery of Saint-Mèdard, legendary French writer-philosopher Voltaire quipped, "God was forbidden, by order of the King, to work any miracles there." Scottish philosopher David Hume wrote, "There surely never was so great a number of miracles ascribed to one person as those which were lately said to have been wrought in France upon the tomb of François Pâris."

In the late 1600s, King Louis XIV tried to purge France of the French Protestant Camisards who displayed abilities similar to the Jansenists. In an official report sent to Rome, one of the persecutors, Abbé du Chayla, complained that no matter what he did, he could not harm the Camisards. When he ordered them shot, the musket balls were found flattened between their clothing and their skin. When he closed their hands upon burning coals, they were not injured. He wrapped them head to toe in cotton soaked with oil. Set them on fire, yet they did not burn.

As if that were not enough, "C.," the Camisard leader, ordered a pyre built; he climbed to the top of it to deliver a rapturous speech. In the presence of six hundred witnesses, he ordered the pyre be set on fire and continued to rant as the flames rose about his head. After the pyre became completely consumed, "C." remained unharmed with no mark of the fire on his hair or clothing.

After I read the final words, the scarlet book closed of its own accord then simply faded away. Velvety blackness filled my mind. In the next instant, I was back at the Tea House sitting beside Camr. I turned and gazed at her, stunned.

"The light picture. I'm not sure what I expected. But I certainly wasn't expecting *that.* Seemed almost sensual! What a unique learning experience. Those with the ability to generate thought-induced phenomena—how are they using their powers?"

There have always been mortals with extraordinary abilities throughout human history. They include your grandfather; medicine men; mind readers; witches; witch doctors; early kings, emperors, and pharaohs; some early religious Icons;

certain magicians, healers, and mediums; Therese Neumann; the Camisards; the Jansenists; others outlined in the Light Picture, to mention just a few. Imposters without such power have been common in every age as well.

Myriads with supernormal powers simply keep quiet and attempt to exert influence. Others feel they cannot change the earth-life system, so they do not try. Some do not wish to. Most do not want their talents known. A host of them become healers or doctors.

A few evolve into mortals like "CS," a fish merchant who lived in the remote Philippine village of San Pedro Etude. Every year from 1987 to about 2002, he commemorated Good Friday by being nailed to a cross as Christ was. When Good Friday arrived, he spent the hours before dawn in meditation and prayer, holding the sharp steel spikes that would soon be hammered into his flesh. At sunrise, he donned his robe and crown of thorns. He was then led through the city streets, carrying a heavy crucifix, to a local hillside. Each year his wounds healed quickly.

I could go on, Jason. I know numerous examples.

"Just all seems so incredible!"

What you think you know was never true. Thought-induced phenomena are the result of varying the frequency of the Energy that all things are made of—nothing more.

I stared at Camr in astonishment. "Forgive me, but all this stuff sounds like—like myths…perhaps even madness."

A noted holy man of India stated he met Hindu ascetics who could materialize fruits, gold plates, a myriad of other objects. He said, "The world is nothing but an objectivized dream; whatever your powerful mind believes very intensely instantly comes to pass."

Scooting closer, Camr said in a gentle tone, While you dream, you do not know it is a dream. Only after you wake do you realize it was a dream. Someday, Jason, there will be a great awakening. You will then understand that your "reality" is a grand externalized dream. Indeed, "a dream within a dream." Dreaming and perceptions from senses are both mental activities. Consequently, the world you mortals perceive with your senses is no more real than your dream world. Most mortals are not awake but do not know it. Awake, if you dare!

Oriental Sage Chuang-tzu, circa 300 B.C., said, "Once upon a time, I dreamt I was a butterfly, fluttering hither and thither, to all intents and purposes a butterfly. I was conscious only of following my fancies as a butterfly and was unconscious of my individuality as a man. Suddenly I awoke, and there I lay, myself again. Now I do not know whether I was then a man dreaming that I was a butterfly, or whether I am now a butterfly dreaming that I am a man."

If mortals could awake from the dream—awake to reality as did Jesus, Buddha, Laotse, Plato, Dante, Emerson, Swedenborg, your grandfather, others known and unknown—would they then perhaps see that Chuang-tzu was not too far off the mark? Would they too unlock the secret that citizens of Earth are not simply mortal beings struggling toward a spiritual experience but in truth spirit beings struggling through endless human experiences? That humankind, like the old sage, is experiencing something akin to a dream?

"Unequivocally mind-blowing! Yet the evidence is compelling. No doubt there'll be those who'll remain skeptical."

Because you could not see germs, bacteria, or viruses, mortals initially laughed at, even ridiculed, ideas like hand washing and sterilizing surgical instruments. Any brand-new or extraordinary idea always has its critics, detractors, naysayers.

"Why is that?"

Hosts mock things because it someway benefits their bank accounts, reputations, or egos. There are also countless fools who speak many words but say nothing. Primarily, however, it is because Man has never agreed on anything since the dawn of humankind—not religion, politics, slavery, abortion, beauty, good and bad, real and unreal, heaven and hell—nothing!

Often it is the loudest, angriest, rudest voice that wins such debates. I can only regard this phenomenon as something in-between jest and tragedy. Many of your established "truths" are only a composition of superstitions, guesses, deceptions; doomed to be refuted by more precise searching means and methods.

I am immensely surprised you find all of this so astonishing, Jason, given the history of your four "miracle" relatives.

Did you not tell me your grandfather had cancer that metastasized throughout his entire body and that he was given only hours to live? In tears, you retreated to the hospital's chapel and engaged in passionate prayer. You subsequently sensed an unseen presence to your left rear. A feeling of warmth, peace, reassurance came over you. Twenty-four hours later your grandfather miraculously walked out of the hospital. He refused the offer of a cane or wheelchair and even chemotherapy; he stated with a confident grin, "I won't need any of that stuff, Doc, but thanks anyway."

"It's true! I know it sounds incredible, but his white hair also inexplicably returned to its natural shade of black. We all teased him and said he was going through a second childhood. He lived a remarkable additional number of active, pain-free years without a trace of illness of any kind.

"Kneeling in his garden to snip the last rose of summer, he called me aside and said, 'I'm getting a little tired. I've had a good life. I've done all the things I wanted to do. Now I just eat, sleep, watch a little TV; next day, same thing all over again. *It's round-up time!*' His countenance appeared serene, happy. What's more, he spoke of his dying so easily, so offhandedly, as if he were speaking of some welcomed vacation departure. Then one moonlit summer night, as promised, he *went home!*"

Also, what about the fifteen-year-old who was raped, beaten, kicked into a bloody pulp, and left for dead? She lay comatose for weeks but awoke after a "laying on of hands" by a Washington, DC family friend.

Then there was the grandmother diagnosed with breast cancer who prayed for a miracle. A dazzling light appeared just inside the living room entryway of her Maryland home. It evolved into "a beautiful lady" who assured her that she would live and that all would go well! Subsequently, the cancer was removed by a Maryland doctor with minimum surgery and no use of chemotherapy. The cancer never returned.

And do not forget the great-grandmother who insisted on being buried in her Catholic Ladies' Sodality uniform. She was not. After her burial, she appeared to four tiny granddaughters one night and retrieved the uniform from a bedroom closet. Next day, their father and aunts searched endlessly. Yet the uniform was never seen again. You have come too near to truth to renounce it now.

"Nearly forgot about my own experiences with the miraculous. You're right, Camr. I actually shouldn't be all that amazed." A flush crept across my face. "Truth is, I have a problem I've struggled with extensively. Women, love—they are a total puzzle. Could you take the mystery out of love for me?"

Camr flashed a brilliant smile that melted into an impish grin. **I am feminine energy. Over the centuries, I have incarnated on Earth as a White, Black, Asian, Hispanic, Mixed Race, virtually every type of mortal female. I have been mocked or scorned for being too thin, too fat, too tall, too short, too homely, or too beautiful and have lived with fervor the life of a harlot, a nun,** a homemaker, a working mother, a manager, a professional, a wealthy socialite, among others.

I have been loved truly, passionately by a man—by numerous men! I have reciprocated with passion so pure, chaste, and fiery that it is a wonder I did not set the heavens ablaze. I am Every Woman! So I believe I can give you a bit of insight.

You seem surprised, Jason.

"More like astonished."

CHAPTER 19

There is Only Love

Come, let us walk.

Camr and I journeyed from the Tea House until we came upon a half-hidden trail in the clouds overlooking the sea. We followed it down the untamed, jagged mountain scape through misty glens, shady groves, fields of daffodils trumpeting their presence in dazzling yellow. In this land of stony hills and rugged mountains, countless other wildflowers also fluttered and danced in the exhilarating breeze. The bleak heights were carpeted in radiant color; every crack, crevice, and crag erupted with blossoms bewilderingly bright. Each individual flower seemed so delicate, yet all together they covered the rigorous terrain like a rainbow blanket flung over the hills.

We eventually reached the great mountain's base. I was greeted by a pristine, sun-swept, sandy beach that enjoyed a special kind of serenity found nowhere else. A whisper-soft breeze stirred. Wisps of spray rose from intermittently dancing waves. Overhead, colorful feathered creatures soared in the brisk sea air. Strange, delicate, internally luminous plant life swayed rhythmically in the background amid silver swaths of dew-bent grasses. The entire setting was bathed in a dramatic, golden, tranquil light that touched leaf and water with a romantic radiance. From high atop the terrace, the water appeared azure, but up close it looked crystal clear.

"What a magnificent body of water!"

Camr fiddled with her hands and moistened her lips. **It is called the Sea of Love. I thought it would be an idyllic setting in which to discuss the topic of affection.**

All beaches reveal a kind of music that lives there; this one was no exception. As the two of us rambled along the captivating seashore, I absentmindedly traced my name in the sand with my toe. I spotted a long-necked ivory bird skimming along the glittering sea, just a breath from the surface of the water. The bird looked in my direction then made the most extraordinary sound. We seemed connected. Everything in the secluded seaside haven seemed connected.

High above the sun and sand in the brilliant blue ether, small puffs of clouds drifted in gentle counterpoint to the white-capped waves below. The clean salt spray blowing in from the sea was like an invitation to the land bound of all that was joyous and free.

As we sauntered across the shoreline's wind-rippled sand, I couldn't help noticing the proud sway of Camr's shoulders; the shapely legs showing through her wispy garment, brushing her flesh like an angel's wings; the rounded silhouette that appeared as firm and juicy as a ripe champagne grape. Camr's tantalizing form moved as graceful as a gazelle in slow motion.

I shuffled across the gorgeous beach, gazing out reflectively over the long, slow swells of ocean. Unable to meet Camr's eyes, my chin dropped. "I used to be a lieutenant in the United States Marine Corps. While fighting overseas in Southeast Asia, I received a message from my sister informing me that my cheating fiancé was dead. She was killed in a way so awful I won't even try to describe it. Didn't think I'd find someone I could ever trust again!

"Years later I met Jackie. The circumstances of our courtship are a bit embarrassing to talk about. So I'll skip that too if you don't mind. Like a wolf, I mate for life once I've found the perfect woman. Jackie and I clicked instantly. I fell in love—deeply, passionately in love. My every sense seemed filled with her. Hardest thing for me is having the courage to love someone. So before I found Jackie, I opened my heart only a little at a time."

Mortal females—you did not trust such creatures?

"It's not that simple. While I was a college freshman, my grandfather warned me many women are like hurricanes. When they first arrive on the scene, they're wild, wet, raging with passion. But when they leave, they take your house, your cash, and everything else you treasure. They whisper, 'I love you.' You buy 'em things until your bank account runs dry. Then you quickly lose them the way vultures fly away when their feasting's done.

"He also said in every woman there's something beautiful, special, something worth finding. Trick is finding it. I found that exceptional something in Jackie.

"I had a king-sized fear of intimacy. It ultimately sabotaged the only real happiness I've ever known. It led to sickening situations of death, deceit, despair. As I look back now, I turn my face away in shame that I was such a colossal fool. What causes such an absurd fear?"

Camr gazed at me with a soft expression. **There is a dilemma common among mortals, Jason, of not getting what you want because you subconsciously feel you do not deserve gratification. It manifests itself in self-sabotaging activities. Such action seems a paradox. On the conscious level, all want deeply satisfying love. But at the subconscious level, many do their best to ensure success in love is never reached. Or that if it is, it does not last.**

Some of your species engage in this astonishing conduct after a challenging love goal has come to fulfillment. Others fall apart

just as their love goal is being reached. Multitudes never get past the wishing-hoping-dreaming stage.

Expressionless, in a deadpan voice I said, "I've seen countless unhappy people living in pain and shame, subtly concealing despair, lies, inner fears. We frantically gulp down alcohol, anxiety drugs, sexual dysfunction drugs, depression drugs, an endless supply of illegal drugs in an attempt to escape hidden torments. Find joy.

"People struggle to achieve, grow old—then die. All of our life's accomplishments, possessions end in dust. Each one becomes laughably trivial the second we depart from the living clumps of stardust we call bodies and arrive here.

"We pathetic creatures called men and women and the madness we call life seem a bit absurd. If it weren't for this universal addiction called love, our brief, brutish existence would be unbearable. If humans discovered Earth was on a collision course with a massive asteroid and we had only minutes left to say all we wanted to say, every telephone in the world would be busy with people contacting other people to stammer or text 'I love you!'

"What is this mystical hunger called *Love*, Camr?"

Camr sat relaxed, with an unfocused gaze. **Love rules without a sword, binds without a cord. The power of love is infinite. The quality of your love determines the quality of your life. For love is happiness; nothing else brings real joy. You grow warm because of its presence, cold because of its absence. It is the fire of life; if it were ever completely gone, you would die. The truth is that half—the most magnificent half—of life is concealed from those who have not loved passionately.**

"Is it important to love yourself?"

Camr's eyes quickly narrowed and looked serious. **The grit of discontent in the souls of mortals causes substantial numbers to be uncomfortable if left alone with themselves for too long. They are secretly unhappy with who they are. Want to be** someone else—someone different. Love who you are no matter what, Jason. For it is impossible to truly love another unless you love yourself. You cannot give what you do not have.

Even during those moments when you realize you are not perfect—moments of guilt, shame, low self-respect—you still need to love yourself. Not only do self-love and love of others go hand in hand, ultimately they are indistinguishable. In the extreme, a false sense of unimportance, unloveliness, undesirability can pass from mere thinking into belief, then into something just shy of madness. You did not establish your worth. The One who created you did, and it needs no defense.

When an elephant is still a baby, a trainer fastens a steel chain to one of his hind legs and attaches the other end to a steel post. The little elephant pulls with all of his might against the steel post numerous times in an attempt to escape. But he cannot. Try as he might, his baby strength is no match for a steel post and a chain. The tiny elephant ultimately becomes conditioned to the idea of his powerlessness. He gives up—resigns himself to his fate.

The young elephant soon grows into a massive six-ton bull possessing overwhelming strength and power. Yet when his trainer ties a slender rope to his hind leg and the other end to a tiny wooden peg, he still will not attempt to escape, even though he then could do so easily.

"Why?" I said, moving closer.

Because this now gigantic bull has been conditioned since childhood to think of himself as powerless. Mortals behave in basically the same manner. You are all mighty spirit beings. Your mind: the most powerful thing in the universe. You are able to be, have, do anything you intend. Yet because you have been conditioned since childhood to think of yourself as powerless—just like a trained elephant—you do not even try to achieve the foremost desires of your heart.

Camr adopted a grave expression; crossed her arms. **Loads of mortals have been ensnared by an ingrained fear of achievement. You have dreams but are afraid to pursue them. Even if you somehow develop the courage to strive for them, you self-sabotage your efforts before your goals are reached.**

Pacing, I said, "What makes us do such clearly stupid things?"

Artists who do not perform, writers who do not write, entrepreneurs who have never created businesses—all have been victims of their Demons. These Demons unyieldingly whisper, "You can't do it!" even though you know in your soul you can. These Demons unrelentingly urge, "Don't bother doing that!" even though you know in your heart you should.

You are not alone if you have been persecuted by your Demons; numerous mortals have. What's more, they, like you, Jason, never even knew the Demons existed. They looked all over for an enemy to blame for their unsuccessfulness but failed to see that the evildoer slinks within.

How many mortals have become alcoholics, drug addicts, or obese; have developed phobias, migraines or mental health issues simply because they avoid doing that thing their souls are urging them to do? Listen to your soul, Jason! Right now its tiny voice is whispering to you, telling you as it has endless times before the calling that is yours and yours alone. You know it; no one has to tell you. Yet you are no closer to taking action on it than you were yesterday or will be tomorrow.

I sucked in a quick breath. "You're totally right. But why?"

Frankly, you have let your Demons make it difficult to get what you want out of life. Your Demons do not have pointed ears or a sly grin. They lurk within the shadowy recesses of your subconscious as thoughts of Unworthiness and Self-doubt. These are the masterful Demons responsible for self-sabotaging actions.

The root of such incredible conduct lies in childhood issues. Hosts of primary caregivers were themselves probably

victims of poor parenting or psychological abuse. They simply followed the model they learned from their own caregivers. As a result, yours may have unintentionally programmed you for self-sabotaging behavior.

What's more, bright females in some parts of your world are caught in a double bind. Multitudes worry not only about failure but also about success. If she fails, she is not living up to her own standards of performance; if she succeeds, she may not be living up to cultural expectations about the female role. Then, of course, Jason, your home on the moon-guarded planet is the land of equal opportunity for all, except—

"I'm thoroughly familiar with that explosive issue, Camr."

Actually, vast numbers of you were placed in shocking psychological dilemmas beginning during childhood. No wonder there is such conflict and anxiety on Earth. You were forced to grow up in a world that is little more than a primitive jungle. Flashy vehicles on your streets, fancy kitchens under your roofs, ornate toilets in your bathrooms do not mean you are not in a jungle! Your jungle is overgrown with clusters of concrete boxes. Worst of all, it is thick with beasts that run in the night who come in human form.

With an ache in her heart, Camr said in a gentle tone, **Too many make the mistake of becoming so preoccupied with the divine dance of preparing for the afterlife that they fail to do those things necessary to successfully live an Earthly life. Such ideas contribute a monumental supply of chaos to your love life, competitive edge, and utmost enjoyment.**

Camr relaxed her stiff posture a bit. **The unforgiven call out from a past forever gone by. Pardon your critics and tormentors, Jason. Most probably had unresolved psychological issues that caused them to criticize you, to hurt you as they did. Forgive them for their ignorance, stupidity, vicious behavior. Forgive them for** being little more than urbane savages, justifying their savagery with smiles as they attacked. Forgive yourself for accepting without question the hate and ugliness they spewed forth. Forgive yourself too for past failures.

Self-condemnation blocks the flow of divine power into your life, robbing you of vitality, bringing only misery and failure. Dwelling on old offenses is like opening a grave: all you find are the bones of a rotted corpse.

You must let madness speak no more. Free your mind of the low self-worth you have limitlessly indulged in. In your quest for self-awareness, you may discover things about yourself, Jason, that may offend your sensibilities. That, however, is part of the journey. You must get in touch with who and what you genuinely are rather than who and what you thought yourself to be. The goal: Like yourself-Love yourself-Value yourself in every way. For as you do so, you will feel more entitled to be successful in love, work, and day-to-day life.

No two mortals are alike any more than any two ice crystals are alike. The Whole created incredible you for a purpose. That is why you are here. It has need of you right where you are; otherwise, you would not be there. It wants to draw on your unique qualities. It expects you to contribute your distinctive brand of beauty to the world. So lead not your life in the shadow of others.

"Absolutely!"

Yet many waste countless days dreading or longing for a future that may or may not come to pass. Their life stories akin to that of the ungratified old soul who grumbled:

> *It was Spring: but it was summer I wanted. I remembered the picnics in fields of daffodils and swimming delightfully in tropical sunrises.*

It was Summer: but it was fall I wanted. I remembered the rainbow-drenched leaves and the crisp, cool air.

It was Fall: but it was winter I wanted. I remembered the snow-frosted emerald green bowers and the sparkling joy of the holiday season.

It was Winter: but it was spring I wanted. I remembered the glittering morning mists and the lavish palette of fragrant blossoms.

I was a Child: but it was being an adult I wanted. I dreamed of boundless freedom, winsome surprises, and spectacular "grown-up" escapades.

I was Twenty-one: but it was thirty-six I wanted. I dreamed of wealth-laden success, legendary fame, and unlimited power.

I was Middle Aged: but it was twenty-one I wanted. I remembered the bold plans, the incredible optimism, and the tremendous energy.

I was Retired: but it was middle age I wanted. I remembered the ingenious thinking, the gracefulness, and the gratifications of a job well done.

It was Spring: I felt stupendous pain! The ambulance arrived amazingly fast.

The Doctor said by sunset my soul would stand naked in the wind. Yet I could not help but remembering: "I never got to be what I wanted!"'

Upon approaching death, multitudes discover they have never truly lived. Whatever path you find yourself on, live in your unique now, for tomorrow is not promised. Countless mortals drift through the days of their lives in a daydream not too unlike this parable. They stand on the sidelines or in the back of the group, waiting for the perfect time, the perfect situation, the perfect opportunity. But if you wait for perfect conditions, you will never get anything done. Begin now! Fortune favors the bold!

In brief, do not succumb to the false belief that your good is somewhere in the future—that it is "always to be." If you do not initiate your goals today, tomorrow will be like yesterday. The moment to do it is now. You need to strike with the fierce urgency of now!

"Is it true our subconscious never rests?"

It records every thought, feeling, impression! This occurs second by second, awake or asleep. This action is continuous from the instant of your birth up until the moment of your last breath.

Camr folded her hands in her lap. **The subconscious does not act differently for the prince or the pauper, the good or the bad, the beauty or the beast. It creates exactly what it is offered. Hold a hideous picture in front of a mirror; the mirror will reflect the ugly picture held before it. Likewise, the world you see simply reflects your mind's own foremost thoughts.**

All life is an effect of which the mind is the cause. Your current life is a condition created by thoughts received in the past. You see the world you have made for yourself by your thoughts, but you do not see yourself as the image maker, though you are in fact purely that.

The one physical element that all mortal life has in common is water. About seventy percent of your body is water. What's more, the surface of Earth is overwhelmingly water. In your watery world's groundbreaking future, circa 1990s, a Japanese researcher performed a series of experiments on the effects of thought on the structure of water.

The doctor typed phrases onto paper that expressed human emotions; taped them to glass bottles of water. Some words were positive, such as "Love." Others were negative, such as "You make me sick, I will kill you." The water was frozen; and ultimately responded to these expressions of consciousness. The water labeled with positive phrases formed beautiful, intricate

crystals with sparkling, diamond-like reflective qualities; the water with negative words became ugly and deformed.

"Actually, I already knew positive and negative thinking had a key impact on our surrounding environment. That idea is simple to grasp, but this remarkably tangible evidence of it is astonishing. If our thoughts can affect the molecular structure of water, which unites all human life, it's mind-blowing to think of the kinds of effects thoughts have on our physical bodies and the people and events that come into our lives."

Humankind's crude instruments cannot analyze a thought. Yet thoughts are "things." They possess substance of a refined magnetic quality. If you ever think a thought, Jason, it is in eternity and "never" ceases to exist. The law of indestructibility of matter functions all the way through to thoughts.

Fortunately, there are invisible wings on the shoulders of all mortals. They are stronger than steel though lighter than air. These wings can carry a weight as great as the eternal portion of your soul. Use them, Jason; let your soul fly away from crippling thoughts of self-doubt and limitation.

You can do and have anything you want in life. But to change your world, you must first harness your thoughts, become master of your own mind. For your state of mind determines what you can or cannot do in life. If you love your current life, then keep thinking your current thoughts. But if you want to change your life, change your thoughts to what you want to see; your world will change dramatically.

So remember, life is meant to be lived in a way that allows you to do that for which you were born; and we were all born for a purpose, or we would not be here. But this requires faith. As a priest, Jason, you should know something remarkable happens when you believe. Faithlessness will keep your little kingdom barren. Yet faith will transform its ground into an amazing

garden of abundance. When the words of your mouth and the thoughts in your subconscious agree, nothing will be impossible for you!

"What you've said reminds me of an article I read flying from Rome to Washington. It involved a horse shying away whenever he came to an old tree stump on the road. Every time the horse came to that stump, he drew back. One day the farmer dug up the stump and leveled the road. Yet for years, every time the horse passed where the former stump stood, he flinched. The horse was shying away at *past thoughts of the stump* still held in his mind. Likewise, I'll find myself always lacking in love, happiness, prosperity if in my mind I'm shying away from these things—consciously or unconsciously—due to thoughts of unworthiness or self-doubt."

Precisely! You are transformed only one way: by the transformation of your mind. Change your thoughts. Change your life.

"Let's get back to true love. Any pitfalls?"

Focusing on my flushed face, Camr said, **The most powerful, unswerving myth about love is that "falling in love" is love. Unfortunately, the rapturousness associated with falling in love is astonishingly brief. Sooner or later you will "fall out of love," not necessarily because you have stopped caring for your mate. It is simply that the magical feelings that characterize the experience always fade away.**

In response to the problems of life, romantic fantasy gives way to reality. You want to have sex; your mate does not. You want to attend a social event; your mate wants to relax at home. You want to save money; your mate wants a brand-new vehicle. You want to discuss work; your mate wants to watch a movie. You dislike a few of your mate's friends; all of your friends dislike your mate.

At some point you "fall out of romantic love." You can then either break up or journey down the fiery, icy path and delight in the wonder of "true love."

"If falling in love isn't love, Camr, then what is it?" I said blinking rapidly.

The truth is, falling in love is a biologically induced erotic experience, a vital, genetically controlled deception that ensures the survival of your species. A major characteristic of this is the illusion that its enchanted quality will last forever. This I promise: it will not. This fantasy has its origins in childhood fairy tales.

"Yeah, those ending, 'The prince and beautiful princess, once united, lived happily ever after.'"

Simply stated, falling in love is the dirty little secret of your genes that tricks mortals into relationships, thereby perpetuating human animals. This type of dishonesty only exists in your world. In this realm there is no marriage; we do not engage in animal sex nor produce young like an animal as you do on Earth.

My mouth slackened. "You have no sex of any kind? Wow!"

Moving closer, Camr said with a slow smile, **Frankly, a good deal of mating and rejoining of former mates does occur. Sex distinction is as real here as on Earth, though of course, its expression is not exactly the same. The truth is, we do "Merge."**

"You what?"

Slightly parting her legs, Camr began swallowing frequently. **At treasured moments, souls merge in order to share one another's memories of other lives. This truly unforgettable experience is tremendously pleasurable. The pair become lost in an orgy of love, friendship, rapturous intimacy.**

My tongue darted out subconsciously. I licked my lips. "Sounds deliciously awesome!"

Will revive your senses! Camr said shyly, looking down, unable to meet my eyes.

A thundering sound of wind suddenly erupted in the heavens. Camr and I gazed out over the Sea of Love intensely. A mesmerizing golden figure driving three winged steeds dominated the sky. Our eyes were overwhelmed by its radiance. The horse-drawn vehicle, its white horses composed of a mysterious substance, came to a halt. It hovered above the seashore directly in front of us.

The beautiful being therein nodded to Camr. She acknowledged it with a nod of her own. I gaped in stunned amazement at the mystical scene unfolding before my eyes. It seemed a bit splashy even for this magical plane.

As Camr was about to enter the dreamlike celestial chariot, she hesitated, gave me a yearning look. She leaned against me, stroked my arm, and said in a soft tone, **When the sorrowful cry to me, I am summoned, for I am a great healer. There is a sore in the heart of a new arrival. Blood drops stain the ground at her feet. Maybe I can heal her. Then, perhaps there would be one less blood drop from her heart to stain the universe. Continue along the shoreline, Jason. I will catch up, and we shall start where we left off.**

I took a deep breath, nodded, gently pulled away. Camr touched her mouth, dropped her eyes; gripped by an unseen force, she was slowly lifted into the air. I paused to experience the wonder of the moment then ambled along the sun-swept seashore in silent communion with the infinite.

CHAPTER 20

❦

There is Only "More" Love

*W*andering alongside the waters of this captivating coastal beach, I enjoyed the sensuous softness of velvety sand between my toes. This staggeringly enchanted place was in a class by itself: the vast glittering openness, the racing free saltiness and sweetness of subtle winds under the fairy-blue heights of sky, the simplicity, the diversity, the related harmony of the myriad forms of elegant celestial life.

Startlingly, a soothing breeze enveloped me; the relentless waves rumbled and sloshed. I closed my eyes, smelled the delightfully cool salt air. When I looked again, Camr strolled the golden sands of that timeless shore beside me.

Sorry, Jason, for my departure. Now, where did we leave off?

"Love and beautiful lovers."

Oh yes!

You see with your brain! Camr said in a bubbly tone, bouncing on her toes.

I frowned. "What does that mean?"

The ultimate outcome of light's fantastic journey through the brain's visual system. That is what you experience when you look at a potential lover and "see" their sexy legs, beautiful smile. Your remarkable brain filters, focuses, translates into electrical impulses and interprets the light sent to it from your eyes to construct the firm derriere, the inviting lips.

Next it flashes your lover's irresistible, sensuous likeness to its frontal lobe forty times a second.

I cocked my head, narrowed my eyes. "Wow! You mean we don't see continuously?"

It is more like a flashing motion picture of your new lover that you see. What's more, closing your eyes and visualizing your new mate stark naked produces the same brain pattern as breathlessly looking at them nude. Not only does your brain not distinguish between what it sees in its environment and what it imagines, Jason, but it also does not know the difference between you passionately making love to your new companion and the same action visualized.

Think of it. The amount of information pouring in from your senses to your brain is absolutely staggering: four hundred billion bits per second.

"Incredible! But we couldn't possibly grasp anything near that huge amount."

Two thousand bits get through to your consciousness. As a result, your brain creates a world—creates a reality—out of the data it is able to process. But, it also suppresses 399,999,999,998 bits of data per second that it is incapable of processing.

My eyes widened. "That must also screen out a tremendous selection of reality."

Camr nodded. **But that is just part of the story. In the middle of your retina, where the optic nerve connects to the eye, you have a blind spot—no photoreceptors. So when you look at your new voluptuous mate, there are huge holes in your vision. Like a skilled portrait painter, your brain impeccably fills in the gaps out of your expectations of what you feel your lover should look like. Your brain does this so superbly that you are unaware it is happening.**

On top of this, astonishingly little of the universe is visible to your naked eye. Mortals are blind to most wavelengths of light; as a result, they are blind to the vast majority of the universe.

"Therefore, we are blind to the vast majority of reality," I said, leaning forward.

Frankly, mortal beings do not see "reality." The wavelengths of light your eye is capable of processing actually create your visual world.

And we do not stop there. Your "emotions" decide what is worth paying attention to.

"Wow! Who knew?"

Camr's bright, glossy eyes began flashing. **They also provide you with the unique capability to block out things you consider unnatural or unpleasant.**

You will not believe this! Your species is limited to hearing sounds only within a compressed frequency range: twenty to twenty thousand hertz. So if your lover whispered "I love you" in a voice below twenty hertz or screamed "I adore you!" above twenty thousand hertz, you would never hear those sweet sentiments.

Now for the surprise: if you lifted your sexy lover incorrectly during foreplay, you would experience a sharp pain in your back. Yet the pain would not truly be in your back. It would actually be a neurophysiological process taking place in your brain. Your brain takes the multitude of neurophysiological processes that manifest as human experience—all of which are internal—fools you into thinking some are internal, others external to the body in the "world out there."

So the sleek texture of your lover's gorgeous hair or the titillating feel of her graceful body beneath your prying fingers is just another series of actions taking place within your brain.

I went pale. "But—but if we only see about two thousand out of four hundred billion bits of reality a second, have a blind spot in the middle of our retinas, feel only our brain's interpretation of neurophysiological processes, and can perceive sounds only within a limited range, what the heck's actually out there?"

Camr leaned forward, spoke with a soft tone. **Reality at large, Jason, is primarily a "Frequency Domain." Frequency is a limitless ocean of vibrating Energy, the eternal motion that never stops and of which all things are a part. The thing that is you is a modification of motion. Your duration of motion—number of vibrations per second—makes you what you are, just as another modification of motion makes a rose or a tree.**

Your brain is a kind of lens that converts these frequencies into the birds, bees, apple trees, of your day-to-day "Images and Forms World." There are clearly numerous things within the frequency domain that mortals are not experiencing—things your brains completely edit out of your reality.

I began rubbing at my brow. "So we're equivalent to those eyeless blind moles that live underground? They too might think they understand reality. But if they could simply behold the endless objects humans "see," wouldn't they be in for a surprise?"

Smiling, Camr said, **The bottom line is this, Jason: the mortal body has become the instrument of illusion, seeing what is not there, hearing what truth has never affirmed.**

When you open your eyes and look around, it is not "the world" you see. In short, you see the world your human senses are able to see, the world your belief system allows you to see, the world your emotions wish to see or not see. Your brain constructs your reality by interpreting frequencies of vibrating Energy. Your material world does not exist, at least not in the way you are accustomed to believing. Primordial Energy vibrating at a myriad of frequencies is translated by your mind into "thought forms" of your own imaginings.

There is no world apart from what you wish. You maintain the world within your mind in thought. The physical world looks concrete only because your brain is able to take this blur of frequencies and convert them into beautiful wedding gowns, diamond

rings, your lover's captivating eyes, or other "real" things that make up your world.

"So there're truly no such things as diamond rings?"

It simply means a diamond ring has two distinctive qualities to its reality. When it is filtered through the lens of your brain, it manifests as a ring. But if you could bypass this lens, you would experience the ring as a quantity of energy vibrating at a specific rate per second.

My eyebrows squished together. "But which one is real? Which is illusion?"

Both are real, or, if you would prefer, neither is real.

The only thing "real" in your world is love. There is nothing else real you can get out of it. Everything else mortals see is only the interaction between their brains and "whatever is genuinely out there." The truth, the reality, the "thing in itself" is hidden from your senses.

"So you're saying the world my eyes perceive isn't real life?"

The fact that what your eyes seem to picture is actually not there is difficult for the unenlightened mind to believe. It sounds like insanity and can be mighty disturbing. You mortals do not doubt that the images your eyes show you are realistic. Yet your faith lies in darkness. Fortunately, understanding will come to lighten every corner of your mind if you clear away the shadows that darken it.

Camr began gazing engrossingly at my muscular torso. **So remember, be not deceived when madness takes a form you think is lovely. Notions like sensuousness, orgasms, sexiness have more to do with what is between your ears than between your legs. Learn to see others as they are in truth, not necessarily as your brain's filter perceives them.**

Camr started stroking her neck, casting a radiant glow. **Real love, Jason, does not involve mates gaping winsomely at each** other's beauty. Love only invites you to be happy and will give you everything that makes for joy. The pursuit of beauty for beauty's sake is pure trophy hunting. You run the risk of winning a "trophy mate" who looks vastly better on the outside than they are on the inside, where it counts. Have you ever met a human being who was enormously attractive, but the more you got to know them, the less appealing you found them?

"You bet!" I said, my eyes watering.

A profusion of mortals are alluring in physical appearance yet have an inner being that is misshapen, dark, grotesque. Conversely, I have observed some a bit plain who had an inner form that was graceful, radiant, and angelic. What's more, great looks have a quaint way of staying behind as age moves on. The trophy disappears: all that is left is a bloated, paunchy, wrinkled old being complete with varicose veins and dentures.

"Talk about crucial obstacles to love."

It would be a huge error to allow your mate's chief function in your mind to become that of maid, cook, nanny, handyman, "money machine," or elegantly attired mannequin to be propped up at social gatherings they find uninviting.

Defying this wisdom is a major reason that the concept of marriage is declining in your world. Of those marriages not ending in actual divorce, numerous stay together primarily because of finances, children, religious concerns.

Simply stated, truly intelligent mortals marry to find their "soul mate," rather than a great homemaker or a great earner.

I became suddenly still. "Thought provoking!"

A sad expression swept over Camr. **Loneliness is a cold river. Hosts have been forced to swim in her icy waters. For multiple reasons, many experience the desolation of being lonely. It affects those of all ages, races, and social strata. Aloneness is a powerful sensation; it can be incredibly painful. It is a feeling of** emptiness, isolation, worthlessness. **Countless become vulnerable, even frightened. Marriage, however, does not ensure freedom from lonely nights.**

I started rubbing absently at my arm. "Why wouldn't it?"

As a result of disputes, incompatibility, infidelity, two mortals can live in the same dwelling, can even be lying in the same bed, yet emotionally, they can be worlds apart. Or two mortals can be like you and Jacqueline—limitless miles apart in the cosmos yet remaining emotionally as one.

Too many seek marriage solely to fill the vacuum of their lonesomeness. Loneliness for love is a possible panic situation. Nonetheless, there is no other facet of life in which restraint has the potential to pay greater dividends than in love. There is nothing lonelier than being married to the wrong mate. Those who are to meet will meet! There is an ideal companion for all, one who is searching for you as vigorously as you are searching for them.

Let go of the limits you have placed upon love; join it where it leads you. Eliminate the barriers within yourself you have built against it. Love will come.

"Reminds me of one of my grandfather's tales. Think it went something like this: A wise but bored king had a huge stone placed in the middle of the kingdom's main road. He disguised himself as a beggar, sat by the side of the road, and watched to see if anyone would remove the hefty boulder. A great many residents simply walked around it. Countless others criticized the king for not keeping the roads clear, but none did anything about the stone.

"One day a gray-haired peasant came along, carrying a sizable satchel of grain. Upon approaching the boulder, the age-old peasant laid down the grain and tried to move the massive stone out of the roadway. After much pushing and straining, the exhausted old man finally succeeded. The weary peasant picked up his sack of grain. Then he noticed a crimson leather pouch lying in the road where the boulder had been.

"The pouch was chock full of gold coins. It also contained a note stating the gold belonged to whoever removed the boulder from the royal highway. In brief, the king taught the peasant what few understand. Every obstacle presents a golden opportunity to improve our condition!

"Granddad cautioned to be patient yet ever alert. He said unlimited opportunities present themselves for love, advantage, success but at surprising times and often in astonishing ways."

I am sure your grandfather understood too that there comes a point in your life when you realize who matters, who never did, who won't anymore, and who always will. So do not stress over mates from your past. There is an excellent reason why they did not make it to your future.

It is the distinctive nature of mortals to wonder about "a better catch." But even if you are prepared to travel the yellow-brick road a bit longer, attempting to find Mr. or Ms. Perfect, how can you be certain that still further down the highway there is not someone better?

I hesitated briefly. "Guess you can't."

What's more, no human female is perfect; all mortal males have flaws. Nothing that breathes on your world is totally perfect. Unfortunately, it is an old human failing to also seek in a lover what one feels he is lacking. They "love" another in order to get something. It may be money, pleasure, recognition, or they may seek to bolster their ego by destroying a mate's self-esteem. Frankly, they will take your soul if you let them! They stay until they sense there is nothing left to steal, then slink off into the night. This is what passes for "love" in the mortal world.

"Sounds selfish, destructive, and childishly egocentric."

I love you. You're perfect for me. Now change! This is the thought process of mortals who are "in love" with a mate they are not totally satisfied with.

"Trying to re-create others to your view of what they should be seems arrogant."

It is also a matter of tampering with the impossible, Camr said, looking down.

Brand-new lovers tend to be on their best behavior initially. So before making commitments, experience a full line of real-life situations with them. But keep in mind that mortal beings will hurt you, disappoint you, let you down. Therefore, if you expect your future mate to never do any of these things, you are expecting the improbable.

"Believe it or not, Mrs. Vassilyev, wife of a Russian peasant, gave birth to sixty-nine children between 1725 and 1765. Got me thinking: what's the difference between sex and love?"

Camr leaned in. **There is a gulf between sex and love where ambiguity restlessly lies. Even so, sex is biological. True love is spiritual in nature. If you love truly, you can never lose entirely, Jason. Within all experiences, no matter how painful, lie spiritual insights. Memories of true love never pass. They linger, instruct, alter your perceptions forever. They endure because of the spiritual nature of true love.**

Honestly, human animals rarely appreciate what they have while they have it but miss it—even grieve for it—once it is gone. Multitudes lament, "I had a great lover/spouse. I'm just sorry it took me so long to realize it." One clear, cold morning in the warmth of their bed, they are struck with the pain of realizing there will be no more hugs, no more special moments together, no more playful or sexy phone calls. What they belatedly realized they cared about most gets all used up! Goes away!

"It's true! Not long after Jackie's death, I stumbled across an old vinyl album in a quaint little Georgetown shop. The legendary vocalist sang Jackie's favorite love song. On many evenings I played that evocative melody, staring off at a midnight star, wallowing in a state of self-pity, bewilderment."

Love is a word that is absolutely bleary, drained, exhausted by overwork. Still, true love is life's greatest experience. When the emotion of romance is added to those of love and sex, Jason, you experience love in all its boundless facets, shades, and colors.

Shakespeare's Romeo and Juliet illustrate a special kind of intensity that accompanies true love. You may not be as young as Romeo or Juliet, but you are sadly mistaken if you think you stop falling in love when you grow old. You grow old when you stop falling in love!

"It seems love's misunderstood—that love isn't a feeling."

Camr took a deep breath, looked me in the eye. **Both male and female mortal animals are basically built to stray. Attractiveness, passion will keep you together only for a brief season. Those who truly love do so because of a firm commitment to act tenderly to a mate, even if loving feelings have faded a bit over time.**

The price of love is possible emotional pain. Human love contains both pain and pleasure. So if you are afraid to risk pain, then you must do without real love—the essential ingredient that makes life wondrous and worthwhile. A full life will potentially be full of emotional distress as well as rapturous joy. But the only alternatives are not to live fully, not to love at all, or to exist in a living deathlike state with an unsatisfied hunger. Souls that do not love go empty in a lonely world.

A coward is incapable of love. Love is the prerogative of the brave. It is a form of courage. Trust anybody—a relative, a neighbor, a friend—and you may be hurt. Depend on someone, and that person may let you down. Love anything that lives—a

person, a pet, a plant—and eventually it will die. Yet do not set sorrow upon a throne to worship because that love is now over. Savor the magical experience in your memories.

In brief, without genuine love, life amounts to a thimble full of nothing.

Staring down at the ground, I wandered a short distance away; returned. "But what in fact is genuine love?"

A beaming smile radiated from Camr. **There is no heaven like real love. All are born for it. But true love is like seeing an angel. All mortals talk about it. Yet few actually experience it. Love is the bridge between a land of the living and a land of the loveless dead; it is alive, free, thrilling, and will always move you! Yet it can never be captured; but awakens naturally within your soul.**

Love grows on you through a myriad of shared intense emotional experiences. Loving feelings deepen as each enjoys a better sense of being understood by the other. So remember, real love has no vengeance. Express angry feelings congenially as they occur, or they will fester, grow, lead to ugly outbursts, distance or worse.

Your soul knows all things, Jason. That's why there are no real secrets, simply unawareness geared to your private needs. No mortal has ever truly fooled their mate. That which is so carefully hidden echoes in their very cells, compromising every word, look, and caress between them.

In spite of the most creative deception, the deceived mate's heart knows everything without hearing anything. What it hears clearly is everything you do not say while you are ingeniously striving to be so charming.

"In short, betrayal makes itself felt."

Want more love? Become more loving!

"What does that realistically mean?"

You will discover that if you love until it hurts, there is no true hurt, but only more love. Learn too that real love is a little blind; its course never does run smoothly. When you love someone very much, you overlook faults galore! Ultimately, of course, there is no other: you are always simply loving yourself.

When you actually meet your true love, Jason, you will find everyone else will see what you seem to be. But your real love will know who you genuinely are behind the mask. Simply stated, your eternal love is not necessarily the one who touches your body and makes it tingle. It's the one who takes your hand and touches your heart.

Clearly, love is no easy game. But genuine love will give you "everything." Pure love is a tender plant; when properly nourished, it becomes sturdy, enduring. Its pain is far sweeter than all other pleasures are. Like a natural spring, the longer and farther it flows, the stronger, deeper, clearer, it becomes.

Love does not fade away with physical death, and you cannot quench it during mortal life. Once it explodes into existence, it is never destroyed. Out of need, morality, or a cause beyond your control, you may conceal it, deny it. Yet it will always be there, shimmering silently within you. There is nothing but beauty in the cosmos, and beauty has only one perfect expression: Love. All the rest is a lie.

"Granddad instructed me, 'Put love ahead of fame and glory. All the glory of the kingdoms of this world will be worthless as a pinch of sand in heaven.'"

Suddenly, Camr appeared melancholy; she looked at me with a pained gaze. **But there is even more. On your deathbed, wealth, fame, power, or poverty will not matter to either you or to your Creator. The Lord of Life will only want to know: 'Did you show love?' 'Have others been helped, inspired, cheered through your having lived?' 'Are there vital acts you have left unperformed, crucial words unspoken? Did your life count for anything truly** worthwhile?' The answers will either bless or torment you after death in ways you cannot now imagine.

Simply stated, perhaps it was not so important to have had the last word in those endless fights. Perhaps instead you should have told your mate how much she meant to you, how deeply you have always loved her.

As you gasp your last breath, what answer will you take into eternity? Did you show love? Or did you squander life acquiring "things" to satisfy your ego? God's point of view on what's paramount in life is clear: there is only Love!

Will your final moments be filled with hope and promise? Or will they find you trembling along a cold lonely road leading to remorse?

Truthfully, the life of mortals is a gallop, a headlong dash to the grave. The dark wings of death are unrelentingly hurrying near. How many ticks you have left, nobody knows for sure. It could be thirty years or thirty days or barely thirty minutes. Your life is slipping away even as you sit there uncovering this reality. Age, health may modify your time, but based on my thirty year example, you have only 10,950 days left, or 262,800 hours, or 15,768,000 minutes, or 946,080,000 seconds.

Choose the time unit that makes you most comfortable, but the cold hard fact is sand in the hourglass of your life is quickly running out!

Death is a black thunder. The unenlightened are alarmed by the sound of it. Yet it will sneak up on you with unswerving footsteps. The beating of its black wings echoes without warning at the door of the young and old, strong and weak, rich and poor. You are all gods in the making, but your body will die like the animal it is. When Death's cold, bony finger scratches at your door, how will you answer: did you show Love?

I sat with unnatural stillness for an endless moment. "Frankly, I see now that I could've loved Jackie a little bit better.

"Aviar touched briefly on karmic debts. Can you expand my knowledge on the law of cause and effect?"

My pleasure.

CHAPTER 21

Law of Life

After an enlightening stroll along the Sea of Love's coastline, we stumbled upon a hexagon-shaped gazebo and decided to rest our sand-encrusted toes. This tranquil retreat enjoyed an off-white marble base, a copper-turreted roof, and built-in marble benches. It abounded in fragrant blossoms and vines laden with deep-purple grapes.

Suddenly, I was startled by the sight of mermaids with long, flowing pale-green hair. They came up very high out of the sea. But they weren't as beautiful as they're ordinarily depicted. In some ways, their faces seemed a bit masculine. They surfaced amid the elegant willowy flora that whispered and sang along the water's edge of a trinity of floating islands. The islands were packed with gorgeous rainbow-colored flowers and numerous strikingly beautiful birds.

As if that weren't enough, tiny humanoid forms strolled about the center isle's lush meadows. Most had wings growing from their backs; several did not. Yet all possessed a semitransparent quality but with white faces and arms. They beguilingly sang a rich harvest of mesmerizing melodies. No flute could have given forth a more melodious sound. Many were singing, circling, and dancing; others seemed to be holding some kind of meeting. Two were hanging delicate, silky cobweb-like stuff over a tuft of grass—probably to make a shelter.

A host of lemon-yellow three-legged frogs gathered on a mist-drenched log and voiced witness to the harmony of the setting. As we lounged on the marble benches, I turned from the magical spectacle before us. "Is karma legitimate? Are people really reborn in one human body after another?"

Camr gave a slow, disbelieving shake of the head. **Why do you think one little girl is born into riches, abundance, loving surroundings but another into poverty, misery, rejection? Why is one little boy a genius while another is mentally challenged? Why is one person blind, diseased, deformed while another is afforded strength, agility, a perfectly formed body?**

The Creator is not cruel. The universe is more benevolent than you suspect. If they weren't explained by "the effect" of causes generated in previous lives, these things would be inexplicable, heartless, vile.

Your soul incarnates in a succession of cycles, as do the trees, the seasons, the universe. Simply stated, your life is a never-ending story. Souls incarnate for the purpose of purging through varied experiences in preparation for their reward.

My head flinched back slightly. "Reward?"

Your soul's reward once it completes its earth-life cycles. "Him that overcometh, will I make a pillar in the temple of my God and he shall go no more out [from the spirit realm to reincarnate]," promises Revelation 3:12 of your Holy Book.

The truth is that you alone are responsible for the circumstances in which you find yourself. You are not the innocent victim of your environment. You are simply experiencing the effects of your own prior actions and beliefs. What you sow, you reap!

"But why isn't reincarnation in the Bible?"

The most important factor was a self-absorbed soul who also loved this seaside gazebo setting. She sat just where you are now, Jason. Slowly, painfully weeping and sighing in voices ranging in

timbre from those of a small child to a young woman, she gave a shameful, ruthless yet fascinating account of how she fought to elevate her standing in mortal life. She greatly desired that which all typical mortal females crave.

I gave Camr a blank look. "What's that? What do all women intensely crave?"

Everything!

Camr's dancing, sparkling eyes suddenly changed to a distant, empty stare; her bubbly voice, to a monotone. **It has been almost fifteen hundred of your earth-life years, but I can still recall the highlights of our talk. Her mortal name was Theodora. She lived between AD 508 and 548. She was a mortal without noble rank or title. Yet armed with the potent age-old weapons of beauty, charm, intelligence, deceit, she became the Emperor Justinian's empress.**

Theodora was the daughter of Acacius, a bear feeder in the arena at Constantinople. She became in succession an actor, a dancer, a harlot. Theodora quickly developed into an accomplished prostitute and bore a male child out of wedlock. Most of her sexual promiscuity, however, is absolutely too disgusting to be uttered aloud.

Once Theodora became Justinian's mistress, her insatiable ambition caused her to set her sights even higher. She was determined to become his empress. But Justinian's mother opposed her with all the power at her command. Although the law forbade males above the rank of senator to marry actresses, this law was abolished by Justinian upon the death of his mother.

Theodora then took her place beside him on the throne. After becoming an adult, her illegitimate child returned from Arabia; he revealed himself to his then empress mother "and forthwith disappeared forever."

Theodora was fair of face, attractive in appearance, and petite. Her gaze seemed always intense and made with contracted

brows. Lavishing more care on her body than necessary was customary for her. She engaged in long, luxuriant daily baths. Then she would dine on a lavish breakfast. At dinner, she also ate and drank ravenously, so much so that she would sleep for substantial periods, occasionally all day and night.

Officials were required to take an oath of allegiance to her as well as to the emperor. The city was full of her spies, who reported everything said against her or the administration. She surrounded herself with ceremonious pomp, requiring all who approached to demean themselves in a manner unheard of during that time. Worst of all, if the emperor imposed any favor upon a mortal without her consent, that mortal's affairs would quickly suffer. He would be dismissed from his office with the greatest indignities then die a horrifying death.

Theodora's knowledge of human animals was expert and innately predatory. Justinian swayed indecisively from one option to another, but she was forceful, strong-minded and inflexible as a steel dagger.

After becoming empress, Theodora turned into an explosive tyrant. Her favorites were catapulted to power, while her enemies died in such vast numbers that the public rose up against the royal couple in the Nika insurrections of AD 532. Justinian was terrified, demoralized; wanted to flee. But tough, unyielding Theodora preferred death to obscurity. She made him sweat it out, stating, "Now every man must die once, and for a king, death is better than dethronement and exile." There was enormous bloodshed. But the riots were subdued.

In short, Justinian subsequently became little more than Theodora's puppet.

Theodora discredited all references to reincarnation in the early Gospels; then she split the church into two warring factions.

Frankly, prior to wedding Theodora, Justinian supported the reincarnational leanings of the Church of Rome.

In open defiance of Vatican protocol, Theodora appointed a lackey—Anthimus—as patriarch of Constantinople for the precise purpose of revoking reincarnational teachings.

The result? Theodora instantly ran into a vigorous battle with Pope Agapetus. The Pope traveled from Rome to Constantinople in severe February weather to publicly censure Theodora. What's more, he reprimanded the outraged Justinian, saying, "With eager longing have I come to gaze on the most Christian Emperor Justinian. In his place I find a 'tyrant Caesar' whose threats, however, terrify me not!"

The emperor, stunned by the pope's actions, made no objection to the pope's suspending Anthimus as patriarch of Constantinople. Saintly, incorruptible Pope Agapetus died the same year. His death followed his triumph so quickly that Theodora was immediately suspected of being instrumental in speeding him here to the spirit plane.

Theodora became determined to have Anthimus reinstated as patriarch. She sent a letter to Agapetus's successor, Pope Silverius: "Make no delay in coming to us, or without fail, recall Anthimus to his own place!"

When Pope Silverius read that, he groaned, "I know very well that this affair has brought an end to my life." But he replied by letter to the Empress, "Mistress Augusta, I shall never consent to do such a thing as to reinstate a man who is a heretic and who has been condemned in his own wickedness."

In a titanic rage, Theodora sent orders to General Belisarius: "Seek out some grounds of complaint against Pope Silverius that will remove him from the office."

Pope Silverius was seized based on false charges and forced into exile. He was fed only bread and water. So he weakened, died. Consequently, Theodora became the only empress in history to succeed in enthroning her own pope, Pope Virgilius.

Emperor Justinian convened the Fifth Ecumenical Church Council. He excluded all but six Western bishops while permitting the attendance of 159 Eastern bishops who supported his ideas. This provoked Pope Virgilius to belated, nonetheless courageous action.

The Pope demanded Eastern and Western bishops be given equal representation, a demand quickly crushed by Justinian. Pope Virgilius refused to attend the council, though his motive might have been self-preservation. He was clearly aware Justinian had put to death Popes Agapetus and Silverius and was not above killing him too.

The Pope was not in attendance and only six Western bishops were permitted to vote. Naturally, the findings of the Council purged reincarnational knowledge within the Christian church. Yet stubborn sects, notably the Troubadours of Southern France, went underground for multiple centuries.

This is the major reason reincarnation does not appear in your Holy Book, Jason. Decide for yourself how spiritually inspired this decision was.

Upon conclusion of our discussion of Theodora, Camr did a slow, tantalizingly graceful catlike stretch; she sat up straight and alert. Her overall enchanting visage started to glow again.

"If we've experienced countless lives before, Camr, why don't we remember?"

Camr's features became expressionless. A host of mortals do remember past lives. A southeastern university in your country studied the cases of over twenty-five hundred children who claimed to have been reincarnated. At around thirty-nine months of age, the children were able to recall specific verifiable details of their past lives. But by the age of five, that knowledge faded.

This great university concluded that the mind and brain are not the same thing. The brain is a portal that consciousness flows through; consciousness, or "soul," untangles itself from a dying physical body, and consciousness or soul "survives the death of the body."

"Just seems like the concept of karma's senseless punishment."

Frankly, it is the law of the Creator that is perfect, not your mortal conception of it. A life in the Earth realm is a way of cleansing your soul. Though admittedly, it may be a tough path at times. All human sorrow comes from your own misuse of the free will given you by the Creator. Do unto others what you want them to do unto you. That is the manner in which to best contend with karma.

Most importantly, it is actually your own soul that steers you into the circumstances you find yourself in. It does so in order for you to evolve by overcoming them. Trials are but lessons you have failed to learn presented once again so you can make better choices. Karma is not fate, simply cause and effect. It is a harsh taskmaster to the unwise, a faithful servant to the wise. The fact is, yesterday's vices and virtues result in today's sorrows and joys.

"What about the Christians before Theodora?"

This brings us logically to the teachings of the Nazarene. His disciples asked him, "Master, who did sin, this man, or his parents, that he was born blind?" (John 9:2). Thus the disciples acknowledged being born blind might have been this mortal's punishment for sins committed in a "prior" life. Christ asked his disciples, "Whom do men say that I am? And they said, 'Some say that thou art John the Baptist; some, Elijah; and others, Jeremiah, or one of the prophets [reincarnated]'" (Matthew 16:13, 14). The Nazarene said to Peter, James, John, "Elijah truly shall first come and restore all things. But I say unto you, that Elijah has come already, and they knew him not, but did unto him whatever they pleased. Then the disciples understood that he spoke to them of John the Baptist [beheaded by King Herod]," thus indicating Elijah had reincarnated as John the Baptist (Matthew 17:11-13).

"Actually, I recall as a seminarian coming across matching views in the works of Origen, Plato, Plotinus, Pythagoras, St. Gregory, St. Clement of Alexandria."

The Nazarene and those other saints of the early church all embraced reincarnation, which was the traditional belief of the Christian faith. In AD 533, the Emperor Justinian unrelentingly, forcefully persecuted all who refused to surrender their convictions about reincarnation.

Resistance was so firm—particularly by rebel Christians called the Cathars—that not until the thirteenth century did the church's campaign of terror and slaughter effectively control reincarnational thinking in the West. Multiple secret mystical groups smuggled this age-old basic Christian belief forward to modern times.

I walked away to regain composure; returned shaking my head. "Reincarnation—how does it work?"

At transition, the quantity of self-aware Energy that is your soul is released from its material shell. Your flesh body falls away along with the ego and conscious mind. All that your soul retains is the total recall of your Earthly experiences stored in your subconscious.

When the cycle of incarnations is completed, when not one soul remains unpurified, when mortals climb from the status of animal up to paradise, the world of human beings will be over. It will reduce to nothingness. Dwindle away. Simply stop seeming to be. The world of Ape Man will end in an illusion. There it was born. There it will end as well.

"I—I don't know what to say. Can we take a short break? My mind's reeling."

Absolutely!

CHAPTER 22

Cordon of Guardians

The sky was greater, loftier, and more resolutely blue than the sky of Earth. The exhilarating winds breathed their own freshness and energy into me, resulting in my cares subtly dropping off like autumn leaves. The pounding surf's liquid melody coursed merrily, soothingly through my sorrow-laden soul. In this idyllic spot, time stood still. Serenity and peace filled the heart. Plus, Camr's sparkling energy was soft, warm, comforting to feel and be around. This multitude of factors made any thought of parting tremendously difficult.

Sitting at the edge of the gazebo's marble bench, I rushed my words. "How long have we been talking?"

As you are now, Jason, time does not exist. A thousand earth-life years are but an instant here.

Frankly, I'd completely lost track of time in this super enchanting world. The hours went by and left no mark, and the days were as fairies that danced on the air and left no footprints.

My head tipping back, I looked skyward, staring off. Afterward, I gave a long exhale and said, "The eye-opening knowledge you've shared, Camr, gives me a deeply satisfying sense of self-worth. There's much more I'd like to learn. It's just that I need to find my friend Jackie O'Sullivan. She and I have dissolved and merged into each other. Without her, my life's reduced to a lonely, confused, pointless struggle. Find her for me!"

Camr's lips pressed together in an intense grimace. **Why do you ask such favors of me? Perhaps I have offered all the impulses of my heart to you, who do not know I exist. Perhaps I would have you satisfy my own strawberries of desire! Perhaps offering what I am to you is like offering myself to the winds of Spring, which no one can hold. Maybe I am conflicted, feel angry. Maybe I hurt. Perhaps you are wiser to ask naught!**

Showing my palms and shrugging, I said uncertainly, "What… What's wrong? What'd I say? What'd I do?"

Camr gave me a brief icy glare. Then soft spoken and almost unnervingly serene, she said, **Your love tale is compelling, but I am not the one to hear it! I seek not to make of your newfound love an enemy. Quite candidly, I am ill equipped to put your mind at ease. The carpenter's son spoke genuinely when he said, "In my Father's house, there are many mansions."**

The world of your experience—the one perceived through your senses—is not the only universe. Coexisting alongside it are countless others in a gigantic, multilayered reality of parallel worlds, some almost identical to your own, others wildly different.

That's why beings travel not from one "place" to another but from one "dimension of consciousness" to another. There is only one boundless universe, and our progress through it is essentially by a change in our level of consciousness.

The higher dimensions, or "heavens," are reached the more inward you go, Jason. The lower heavens, the more outward. Each heaven has multiple separate dimensions. Each dimension envelopes multiple smaller dimensions.

"How immense is this stack of dimensions?"

Slanting her body away from mine and using a carefully controlled tone, Camr said, **The Great Rays have searched far and wide for its ending. The result seems a bit fantastic. They concluded that this progression of dimensions continues to infinity.**

There is a brief poem the elders teach that sums up this phenomenon. It goes, "Big dimensions have little dimensions that rest themselves inside them; and little dimensions envelop even tinier dimensions, and so on—ad infinitum!"

Truthfully, the universe Earth inhabits is only a tiny fraction of the vast, mysterious Whole. The dimension we are presently in is merely a stepping stone to another heaven. Beyond this second heaven, there is the Third Heaven—a bright, serene, wondrous landscape without terrain, a reality so brilliant and formless that to human perception, it appears only as a streaming of light. I saw things, heard things there that are unutterable! It is something you actually feel!

The higher the dimension, the brighter they are, and the more frequency-like they seem. The highest realms appear to be pure frequency domains, which frightens many souls. Unfortunately, Jacqueline could be in any one of them.

I gave a heavy sigh. "Is there no one who can help me?"

We have elders who have gained mastery of the sublime mysteries of the Light. They are well able to help unhappy beings resolve whatever problems plague their souls. They are known as "Preeminent Teachers-of-Light."

These revered souls have reached the Creator directly, retain no trace of worldly limits, remember their own Identity perfectly. Although they are no longer visible, their images can still be called upon. They reside on a peerless world at the heart of the Whole. Yet they will appear when, where it is vital. All needs are known to them. Most importantly, they will provide all the help you can accept.

"How do I reach these teachers?"

You will find one at the Temple of Wisdom, here in the second heaven.

"Located here? Where?"

In the northeast sector of Dimension Three on the Mountain of Solace. Actually, my own dwelling is located in a village not far from there. The temple is not hard to find once you get to the mountain. There is danger, however, in taking such a journey. You must only travel there escorted by a cordon of guardians.

"But what possible danger could there be to me in the spirit realm?" I said in a disbelieving voice.

Even here, certain dazzling but unclean essences attempt to prevent souls like you from soaring to the heights. Level Three abounds with bright essences of disembodied spirits who have lost their souls and who will attempt to draw you to themselves to steal your light.

These unclean spirits want to entrap you, Jason. They want you to defile your soul, cling to them, not rise further. They will show you future events; sometimes they will show you untrue things. But whatever a soul receives from them is untrustworthy. To help reach your destination safely, I will ask Archangel Rotaar to accompany you.

Camr closed her eyes, bowed her head, and remained motionless for an instant. She then opened her eyelids; glanced over my shoulder and flashed a dazzling smile. I turned, came face to face with one of the most amazing sights I've ever witnessed.

There stood three colossal, overwhelmingly powerful, breathtakingly beautiful beings ranging in height from about thirty to thirty-six feet. All were glowing in radiant white. The Archangel Rotaar—the tallest—had its spectacular brilliant-white wings at full span. I could see the wings of the other two—Janaar and Xaraar—folding behind their bodies as both slowly got into position. Their wings seemed a dusty grayish white. They waited silently in front of a mammoth rock right behind their leader. I staggered out of the gazebo in stunned amazement.

"Wings! Holy Shit! They actually have *wings*! And I thought all angels were about my size," I said with a gasp, stumbling back a step or two.

My emotions were still midway between shock and astonishment. Yet I managed to notice that their long white-blond hair, ice-blue eyes, and other facial features all appeared identical. Like Aviar, they seemed to have no gender. Their essences also appeared illuminated from within and surrounded by bands of white, gold, purple, and silver-blue rays.

Without appearing uncongenial, they never smiled, never frowned, never changed expression. Each radiated an aura of pure, powerful love. It touched the deepest reaches of my soul, causing a sense of profound peacefulness. What's more, each enjoyed an individual energy.

Rotaar projected a powerful, reserved aura; his wings seemed relaxed. Janaar radiated a friendly, assertive, outgoing energy. His wings fluttered softly, creating a wispy breeze. Xaraar, the smallest, emanated a sadness—well, not quite sadness, but a sort of melancholic energy. His mild form of melancholy seemed mixed with a strange blend of shyness yet had aggressive traits. Xaraar's wings remained tightly folded against the skin of his back.

Camr familiarized Rotaar with the mission. The colossus folded his wings to his side; he said emotionlessly, **Let it be done!**

Camr turned to me, smiling, leaned forward.

The Temple of Wisdom is easy to find. Even so, I will draw you a map from Pale Radiance Trail—your drop-off point—to the shrine. The teacher can usually be found in the solarium occupied by his favorite pastime.

"Which is?"

Engaging in deep contemplation of some unique mystery.

"What's his name?"

We here address him as Teacher or Master. He is wise and loving, and his knowledge is vast.

"Well, how will I know him?"

Citizens here seem to change their appearance as frequently as you mortals change clothing on Earth. The teacher is no exception. He typically emerges in one of three forms. The master may appear as a majestic angel arrayed in shining armor, wearing a bluish-purple cape. He will have long silver-white hair, penetrating bluish-purple eyes, and will be wielding a sword of violet flame. He also could appear as simply a bearded old man. Or the timeless sage may come forward as a sphere of intensely glowing bluish-purple light.

Camr then extended her dainty hand. Here is the map to the temple at Mount Solace.

I placed the small map under my garment's off-white sash. "Thanks, gorgeous! You've been super!"

Camr's eyes became bright, glossy; her appearance flushed. Earlier, I implied your journey will be dangerous. Yet angels have great power. If I were to highlight everything I have seen, you would scarcely believe it. They can annihilate anything simply by their will or by a look. I have observed mountains teeming with dark spirits, shaken, leveled, overturned. I have witnessed cliffs split down the middle to their very base, the evil ones on them swallowed up. I have also spotted angels scattering evil entities, casting vast hordes into the Black Abyss.

You are in excellent hands. Rotaar is one of the most powerful of all.

Around Camr there suddenly seemed to be a tangible sense of quiet. Attractive and effervescent, she nonetheless carried the vaguely haunted look of one who's suffered a staggering loss of love. The pain of that memory appeared to briefly darken her features. She smiled at me, but two tears slid down her cheeks. I stood there like a well-meaning friend, but I didn't know what to say. Momentarily confused, I looked up at an empty space in the sky.

The moment's quiet solemnity was broken as Camr reached out, touched my face. Then with a soft voice she said, **It has been an unexpected pleasure seeing you again, Jason. I pray the old master will be able to soothe your aching heart.**

We stood there, the two of us, two beings struggling to understand the meaning of the powerful, soaring "something" between us. This "power" wound around us like a boundless coil of ribbon binding two beings that otherwise had little hope of understanding one another. I was completely unprepared for the never-to-be-forgotten experience that followed.

Camr caressed my arm and looked into my eyes; she felt an empty, lonely feeling deep inside her. A long, torturous silence passed; Camr's heartbeat quickened. Her pulse throbbed in her throat as she said, **I do not know how to reconcile what I am feeling with who I am. The white fire of love touched my heart in times past, burned it deeply. Still, love's fire will not leave me alone. I have whispered to you in the perfume of a rose, but the flower soon faded and was, like me, forgotten. Now you would forsake me and desire another!**

I am offering ripe strawberries to one who does not appreciate their delectableness; I am pouring my sweet wine for one who cannot taste it. This is tremendously hard on my soul!

Then Camr's moist lips passionately melted into mine; her eager, seductive tongue entered my mouth. She kissed me with rapturous warmth, exquisite tenderness. I drifted into a sort of twilight ecstasy. I felt as if I were floating above the clouds, my lips gently caressing those of the beautiful creature for time without end. Her subtle, sweet scent titillated my nostrils. Clouds soft as down magically sprang up beneath us. We rested upon them with the lightness of a puff of air like two butterflies fluttering in the midday sun. It was an experience beyond enchanting. When I opened my eyes, the lovely creature was gone.

I stood leaning against the gazebo in great shock. Unabridged ecstasy had bewitchingly delighted every member of my body. I'd experienced the wonder of something moving, distractingly exotic. Biting my lip, staring down at the ground, I wondered what that hazel-eyed beauty knew about us that I didn't.

Rotaar jolted me back to reality by reaching down his massive right hand and clasping my own, which produced a tranquilizing sound. His huge palm seemed warm and comfortable in mine. I felt a serenity seeping into me like a balm soothing my emotions. The winged warrior raised his left arm to heaven. Upsoaring like oversized eagles, we ascended swiftly from the white sandy beaches of the Sea of Love. Gracefully, effortlessly, we sailed into the deep, limitless upper heavens. Each star of night I beheld seemed close enough to touch.

And that was only the beginning! I could go anywhere in anytime—past, present or future—in my immortal spirit body. I became unexpectedly emboldened surrounded by my commanding angelic escort. I released Rotaar's hand. I sailed, floated, soared; I straddled an auroral beam. My soul seemed like an enchanted boat floating upon the silver waves of winds. I glided down, around, into a zesty sea of profound ever-spreading exhilaration. Catching the pristine winds that fan heaven, we sailed on, away, afar without a course, without a guiding star.

What's more, I passionately pleaded for a side trip to the universe I'd left behind, which was then fading like a dream only half remembered. Rotaar hesitantly agreed.

We entered a great dark opening in the fabric of space. Its walls glowed brilliant white while tiny, bright, colorful "clouds" rotated clockwise around the interior. We exited from the tunnel and entered a pale-greenish haze. Subsequently, the Milky Way's northern constellation Cygnus came into view. There was blackness all around.

With my supersensitive spirit vision, I pierced beyond the familiar rainbow of visible light to a much more vibrant world, for the heavens blaze across a spectrum of energies far broader than the human eye can behold. Black holes were uncloaked by bright X-ray bursts as matter spiraled into them. Joyously, I roamed in and around the seventy billion trillion stars of the physical universe.

We explored massive conglomerations of galaxies clustered like grains of diamond dust to a celestial veil projecting kaleidoscopic bubbles of primeval light. We navigated through a universe without stars. We witnessed the iconic pillars of the Eagle Nebula soar four light-years high against a turquoise hydrogen sky. I marveled at a sudden lightning flash of radiation that etched an afterimage of the Big Bang across the heavens.

We drifted beyond the outer edge of the rings that make up Earth's multiple planes. I could perceive Earth in the center with semitransparent radiant globes around it, each one separated from the other by fractions of an inch. I looked closer at Earth and saw this very, very thin royal blue line along its horizon. I cringed then shuddered as I realized it was Earth's atmosphere and that that was all there is of it. Earth's wispy dome appeared about as thick as the fuzz on a tennis ball—and that's all there is to protect humankind from the deadly ether of space.

We soared to the far shores of light. Beyond that point a dense fog of superheated plasma impeded light's progress; I became mesmerized, frightened, confused. I chose to go no further...

Rotaar halted in midair; he took me by the arm and held me much like a loving parent clutching a tiny infant. As he cradled me securely in his powerful right arm, we floated even higher into the blue, blustery, transparent layers of ether. There was

a sensation of wind flowing before me…around me…faster…
faster…then silence…I passed out.

Dawn broke with spectacular rosy rays; the elegance of the night
stars faded. Squinting, my eyes gradually opened. I had a strong
sense of being encircled by love: felt warm, sheltered, at peace. I
awoke on a makeshift bed of soft meadow grass, leaves, and pine
needles. My mind felt clear, fully awake, aware of a sense of peace
and heavenly freshness. It was lovely, good, and freeing slumbering
under the open sky amid the wind's unfettered spirit.

Rotaar, Janaar, and Xaraar were standing around me, looking
down expressionlessly. Enthralled, I began to survey my surroundings. My eyes reveled beauty never seen upon the Earth. *What tender colors, what exquisite forms,* I thought.

I turned toward my three gigantic companions. "I should be
OK. Camr drew me a map. Appears to be a substantial hike from
here to the temple, but I need to walk and collect my thoughts before meeting the old master. Thanks, all of you!"

Moving closer, Rotaar said, **The Light is the source of all good;
we are merely one of Its channels.**

I felt a warm radiance of gratitude surge through me. As the
three glowing celestial knights ascended into the sky, I shouted,
"Maybe we'll meet again someday? Stay in the Light!"

The powerful trio flew around me in a broad circle several
times before soaring into the heavens, fading into the blue.

CHAPTER 23

❧

Village of Tranquility

I wandered down mildly sloping Pale Radiance Trail toward a grassy meadow. On the other side there was a luminous marble boulevard that Rotaar referred to as "The Path of Light." A tranquil stream flowed melodiously alongside "Light" Boulevard. A covered bridge connected it to a picturesque little town. The bewitching wooden expanse was fragrant with the perfume of huge almond blossoms running along its top and intermittently cascading down its sides.

Gorgeous white-feathered creatures—dozens of them—were serenely afloat on the calm, crystalline surface. They glided gracefully under and around the stunning structure like swans flowing under a bridge of enchantment. In pure wonder, I crossed over the span to get a better look at the charming hamlet.

There was a quaint, etched, bronze signpost at its entrance.

"Welcome To Tranquility. Population: There is only One of us here!"

I stepped from the delightful bridge into the most breathtaking little village you could possibly imagine. Its beauty far surpassed any concept of beauty accessible to human sight. There's no way to adequately describe its elegant, understated grandeur. Still, something should be said in order to provide at least some idea about it.

A multitude of its dwellings were positioned one near another, arranged in the form of a city with streets, lanes, and public squares just like the ones you'd find on Earth. Others were set apart on oversized parcels of terrain located on hills or in mountainous areas overlooking the captivating cityscape.

The lodgings were crafted out of wood, stone, brick, gold and precious gemlike substances. There seemed to be every type and style imaginable. No two looked alike. I didn't spot any smog, litter, or even insects. Everywhere I turned, the surroundings appeared sparkling, pristine, quiet except for the hauntingly beautiful music breathing throughout the village. A great choir seemed to sing to a harp, but I could only hear, not see, them. It was soulful and transcendent, containing every joyful noise I had ever heard. I gave pause, listened passionately, felt moved.

When I mentioned I was a friend of Camr's, her congenial neighbors showed me great kindness. The truth is, in the spirit realm, doing good for others is a sought-after joy. I was permitted to stroll along the lanes, to look around wherever I wished. At times, my gracious hosts gave me a glimpse into their charming homes. Each masterwork had rooms galore, including multiple bedrooms, but none possessed a kitchen, bathroom, or lock on any door.

Everything in the stunning residences sparkled as though made of precious stones. Even the unconventional oversized windows enhanced the numerous shadings of light throughout each dwelling. A host of objects looked like diamonds with similar variegations of light. The walls were translucent; within them I could see fluid forms representative of heavenly things in endlessly changing variety.

The dwellings also possessed superb lawns complete with flower-bedecked gardens you'd simply fall in love with. What's more, they were surrounded by rows, clusters, and natural archways of trees unlike any others. The trees and flowers changed from day to day; those transformations made the exhilarating views unswervingly new. I observed vastly more in those architectural works of art, but those things can't be described using human terminology.

Near the center of the lovely village stood an incomparable "House of God" fashioned out of matchless glass and gorgeous wood. Its twin-carved doors, superlative. The silhouette, bold, dramatic, which caused it to appear more like a gigantic sculpture than a place of worship. Though it appeared virtually devoid of artificial splendor, it was a magnum opus of clean lines and design. The unparalleled edifice stood towering in a ruggedly beautiful landscape amid a grove of extraordinary, brightly glowing trees. When the airstream swirled, their shining leaves glistened in the soft breeze like sinuous gold.

The pulpit was situated in the east end with seating arranged in a semicircular configuration. Every seat possessed an excellent view of the podium. The floors, seating, and pulpit were all crafted of a preeminent version of the same gorgeous wood as the building's exterior. I didn't notice any bells, books, candles, or recognizable religious symbols on display.

Beyond the seating area stood a water-lily pond teeming with colorful, shimmering koi. Abutting the pond on each side were beds of exotic blossoms winsomely intermingled with exquisite hanging floral baskets and graceful trees. A heavenly light shone down from the pale-blue ether, bathing the seating area in a blissful radiance. The interior of this holy space was a stunningly sublime indoor paradise guaranteed to restore even the most burdened soul. I was there only briefly, yet I was transported into a state of utter deep serenity so profound it's impossible to explain.

Next door to the "House of God" stood a library. I entered the vast ultramodern structure and caught my breath in wonder. It wasn't the architecture that astonished me but the unlimited volumes. I wandered aimlessly among the shelves and selected at random a thick red book from a middle shelf. It was a book by a

Renaissance physician and alchemist printed in large black type. It stated that angelic spirits were divided into two distinctive groups, celestial angels and dark angels. A ravishing doe-eyed librarian with full, pouting lips approached.

She gifted me with a dazzling boundless smile. **I am Layla. You have questions?**

"Library in the spirit realm! Why?"

For the same reason you find one anywhere. New arrivals usually think upon entrance to this plane that they will intuitively know everything, perhaps be able to prophesy the future like fortune-tellers. Souls do not suddenly become all wise! Countless souls here are nearly as intellectually blind as they were in Earthly life. Hosts are able to pick up the knowledge that they had forgotten. But in truth, if you lacked intelligence on your plane, you will still be dull upon your arrival in this realm. Of course, there are academies for all who wish to attend.

It would perhaps surprise you to know there are dim, lazy, unambitious spirits here as on Earth. There are also brilliant, fascinating spirits whose very presence is rejuvenating.

"This hefty book I selected on angels would probably take me weeks to read. Maybe you know the answer. What's the difference between celestial and dark angels?"

Layla leaned forward, her eyes wide and glowing. **Celestial angels work toward harmony with the laws of God; dark angels work against such harmony. In the archives of the angelic regions, there are cases on record where a virtuous angel has become evil or an evil angel, virtuous. But those cases are rare.**

I have never given my soul to the keeping of an Earthly body. Yet I suspect you are a new arrival from that Valley of Forgetfulness.

"You can tell, huh?"

As your soul travels down the road of future hopes, be wary of dark angels. I myself have been urged by such spirits to join

forces with them. Their arguments are often tremendously plausible, and the temptations presented are tempting.

"What's the best way to spot dark angels?"

Both types are extremely brilliant and beautiful. But there is a difference between the two perceptible at first glance. The eyes! The eyes of celestial angels sparkle with love, while the eyes of dark emissaries are evil and extraordinarily unpleasant to encounter. By their fruits, the dark energies shall reveal themselves.

Layla's eyes grew wider. **I will share something essential for self-protection. There are spirits on this plane and spirits on your plane; the difference being mostly a difference in garments. One wears mortal flesh. The other wears a subtler body made of energy that is vibrating a bit faster.**

Saintly spirits here are powerfully drawn to Earthly spirits whose ideals are in harmony with their own. They carry with them the memory of your world, while numerous mortals have lost the memory of theirs.

The magnetic attraction between mortals and spirits is strongest when mortals are experiencing some intense emotion. It could be love, hate, anger—anything. When you are excited, spirits draw near you. They are overpoweringly attracted by fiery, explosive emotion.

Layla clutched her hands anxiously. **When you lose your temper, you lose control of yourself, and another entity may momentarily assume control of you. This plane is filled with hateful spirits. They love to stir up strife here and on your watery world. They enjoy the excitement of anger in others and are thrilled by the poison of hatred. As certain mortals revel in drugs, so do they revel in inharmonious passion. Any tiny seed of anger in your heart, they feed and inflame. These evil spirits attempt to stir you up again, even after you have calmed down.**

Unfortunately, a dark spirit may find that by attaching itself to a certain mortal, it is sure to receive a daily thrill of angry excitement as its victim continually loses his temper, storms, rages. Carried to its ultimate, this situation could become obsession on the part of the dark spirit; end in insanity for its victim or even result in two separate entities attempting to occupy one human body at the same time!

I looked down a moment, at a loss for words.

"My friend Aviar actually took me to the realm of dark spirits. Yet it still sounds incredible! Evil spirits inhabiting heaven—inhabiting this sacred realm."

Layla's eyes narrowed. **You are not in "heaven." Oh, don't look so shocked! You are not in "hell" either. What's more, the inner world is no more essentially sacred than Earth. The earth-life plane is simply a lower dimension of this one.**

Feeling a bit overwhelmed, I said solemnly, "Thanks for the warning, Layla."

I handed the thick volume to my beautiful, smiling librarian, returning her smile as I exited the building with almost drunken-like steps. I seemed to communicate with souls like Layla about the same way I did on Earth. But as time went by, I began to converse more and more by projected thought.

I continued my journey along the shady lane. Subsequently I found myself absorbed in lively conversation with a fascinating little boy; I believe he said his name was Joseph. He looked about twelve, possessed European features, and seemed wise beyond his years.

"You are a remarkably wise child!"

His huge, honest blue eyes gazed at me with an incredulous stare. **I am not really a child at all. I am as old as the stars, as you—or as anybody. Have the spirit guides not informed you that we are all immortal—without end or beginning—that we live an abundance of lives upon Earth?**

I recently transitioned back here due to an accident. **The call of matter, the eager, terrible call of blood, warmth, food, sex—of activity raised to the nth power—has again infected me. I want to resume my incarnation quickly. I am searching intensely even now for another woman, the right mother, to bear me. Maybe I will run into you again sometime in the future. Perhaps then I will have the adult body and you, that of a child.** Though young in bodily form, Joseph was old in mind.

To my utter amazement, I spotted an entity with Asian male features riding in what he termed "**Simply an old-fashioned toy.**" The toy appeared to be an atomic-powered hovercraft-type thing; it was noiseless, open sided, silver in color. It hovered about twelve inches above the terrain. It was aerodynamic, could hold four passengers, and was operated by means of the mind.

Its operator said, **Usually I just think myself to wherever I want to go. But sometimes I enjoy jumping into this old antique and taking brief pleasure trips alone or with friends.**

I discovered bewitching things everywhere I turned. I saw mansions so magnificent that they were beyond description. Each palace seemed more impressive than the last. It was the same inside. The generous rooms were graced with stunning things, all glittering like gold, silver, and precious gems in amazing forms that varied bewilderingly. Many represented unutterable, divine things of infinite wisdom. Again, there were numerous things I set eyes on—things that wouldn't fit into human words or concepts.

As I wandered the rustic, sun-swept footpaths enjoying the mingled scents, the play of light and shade, I happened upon an ornate iron gate highlighting beige stone pillars. Inside the gate winsome plant life shrouded a meandering path. Suddenly there was great rustling among the leaves. Startled, I glanced down. In the dimness, all I could see was a remarkable-looking rabbit rubbing up against my leg. Upon closer inspection, the extraordinary bunny turned out to be a dazzling white feline.

The handsome cat boasted white velvety-fur, a pink nose, and a bobtail. Its left eye appeared green, the right, blue; its ears were long, tufted. The bobtailed cat strutted past the open gate along the winding, crystalline path for a few feet; it paused, looked back as if beckoning me to follow. I hesitated. But my curiosity seduced me into crossing the leafy threshold and exploring the world beyond.

Sparkling stones crunched underfoot as I crept warily along the pathway; I happened upon a soft glow gleaming through the windows of a thatch-roofed stone cottage nestled among trees and a magical garden—a dollhouse cottage virtually any woman would love to live in. It overlooked a sleepy stream fed by a peaceful creek a few yards away.

A gracefully arching stone bridge led over the stream to a grove of trees that blazed orange, gold, multiple hues of green. The stippled light of willowy trees and dew-drenched blossoms shaded a picturesque gazebo. On every breath of wind, the fragrance of the lavish garden offered special delights to my senses. This intimate and utterly charming hideaway was a haven that dazzled the eye.

The rich palette of morning radiance offered a breathtaking view of the sparkling stream. Its warm brilliance peeked through cloud-like forms, illuminating the cascading brook in an enchanting spotlight. Its dancing beams dazzled the scene with subtle flashes of glistening color. The host of sumptuous flowers, the cheerful melody of songbirds, the tranquil flowing water all came together in a joyous display of colors, sounds, and fragrances. I couldn't imagine a more ideal place to rejuvenate the mind. It seemed too perfect to be real.

I retraced my steps along the path winding through this symphony of rainbow blossoms; exited silently. I glanced over my shoulder at one of the stone columns guarding the gateway. A weathered bronze plaque bore the name "Camr."

The Village of Tranquility was a lush valley bordered by majestic mountains and cliffs. It nestled charming cottages, striking mansions, mighty castles—each with its own distinctive character—in a mystically serene setting rich with remarkable beauty and natural drama.

The surrounding hills and valleys possessed vividly blended green, brown, gold, russet, mauve, and plum hues. Emerald-green swells and dips were also delightfully situated throughout this incomparable region of charm and grandeur. What's more, heavenly bodies could be seen floating in the cool, clear daylight ether. Their colors were deep, sumptuous mottled tones glittering like liquid jewels.

Every magnificent home within the glorious village was a fusion of stunning design and amazing materials most unknown in our world. In no fantasy have I ever seen anything so exquisite. Nothing I've encountered, sleeping or waking, comes near to such loveliness. The smallest leaf, a thing of wonder; each blade of grass, a perfection.

CHAPTER 24

※

No Less a Woman

*I*ncredibly, in this storybook village of gorgeous glistening wonder, I saw few children; mostly adults all looking about thirty. But there were ample pets roaming about: dogs, cats, horses. Plus there were baffling species like "Carriers." In the bald and barren northland, Carrier Birds nested among the reeds of the Silver Lake Region. It was so named due to a surrounding silver-leafed forest boasting ice-blue blossoms.

Suddenly from out of the mist, astride a handsome white horse stepping through the tall grass like a conqueror came tantalizing Mia, her flowing white garment short to the knee, her arms bare, her hair in wild disarray. Nevertheless, she was enchantingly beautiful. Camr's alluring neighbor Mia had been functioning as my unofficial tour guide. With eyes twinkling and an effervescent smile, she gracefully dismounted her commanding stallion.

She was petite, exquisitely beautiful with large brown eyes and dark, slightly wavy hair down to her shoulders. Her face was smooth, lightly tanned with features that appeared to have touches of the Orient, Middle East, and Europe. Her sensational body was erotic perfection. She was no less a woman because she weighed perhaps a kilogram instead of 120 pounds.

I gripped my sash, looked her directly in the eye. "Mia, seeing you riding out of the mist on that white horse brings back a memory that's unrelentingly haunted me. When I was around sixteen, my grandfather took me on a trip to Cornwall in southwestern England to visit relatives.

"Late one August afternoon, I was exploring on Loe Bar, a stretch of the Cornish coast. As I gazed here and there, I was astonished to see a petite, attractive young woman with long brown hair atop a white horse. She wore a loose, off-white medieval-type garment. The woman leaned forward on her flaxen horse with one hand on a sheathed dagger, staring at the site where I stood. Eager to have a closer look, I stepped forward. But as I did, she vanished as suddenly as she'd appeared.

"I returned to the same location years later. That time I had my friend Jackie O'Sullivan at my side. Incredibly, a vision appeared of a band of medieval warriors in chain mail. Some wore cloaks of red, others, white, and several, black; their horses wore matching ornamental coverings. One rider dismounted, staring at the exact spot where Jackie and I were gaping in astonishment. The vision vanished within minutes, just as it had years before.

"It would be an understatement to say that I was stunned. Biting on a fingernail, I looked at Jackie and wondered if she'd seen what I had. 'Jackie, what did you see? Tell me precisely! In detail!' I said in a stiff, inelegant voice. Her reply was identical to what my eyes had observed.

"We returned to the charming inn where we'd secured lodging completely shaken. About six thirty that evening, we decided to get a bite to eat. The inn's dining room featured arched ceilings, heavy drapery, ornate carpeting. Fresh-cut roses jutted from crystal vases on damask-draped tables. Men wore jackets, chefs wore toques, servers wore suits. The food was superb and dramatically presented on gorgeous china. This old country inn had long been saddled with an adjective that does it justice: perfect.

"Over an excellent steak dinner, Jackie and I began to rehash the day's perplexing incident. The owner of the inn, Arthur

Weston-Dalks—or 'King Arthur' as he was affectionately known by staff and guests—overheard our conversation. He strolled over to our beautifully appointed table, introduced himself, and sat down without invitation.

"King Arthur didn't seem surprised in the least when we relayed our story to him. He said he'd heard similar accounts from numerous guests over the years. I thought my two experiences were incredible. But the hospitable innkeeper proceeded to share with Jackie and me an extraordinary tale of his own. After several sips from a cup of black coffee, King Arthur began in a hushed voice:

"'A country physician here in England considered himself a hardheaded man of science, but an experience he had in the early 1930s shook his faith in conventional ideas of reality. One of "Doctor M.'s" patients was "Lord C.," who lived on the Isle of Thanet. The front steps of his estate, christened "Bentcross," led to a semicircular driveway opening at either end onto a country lane. A hedge screened the mansion from the road.

"'Lord C. was greatly ill, and the seasoned medic saw him daily. During a visit, Doctor M. stood at the top of the steps, deep in thought about his patient. As he told the story later to my father, he was not much mindful of his surroundings when he happened to glance up toward the hedge.

"'But there was no hedge! Nor did a road lay beyond where the hedge should've been. Try as he might, Doctor M. couldn't see a single familiar landmark. There was only a rutted, muddy path stretching across empty fields. Odder still was the man walking up the path toward the estate. He carried a flintlock rifle. What's more, he was wearing breeches, riding boots, caped overcoat, and a top hat with a narrow crown—a style long out of fashion! He appeared to belong in another century, perhaps the late eighteenth or early nineteenth.

"'The physician stated to my father that the stranger seemed to see him as well. The result? The stranger stopped midstride. The two men gaped at each other. Trying to orient himself, Doctor M. said he turned to see whether Bentcross was still behind him. It was. When he turned again, he found the landscape had righted itself. The hedge and the road were in their accustomed places, and the stranger had vanished.'

"Your thoughts?"

Mia tossed her hair back with a shake of the head. **There is a vast mystery and beauty surrounding the human mind. It is understandable that wonder grows with every new discovery about its marvelousness. Today, your species stands on the threshold of ever greater discoveries. Your mind is all powerful, Jason. It can even act as a sort of time machine through which your spirit can travel to whatever past, present, or future era of life you choose.**

"Ghost sightings," or visions of historic figures reenacting deeds they performed in life, are nothing more than spirit beings consciously or inadvertently utilizing their minds to transport their astral bodies into your present reality.

"Aviar also expanded my horizons. Your combined explanations give me an entire new perspective. Thanks!"

Would you enjoy a ride on one of my beautiful pets? Mia asked, graciously offering me a chance to ride her pet Carrier Bird, Rolf.

"You bet!" Peering through a grove of silvery trees, my eyes bewildered, I caught a glimpse of Rolf drinking from a spring and quickly had a change of heart. Her *pet bird* was several hundred feet long and who knows how wide. His legless, serpentine body was covered with glossy emerald feathers, but his feathery tail was gold-tipped, his gigantic feathered wings, dark grayish-blue. These enormous reptilian birds possessed the disposition of pet dogs, plus they repeated, parrotlike, any words they heard frequently.

After being formally introduced to Rolf, I said, "On second thought, I'll take a pass. Maybe another time." Mia drew gently near Rolf. The great reptile looked at her tranquilly, neither startled nor afraid, and allowed himself to be stroked and petted. Following several affectionate pats, Mia uttered a shrill screech-like command: **Eeeeeeick!** The gigantic feathered dragon beat its wings into a whirlwind, leaped into the air riderless, and swept through the ether swift as a gale. Noble in form, majestic in flight, soaring in the blue serene, the great reptile's feathers sparkled with a magical golden hue.

Sensing my wounded male pride, Mia quickly presented me a face-saving riding alternative: Camr's horse, Yago. The graceful, spirited, finely chiseled stallion who began snorting and pawing the ground also seemed a bit much for my limited riding skills. Humiliated, I attempted to graciously decline to mount the hot-blooded charger as well. But after prodding from Mia, I reluctantly climbed on the prancing, handsome dusty-white creature. Mia and I then rode bareback, galloping like playful, carefree children among the blue-flowered hills and lowland valleys of the Silver Lake Region.

Dust from Yago's hooves swirled backward dramatically. In the lead, I galloped with my body hunched forward, coaxing the utmost from my mount. The uneven road dipped, rose again, curved through a small wood and then plunged into a ravine. Yago flew on the wings of the wind. Laughing and giggling at the wonder of it all, Yago and I dashed over hill, over dale, over clover-rich windswept trails. Residents referred to pets as their children.

The lion's share of the community's inhabitants appeared blessed with eternal youth. Their complexions seemed flawless. Most had dark hair. Each possessed a subtle inner glow. Nearly all seemed to be about thirty with athletic builds, and they were of every nationality. They appeared approximately the same size with males bigger, taller than females. Oddly, newly transitioned elders seemed to sleep a lot. Yet, they all grew progressively younger looking and also ended up appearing thirty.

Most citizens seemed clothed in garments that were some shade of white. I counted at least twenty-seven different whitish tints before losing track. Only a tiny number dressed in other colors. But virtually no two dressed exactly the same. Clothing styles ranged from the most modern to the most ancient. I even got to thinking I might enjoy wearing my old Marine Corps dress blue uniform. Some beings also could be seen without bodies. They appeared only as floating balls of energy in various hues and were about the size of tennis balls.

Life in the village was unhurried, rich, and supremely satisfying. The air was fragrant with the perfume of compassion and love. The "village folk" seemed as natural and informal as the welcoming wildflowers that lined the bucolic cobblestone lanes.

Everyone worked in specifically useful occupations half the time, played half the time, and enjoyed their work as much as they did their recreation. I think the happiest spirits I met were painters. Their pictures, a feast of exquisite beauty. All beings delighted in at least one hobby and appeared tremendously carefree. That included me. Heavenly bliss flowed in the deepest recesses of my soul. I felt joys both indescribable and innumerable, almost to the point where I couldn't bear anymore.

The south side of the village featured a wonderful park where delicate flowers bloomed and gigantic trees stood as proud, silent sentinels. These leafy mammoths guarded the tranquility of a setting where streams, trails, grassy fields came together in perfect harmony. Just inside the entrance was a timeless millpond occupied by distinctive aquatic creatures. They ranged from odd to outlandish; all swam in charmed circles and made extraordinarily beautiful sounds.

Nestled beside the vintage pond was an enchanting fruit-drink bar. Disguised as a quaint grain miller's cottage, the bar doled out in compact crystal goblets an assortment of exotic juices. The most popular was barley water flavored with mint. This fieldstone charmer was as inviting as they come, its rustic wood-adorned interior glowing with a hearth-like warmth.

The terrific drinks, wood-beamed ceiling, and stone fireplace reinforced the feeling that I was spending an evening by the fire in my favorite cozy ski lodge. The friendly, comfortable pub seemed to be the social center of the village—a place where neighbors met, friendships were built.

Mia invited me to some much-needed relaxing entertainment. It was a form of soccer. Both teams had equal numbers of male and female players. What's more, there were no referees, no scoreboards, no shoes; all played in their bare feet. The playing field resembled brilliant-white sand enclosed by a neat azure border with azure balls, white goal posts, and nets.

This setting seemed idyllically framed by the park's luxuriant trees and blossoming vegetation. There was also a sizable gallery of lively spectators literally resembling a United Nations assembly, which Mia joined. They exploded in super animated cheering whenever a player scored a goal.

I watched the unique soccer match while reclining against a mesmerizing butterfly tree. Its pale limbs were in full bloom, casting a dappled shadow across the landscape. I sat in the shade of its canopy, marveling at its stand and breadth and reach of branches. Each limb was crammed with colorful blossoms, scarlet berries, and swarms of beautifully bizarre butterflies. These elegant creatures danced by the thousands about the picturesque tree. The lavish profusion of multihued wings, flower clusters, and berry-tipped panicles created astonishing dreamlike rivers of color.

A rainbow-hued butterfly fluttered down from a towering bough, alighted in my palm, and gracefully opened its wings. I stared alternately at the intriguing butterfly and the lively game. But my mind was clearly elsewhere. I was reflecting on the fact that I felt a deeper happiness in Tranquility than words could express. I began to imagine how it might feel to forever be a part of such a serene haven. I looked up at the horizon. Blanketed by the clear blue ether, the vibrant radiance of sunlike luminescence gifted me with a moment of considerable exquisiteness.

The song of a lark in the vivid, dense foliage interrupted my thoughts. I yearned to stay but knew I had to go. Amid a mist and shadow of sadness, I meandered across the park. As I passed, a flock of white doves flew out of a black cypress tree, circled the tree, and landed again.

I continued along the well-worn route over an old stone bridge that ended at the Path of Light. I glimpsed a gathering of remarkable water fowl dotting the stream and its banks as I crossed over. Each intently observed my sad exodus without comment. With a downcast glance, I exited the timeworn bridge, resuming my journey along the boulevard. I walked on deep in thought.

CHAPTER 25

The Gates

I saw a double row of dark-topped trees like cypresses, and at the end of Path of Light Boulevard was a pleasing softly diffused luminosity. The light as I approached it was softer than moonlight, though clearer. Yet this delightfully inviting radiance seemed to come from nowhere. It simply was.

As I approached I saw two angelic beings walking toward me hand in hand. There was such a look of love and happiness on their faces as one never sees on the faces of people on Earth. The couple did not even look at each other as they strolled; the touch of their hands seemed to make them so much one that nothing else could've added anything to the romance of their rapturous mood. Here and there along the avenue meandered numerous other male and female beings. Two by two or in groups they walked, smiling to themselves or at one another.

Far off in the distance stood a magnificent castle sitting atop the foothills of Mount Solace. The castle and its surroundings were ringed by three belts of water, two of land. Each belt was separated by walls of pearly, rough-hewed stone. Spanning the canals was Path of Light Boulevard, which ran in an unswerving line up to the castle region.

At each of the six gateways along the boulevard, a pair of angelic sentries stood at attention. At the first walled entrance, beyond which appeared the first sparkling canal, were two mighty angels whose wings were snowy white with gold tips. I bit at my lips, cleared my throat as they turned toward me.

Infant of the Sixth Race! You seek the Teacher's wisdom?

Not meeting their gaze, I said, "Camr, a member of The League, sent me."

We perceive the chant of brotherhood in your soul. Enter, you may! The Teacher's words are not just wind. His words have something to say. They sing beneath your mind like a storm of pure, perfect truth.

At the second entrance, beyond which stood the first belt of plush green fields, were two angels whose wings were white with silver tips. At the third opening and the second dazzling body of water stood two angels with pale-blue wings. At the fourth access and second belt of blossoming meadows were two angels with green wings. At the fifth entrance and third radiant waterway stood two angels with wings of deep purple. At the sixth entrance were two magnificent angels whose wings were a solid, glittering gold.

All the other angel-lookouts were clothed in long, loose brilliant-white garments. But the two golden-winged sentinels at the sixth gate were powerfully, athletically built—and naked.

I left the avenue of cypresses and sauntered along a rustic road. The sweet fragrances of spring were in the air. Handsome flowers bloomed along its border and were laid out in designs never seen or even possible in our world. The bucolic lane appeared to be painted with luminous silky-white particles of some kind. Upon closer inspection, it seemed to be made of broken pieces of a white stonelike substance.

I picked up a tiny piece of the rock. It felt supple. Further down the way, I came to a crystal bridge with whiter-than-white stone pillars spanning a rushing brook. The stones of the bridge seemed to be massive pieces of the stonelike stuff. "Remarkable stone," I said, doing a double take. "So white and soft yet amazingly strong!"

After walking another few hundred yards, I came upon the strangest yet most enthralling landscape. It appeared shrouded in splendor. It seemed like a fairyland: the intense blueness of the heavens, spotted with only an occasional white cloud-like form; the vivid variegated foliage, in more shades of green than there could ever be; and the distant mountains, white capped and majestic.

Stately trees along the sides of a winding road were covered with the luminous white substance. As the soft breeze swirled, the silky particles lifted up into the air. They tinted the trees until those nearest the road looked like snow-frosted holiday decorations.

I jogged down a green granite stairway to a garden surrounding a petite thatch-roofed villa, where, in sunken sections, picture-perfect flowers were blooming. Oversized grass paths wound among engaging flower beds in sweeping curves. Suddenly an irresistible beckoner demanded my attention. My startled gaze witnessed an unexpected visual pleasure. On a tiny desolate island in the center of a translucent lake stood a futuristic, silvery angel sculpture towering sixty feet high. A dazzling light unlike any other illuminated its graceful torso, wings, and halo.

Straight ahead was not a castle, as I'd initially thought, but a magnificent cathedral—a finely crafted edifice of white marble, stained glass crowned with a roof of pure gold. At its summit, a unique emblem identical to the one atop the pyramid in the Garden of Light. The main entrance to this celestial masterpiece was superbly enhanced by three sets of colossal solid-gold double doors. Each twin center door had a sizeable gold ring at its midpoint; the portals to the left and right of them did not. But all six doors were exquisitely etched.

A massive set of twelve stone steps led up to the multiple-door entryway. The steps seemed inspired by downward flowing water, each step flowing into a widening step like a wave into a wave.

It was a place of pure magic. The spirit of God hung heavy in the air. The wind in the trees whispered of the Creator's love and majestic power. Incredibly, I was there in the midst of it, immersed in the dazzling energy of the hallowed realm of Light. I heard soft rustling in the distance. A profusion of branches shifted; their luminous leaves breathed forth precious ether. I gathered up my courage, proceeded toward the terror and grandeur of the flowing stone steps.

CHAPTER 26

※

Mountain of Solace

As I uneasily ascended the cathedral's stone staircase, my bare feet touched one step after another, obliging me to notice their rough-hewn texture. I reached the top and stood anxiously before the commanding gold doors. Within there was chanting. The rhythmic intonation, the pauses, the very response my soul gave to the transcendent sounds indicated some sacred mantra was being expressed.

As the chanting reverberated through the Gothic arches, I marveled at the beauty of the cadence, the maintained antiphon, the unison of diction, the perfect melodic phrasing. It sounded like a song, not in the conventional sense, but like an endless source of voices blending together in the most extraordinary tones.

With a feeling of half-awe, half-excitement, I breathed deeply and stretched out a trembling hand. The smooth, radiant gold felt cool to the touch as I took hold of the rings. I gave three knocks then softly pushed one of the doors. The massive burnished portal easily swung open. Gradually, the dimly lit interior was revealed as the great hinges swung back. The chanting instantly broke off. I retreated into the shadowed doorway onto the vestibule's luminous marble floor. But I stopped in midstride, bewildered.

Floating above me in midair was an immense, three-dimensional holographic panorama—a mysterious depiction of something I couldn't quite grasp. A brilliant light illuminated it from above. It was delightful, magnificent, sublime. Its breathtaking power and grandeur inexplicably terrified me. I felt utter shock followed by quivering disbelief then simply stunned amazement. Yet at the same time, there was something about it that also filled me with a peace that passed all understanding. I stood transfixed for an instant before turning in wonder and exploring the rest of my surroundings.

The temple was a dazzling testimony to the skills of talented celestial artisans. Its off-white graceful arches' ribs rose until they faded. Its high-domed ceiling, fashioned of pure gold, boasted dramatic crown moldings. The overhead surface also enjoyed a stained-glass center comprised of glittering well-known and unknown colors. Captivating stained-glass windows were elegantly incorporated into this holy space as well, each engorged with the most beautiful blue, gold, green, and purple hues I've ever set eyes on.

As I stood there steeped in bliss, I could feel the warmth of the windows' delicate rainbow glow. The vivid colors beamed out, penetrating my mind and cleansing my soul. Shafts of light fell picturesquely across the sanctuary's glossy floors. The air smelled of some splendid fragrance. Everywhere stood grandeur beyond the power of words to describe. I felt completely overwhelmed by the solemnity, the stillness, the magnificence of the scene.

Near the front wall, I noticed mystical moist balls of light varying in coloration. They looked tennis ball–sized and glittered dazzlingly bright. They seemed so numerous, glowed so incandescently that I felt compelled to close my eyes. I opened them gradually and approached the host of lights with caution. They continued to glow. Abruptly, they began to dance, sparkle, and merge, creating a radiance so bright I again shut my eyes.

When I opened them that time, one of the balls of light was floating directly in front of my face about eye height. It quickly evolved into a petite Asian woman softly brushed with beauty.

Brother, I heard your footsteps passing in the darkness.

"I'm looking for the Teacher." My breathing quickened.

The Master can be found one level below. May I show you?

"Just point me in the right direction. I'll find him."

Clearly you chart your own course, she said smiling.

The young woman motioned to an opening to my right. She then resumed her form as a sphere of light and rejoined the cluster of lights at the front of the sanctuary.

As I advanced toward the far wall, the white-marble floor beneath my feet gave way to luminous gold that sparkled like fire. The walls were covered with a pale, mottled crystal of ineffably exquisite hue. Within them appeared an ever-changing panorama of achingly beautiful color scapes and sacred symbols. These divine depictions were similar to those I observed in prominent homes in the Village of Tranquility.

I looked along the wall for a door. I came upon instead an archway circumscribed by elegant gold moldings and marched toward it. I continued through the arched passage, spotted a golden spiral staircase. Its white-marble steps appeared well worn and led down to the solarium.

At the foot of the stairs, a magnificent reception area emerged. I strode across the enormous, elegantly appointed lobby into a circular room. It was pristine, exhilarating. I murmured in stunned amazement, "I've been in here before. I know I have! But why? When?" Still reeling from the shock, I took a deep breath of refreshing ether and treaded warily past a masterly crafted desk. I stared at the items on the desk. All looked unconventional, futuristic yet familiar. I picked up a silvery thing, muttered, "Name's almost on the tip of my tongue."

The floor appeared to be composed of a warm honey-hued wood. It was accented by a glowing golden fleece that soothed my bare feet as I strolled across its creamy softness. A fire warmed the room from a massive white-stone fireplace. A trio of lancet-arched windows let in a fragrance-tinged breeze.

The scene from the windows was of a distant waterfall cascading into a small lagoon, clear blue and serene. The view was enhanced by the windows' wispy, silky hangings, which gracefully undulated in the soft breeze. Twin off-white, ultramodern chairs waited side by side. Rubbing my neck, I sat on the one to my left. My breath slowed.

Biting at my lip, I glanced around the circular room; from the stillness to my right I noticed movement. I witnessed waves of changing textures and intensities of dazzling patterns: kaleidoscopic clouds of color shot through with light, intricate images, glistening shapes, wispy mists, and incredible sounds. This explosion of mists, patterns, colors, and sounds evolved into a dazzling silhouette with a fiery face of raging violet flames. Its intensity diminished.

A figure approached, humanoid in form, surrounded by a glowing aura of brilliant-white rays shooting out thirty to ninety feet. He seemed wise and venerable in appearance—far older than any man could ever be—and had long, flowing silver-white hair framing a bearded face that was unlined but mature. His eyes seemed bottomless, extending from the center of the great blue void unto the region of God's highest thunder, and were dark bluish-purple in color. His silvery hair danced like white flames when he moved. Just to be in his presence was to be intoxicated by a sudden passion for God.

He wore a long whiter-than-white garment that reached almost to his ankles. Light shone from him so that the great room was filled with brightness. Surrounded by a blinding, blazing splendor, he sat in the empty chair opposite me. An all-encompassing peace and serenity enveloped the atmosphere.

The saintly being waited calmly with gestures that bespoke a fatherly affection. I immediately sensed his all-powerful, unconditional love spread over me, through me, until it was part of me. I felt enormously blessed by his presence. I also found myself fascinated by the beauty of his face and the sweet indefinable aroma emanating from him. At length, a deep, rich male voice resonated in my mind.

There are matters that occupy your mind, my child. I come to aid thy wish. Let thou voice be heard.

There was an unexpected feeling of awe. I squeezed my eyes shut, nearly prostrated myself. I sobbed and wailed like a wounded child. "My Lord and my God!"

No, little one. No god here, not as you mortals think of it. I am simply a traveler from an antique realm, a channel of the vast Whole, as you are.

I deliberated a few moments before speaking a second time. *How should I begin,* I wondered. I felt a weakness come over me, and with it, a simpleness of heart and mind. I was like a tired-out infant who needed to rest in his mother's arms. I buried my head in my hands and wept. My entire body convulsed with remorse, sadness, guilt. It's impossible to describe the grief and hope that tormented me. I couldn't look at the old master. Staring at the floor, I poured out my soul:

"God have mercy on my utter stupidity. What a shameful life I've led!"

Out of nowhere, there appeared beside the silver-haired being a most extraordinary-looking dog. He had a soft, fuzzy pushed-in face, floppy ears, and a bushy tail curving gently over his back. He also possessed big, round, mysterious dark bluish-purple eyes; a slightly wavy cream-colored coat with splashes of sable around the head, back, tail; and front paws that turned slightly out. His head was carried well up in an arrogant, elegant carriage.

What's more, he appeared muscular, about twelve inches tall, and seemed to prance proudly rather than walk. Around his neck dangled a golden collar with an enormous star sapphire suspended from it on a gold chain. To my astonishment, he possessed an aura identical to that of his master. The age-old being began absentmindedly stroking the cute little dog while stating, **You can call me Pete.**

I wasn't quite sure whether he was referring to himself or to the remarkable-looking little dog. So I timidly replied, "Yes, master."

Reading my thoughts, the master said, **My name, child, you need not know. A name is a limitation. I desire to quiet all self-limiting notions.**

The tiny dog came over to where I sat, lay down, and rested his large, round, soft head on my foot. It felt like a warm cloud. Instantaneously, as if by some magic, I felt better, lighter, and at peace. I quickly regained composure. Memories of my past surged from my lips like the waters of a rushing brook, this time without the tears:

"My father was a child-molesting tyrant. My mother a drunken slut. I spent most of my adult years plotting how to exploit those weaker than myself. I thought of women as disposable pleasures rather than meaningful pursuits. Marriage seemed sentimental foolishness to me.

"Worst of all, I'm a priest who took a sacred vow of celibacy. Nonetheless, I fathered a baby with a married woman. I saw her, I sought her, yet I did not mean to love her—but I did! I hate myself for it; but I was passionately, rapturously, overwhelmingly enthralled. Our love, however, was born of blood and tribulation. It resulted in a man's gory self-slaughter; my unborn child being crushed to death; and the mutilation, drowning of my baby's beautiful mother, the only person on Earth I ever truly loved.

"I was half-drunk, arguing, driving like a mad man. I lost control of her convertible, went over a cliff, and exploded it into a fiery private hell. My precious Jackie became engulfed by a white-hot inferno that nearly cremated her while she was still alive. There was burning, screaming, excruciating pain!"

I stared down at my feet for an instant then covered my face with my hands.

"She—she probably just needed some emotional support when we met. The disgusting truth is maybe I betrayed her trust. I've walked a dark trail, living like a dead man. I'm dying inside because I killed her…Just the same as if I had plunged a dagger through her heart. And the blood clings to the blade! It won't come clean! I deserve the broken end of a bottle twisted in my face in some piss-soaked dark alley, ending the knotted riddle called my life."

Shhh! Say no more! Frankly, we all make choices we regret.

My remorse then manifested in anguish and tears of a visceral intensity I'd never experienced before. The timeless being gazed at me with deep compassion in his penetrating bluish-purple eyes.

A few observations. First, what is the chief makeup of you mortal children?

I shrugged. "Honestly, I don't know."

Desire! The unstable scales of desire—this age-old torment is what drives you. You are all walking bundles of desire lusting, panting after endless cravings. You have a hole in your soul you keep trying to fill with "things." No matter what you have, you always yearn for more! Your hearts beat, your blood flows, your bodies move solely to satisfy intense, aching longings.

"What's the object of all this desire?"

Uninterrupted happiness, however you may define it. But on the earth-life plane life has an annoying habit. It is called the "Out-of-the-Blue Syndrome": out of the blue you are short of money; out of the blue appeared an inoperable tumor; out of the blue you felt sad, depressed, so empty.

Truthfully, there really is no such thing as "out of the blue." There is always a prior cause that precedes any effect or event that arrives like a bolt out of the blue. Somewhere in your past, a negative seed was planted. You human animals destroy forests, oceans, Earth's atmosphere. You humiliate, enslave, cheat,

torture, rape, kill each other. These types of causes will, without fail, produce matching effects.

"What's the best way to stop experiencing problems?"

The greatest discovery you can make is that there is a Boundless Power resident within you. What's more, It enables you to rise above all hurdles and equips you with all the necessary capabilities to make you master of your fate and captain of your soul. This is the secret of all power. In order to utilize this power, however, you must "seek ye first the Kingdom of God," as your Holy Book instructs.

My gaze clouded, went distant. "What er, is the Kingdom of God?"

The master raised his eyebrows. **The only thing that exists! The Kingdom of God is the consciousness of God. As you think the thoughts of God, a rich harvest of tranquility, abundance, delight will mystically flow into your life. When you think the thoughts of God, you shall have entered the Kingdom.**

But the key is to carry out the Creator's will for your soul first. "And all other things shall be added unto you." There are numerous successful but miserable human beings wallowing in painful pleasures, tragic joys. They fear more wealth for the many means, less for the few. They shun the Creator's wishes, disregard the law of cause and effect, consequently hindering their own happiness.

Humanity's ever-present stumbling blocks are self-interest, self-indulgence. All misdeeds, offenses, atrocities result from these great errors. You children spend your entire lives chasing the toys and trinkets of your world in the pursuit of happiness. You all want to see yourselves better off than the others. Hosts even try to be content because another seems to suffer more. How pitiful and disgusting are such thoughts! For who could suffer less because they see another suffer more?

Myriads constantly misuse the power of their minds and have forgotten most sacred knowledge. So you stumble along

blindly on rocky routes to nowhere. **The shadowy paths you travel are carpeted with leaves of false desires, leading only to disappointment, anguish...**

"And what, master?"

It makes me cringe to think of it...Nonetheless, you continue to do what you do in an attempt to get rid of "that feeling."

"Feeling?" I said, my voice trailing off.

That empty feeling of "Is this all there is to life?" Many try to make this feeling go away by acquiring grander and ever grander houses, flashier and ever flashier motor vehicles, trendy shoes for every day of the year, a "trophy" significant other, or "the latest new thing."

"Then how can you make this feeling go away?"

A thoughtful expression crept onto the master's face. He said, **The test of human progress is not whether you add more to the abundance of those who have much; it is whether you provide enough to those who have too little. The Father-Mother shall not sleep peacefully upon the wind till the needs of the least of your brethren are satisfied. Simply do something—great or small— for someone. Let them lean their tired heads against your shoulder as they rest awhile. The more of it you do, the more joy you will obtain. See for yourself.**

Countless rich mortals wear themselves out rushing around on business, piling up more wealth than they could ever use. They want to live on top of the mountain but don't realize happiness is obtained by the journey taken—by helping others along your way to the top of the hill. For you reap only what you sow! On that spherical "Garden of Agony" upon which you children briefly reside, keep in mind you are all beautiful, powerful immortal beings. Immortal beings should define success as "Am I happy?"

"The greatest happiness possible" is what powerful human beings are seeking with their power, what rich human beings are seeking with their wealth.

Leo Tolstoy was fifty-two years old; his two greatest novels were behind him. He found himself in a crisis. Tolstoy was of noble birth, was famous, had a family, land, money, but it all seemed empty. He was unable to write, had trouble sleeping, and contemplated suicide.

Tolstoy took a remarkable walk in the woods and discovered God. The result was that he renounced alcohol, tobacco and wanted to give his money to the poor. Tolstoy went from contemplating suicide to feeling "alive!" and "happy!" He said, "At the thought of God, happy waves of life welled up inside me. Everything came alive, took on meaning. The moment I thought I knew God, I lived!"

When you approach death's door, do you want your life to have resembled Tolstoy's or this icon of human success who made this observation around 30 BC: "I have now reigned over sixty years in victory or peace, beloved by my subjects, dreaded by my enemies, and respected by my allies. Riches and honors, power and pleasure, have waited on my call; no Earthly blessing appears to have been deficient. In this situation I have diligently numbered the days of genuine happiness that have fallen to my lot. They number seven."

"Think I know who—"

A being's mortal name matters not, child; only the example set by their immortal soul. My second observation. All the unpleasant people, situations in your life merely reflect one of your uglier traits. They are like a mirror of your character. Accordingly reform a piece of your personality; "your mirror" will reflect this transformation. As you refine yourself, situations will begin to change for the better. Everything in your life is there for one reason: to offer you the opportunity to grow.

"Too bad we don't encounter these truths before we depart Earth. It's probably like my granddad always said, 'God is always trying to talk to us. But we just don't listen!'"

The master gave a deep sigh. Then in a soothing tone, he said, **Your love affair with the evolving soul known as Jacqueline Sophia O'Sullivan has clearly caused you tremendous anguish. Know this: carefully or haphazardly, all mortal beings choose their own Earthly circumstances and must suffer the consequences thereof. You were part of a tragic situation. But your mate and her companion of convenience unilaterally chose to end their mortal lives prematurely. You did not choose their unfortunate solution for them.**

Therefore press this guilt not like a crown of thorns against your skull, nor nail yourself to it.

Know too that all the desires of the body have their rightful place in human experience. But they are to be used, not abused. There is each day set before all beings life and death, good and evil. You must choose. Still, it should be kept in mind that there is a consequence associated with each choice. For what you do not learn through wisdom you will learn through pain and suffering.

Into these karmic equations, however, is always added the factor of love: "Did you do it out of love?" The major reason beings incarnate on that pinch of dust orbiting a minor sun is to learn love is the key. Learning this lesson is crucial to both your biological and spirit existence in ways you have not even begun to grasp. The answer to this question can adjust your ultimate karma.

There are affairs in which powerful emotions join forces with sexual magnetism to create an adulterous relationship of genuine affection. Was yours such a relationship? Only your soul knows for sure. Nonetheless, all involved in this tragic earth-life drama will face suitable karmic consequences.

You children see the past and persist in putting it in the present. Forget the time of terror that was so long ago. Learn from the experience. Forgive yourself. Try to forget things better forgotten—and move on!

"It's no secret humans have had it drummed into us that acquiring great wealth is crucial to virtually *everything.* Practical wisdom we can rely on?"

The master covered his mouth to hide a smile. **Permit me to answer, little one, by way of an age-old tale.**

Long ago there was a poor cobbler's son named Jayrr. He was a strong, handsome young lad married to the fair Carlianna. They heard of a mysterious land called The Island of the Enchanted Silver Spring. In the exact center of this island, there was a magnificent spring gushing crisp, pure, refreshing water. But for exactly three seconds every twelfth day at precisely 6:00 a.m., this enchanted spring also erupted a shower of glittering silver nuggets high into the air. Consequently, silver nuggets were more abundant on this island than pebbles.

So Jayrr and his beautiful bride, Carlianna, left their home in an impoverished northeastern region to set out for its major seaport. There they learned that The Island of Silver Spring truly did exist, but they would have to hurry. A great three-masted sailing vessel christened *"The End of Time"* sailed to the island only once every nine years. What's more, it was leaving within a matter of hours! So Jayrr and Carlianna rushed aboard.

When they arrived on the island, they found what they had heard was true! Sparkling silver nuggets were indeed everywhere, like sand on the seashore. Falling to their knees, young Jayrr and Carlianna began filling their pockets with the dazzling nuggets, dreaming of how rich they were going to be back home.

At that very moment, old Reg-jo-hen, the wizard, approached them. It was rumored he often flew around Silver Spring astride

a swift, frightening black creature. "You're wasting your time filling your pockets with those worthless nuggets," he said. "Since
you're going to be here for nine years, you'd better have a way to
support yourself. Do you have a trade?"

"Why, I'm a cobbler," said Jayrr.

"Very well. Then you'd better start quickly making shoes,"
he told them.

That is exactly what Jayrr and Carlianna did. She designed
the shoes; he made them. Their shoes were fashionable, finely
crafted, astonishingly comfortable; very soon they had a hugely
successful business. In fact, Jayrr and Carlianna became the island's leading couple. Before they knew it, nine years had passed.
Then one day, on the horizon they saw *The End of Time* speeding
toward them under full sail.

So Jayrr and Carlianna quickly packed up all their possessions and jumped onboard. When they returned home, family
and friends eagerly looked in their fancy luggage then stared
at them in amazement. "Where is all the treasure?" asked their
relatives. "The two of you were gone for nine years; all you've
brought back are bags loaded with shoes!"

Jayrr and Carlianna looked at each other and just laughed.
Didn't they understand? Shoes had made them a rich, famous,
powerful couple on the island! But just as Jayrr opened his mouth
to speak, the truth suddenly dawned on both him and Carlianna
at the same time. They both had forgotten the true purpose for
which they had gone to the island. Therefore, they had nothing
more valuable than when they left home.

In brief, your physical world is akin to an island in the universe you are temporarily visiting. The silver nuggets are the
opportunities for loving, sharing, evolving into a mature spirit
being that exists all around you. Because they are as numerous
as the stars in the sky, you become oblivious to them under the

seemingly urgent needs that day-to-day life on the water star imposes on you.

You and Jacqueline, like a myriad others, simply got caught up in the artificial values of the "island of Earth." You children just forgot the real purpose for which you incarnated on that tiny blue world.

Simply stated, you are there to love, laugh, assist each other—evolve into a perfect miniature of the Creator.

I trust this timeless tale gives you new insight.

"The more I learn, the deeper the mystery. What does it all mean, really?"

CHAPTER 27

What Does it all Mean?

The old mystic rested his hand upon my forearm. His touch was soothing, light as air. I glanced upward, somewhat startled by the presence of a brilliant-white light near the ceiling. As I gazed at the glow, the ceiling disappeared. Then the walls also dissolved into vacant, colorless space. We seemed surrounded by nothing but clear, boundless sky. The master released my arm. I was astonished to find myself seated next to him in front of the white-stone fireplace. We were both sitting cross-legged on the honey-hued wood floor, our bottoms cushioned by a plush, velvety golden fleece.

The age-old sage appeared unruffled by our sudden change in location. I stared at the cushiony chairs we had once occupied then turned back to the delightful blue-and-yellow flames entwining the logs in the fireplace, surprised, confused, uncertain of what to think.

Something wrong, child?

Staring again at the empty chairs in disbelief, I said, "Well… no, I guess not."

The master offered me a wide grin, and his eyes squinted with a twinkle of mischief. Then adopting a more serious demeanor, he said, **When you climb an alpine mountain, you do not go directly from the bottom to the top. Rather, you zigzag, go around and** through before eventually reaching the summit. So it is with acquiring understanding. Permit me to bring light to the darkness you are experiencing with a brief soul-healing review.

The Source is the origin of everything. It is what humans refer to as God. This Primordial Universal Energy possesses a higher vibration rate than conventional matter energy, finds an outlet through everything that lives. This Chi/Energy is even now expressing Itself through you; without this expression, you could not live. That is the meaning of the mystical saying "In Him we live, and move, and have our being" contained in Acts 17:28 of your Holy Book.

The Divine Mother-Father is your source of life, the life within, the air you breathe, the food by which you are sustained, the water that renews and cleanses you. It is a limitless sea of Consciousness, a never-ending ocean of luminous Energy Whose Body is the Pool of Eternal Life. It is the Original Cause out of which we all are made. That is why your Holy Book calls you "the children of God."

The most fantastic delusion mortals have unrelentingly held is that The Source of Life and Love becomes like a clenched-jawed, ill-tempered, vengeful child if It does not receive lavish adoration. In truth, sweet talk will gain you no unique advantage. It is the way of the Source to have no favorites. It simply manifests whatever you intensely believe. As your Holy Book correctly states, "It is done unto each one of you as you believe."

You were greatly mistaken if you thought you lived apart from the Whole as a separate entity that moved in isolation, unattached and housed within a hairless ape's body. Realize the "something else" you thought was you is an illusion. See the Source as It actually is, child, then you shall understand yourself as you actually are. As it happens, you are an extension of the Source. This is what we all are because we could not be anything else. For there is nothing else in existence!

"Fortunately, I also now understand master, we humans foolishly think of life as an endless well. Yet everything happens only a certain number of times, and a very small number of times, actually. How many more times will we get to see someone so deeply a part of our being that we can't even conceive of our life without them? Perhaps twenty or thirty times more. Perhaps not even that. And yet it all seems limitless.

"Truthfully, my major reason for coming here—"

Yes, yes, child! When your Jacqueline arrived empty and dark, she raised her broken heart's lantern, and even now the guardians of the flame are serenely refilling it with love's light. When souls whose hearts have become heavy-laden with the grief of being separated from one they love come home, they require something more potent than an energy shower in order to get them safely through their emotionally painful withdrawal experience.

"Energy shower! What's that? I don't remember getting one."

After a new arrival's initial meeting with welcoming loved ones, those who require it are propelled to a special location where they receive a healing shower of primordial energy. It rinses away all the destructive emotional influences of physical incarnation as a human animal. But Jacqueline needed more.

Your Jacqueline has also been dispensed the breath of life and the precious water of animation and has been put into a healing slumber. She shall remain enveloped in soothing wings for as long as it takes her to feel complete again. In such matters, one must engage in the sport of truly enlightened beings.

Frowning, I said, "What sport is that?"

Patience! Jacqueline is receiving tender care and will be absolutely perfect just in time for first light. It has been taught in seasons long past that certain souls are linked across time. These

souls are connected by an enduring love that echoes through the ages. You children are numbered among those souls. So rest assured that not even the ecstasy of being home again is overwhelming enough to diminish this remarkable love. It actually expands it and causes it to grow deeper. On this plane, the flame of love burns at its most intense.

In truth, love knows not its own depth until the moment of separation. Your Jacqueline, now separated from you, tarries in the house of love's raw, stupendous sorrow, which you cannot visit, not even in your dreams.

I turned away briefly to gather my thoughts. "What does all this mean for me?"

Simply stated, think not that you can direct the course of love; for love, if it finds two beings uniquely suited to each other, directs their course. You and Jacqueline were born for each other, and together you shall be forevermore. Yet there must be spaces in your eternal togetherness. That is where patience fits in. You must suffer the winds of the heavens—when karma dictates—to dance between you and your beloved for a season. Unfortunately, karma decrees you must now resume your journey.

I gave a slight bewildered headshake. "I—I don't understand. Resume what journey?"

Your soul's evolutionary journey to obtain the contribution you are to return home with. At present, your soul's great gift is virtually nonexistent.

I tapped my fist against my lips. "Gift? I still don't understand."

God extended portions of Itself that It might add to Itself. The contribution you are to return with after each incarnation is more experience, more love, hence more of yourself. The Creator wishes you to add to yourself by blending what you are now with what mortals call earth-life experiences. It is the total of that experience, the growth of your soul that is your gift to God. Your wonderful contribution, your earth-life experiences will give the Creator dreams to dream.

But at this time you are incomplete. The contribution you would offer, too small. You must acquire vastly more experience before you can transition worthily from your incarnation as Jason Xavier Roberts. So you will return to the body.

I grimaced. "Not that! Anything but that! Please! Don't send me back to that rotating insane asylum. Not now! Not this soon!"

The master lightly touched my shoulder. **My child, the mortal world of brutality, vengeance, betrayal does nothing. It has no effects at all. It merely represents your thoughts. This world may seem to cause you sorrow. Yet this world, as causeless, has no power to cause. As an effect, it cannot manufacture effects. As an illusion, it is what you asked for. Your senseless wishes represent its pains. Your bizarre desires bring it evil dreams. Your notions of "death" envelop it in fear.**

Realize its truth as but a wispy veil before the Light—an artificial bank of dark clouds only seemingly solid. Yet in this dim cloud bank, you see realistic mountains, lakes, cities all rising in your imagination. Your perception assures you they are there. Figures come, move about, go; actions seem real; forms shift from magnificent to grotesque. Back and forth they show up and go, as long as you play this game of children's make-believe.

There is no step along the road that anyone takes by chance. It all appears arbitrary. Yet there is a plan behind appearances of people and things. You dwell not here or there but in eternity. You travel but in dreams while safe at home. Your incarnations in flesh, blood, and bone are designed to make you ready for the final step of the journey inward. The hard-hitting truth is: no matter where you believe you are, the only place you can possibly be is in the Mind of God.

"So none of it's real?" I said, looking down, running my hands through my hair.

Nothing is real, child. Yet nothing is unreal. Plainly, little one, you have grown a pinch. But now is not the time for your homecoming. Your present incarnation is still an unfinished symphony. You must again cross the great deep and resume your imperfect life.

"Please, master, I need more time! Is there something wrong?"

If you fail to act quickly, you will lose your earth-life form.

I felt a tiny shiver. "But—but how can this be happening? I've been permitted across the frontier between life and death. I'm now beyond the border—past the barrier."

There is a master plan overriding such things. It decrees, "Each being must live out the full tenure of every incarnation"— that souls who come home mid journey must immediately return and cope with the difficulty prompting their untimely departure from earth-life.

What's more, many have had near-death experiences, out-of-body occurrences, encounters with deceased loved ones. This has forced them to ask themselves, "What is reality?" Their mental stability could actually rest upon their uncovering the straightforward truth.

I felt dazed; my mind was spinning. "You're talking about millions, countless millions!"

Your mission is to take the growing numbers who believe themselves to be no more than remarkable apes evolved out of the slime and to tutor them. "Un-ape" the children of the apes. Remind Homo sapiens they are divine beings.

Your entire species remains restless, unfulfilled; few have any realization of permanent peace. Your world is in agony, rapidly evolving into a lost colony of broken, badly informed, degenerate souls. The great nations are lost, rotting. Sons are dying

before they are men. Daughters are mothers before they complete childhood. Violence in homes, savagery in streets, shocking drug abuse are unrelentingly increasing.

I swallowed hard, rubbed at my exposed forearm. "My mother belonged to this group. Many nights I'd find her lying on the ground in our backyard staring up at the stars. She'd be naked, aloof: out of reach of sobriety, self-respect, common decency."

The master offered a deep sigh. **There are none so good they have no faults, none so wicked they are worth naught!**

Under the influence of drink or drugs, courage is quickened; fear is banished briefly. It makes you feel you can do what you had thought you could not. This wealth of confidence passes away as you either grow sober or get higher. But while it lasts, it is like being possessed by a super power that gives you a clear advantage. The sense of enormous power it can give is only a sign that shows mortals the abilities you now possess are only shadows of your real strength.

The greatest problem beings like your mother have is accepting the vast power of their minds and comprehending that they have been creating their own reality twenty-four hours a day. Help your species realize they have forgotten who they really are, where they came from, and where they are going. Then what you children now call the miraculous will become common on Earth.

We are depending on you, Jason Xavier Roberts, to revise this shocking situation.

CHAPTER 28

Mystical Shades of Blue

stared out the solarium's colossal windows. In the distance, a stream whispered down a leaf-green mountain, misting exotic plants that fragranced the air. At its base: the dragon-green depths of a luminous lake and a sweet-scented orchard where beautiful creatures frolicked about. Then turning my eyes skyward, I noticed for the first time the rounded room's ceiling. It was created out of something akin to ivory; variegated with gold and silver and a copper that sparkled.

Suddenly aware of the master's patient gaze, I became self-conscious and humiliated. In a choked voice while staring down at my empty hands, I said, "Master, will Jackie also be forced to return immediately? Will she be going back with me?"

No, no, no. Jacqueline was already dying due to complications connected with her injuries. Unbeknownst to her, she had barely more than seventy-two hours remaining to live in your world. What's more, her premature return resulted from love. The note she left said it all. Clearly you have touched her perfect body, her pained mind with your love. Nonetheless, you must return to Earth alone. Look neither ahead nor backward, child. Look straight into the present and sleep with a prayer for Jacqueline in your heart.

Customarily, before entering the earth-life plane, souls pass through a mystical barrier that serves to lower the vibrations of consciousness. Their memories are completely wiped clean. This

intentionally induced amnesia is vital in order to prevent relentless pining for the splendor left behind and to prevent echoes of past lives from restraining future potential.

Child, the Holy One has permitted you to wander in Its winds, to absorb everything you found. It now desires you to take all that has been revealed and share it. So, the act of bathing in the elixir of forgetfulness will be waived for you. Your memories will remain intact after you reenter your animal body.

Voice quivering, I said, "But I'm not the one for this mission. I wouldn't know what the heck to say. If I tell people the truth, they'll laugh, believe I've experienced hallucinations. Or they'll give me that 'look' and assume I'm a straightforward lunatic. People aren't used to the truth! Fact is, the vast multitude are hypnotized, think whatever they're told to think."

Today's idea may seem quite sobering. Nonetheless it is but pride that would deny a call from the Source Itself. If the Creator believes you worthy, so you are. It is simply arrogance that judges otherwise.

Truth is neither obscure nor hidden. Only time can teach what is truth and what is purely the legends, fantasies, superstitions of centuries-old storytellers. Therefore, accelerate time! Let the veil of ignorance be slashed so ignorance finds no hiding place. The Creator's children sleep and must be awakened. But beware, mortals tend to resist the new. The cold chill of fear causes multitudes to cling to countless dead ideas, lifeless old beliefs. Your mission is to set free the long-imprisoned spirit of truth on the water star.

Let not the mouth of the misguided hinder those "awake" enough to see. Let not their lips prevent said souls from observing the beautiful naked truth. Still, make your appeal only to those who hear and are convinced. For humans persuaded against their will are of the same opinion still.

Prisoners endlessly bound with heavy chains of ignorance, with eyes so long cast down in darkness they remember not the Light, do not leap up joyfully the instant they are set free. For a host, it takes time to blow away the puff of madness that so unyieldingly swirled about their souls. Yet those who hath eyes will see. Those who hath ears will hear.

"You're asking me to accomplish a feat of epic proportion," I said, wincing.

And yet I ask even more, child. You mortals possess an impressive supply of blind and naked ignorance. Seek to relax human indulgence in at least the preeminent variety.

"Preeminent variety?"

Early human males regarded females with a strange mixture of mistrust, fear, fascination, suspicion, and contempt. Consequently, the molders of your world's myths were all in agreement that "woman was the root of all evil."

This astonishing notion of the "evil female sisterhood" was a view sacred not only to Hebraic and Christian tradition, but also to numerous pagan mythologies as well. This reinterpreting of reality—this bestowing on females a mantle of Devious, Deceiving, Wicked—was a way to justify keeping them submissive, powerless, and under control. Evolving customs and morals have provided increasingly better treatment for mortal females. Yet the need of further evolution is clear.

"Plainly! Are there other issues born out of ignorance we've indulged in?"

Two thousand years before the arrival of quantum physics, the Jewish mystical tradition of Kabbalah revealed that reality existed in multiple separate dimensions. The Kabbalists compiled a set of twenty-three books known as the Zohar. They talked about ideas centuries ahead of their time. In an age where science determined the world was flat, the Zohar depicted the

Earth as round, with mortals experiencing day and night in different time zones. It described the moment of the creation of the universe as a "Big Bang–like explosion."

Concepts such as parallel universes, space travel, black holes in space, healing, cholesterol, origins of heart disease were also encoded into the Zohar.

"The Kabbalists must've been highly acclaimed. Were they given prominent positions, honors, riches for their discoveries?"

The great Kabbalist sage known as Akiva was publicly skinned alive by the Roman Empire in front of twenty thousand spectators. The Kabbalist Ishmael, the son of Elisha, was flayed, his face torn from his head and given to the daughter of the Roman emperor. The sage known as Gamaliel was beheaded.

"I get the picture. But why such primitive persecution?"

For revealing what humans now take for granted. Olden mortals considered the revelations of Kabbalists sacrilegious, frightening, not in line with their preconceived ideas.

"Even so, why all the defense against revelations? All the reinterpreting of reality?"

First, it is the nature of humankind to fear what they do not understand. Second, due to the limited understanding of unsophisticated human animals many distort reality to better fit their biases, comfort zone, preconceived ideas. They do so by reinterpreting reality to suit their notion of how they think things "ought to be." Third, Homo sapiens are an arrogant species; they seduce themselves constantly by the illusion that they are enlightened. Yet more often than not, they only embrace ideas supporting what they already believe.

Light is often too painful for those who want to remain in darkness. With the things of God, there is enough light for those who want to believe, enough shadows to blind those who do not. Consequently, it is difficult to teach children of Earth the plain truth. Myriads have minds like empty rooms. They appear obsessed with ideas of the past—they are bookworms rather than thinkers. Nonetheless, truth is unalterable. It can be unrecognized, but it cannot be changed. It merely is.

Simply stated, one cannot expect a blind mortal to appreciate beautiful patterns or a deaf mortal to listen to bells and birds. Blindness and deafness are not confined to the body alone—the understanding has them too.

On that primitive ocean world, where God's laws do not prevail in perfect form, can you yet do one perfect thing: take ignorance, ever so gently, from your brethren's hand. Feed them truth with humility and with much tenderness. Lovingly encourage them to reexamine all they have been told.

Still, you may come across those with good hearts and good intentions who just do not agree with you. Therefore, you must be clear eyed and calm about these things, child. For who among your fellow Earth dwellers would profit more from prayers alone? Who needs but a smile, being as yet unready for more?

My expression turned serious, solemn.

If you come upon children who fall into the category of unbeliever, your message is not for them at this time. Truth knows neither yesterday, today, nor tomorrow. Bid them go in peace until their spirit is ready, whether it be later in their present life or the next or the next. Keep in mind, little one, that for those not ready for more, your present sacred customs are an enormous step up from the religions you humans once revered.

I dry washed my hands. "What was so bad about our old religious rituals?"

Let us look at the record. To appease the god Baal Hammon, Carthaginian General Hamilcar Barca, father of the great General Hannibal, sacrificed children in white-hot flames.

Affluent Carthaginians resorted to buying children from other nations, rearing them in secret, and then offering them to Baal in lieu of their actual offspring. Brass statues of Baal Hammon stood throughout Carthage. Baal's outstretched hands slanted downward so a tiny child placed on them could not lie there but rolled off, plummeting into a fiery abyss below.

On one occasion a numb, heartbroken mother walked in tearful procession to her god, pale with fright, then chained down her diminutive, sleepy-eyed, weeping infant and offered him up to Baal. A profusion of wispy children were subsequently offered up for sacrifice—after each staggering occurrence, onlookers gave a gut-wrenching shudder of horror. Every time a tiny toddler was presented, the priests laid their hands over them to place upon the elfin bodies the sins of their race.

The young victims hardly reached the edge of the fiery pit when they disappeared—like a tear on a red-hot iron—causing a plume of white smoke to rise above the scarlet glow.

But there is even more. Worshipers piled the petite victims onto Baal's hands bound in immense chains. They wanted to count the young children, to ensure their number corresponded to the days of the solar year. But as the pile of miniature offerings mounted, the flailing of their delicate arms made it impossible to distinguish them.

As if that were not enough, the "religious worship service" went on for countless hours. The inner walls of the temple took on a dark glow. Burning flesh became visible. Sizzling flames died away, leaving only a pyramid of black ashes about the god's knees. Baal's brass body was drenched in deep glowing red like a giant who had bathed in babies' blood.

Incredibly, the parents themselves brought their little ones to the bloodthirsty god. They comforted their babes so the children would not weep while being roasted alive. The "godly" fathers and mothers stifled the heartrending cries of terrified young ones with kisses, caresses. Shockingly, these parents told the frightened babes that they must not shed tears, squeal, or scream, as the noise might disturb the spirits of those dear toddlers previously burned to a crisp.

And that is not all! Your ancestors ate the flesh, drank the blood of male tribal members whom they deified then fattened for sacrifice. Think of it: your forbearers sent messages to their gods; and in one tribe the chief, to convey such a letter, recited it verbally to a slave then cut off his head for special delivery. If the chief forgot something, he sent another decapitated slave as a postscript.

What's more, virtually every animal in nature, from the Egyptian beetle to the Hindu elephant, has somewhere been worshipped by you mortals as a god. The truth is, human sacrifice has been honored as a sacred religious practice at some time or another by virtually all cultures. In short, from age-old civilizations to current times, "good people" are defined in terms of religious ceremonies unquestioningly performed and unswervingly financed.

Hands up, I backed away with a shudder. "I get it! I get it! Can we move on?" Coughing, I said, "Feel like I'm gonna vomit!"

Yes, yes, child.

"Would you be disappointed, master, if I confessed I'm still a bit uncomfortable with what's being asked of me?"

A spiritual warrior must be willing to stand tall when standing is not easy. Even so, worry not, little one; you will not leave this realm friendless nor be forced to rely on those two aging conspirators, hope and luck. The Power, the Force will guard you along the way.

I scratched at my cheek. "The Power and the Force?"

The master gave a subtle nod. **A being appeared in Palestine whose power was extraordinary. The people conferred upon him** the title Great Prophet; his disciples called him the Son of God. He raised the dead and healed a multitude of diseases.

Tall, well built with an air of seriousness in his expression, he quickly attracted the love and reverence of all who saw him. His hair was the color of new wine—a golden brown, yellow red—from the roots to the ears, and from there to the shoulder it was curled and fell down to the lowest part of them. Upon the forehead, it parted in two like a Nazarene's. His forehead was flat and fair; his face, without blemish or defect and adorned with a graceful expression. His nose and mouth were very well proportioned; his beard was thick and the color of his hair. His eyes were piercing, blue or bluish-gray, and extremely lively.

In his reproofs, he was terrible, but in his exhortations and instructions, amiable and courteous. There was something wonderfully charming in that face with a mixture of gravity. He was never seen to laugh but had been observed to weep. He was very straight in stature; his hands were large and spreading, his arms, magnificently muscled. Long tapering fingers, nails well kept. Long nail, though, on the left smallest finger. He talked little but with a great quality.

This illuminating soul, this elder brother, walked your world as a carpenter's son. The sound of truth was mighty on his lips. This same soul is a Force in the universe. You may call on the Force to aid you in becoming better in all things beneficial. The Force can also correct any illusion by dispensing what mortals label miracles. This mighty being can be called on anywhere, at any time.

"Will I be able to see the Force?"

As you should know by now, you children look upon your little blue world with a gaze made not to see reality. Thus, you cannot see the reality of the Force. But you will be able to witness the Force's miracles manifest in your circumstances.

"How many miracles am I entitled to in my lifetime? One? Two? Three?"

Three, three hundred, three thousand—whatever is required. Each human's life and needs differ. There is nothing special about miracles. They should be prominent in the lives of all humans every day. If not, something is clearly amiss. Of course, beings must first purify themselves then possess the necessary faith to call them forth. Your Holy Book is correct when it insists, "Ask and ye shall receive."

The master's eyes began to widen and glow. **But that is just part of the story. The Power is the Voice for the Creator. This vast, complex conglomerate of energy fields has been called by numerous names, including the Christ Mind, the Holy Spirit. You also cannot see the Power, even though it remains closer than the thoughts of your mind every second of each day.**

The Power is in you in a very literal sense. You will know of its presence by its fruits. With this powerful Helper, you will be able to do things you have not been able to do before and accomplish things you could never accomplish on your own. Its voice is quiet. It will not argue, demand, or command. Most importantly, it will not delay in answering your every question regarding what to do. It knows!

"Do the Force and Power cater only to those with assignments from the Creator?"

Both remain ever ready to lift the crown of thorns you humans have placed upon your bleeding heads and set you free! Yet in your lonely, senseless wanderings, this mighty duo's assistance is amazingly disregarded. Your brothers, sisters go idly about, aware of the futility they see all around them, perceiving how their tiny lot quickly dwindles. Still they meander on in misery and poverty, though this powerful pair walks beside them bearing potential aid so great that everything the mortal world contains is valueless before its magnitude.

The master's face drooped. **To those of us who walk the sky, Earth dwellers seem sorry figures—weary, worn, defeated. Countless are in threadbare clothing with bloody feet from the rocky roads you walk. You work hard to get money to buy food to get strength to work hard to get money to buy food to get strength to work hard to get money, etc. This is no life worthy of children of the Light.**

I stared down at the ground intensely. "Is prosperity in our very own hands?"

The master's eyes widened, and he became suddenly still. **You wish to live in a congenial environment peopled with friends who genuinely love you, surrounded by all that is beautiful?**

"You bet!"

Then forget all else, think only upon what you want. Control all thoughts that deny your desired reality, and as mist disappears before the sun, so shall all that hinders your goal melt before the shining radiance of what you set your heart on. Nothing happens by chance. You create your own reality every time you think.

The Creator works like the soil. It receives the seed of your thought and quickly begins to manifest your desire out of Itself. Universal Mind will accept whatever you give to It and will "grow" or create then give back to you whatever you thought into It.

Simply stated, we are surrounded by a Creative Mind from which all things come. We think into It; It does the rest. What we ultimately receive will depend entirely upon the thoughts dwelled upon in our minds. If you intensely believe in a huge result, Divine Mind will do a huge thing; if you only believe in a tiny way, the result will be a tiny one.

Souls who dare to cast their thoughts out into Universal Mind and dare to claim all there is soon discover God will honor their requests. What's more, you dishonor the Mother-Father when you

claim less than all It has to give. The universe abounds with prosperity simply waiting for you, but you must believe—then take it.

The Creator envelops you, flows endlessly through you, becomes operative through your thought. Therefore, if you remain sick, miserable, poor, do not blame God, devils, others—it is your own fault.

There is nothing more frightful than ignorance in action. Naïveté is a mighty thin cloak to keep out the frozen misery, icy grief, cold despair of mortal existence.

I licked my lip with cautious hope. "Would it be possible to be given assurance the Power's there when I need help?"

The master gave me a disapproving look. **You children of Earth, your need for such toys is ever a baffle to my age-old hoary head. Nonetheless, touch Pete's collar.**

I leaned over and touched the collar of the little dog whose head was still resting on my foot. A dazzling deep-blue ray shot out from the sapphire dangling from it. Afterward the tip of my index finger began emitting a subtle glow. As I sat up in my chair, I became lost in rapturous awe at the power and glory of the spectacle unfolding before me. The powerful blue ray split into a myriad of images that began to circle round my head. There appeared a glowing white shape, a hooded figure, a little dog, the color blue, a human hand, an entity called "Sam," and a mystically beautiful lady.

"That hand! My grandfather spoke about 'The Big Hand.' The truth is, I thought his comments were generated by a bit too much bourbon.

"Which should I choose, master?"

You do not choose, little one. A symbol will choose you.

After encircling my head a dozen times, the parade of symbols came to an abrupt halt. The color blue stopped directly above my head. All other symbols instantly disappeared. Pete eyed me with an extraordinary look, made a soft guttural sound.

You have been chosen by the color blue. It is your symbol aid is ever near.

The master closed his fist, waved his hand for a second. Then he opened it and said, **Lo!** In his palm was a crimson pouch. He opened the petite velvet bag and took out a tiny blue object.

This blue stone can increase your vibration rate to a level in harmony with divine forces, thereby making it easier to receive their insight and protection.

He handed me the astonishing stone. It pulsed as if it were alive. With each subtle beat, its color changed cyclically from azure blue to violet blue to greenish blue.

I felt a staggering jolt through my body as I said, "Hope I don't ever lose it!"

Clawing at his cheeks, the master screamed at me in horror, **No, no never can it be—never, never can it be, child! This eye of light will bring stupendous loss, huge misfortune, a horrifying death to anyone other than you, its adoptive father!**

The master reached out to touch me, quickly pulled back and instead clasped his hands together in his lap. There was a great thunder of silence. **Forgive my explosive outburst, child. But, it is vital to utilize exceptional care with your potent new gift. Hold this mighty stone in your hand in the sunlight; it becomes a looking glass wherein you see the mysteries of all the worlds. Tap it to your forehead, the stone's storage of energies will provide undreamed of power. Most importantly, it will facilitate your soul's safely taking leave of your mortal body while you sleep for its tutoring.**

I rubbed my chin. "Tutoring?"

Your soul's travels to the various universities of the Spirit to study with angels, masters of wisdom who have gained mastery in their fields of specialization.

"Do all souls ascend to celestial academies, and commune with spirits nightly?"

Only those who are worthy! Amazingly, you mortals seldom remember at dawn the journeys your souls made at midnight. One moonlit evening you actually danced with me in a garland of glad souls; but you left us when the eastern sky grew rosy. Why did you leave so early? Do you fear the rose-colored sky?

Forehead wrinkling I mumbled, "I, er..."

Last but not least, the blue stone is not a psychic toy! If used selfishly, it can violently rip its user into pieces! With the Force, the Power, the blue stone at your disposal, all power and wisdom in heaven or Earth will be at your beck and call.

The silver-haired being arose, motioned for me to follow him to the great hall's glistening staircase leading to the main level of the temple. Warm radiance washed through me then faded as the glowing figure moved away. I hastened after him.

"Wait!" I shouted at the top of my lungs. "Before I go, master, just one additional thing! The more I've researched the confused course of religion, the more farfetched the notion of *God* has become. I am ashamed to admit that I'm a failure as an atheist too. Can't seem to cure myself of praying to a God I no longer believe in. We've talked a lot about the Light, but I need to know straightforwardly: is there actually a God? You know, like the one I learned about in Sunday school as a kid. Or are the growing numbers of atheists simply unmasking cold hard truth?"

CHAPTER 29

Is There Truly a God?

I stared up, enthralled by the commanding hall's awesome columns and archways. My eyes were filled with wonder and amazement as I pondered if those masterpieces were also possibly invested with profound spiritual meaning. Of all the mystic places I'd encountered on my wondrous journey, the most unconventional was the solarium's magnificent, sparkling copper and glittering gold–covered lobby.

I started to speak but hesitated due to an extraordinary look on the master's face.

The master gazed sadly into my eyes. **Listening at the door of Earth, it is clear your species is far from being spiritually well. Attempting to prove the existence of The Divine Presence is akin to looking for a needle that no one ever lost in a haystack extending to infinity. God makes no attempt to hide from us. You mortals try to hide from It and suffer from deception.**

The much-abused human utterance—"God"—has given rise to bizarre beliefs and delusions of ego, such as "Our God is the only true God! Your God is false!" and even "God is dead." You foolish children are like occupants of a towering building with a multitude of glittering windows; you peer out of different panes at the same light. You each formulate opinions of what you observe. Then you each insist yours is the only realistic interpretation. So

beware, little one, when you search for spiritual truth. You may not like the answers you receive.

At the end of the journey, you shall not be the same person you were when you set out. There will be no going back to innocence.

"I still want to know the hard facts."

The truth is, child, you recognize, however dimly, that we carry within us the wisdom we seek without. Forgive your antiquated sibling, but I cannot give you the all-embracing answer your uncertainty seeks. It lies only in you. Turn you to the majestic calm within, where in hallowed stillness dwells the Creator you never left and who never left you. The Light will assist you in remembering what your soul has forever known. Be still an instant; go home with It. Be at peace awhile. In silence are all things answered, every problem resolved.

Ask! Be still! Listen! Your request is one whose answer has been waiting long to be received by you. What do you feel? What do you hear? What do you see?

I stood riveted in front of the colossal lobby's golden spiral staircase for an eternity, thinking, *Let the Light shine through this appearance known as Jason Xavier Roberts. Let this shadow vanish before God that I may see reality as it is in truth.*

A titillating warmth came over me. I no longer felt separate. The stars, the planets, all that exists seemed to be a pulsing part of me. I felt a oneness with the Absolute.

No Earthly bliss can compare with the boundless ecstasy engulfing those who cross the threshold of oneness with the Source. Through infused mystical knowledge, I suddenly knew no rituals we've set up in which the dance of death delights us could bring extinction to our souls. I didn't just believe I'd enjoy eternal life someday; I was certain I possessed it already. The overpowering rapture enveloping me wiped out all fears as my soul seemed reabsorbed into the seamless oneness of existence.

Gradually, an astonishing Door of Light opened.

"Master, where am I going?" I said, cutting my eyes toward the gleaming door.

Wherever the Creator would have you go.

"What am I looking for?"

The real, the unreal are all there are to choose between and nothing more.

I felt my heart racing, a drumming in my chest as little by little, my entire being became illumined with a Divine influx, a flood of light so bright that I couldn't see my own hands. At last, the dazzling brilliance slowly diminished.

I thought, *What the devil!* There before me stood a frightening monstrosity complete with hoofs, horns, and a tail.

"Hadn't thought of me before, had you," sneered the evil-looking creature.

I was enormously distraught and alarmed by its appearance. Shockingly, it looked, with all its unlovely accessories, like a replica of me. "Go away!" I shouted.

"I can only go where you go," it screeched.

"What do you mean?" I said, cringing.

The specter roared, "I am your Dark Side! All beings have one. I wear countless faces: angry, greedy, evil, vindictive, manipulative, controlling, selfish, critical, judgmental, weak, lazy, fearful, and on and on.

"I act as a secluded storehouse for all these offensive sides of you. I am a guarded repository of all the things you pretend not to be; all the traits that embarrass you; all the faces you don't want to show the world—faces you don't want to even show yourself."

"Can I never get rid of you?" I yelled at the revolting beast.

The apparition glared menacingly. "Yes, you can get rid of me."

"How?" I said, leaning away from the hideous organism.

"By getting rid of yourself!" It snarled, breaking into a thunderous wicked laugh.

"Wow! You've given me an entirely new perspective on good and evil."

Suddenly, beyond my twin self, beyond the stars, past everything I could see, there appeared an arc of golden incandescence stretching as I looked into a great shining, hollow ring of luminosity. The ring filled with Light before my eyes. The borders of the shimmering ring disappeared; what had been in it was no longer contained at all.

The Light expanded, covered everything, and extended to infinity, forever glowing with no breach or boundaries anywhere. Within it everything was joined in perfect endlessness. It was not possible to imagine anything could be outside, for there was nowhere this Light was not.

There appeared within this halo of brilliance the glorious radiance of a thousand suns that made the Creator visible to all. Robed in a fury of light, the Creator's image was mirrored in the sparkling crystal flood. Fearful and trembling, I beheld a veil of flames, a fiery mist, a brilliant glistening in front of me. I looked up! Any fear I'd had was forgotten in awe and astonishment. A Female Form clad in dazzling white hovered in midair: she was beautiful, breathtaking, majestic, beyond description.

She looked right at me; it was blinding. Suddenly there exploded into my mind a flash of shocking, exhilarating truth. It came not in any form of language but rather in a wordless, formless wonder; too vast for the limitation of thought. I fell upon the ground and lost consciousness—how long a time, I do not know—I awoke, got up, and looked about bewildered.

After I subdued the inner quivering of my soul, I recalled the experience that had been too big for me while I was feeling it. I cried but was shivering too. I could not speak, for I went from inner quivering to where words fail entirely.

I thought, *Here is the memory of what we all are—a part of this, with all of it within. My actual self is not a body of bloody meat and bone. No body that ripens into rotting flesh can contain my spirit nor impose on me limitations God did not create.*

My twin self journeyed along an elliptical arc to a second portal; a magnificent Golden Door swung free. Timeless wisdom suddenly reechoed in my memory, gathering clarity as I became willing to hear its subtle voice calling from far away in myself. I saw that before the Earth, moon, stars; before time or space; before history came alive there was only one naked reality—**ENERGY!**

Sounds fantastic? Yet in mind-blowing shock and awe, I witnessed a dimly visible image without substance, a shape that had no shape, an incandescent mass that was in no place, in no time; it was a boundless, swirling, luminous mist of **CHI**. I observed as well this fine, radiant white essence forever falling into everything.

I understood that flowing through me is a living crystal river that can never be completely grasped by human thought. I am an extension of the One unseen Life that dwells in the depths of Its own being. At times, It assumes form briefly to experience Itself as a pebble, a leaf, a bumble bee, a dolphin, a grandmother, a star. I then realized the Creator's not "up there" somewhere judging our world from above. It's orchestrating, "playing" the universe—and all things therein—from the inside out.

Finally my twin self journeyed to a third portal, a massive Red Door. I was surprised to find the Archangel Gabriel behind its spectacular redness. He was kneeling, palms together, facing east, as if in prayer; mighty wings protruded from his powerful, hard-muscled back. Without turning, the colossal being said, **What secret torment has mounted your soul with spiked spurs?**

"I've given, cared, worked, worried, dreamed, planned. Yet nothing in my life turned out as I intended. Loads of things actually turned out exceptionally bad."

Gabriel turned toward me, relaxed his posture, laced his fingers behind his head. **There was an old sage whose rare thoroughbred stallion ran off. When his twin brother came to console him, the sage replied, "Who knows what is good or bad?"**

When his stallion returned the next day with a herd of wild mares following him, the foolish twin came to congratulate the sage on his good fortune.

"Who knows what is good or bad?" said the sage.

Then, when the sage's daughter broke her leg trying to ride one of the wild mares, the twin came to comfort his brother again. "Who knows what is good or bad?" said the sage.

When the king passed through the village forcing young women, against their will, to become one of his numerous concubines, he passed over the sage's beautiful daughter because of her broken leg. When the foolish twin came to congratulate the sage because his daughter would be spared, again the sage said, "Who knows what is good or bad?"

Jason, you say nothing in your life turned out as you intended. I say, who knows if that is good or bad!

The Red Door closed. My primitive Dark Side vanished. The dazzling illumination enveloping me also disappeared.

Perfectly tranquil, the old master had been observing me. A subtle, knowing smile beautified his wise face. **Knowledge comes from the altar of truth within. You called it forth splendidly. Yet I shall awaken your spirit further.**

There is a timeless saga about three blind humans and an elephant. The first blind human grabs hold of the elephant's ivory tusk, describes the smooth, hard, tubular surface he feels. The second blind human grabs hold of the elephant's left hind leg. He describes the rough tree trunk–like form he comes across. The third blind human grabs hold of the elephant's right ear, describes the huge fanlike massiveness his fingers touch. Since their descriptions are so unalike and none can see each other, each thinks he has grabbed hold of a different living creature.

Throughout your vast history, human animals have been as much in the dark as the three blind humans of my story, thinking the limitless attributes of the Creator were actually different things or phenomena. In truth, all that exists are simply various aspects of one underlying Whole. The many names you little ones gave Its aspects have distorted what you see but have not interfered with reality at all. What you children of Earth have stammered since humankind's beginning are fragments of one immortal name.

Forget everything you have heard about reality, for life is not about a myriad of individual things each wiggling in a distinctive way. Life is One Solitary Thing wiggling Itself in countless ways. Subatomic particles, all else in the universe are no more separate from one another than different patterns in an ornate Oriental rug. Everything is a seamless extension of everything else. Yet each thing possesses its own unique qualities much like the features of the elephant the three blind humans were struggling to "see."

Now for the surprise: heaven, Earth are actually within you. Life as you experience it is a projection of your soul. The

three-dimensional world is akin to a huge movie screen that allows mind-patterned creations to be visible. What you children take to be your body—the flesh, blood, bones that feel so genuinely real to you—is also simply a projection of spirit. In a nutshell, your soul creates by thought projection the experiences you have in the "movie" you call life. You do not live in a world. A world lives in you!

The circumstances of your life are as easy to change as it is to place a different movie in a movie projector. You know what it is like to see a movie; you get caught up in the picture. The movie is hypnotic. You forget your own reality and enter that of the movie. So it is with the movie you mortals call your Earthly life.

I experienced a quick tensing of my body. "Clearly we possess astonishing ability, and our mighty mind is the key."

It is even more potent than you think. The mind can heal. The mind can kill. Your mind, child, is frankly the most powerful thing in the universe.

The master's hand clasped his chin briefly. He then casually settled back. **Let us not get sidetracked!**

Unfortunately, The Human Family personalizes the Creator; it makes of It a "Being of Form." Incredibly, they give It a body modeled after their own apelike form. The ancient Ethiopians said their gods were snub nosed and black skinned like they were; the Thracians, that theirs were blue eyed and red haired like them.

No doubt about it if cows, horses had hands and created the works of art that humans make, horses would draw the figures of their god like horses and cows like cows. Truthfully, the real you—your soul—is made in the image of the Creator, not your animal body.

The master's posture loosened a bit more. **I must again ask too much of you, child—to bow to this reality as well. The illusory world mortals see is governed by laws of overwhelming pain. You** are born into it through pain and in pain. Your growth is accompanied by suffering; you learn of sorrow, fear, death. Your minds seem to be trapped in a "meat-bag" brain. You seem to love, yet you desert and are deserted. You appear to lose all the people, pets, things you cherish.

After a lifetime of misery and hardship, your bodies wither, gasp, end up rotting in the dirt, and are no more. Multitudes are filled with images of a god who is a father in king's robes with scepter and crown; a god who is a jealous, hot tempered, vengeful, arrogant eye in the sky, watching, waiting for you to falter and fail him. Hosts subconsciously believe that God is cruel. The truth is, if this was the real world, God would be cruel.

The legendary storytellers who believed and passed along these childlike notions may have been sincere; yet they were sincerely wrong. Presenting attractively wrapped fairy tales as real-life is a major cause of the rising atheism among thinking mortals. Given the current trajectory, the things of God will soon become only the province of the dimwitted before being dismissed altogether as a charming myth. Harsh realities but nonetheless the truth.

To be quite candid, child, atheists are simply unenlightened. Yet their skepticism is understandable, for the god they were asked to believe in does not exist—and never did.

"At last—think I honestly get it! There's *Something* that makes things out of Itself by becoming the things It makes. Its the Absolute Essence of all that is. The only thing in existence is *this Creator* and a limitless number of Its Self-expressions in a birthless, deathless, ageless sea of Self-Aware Energy some would call God. I am that, you are that, all of this is that—and that's all there is! Anywhere. Ever!" Suddenly I was at a loss for words; I clutched at my gut. In a voice choked with tears, I stammered, "It's…"

The master gave me a soothing pat on the back and in a quiet voice said, **Yes, yes, child. I know!**

Ultimately, I regained my composure, said, "Does It, God, have a name?"

No, no, no. It is simply the "I Am that AM—I become that which I become."

I asked whisper softly, "Is God male or female?"

Wrinkling his brow, the master looked at me with a thoughtful expression. **Refer to It as Father or Mother—both mean the same. For the Divine Presence is both male and female Energy—apparent opposites that are in fact complementary, different phases of an essential unity. Each is necessary to the other; each bears within it the seed of the other. Contending yet in harmony, the two forever flow into one another in stately cosmic rhythm.**

Then with solemn eyes and a voice devoid of emotion, choosing his words deliberately, the master said, **This is the point-blank truth: there is a God, but there is no God in the human realm— only the Law of Cause and Effect. God is an Energy Being! An infinite ocean of Self-Aware Energy. You are truly made in Its image and likeness because you are a literal extension of God Itself. In brief, you are a vital "cell" within Its boundless Energy body.**

A human cell living inside you cannot get outside your body to see and prove to itself that you, Jason Xavier Roberts, exist. Similarly, you cannot see the Creator to prove to yourself that It exists because you live "within" the Creator, and the Creator has no outside.

God cannot be seen—only understood, only experienced. It is the invisible Life Essence of all that is. The Intelligent Energy running through every portion of the Whole. The Life we all "feel" but do not see. You see only what It does, never the Creator Itself. You are one with the Creator. You are a bit of Its body. You are a miniature god. Your mind is a pinch of the Mind governing everything in existence.

Your Holy Book sums up this truth in Isaiah 46:9: "For I am God, and there is none [nothing] else!" The Creator said

straightforwardly, "What you do unto those who are the least among your brethren, you also do unto me."

One thing's for sure: the tiny within Creation are not unimportant; the great, not as important as you have the habit of supposing. That's why actual superiority and inferiority between beings is genuinely impossible. To God there is no high, no low, no great, no small. The perfect functioning of the God-Creator depends on the work of every cell! Therefore, each is precious. All are vital. You are a unique, irreplaceable bit of God. All that exists, exists within the Creator—the Lone Presence—Who is a Universe of One!

This is as I know it to be.

"Endless mind-opening revelations! How do you know all this?"

Moderately wise each being should be, not overwise! For a wise being's heart is seldom glad, child. You listen with joy to my music, but I am only a hoarse minstrel. In truth, all wisdom comes from the Creator; I am simply one of Its myriad channels.

The master's face underwent a fascinating change. It became one of surpassing beauty. His entire being became radiant with internal light. Boundless love exuded from his captivating blue eyes. He motioned for me to kneel. The age-old teacher placed a powerful, electrifying hand on my head. I felt a warmth emanating from his palm that seemed like a sort of liquid sanctification; it coursed through my body and penetrated my soul. From the immortal sage's mouth drifted an appealing fragrance of roses and violets that bathed my face as he said:

Fortunately, your destiny and you are not at odds. You do not walk life's path alone. Make no illusion, friend. In truth, the Power, the Force are your only friends. Here is the answer to every difficulty that will confront you today, tomorrow, and throughout eternity. Whenever a problem assaults you, hold your mind in silent readiness, hear only the Power's voice. Go past all the explosive shrieks, sick imaginings concealing your link with the Eternal. Sink deep into the peace waiting for you.

You will find yourself immersed in the answers to all the problems of the universe. Have faith in this Power who already has faith in you. It can put into action any activity necessary to make you the victor in all circumstances of your life. The Power will tell you what to do in the hour of need. You shall be told everything you ought to know when the time of need arrives, and you shall not be misled. In the dark places of human ignorance, the Power shall guide you into the perfect way.

Some of the ideas presented, you will find hard to believe; others may seem truly startling. Yet they are mighty forces to be used, not held idly by. Remember only this: you need not believe them nor even welcome them. Some, you may actively resist.

Apply these gifts as your circumstances dictate. Nothing more is required. Their results will be more convincing than my words could ever be. Freedom from oppression by life's misfortunes lies not in mysteries or occult performances. It rests upon the intelligent use of truth, natural forces, and universal laws.

Commit what you have experienced to those practical symbols mortals refer to as printed words; that it may be given unto their children, and they unto their children, and it shall not perish from the Earth.

Speak of the Creator's love so clearly that even the blind and deaf could not fail to see and hear this truth. For the mythmakers and monks who made up your stories have permitted a storm of fantasy to scatter the Whole. Gather God up again in a vessel pleasing to the Source of Life. Portray the Divine Mother-Father not with silver or gold but with colors made of berries and bark.

Everything needed to be said about God, love, the nature of being has already been said. But since no one was listening, everything must be said again. The animal called human was given, grasped, then let fall again those ideas. They were too warm, in seasons past, to be comfortably held by hands cooled in the labors of childish selfishness.

Leave any "Holier-than-thou" attitude to smaller minds. Most importantly, you need not try to change the entire world. No one needs to be saved except you and those enlightened ones who hath ears to hear God's truth. The Creator is depending on you to be the means through which Its' voice is heard in your world. Through you, little one, will be ushered in a world unseen, unheard, yet truly there.

Then, as if freed from a great weight, I arose.

"Like to say good-bye to Camr before I go. What's the fastest way back to her?"

Mount Solace's timeless trail is the quickest way to get back to where you need to go. You will find an opening to it about three hundred yards northeast of here. Take note; it is tremendously steep with poor footing in places.

Now, back to the dream. Bring light to the tired eyes of those as weary now as once you were. Flood the outer world with the truth about reality, the truth about The Kingdom of God.

I gazed intensely into the master's solemn face. "Will I ever see you again?"

The old sage's features softened. With a beaming expression, glowing cheeks, he said, **The path of life is a circle; be assured we shall meet again. When you hear a sound in the distance, like the brushing of a butterfly's wing against the shoulder of the morning—I will come walking down a ray of light.**

The master then blessed me, smiled—blue eyes sparkling—bowed, turned, and walked away. The moment seemed one over and above self-pity, sadness. I was setting out on a journey I would've given anything not to make.

CHAPTER 30

Return to the Dream

I ascended the vast lobby's golden staircase, proceeded through the archway into the silence and majesty of the cathedral. I paused, lost in frozen gaze, mesmerized by an unforgettable sight, my soul poised between the transitory and the eternal.

Then I realized the enormous hologram floating before me was not just some magnificent abstract portrait. It depicted a three-dimensional image of the Creator complete with saffron swirls of the quivering heavens—an image so holy, so beautiful that I could scarcely refrain from kneeling at its feet. Impulsively, I stretched out my hand and touched the face of God—or at least a holographic depiction of It.

Surrounding the Creator's dazzling panorama were bright flames of violet fire that blazed up as I stood before them. Shooting out from its center were seven powerful rays of sparkling light, each ray wrapped in a cylinder of vivid, glowing, unutterable color. The truth is, I saw more than I can tell and understood intuitively more than I saw. How can the inexpressible be expressed? How can the unspeakable be spoken?

The silence said what I could not. Bringing a shivering hand to my forehead, I stirred from an enchanted moment frozen in time. Overwhelmed, shaking all over, I staggered with a dreamy, wondrous feeling back to the entrance hall's gigantic gold doors. I stepped outside into the sunlike illumination and slowly descended the pallid stone steps.

As I moved one foot before the other, I experienced a sense of freedom from the shackles of past wrongdoing. When I reached the bottom step, there was a sublime feeling of completion.

I stood there, eyes closed, thinking about my strange and wonderful adventure, the limitless revelations received. The spectacular images I'd witnessed. The exotic astronomical views encountered. The ebb and flow of tender, haunting music. The intoxicating lifestyle where every day is a different, exhilarating journey. Camr's rapturous farewell kiss—my heart still throbs and tingles whenever I think of it.

The total occurrence struck me as an elegant fusion of art and reality. The entire incident had been the most astounding of odysseys, a voyage into realms more bizarre and more beautiful than could ever be imagined.

Life is strange, but here in the spirit realm it seems so very precious. Here you experience beauty and truth in their purest forms.

How many minutes passed while I stood with my eyes closed, musing, I don't know. I gradually opened them; caught one final glimpse of the stately pillared temple of whitest marble and golden roof. Then I resumed my journey to Mount Solace Trail, still lost in thought.

In no time at all, it became apparent that I was rushing down the steep mountain trail much too fast. The way down appeared crooked. There were exposed roots, loose rocks, slippery spots just as the old master had warned. Collapsed trees lay across the path. I felt a bit nervous about these hazards, but my legs seemed to possess a will of their own, carrying me down the incline at almost a dead run. I let my feet single out the best spots, permitted myself to fly up over the fallen trees. I was sailing down the pathway's sharply sloping terrain too quickly but in perfect harmony with its magical forest, its liquid air, the finely jeweled droplets on incomparable plants and trees.

I remember breathing deeply, entirely satisfied to be where I was, pleased with each second, wishing for nothing. My life, for those enchanted moments, seemed as clear and resonant as a crystal. Spellbound by the grandeur of my surroundings, I didn't notice portions of a tree root protruding from the trail until too late. My foot caught the tip of the root, causing me to stumble headfirst off the east slope of that leafy peak. I felt the wind on my face for a moment; then the most merciful blackness swallowed me like a peaceful midnight dream.

An incomparable sense of warmth came over me. I felt a strange sensation in my brain. It seemed as if my soul were being exhaled out of the Whole and sucked again into the tiny vessel of a human body. An entrance had opened to a different dimension, another reality. I'd fallen off the edge of a magnificent world into a greatly inferior one.

I had a sense there was a light shining on my eyes; then I felt weariness in my arms and legs with an accompanying desire to move them into a different position. When I attempted to move my legs, however, my feet fell, jarring my entire body. I opened my eyes, was surprised to find tears running down my cheeks. I felt both stirred and depressed at the prospects of *being back*—back to the fear, hate, pain people call life.

I glared through the tears. My feet had slipped from the brown-leather ottoman and had struck the floor. There was an electric light at the side of my head: my reading lamp. I was back in the oversized leather chair. The fire in the fireplace was still going. The room was comfortably warm and very quiet. Nothing but the occasional crackling of the burning logs disturbed the serene stillness.

I felt hot, sweaty, tired. I sat up in the chair, experienced painful cramps in my legs. I rubbed them for a second, tried to get up, but I couldn't walk. I felt dizzy, barely able to move. But the heart attack—the pain in my chest—was gone! I was still alive! Except my body was shocked: it felt very cold, my blood pressure was low, my pulse rate seemed slow, my heart twitched periodically. As I started breathing normally again, my aching body began to slowly thaw out, but my muscles felt painfully stiff.

I suddenly became aware of sounds coming from the grandfather clock in the foyer. It was just concluding its twelve bold strokes. It was then midnight! Sounds incredible, yet during the mind-blowingly brief interval of the first and last of those twelve chimes, I had died, journeyed to and from a dimension of light all in a matter of just...microseconds? But how could that have possibly been?

These thoughts rushed to my mind with such explosive force that they caused me to jump straight up out of the chair in one single reflex. I stumbled about the partially moonlit room, disoriented, nervously pacing, thinking, muttering unconscious comments; my mind was in a daze.

I plopped down in the huge leather chair and became lost in a state of deep thought: *It seems the stuff of science fiction. Was it all just a dream? A nightmare?*

I felt something hard and looked down. Then I saw it. Lying atop a rear corner of the chair's cushion was the mysterious blue stone—my gift from the old master. At that moment I realized unequivocally it wasn't all a dream. What's more, that I'm an incarnated soul—a sort of dual person. The flesh and bones of my body are of the family of Man. But my personality, my mind are of the soul. I no longer seemed to be Father Jason Xavier Roberts but a channel of the Source with an essential mission.

Days passed; my body returned to reasonable operation. But it took me endless weeks of reflection to recuperate from my experience in the realm of Light. But the essence of me certainly did not recover, nor will it ever. There isn't simply a different overview but a remembering of unlimited freedom, an ever-so-slight glimpse of who and what I truly am. Every minute it becomes harder and harder to stay here. I yearn to live. Yet I wish I were "dead." I long to get back home, where I am more "me."

Some of the shock of returning to the body has worn off. I've begun to be conscious of emotions. Sometimes the sadness is so intense I want to cry. There's nothing else to do. Now I see why accepting the elixir of forgetfulness before incarnating on Earth is so helpful. It eliminates homesickness, nostalgia. It stops the pain. I used to meet a person on the street and think he or she was another person. Now I realize that when I seem to meet another, I'm simply meeting a portion of my Self.

I've glimpsed eternity and enjoyed the luminous, tranquil kingdom where time will be no more. I now know physical birth is not the beginning, and death is not the end; this hard-hitting truth released me from sadness, anxiety, and even death itself.

Those of us who've tasted the spirit dimension's richness understand unequivocally that we've visited the ultimate reality. It's the plane of consciousness from which we embark on successive trials of incarnation and to which we return at the death of the body—the laying off of an old physical garment and the donning of our natural celestial one.

One lesson from my journey "home" stands out above all others. As long as the boundless, wispy, breathtaking freedom of true reality remains frightening to you, you'll continue to dream of a physical reality "out there" for yourselves that is comfortably solid, even though "out there" does not exist!

The essence of everything I've shared with you is true. I might've said much more had it been permitted me. I may not have convinced you that you dwell not here but in eternity nor convinced you of the reality of the spirit realm. Most who've experienced it don't even try; their individual knowledge is enough. Here in the midst of it, the physical world does seem real. Here you are part of it. Yet from above, the perspective shows you the battle's not real and is easily escaped. It shows you that there's really nothing to escape from except illusions!

What is false is false; what is true has never changed! And so my story ends. Well, almost.

CHAPTER 31

The Rainbow Bridge

*J*drove out to Jackie's grave, which mysteriously gave off the scent of roses. My route took me past townhouses oozing with colonial charm that date to the eighteenth and nineteenth centuries. The residences were decorated with lovely glittering ornaments, fragrant woody pinecones, scarlet berry clusters nestled among dense greenery. A wealth of festive wreaths, candy-striped garland, and rainbow-colored lights also adorned these timeless charmers. All boasted a treasure trove of opulent holiday decor reminiscent of the beauty of a vanished world.

Considering Georgetown's river views and brick sidewalks lined with meticulously kept, beautiful period homes, it's not surprising Jackie adored this historic treasure's every brick and cobblestone. Now this oasis of the rich and powerful—even bedecked with its magnificent red, green, and gold holiday trim—felt more like a doorstep to despair.

There seemed to be exceptional drama and energy at Georgetown's tiny Eternal Mystery Cemetery on this evening, courtesy of a fiery golden sunset. I brought flowers, which I placed at the base of Jackie's headstone; then ran my hand over her name, wiping dust from the engraved lettering. Suddenly a voice pure as the naked heavens whispered, **Jason! My heart aches for you.** Then a faint high-pitched buzzing sound echoed about me. I felt slightly dizzy. My surroundings started to spin. My sense of a physical body slowly faded.

I ascended to an astonishing world of clouds—a great white plain with snowy hills and mountains. I found myself effortlessly floating in the air on one side of a shimmering rainbow bridge. On its opposite end there was a glowing sphere mauve in color. My breath stopped. Hands up in a defensive stance, I slowly, cautiously crossed over, reached out, and touched the *thing* before pulling back quickly. It was an odd, tantalizing experience.

Backing away, I retraced my steps. Seconds later, the radiant object gradually began to change. It slowly transformed, as if by magic or sorcery, into an alluring shape wearing a white, loose, short garment. It was elegantly crafted of delicate, wispy stuff that rippled in the silky breeze.

My face became bathed in wonder and bewilderment. The luminous form drifted across the gemlike bridge toward me, and with a soft voice said:

Do not pine for me in that garden of tombstones, dry bones, and rotting flesh. Do not seek the living among the dead. I came out of my mouth with the bubbles when my body sank to the bottom of the Potomac River. My spirit's stronger than any river's embrace. We cannot die! But we can confuse ourselves with things—like bodies—that do. Our lives are not a part of anything we see. They stand beyond the world. It was my body that died. Not me!

I am no colorless ghost dripping with grave dew. I'm real! I'm vibrantly more alive now than when you knew me clothed in animal flesh. Throw aside the black robe, Jason. Laugh at death! We are as immortal as God Itself. The truth is, there is no time, no

space, no beginning, no end. Death is but an imprudent thought in the childish mind. An opposite of life does not exist. Nothing has ever been "unalive!" We are extensions of an eternal flow of Energy that is ever conscious, ever alive.

The age-old journey all began, will end in the Invisible Boundless Reality beyond the veil. Some believe these homecomings to be a bitter hour of raw terror. Yet releasing your soul into the arms of the Mother-Father is akin to a swan hesitantly lowering itself into a rushing brook. The water gently receives her, and softly yielding, it flows back beneath her in graceful waves, while she, totally serene, with elegant savoir faire, allows herself to glide evermore. Nothing dies! All simply returns from whence it came.

There she stood, looking just the same as the Jackie I had known before the car crash: tall and slender with long, dark hair; ravishing good looks; eyes bright and dazzling as a spring sunrise; an alluring smile that made all else in the spangled firmament pale by comparison.

She was a brilliant radiance of beauty, a sensual mound of feminine physical appeal. I was so excited that only slowly did a strange thing dawn upon me: *her perfectly formed body appeared transparent.* What's more, it possessed a warm, soft, comforting glow. Her coloring was a beautiful silvery hue I'd never seen anywhere else—a tincture beyond the color frequencies we have words for.

I was half-afraid that if I even trembled, her essence might mystically dissolve like a fleeting dream.

Jackie sprang into my arms. **Jason! Jason! Jason! Hold me**, she yelled breathlessly. **A thousand and one nights I woke up in heaven screaming, craving your touch.** Hesitantly, trembling, I caressed her, and she, me. Was it self-deception, or did she really feel warm to my touch? I kissed her lips—a long, lingering kiss— and felt them, soft beneath mine. I touched her shoulders, arms, and thighs—soft warmth greeted my fingertips. With unutterable gratitude and joy, I put my arms around Jackie tightly, squeezed her tenderly. She smiled into my eyes, blushed.

She was dressed only in the exquisite, delicate, loose-fitting garment that floated about barely touching her skin. My eyes filled with liquid delight. I surrendered completely to the spell of bliss supreme. The glittering of my tears attracted her eyes to mine. Perhaps she also heard the raw power of my love multiplying the beat of my heart.

All the repressed grief in my life reached critical mass. There was a titanic explosion. Clutching at my gut, I said, "Didn't realize I could miss someone so much! My life's so empty without you that it shivers in anguish. I'm not letting you go again. I can't! It hurts—"

She cut me off abruptly with a gentle voice that was soft, angelically tuned. **I know it's been difficult. I've just awakened from a wondrous sleep. The old master arranged it so I could come for a brief good-bye. I couldn't wait another minute longer. Your name was on my lips when the waters of the Potomac overpowered me. I came directly where I knew you'd be.**

"How—how'd you know where to find me?"

I heard you.

I stared at her incredulously. "You could hear me?"

Frankly, all the blessed dead are standing about you mortals watching and listening with great pleasure.

Jackie began lightly stroking my arm. **We hear a rich source of Earthly sounds from the other side, especially music. Human voices seem a bit muddled, though, unless you train your ear. I trained mine to be in tune with your voice.**

I heard you many a night calling my name, weeping, listening to my favorite love song over and over again. I came to you night after night while you were sleeping and covered you with my kisses. But you never woke to see my shining silvery form bending

over you. I've watched at your window when the raindrops beat upon it. You did not notice my presence; you seemed aware only of the rain.

I now see that if I had to live my Earthly life over, I would dress simpler, speak more of what I felt, less of what I thought, and bare my body and my soul more before the sun. But despite our numerous ups and downs, I'd still choose you. You are the sum total of everything I've ever wanted in life. You're the object of my love, the keeper of my spirit.

I—I know I've said, done some impossibly stupid things…

"Who hasn't? I still love you totally, passionately, endlessly."

Makes me want to fall in love with you all over again.

With visible shakiness, Jackie continued. **I'm perplexed, Jason, and haunted by feelings of guilt. You have my heart. I have yours. Yet our love has instilled in my soul feelings of absolute selfishness. I don't want your lips to touch another's today, tomorrow, ever. What I want is every single precious ounce of your love, every drop.**

When finished speaking, she paused for an instant. Her lips broke into an exquisite smile. There appeared such a warm wealth of feeling in the air, such a tremor. Her words seemed sheer beauty to me. They charmed my broken heart; expressed everything I vitally needed to hear.

"I like my body best when it's with your body. I relish kissing your electric softness. Love the delectable sensation of your body when it's under mine. I yearn to be closer to you than breath, nearer than the beat of your heart." The sound of my voice and what I'd expressed made me feel self-conscious. When I began to sob involuntarily, driven by self-pity, I felt even more ashamed. Then I lost any vestige of control. I gave myself fully to feelings of boundless despair.

A whirring noise abruptly resonated from the distance. At first, I thought it was the sound of billowing wind. But there was no wind! Jackie's head dropped.

"Is it time?"

My hour has come. Jackie said as her sparkling eyes appeared to dim.

I have to leave, but you must linger here where darkness rules, she sighed.

With a quickening heartbeat, I leaned forward; my fingertips traced along her elegant cheek. "You are, and will always be, the joy of my life!" We embraced, weeping. Her gentle softness surrounded me with comfort and love. I started holding Jackie extra tight with eager straining. Life is all about moments. I intended to treasure this one.

In that instant, the radiation of her love was overwhelming. There was neither day nor night, only my love and hers. It seemed there could be no greater degree of bliss, no greater level of delight than the rapturous sensation I felt at that very second. But Jackie placed her lips to my ear, whispered, **I love you!** And the world stopped completely...

Her sparkling eyes were luminous with emotion. It was there—all of it—in those tears faceted like diamonds, glittering in the clear, cool light. Her drops of sweetness momentarily quenched my forlorn thirst. They spoke more earnestly than language could.

"How will I ever find you again? Is it all lost like tears in the rain?" I said in a despondent, husky voice. Jackie, tears of love trickling down her cheeks, caressed my lips with hers, held me tight, and broke into uninhibited weeping. I kissed away her tears, fondled her silky tresses. "Don't cry, babe! You're why I live and breathe. I'll search for you through a thousand worlds and ten thousand lifetimes until I find you, if needed."

Then my lips got lost in her kiss. I loved all of Jackie's kisses, but this last was the sweetest. We melted into each other, like the waters of a rushing river intermingling with the sea, and became one being. I pressed my lips to hers delicately, then passionately, trying to draw her soul within my soul. When we finally withdrew from each other, there was a sensation of pain starting in the upper region of my heart.

The Garden! What about the Garden? We'll meet in the Garden of Light on the Tea House terrace. I'll come every seventh of August earth-life time, the anniversary of the day we met. Wait by the fountain for twenty-four hours.

"My incarnation—I don't know when it'll end."

Jackie placed her hand over her heart. **It doesn't matter! I never stopped thinking about you. About us. Now I again have hope— no, a knowing we'll be together for all time! So each seventh day of August, I will close my eyes; I will dream about your partaking of the gifts lying chaste yet smoldering within my depths, and when I reopen them…one day you'll be there. I'll continue to come, continue to wait until your lips again taste mine. Love cannot be obstructed by the barrier of "death." Love reaches out past death, past time, beyond space.**

Jackie started to slowly back away. Tears were streaming down her cheeks. A mighty, unyielding *something* seemed to be pulling her. Jackie reached out her arms to me. I reached out for her. But already she was far away, silently calling out to me with her eyes, all the while melting into a sphere of soft mauve luminosity that ascended and floated above the snow-crested, misty mountaintops.

My deep serene joy was quelled; my mouth, sad beyond all reasonable inducements. Motionless, wondering and with a never-satiated gaze, I watched my sweet bit of loveliness disappear in a rainbow haze toward the east.

After that there was blackness…intense blackness…blackness with texture and a vigorous wind. Then perfect calm. I opened my eyes and looked through the tears. I found myself again at the cemetery in front of Jackie's headstone, filled with a raw sadness beyond words or emotion.

CHAPTER 32

⁓

Teardrops Amid Snowflakes

I looked up. A tall, blue-eyed gentleman with silver-white hair was smiling at me. He wore a well-tailored white suit. He stood on the cemetery's gravel footpath, leaning on a mahogany walking stick with a brass horse-head crown. His custom-made white shirt bore initials on the rim of gold cuff-linked French cuffs. His off-white silk tie boasted a perfect Windsor knot. He was clutching a petite pine wreath trimmed with ruby-red holly berries.

He examined me with unparalleled eyes. "You know her, then?"

"Very well, but not for very long." I said, eyes red, sniffing, wiping at my nose.

"Ah," he said with a sigh, as though a great mystery had been solved to his satisfaction. "I've passed by here often and wondered about her. That quote on her headstone—'Death leaves a heartache no one can heal; love leaves a sweet reminiscence no one can steal'—is incredibly charming. My wife's down the path a bit."

I gave a soft tap to his arm. "I am truly sorry for your loss."

"Forgive my frankness, young man, but when I look beyond your painted smile, I see a tremendously sad face. Still hurts, huh?"

I stared at him with a long pained look; my watery eyes broke contact as I said, "When I gazed upon Jackie's grave for the first time, it was with the overwhelming feeling of an insane man staring rivetingly at one single hopelessly dark spot. I wept without pause for three days and three nights. Her life was like a buttercup: a flower quick to blossom in spring and all too quick to die. No sooner does it bloom than its petals fall away in the wind.

"I know this might sound like the mushy nonsense of some romance novel. But I miss her in a quite simple, desperate, human way. I miss seeing, hearing, tasting, touching, smelling her and holding close her fragrant softness in my arms. When she died, she took with her the best part of me. The sense of sweetness that sprang from our brief time together still trickles in my heart. It left me hopelessly in love—helplessly addicted. Not just to a beautiful face and form but to the essence that is her."

I pressed a fist to my lips. "When Jackie died, my heart died too. And the wake continues long into the night. I've discovered a black despair that's bitter, relentless—a lonesomeness so profound it seems impossible to come out of. Sometimes it's like she's right inside of me. I can hear her voice. Feel her breath…"

For an infinity all went silent.

"Here's a perspective from an old man, for whatever it's worth. No accident or chance is possible in the universe. Things come, remaining for just as long as they're needed; then they go. The same is true of people. The same is true of those we love."

I swallowed hard. "Think you're right. But I also believe all who meet and seem to part will one day meet again. I know this'll happen for Jackie and me; it's only a matter of time."

"You really believe God looks out for ordinary people like us, young fella?"

"She must! Don't think we'd make it a day otherwise."

"Then why aren't there more happy endings in life? Take a look around at the world in all its grime and torment. How many people have you met who are truly happy? How many have obtained their heart's desire? Or, having obtained it, are satisfied?

"A great number struggle through countless days, endless nights of quiet desperation. Many people meet with failure, disappointment, injustice, betrayal, impoverishing loss. We struggle to get possessions and soon discover they possess us. Worst of all, while navigating through our intense, nasty existence, we invariably find ourselves in dark places, alone, and afraid.

"The current state of the world, my life, is not at all what I expected it to be. It seems few things occur exactly the way we imagine; most turn out either a little better or much worse. From a distance all things seem bright and beautiful, but the world's not a pretty thing when you look at it too closely."

I cleared my throat. "This world always was, is now, and forever will be a pit of despair. Whenever one problem's overcome, another, huge or small, always pops up to take its place. Life is a fight! You must conquer it, or it'll conquer you! Life isn't about waiting for the storm to pass. It's about learning to dance in the rain! No one's life is neat, perfect, antiseptic. Everyone's existence is a bit messy, sometimes even chaotic.

"Love is the key to keeping sane in an insane world. Wealth, position, power alone won't make life worthwhile. We all need love to make living happy and complete. I was just a normal guy battling the days of an ordinary existence. Then something magical called *the love of a woman* raged into my life. At that moment, the brutishness of day-to-day existence started to decay."

I leaned in. "This time, like all times, is a very good one if you know what to do with it. You carry within the capacity to imagine and to give shape to your world. All must realize this truth, come to terms with it, cope with life's inevitable trials whenever they rear their ugly heads. Everything that happens, happens for a reason, and it teaches us, causes us to grow into mature spirit beings. Ultimately we'll all experience a happy ending. It's impossible not to!"

The debonair old gentleman looked intently at me, smiled broadly, as if especially pleased with my replies. "Bravo! You have learned well." He walked up closer and shook my hand. "Jason, do you know who I am?"

I gazed into his incredible blue eyes a long time. "Aviar? Aviar— is that you?"

"The master sent me to ensure the meeting he arranged between you and your mate went off smoothly. He will be pleased to hear how well you have expanded your spiritual knowledge."

"Certainly look totally different from when I last saw you!"

"The majority of us, while visiting your plane, adopt a form that looks just like an ordinary mortal's. Nothing about our dress or speech would make us different from others present. Did not your Holy Book's Saint Paul warn mortals to 'show hospitality; for by that means some have entertained angels without knowing it?'

"Ever been visited by a spirit in one of our numerous disguises before this?"

"Think you're the first."

"Spirit beings are minds without bodies. Actually, we can be near you, observe you, even protect you without assuming any physical form whatsoever."

Aviar then turned, casually walked away. He appeared to be walking at a normal pace. But he covered distance so quickly that it seemed like only a matter of seconds before he'd vanished. What's more, he left no footprints in the gravel path.

A car stopped and the doors opened; withered faces peered out from a midnight-black hearse. A widow stepped out, her elegant hat pulled down low; it blew off and skidded across old, moldy graves. Something creaking rolled passed me, dragging a flag-draped coffin; I flinched. Whenever those processions plod so heavily by, I'm secretly afraid to look. I'm afraid the cold-waxen hand, so naked and near, could be my own.

The somber casket was followed in close succession by a black-draped parade of moist-eyed mourners. Georgetown took on a sacred serenity; it became peaceful, placid, still. Solemnly, I listened to the bugler play, felt a sudden chill.

As the sound of taps was being played, I caught sight of the widow's face which was drawn and hollow with fatigue-etched eyes that spoke of struggle and loss. Suddenly, the soles of her trendy heels collapsed. The widow removed her shoes and stared at them while standing barefoot, bewildered, shaking uncontrollably in the icy green grass.

She hung down her weary head, her thoughts magnifying her worry into fear and her fear into terror.

A short priest in a raven-black robe offered a long soothing prayer. The widow, her two tiny toddlers sat staring at the lavish bronze box. Those still not crying couldn't hold it back when the young mother erupted in loud, choking sobs. Then came the whir of an ungracious motor. The warrior's body descended deep into moist-mud darkness and was left to the mercies of worms and black smells.

Something moved on the ground near Jackie's tombstone. I stepped back, shuddering. In front of her headstone lay an old dog. It was Riley, the closest thing on Earth to an angel's love, the faithful, cuddly stray mutt of unknown age and pedigree that Jackie had adopted and adored like her very own child. He was hungry, weak, and encased in grimy, tangled fur. Riley immediately recognized me and had the strength to lift his head in greeting, but he could do no more. His sad eyes reflected a hint of joy at seeing, once more, someone who loved him.

I knelt on the frozen ground, held him, cried. He licked the tears off my face; then his head sank down again, and he died. I looked up, stared off at the twilight vista, and witnessed a lone sunlit peak in the midst of darkening sky. The next day, Riley was lowered into a grave on a tiny hill above the sun-swept meadows he had loved to run and play in at Argotique.

I walked slowly out of that desolate place, down a lonely street, listening to the sound of my own footsteps. Images of the frightened widow crying, her trembling toddlers, and Riley's shocking death refused to leave me. The weather seemed chilly, but December in Georgetown usually is.

The sun sinking into the horizon compelled afternoon and evening to kiss good night. It was the holidays. The historic, vibrant village resembled a storybook world of glitter, lights, music. It was the midst of the December Merriment-in-Georgetown "happening." The countless tourists walking its cobblestone streets all seemed to be bursting with love, excitement, and joy.

The utmost enjoyment of the holiday season is found wherever there's love. I urgently needed a king-sized dose of that wondrous kind of love. My empty heart felt battered, dried, withered. It was haunted by Jackie's voice on her answering machine, saying, "Hi! I'm not here," the nth time I called after her death.

The air seemed clean, bracing; it was a star-filled night. There was only a crescent moon, but the stars sent down their own bewitching light. I turned up my coat collar, shielding my grief-whipped face as a drowsy numbness pained my senses. I marveled in wonder that what had started out between Jackie and me as sensuous, passionate, forbidden had expanded into something lofty and astonishing.

I hummed a Christmas carol, strolled on, watching frost fluttering in the snow-laden sky amid naked birch trees. Borne upon the wintry breezes, crystals of snow, white and wild, also began falling into the C&O Canal's relaxing waters.

I took out my pipe, found a solitary match in a pocket crease. I lit it, holding the pipe to the tiny flame until it almost licked my finger. So much left behind—so many warm, wonderful memories. All the happiness I'd ever known buried in a frozen Georgetown grave. I exhaled a thin stream of smoke, watched it drift away. Magically, a rich fall of snow beautified the night. A dazzling white owl floated nonchalantly overhead, its shadow dancing on the moonlit snowdrifts piled white and deep.

I could see lights far off across frosted lawns winking through the trees, could hear the sweet sound of voices singing. Beneath towering pines crusted with snow stood a charming old townhouse, its miniature sugar-coated yard accentuated by a delightful snowman. He cut quite a dashing figure in his red scarf, carrot nose, black top hat with a sprig of holly jutting from its crown. It might've simply been a case of projection, but I thought he too seemed a bit sad.

Leaning against a black cast-iron lamppost, I heard the clip-clop as a six-white-horse-drawn crimson sleigh with Santa at the reins wound its cobblestone way out of old Georgetown. Santa's sleigh was bedecked in forest green; the scent of fresh-cut juniper was intoxicating. Close behind, out of the snowy mist appeared smiling, joyful carolers, their eyes twinkling brightly. I watched the oncoming procession wind its way closer, heard the people singing, their crisp voices echoing in the tranquil night air.

I drifted toward the approaching carolers, toward the marching ranks, toward lanterns swinging blotches of light on the historic brick walkway. I watched the carolers stride by, the glowing light of their lanterns fading in the mist. I stood there for an eternity in the cold afterlight of evening, my head down, lost in thought. A profusion of loneliness dripped from my heart onto old memories like a shower of icy rain.

I reflected on the times Jackie and I meandered along picturesque C&O Canal, her cheering me on during rollicking soccer games at Rose Park. After working up an appetite, we'd stop by a charming café, have a cup of coffee and a peanut butter and jelly sandwich. Then we would wrap up the day at a cozy bistro that served French wines by the glass. Summer nights we'd sail along the Potomac, gazing up into the moonlit heavens. Now she, my son have sailed away up to those very heavens, leaving me to wander alone and lonely in a state of exalted misery that feels pitch dark and empty.

I paused in the deep blackness of my loneliness, just then realizing that sadness has no end; happiness does. Downhearted, devouring my own soul, I wandered like a solitary thought alone in the night. Dizzy with overpowering echoes of *déjà vu*, I intended to stroll Georgetown's moon-washed streets till dawn's silvery light. The snow-blanketed avenue was hushed except for the rumble of a passing snowplow along a cobblestone lane that interrupted my thoughts. When I looked up again, the caroling procession was down Pennsylvania Avenue.

The crisp, glistening snowscape decorated sills, trees, and a host of distinctive rooftops. They called Georgetown old even long ago. People now reckon her age in centuries, the way they do with forests. I ambled along her glittering lamp-lit streets past a centuries-old orthodox synagogue, a Catholic church celebrating mass in four languages, a Methodist church that'd been there since the 1700s, past a charming old-fashioned pharmacy and a wealth of one-of-a-kind boutiques. Surprisingly, I discovered I'd wandered down to the waterfront.

I hiked the banks of the Potomac a thousand steps or so. A sad, nocturnal silence was my shadow. Numerous people huddled together in the cold, sleeping, and suffering strange agonies along the river's crystalline borders. Misery permeated the sound of the wind blowing in that bare place. I wondered about the lives of those folks and what had led them to be homeless in Washington, amid all the wealth, glamour, and magic.

I halted on those frozen banks near Key Bridge and gazed out over the gently flowing icy winter river. Colorful boats at anchor drifted to and fro. The only sound was their snapping flags twisting in the wind. The river appeared somehow different that night, seemingly despondent, remorseful that it had taken the life of someone we both loved so dearly. I responded in a faint whisper, "I know how you feel. We both miss her. But it wasn't your fault. She loved you, of that I am confident. And to my utter amazement, she also loved me."

This is the age of the Messiah, some say. But the Messiah will not come in the form of a dazzling celestial being. The Messiah will come to the children of God in the form of dazzling Thoughts of Truth—a Truth that will liberate those who grope about in darkness, fearful of shadows, afraid of things unseen and unreal. I foresee an eventual reevaluation-of-religion-movement, composed of lapsed Christians, freethinkers, and atheists, in which numerous "facts of religion," scrubbed clean of *holiness*, will be found to not be *pure* fantasy.

I'm just an ordinary guy who's given a frank account of the things I've experienced. Perhaps my interpretations may occasionally be wrong. Nonetheless, to the best of my ability to communicate it, this odyssey constitutes my truth.

Eyes that look are common; eyes that see are rare. Those who have eyes to see and who have journeyed through my memoir this far, I hope you too are able to see the true nature of being. Those who have ears to hear, listen to your own soul during moments of quiet reflection. Love's Voice will reveal memories of your own journeys to the realm of peace, joy, and everlasting life.

If you're still unconvinced at this point, it's not because the things I've shared are untrue; it's solely due to my inability to adequately portray this truth. For this, I apologize. I have diligently searched beneath the heap of Man's worn-out and faded words to find the right ones to describe what I've lived through.

I now realize no words I could write would transfer fully this truth to another human mind. I can't tell you any spiritual fact deep within, you don't know already. All I can do is remind you of what you've forgotten. Truth cannot be learned, only recognized. Living truth, ancient and yet ever new, lies within. After "death," you'll uncover the cold hard truth for yourself, and then we shall have much to say to each other on the subject…

A clock chimed in the distance, disrupting my thoughts. I resumed my stroll along the glass storefronts of Georgetown; they captivatingly displayed twinkling winter scenes loaded with adorable holiday characters. Ambling through the soft, slumberous snow, I absentmindedly fingered the mysterious, pulsating blue stone, cuddled up in the folds of my pants pocket.

Suddenly there erupted a thunderous ***BOOM!***

CHAPTER 33

Boom!

There was a startling shift in the heavens! A glittering of whiter-than-white light! I found myself enveloped in brilliant velvety whiteness. Feelings of serenity and sumptuously divine warmth surrounded me. Little by little, this sensation drifted gently into the very core of my being. I could feel an incredibly powerful spirit so close behind my shoulder that I could've touched it with my trembling fingers.

I peered uneasily through the window of a quaint little shop charmingly decorated with reindeer, candy canes, toy trains; I beheld its reflection in the glass. Stunned, I was unsure of how to react. My gaze met the form of a commanding being in a monk's dark, hooded cloak. His face was guarded by the cloak's jet-black hood. He moved with slow, majestic steps. I felt mesmerized by the grace of the being's towering form and regal air.

What happened, I wondered. *Did I inadvertently summon the Power?* Puzzled, I called out, "Are you the Power? The Force? Aviar?"

A booming voice said, **I am the self that I am!**

A sudden breeze blew back the covering on the being's head. The gust revealed a look of dark splendor. Majestic! Beautiful! Terrible! His face was like that of a hawk. It radiated an astonishing blend of power, evil, goodness, and love with a mystical beauty both superhuman and subhuman. An extraordinary icy aloofness emanated from the creature's spellbinding eyes, which startled me by their force.

As if that weren't enough, its riveting countenance virtually glowed with foresight, authority, raw power. What's more, its features appeared deeply marked with lines of regret and pain resulting from an eternity of intense struggles.

My chest tightened and my insides quivered violently. "Who—who are you?"

The specter threw back his head with an arrogant motion. **One who can resolve any despair! I can shorten any gloom or horror you are suffering through.**

"You could do that?" I said with a rise in vocal pitch.

A slight smile curved the frightening features of the hair-raising being. **I could!**

My body posture perked up. "How?"

It lies in the mind, snarled the scary life form. Coming nearer and assessing me with eyes like smoldering lakes of flame, he thundered, **It lies in the power of my mind!**

In the future never peer too long upon the ground; you might miss the vision. Some night when you least expect it, I may again thrust my form through the wispy veil hiding me from you. Simply stated, your blue stone makes you a magnet for forces like me.

Beads of sweat formed on my forehead. "Frankly, you don't look like an angel; you seem more like something from a bad dream."

How wise you are in your ignorance. I feel strongly compelled to share an age-old secret whose time has come.

I felt a quiver in my stomach.

All life is a dream, Jonjaie—but we are not *The Dreamer!*

Frowning, I said in a shaky voice, "In plain English, what does that mean?"

The truth is, you will have to experience it for yourself. We unmask The Dreamer in our own time.

The remarkable spirit then observed me for an instant with a questioning gaze. **Have you misery in need of defeat?**

"I've walked past too many coffins, experienced endless shades of pain. The question of *priesthood versus husband* has tormented me to the brink of what a soul can bear. One summer night I lay half-asleep, listening to the sound of rain on the roof. Cool and comfortable, I closed my eyes, retreated into my spiritual depth—into a place deeper than thought where the restless waves of life are still.

"My soul stood face-to-face with itself. Ungratified priest or husband and father? My heart chose the latter. This can't be wrong!"

There are no absolutely right or wrong answers, only endless questions—and the journey.

"I learned too late that love's the key to happiness. I had real love yet let it slip away. That stupid mistake rages within me and mocks at me. My life's become an open wound full of pus. It festers, rots, won't heal. Wish I'd married Jackie when I had the chance! I'd give anything to unring that bell. But there's nothing I can do at this point to put things right in my life."

Clearly no one can go back and make a brand-new beginning; but one can begin from now and make a brand-new ending. The spirit said in a soothing tone.

"The prospect of living without Jackie's terrifying. Can't stop thinking about her. I don't know what's come over me."

When you love someone genuinely, you have no power over romantic feelings, Jonjaie.

The mind-blowing angel stepped even closer. **One's life, destiny are based in regions beyond human reason. Each experience is simply a lesson God would have you learn. It appears you have learned the lesson of love, although a bit belatedly.**

The love in you, Jonjaie, remains as radiant as a star, as pure as light, as innocent as love itself. That is why your agony shall not eternally endure. What's more, your unyielding

refusal to lose hold of the rock that has steadied and sustained you is truly laudable. Your mate sounds like a real never-to-be-forgotten gem.

Nodding, I said, "Kind of woman I've always dreamed about."

I must now return to what you just could not imagine.

"What's that?" I said with a troubled and baffled look.

Your future!

I heard a gripping noise—a pounding surf-like roaring but deeper, like the beating of a thousand eagles' wings. The noise instantly diminished. The deserted streets blackened once more. The dark-shrouded presence was there. Then it simply wasn't. My soothing serenity also disappeared.

Georgetown's picturesque streets remained silent, except for a little sigh in the wind. I stared in blank apprehensive dismay at the glittering lights decorating Pennsylvania Avenue. Something extraordinary had just happened to me. Frankly, I wasn't sure exactly what it was myself.

Suddenly there was an indescribable, deafening sound. I felt the sidewalk giving away under me. I yelled! My voice echoed strangely. Then I saw the street open wide. I fell or was sucked by something like a powerful magnet into this "opening."

Seconds later I heard a thunderous *Whoosh*! I seemed to be hurled from a great, dark, whirling mass of icy air. My widening, bulging eyes did a double take. I bolted upright to a seated position and cried out, "Where am I?"

"You're at the hospital in Saint Michaels, Jason."

"Jackie! You're alive!"

"Of course! Why wouldn't I be?"

"Because…hospital! Why am I in a hospital?" I said, jerking my head back.

"You were running along a trail. You must've tripped, hit your head on a rock. You've been in a coma for almost three days now."

For a moment, there was utter silence in the room.

"Coma!" I said, a bit frightened, dazed. "It's been more like a whale of a nightmare! Felt so real! It seems like I've come back from a state of being, from some *place*, some*where*," I said confoundingly. "I know I'm not making any sense. I realize my babbling sounds insane. It's just that my 'coma' seemed as real and solid as the chair you're sitting on. It was beautiful, bizarre, illuminating, and frightening all at the same time. In it everyone died: you, Ethan, even Riley! I drifted about alone, angry, depressed.

"Then I died too, went to heaven, hell. Was told incredible, crazy notions about—about *everything*! I was even given a mysterious blue stone by a strange old man. It's all so fantastic! As if that weren't enough, I think I was supposed to remember something vital—to do something involving symbols."

"Symbols! Like what?"

"Can't remember. Yet I'm certain it'll all come back to me in time. But most importantly, soon as the doctors release me, I'm taking you to London, Paris, and Rome. I want us to spend some quality time together—actually, loads of it."

"I don't know what's come over you, Jason, but I like it. Seems like that bump on the head did more good than harm."

"Does Doctor Goldstein concur with your prognosis?" I said, sitting on the side of the bed, smirking; I gave Jackie a playful pinch on the butt.

"That reminds me, I'd better call Abe Goldstein. He made me promise to call him when you awoke. He arranged for this wonderful private room. Best of all, he fixed it so I could sleep on a cot next to you.

"I'm sure he's at your sister Liz's place."

"What's he doing there?"

"If I had to guess, I'd say he was passionately penetrating a special area of Liz's sleek torso right about now."

I hid my face and yelped with surprise, "Holy Shit! How—when did all this happen?"

"Maybe one moonlit evening both reached for your bedpan, casually touched, and magically love came tumbling down. All I know is Liz richly deserves a great guy and Abe's one of the greatest. Last time they were here, if Liz had stood even a pinch closer, she would've been in his hip pocket. What's more, Abe seemed to be examining her shapely body more intensely than he was examining yours," Jackie said, chuckling.

"Liz told me, 'My father's sick behavior compelled a voyage into darkness that's been long and cruel. I sought blackness so complete that I could hide from the ugly truth forever. Since I met Abe, the darkness in me has been brought to light. Now I realize that I'm not afraid of love, but only of what my father's vileness made of it for me.

"'It's been a painfully slow journey, Jackie, but I've finally found someone I'd enjoy spending the rest of my life with.'

"I said to Liz, 'It does not matter how slowly you go so long as you do not stop.'

"You'll also be glad to know James graciously offered to take care of Riley."

Jackie's eyes narrowed, and she started tapping the top of my nightstand with her fingers. "Last but not least, Bobby stopped by with Mama Jones. She brought a homemade batch of your favorite chocolate-covered peanut butter and jelly candy.

"Unfortunately, Bobby's pet nympho, Sunny Day, tagged along as usual. Sunny leers at you whenever she thinks I'm not looking." Jackie paused, said icily, "That bitch!"

"Retract your claws, tiger-lady. I've seen Sunny's boyfriend. I am not her type!"

"If someone offered me the tiniest proof she wanted you, I'd scratch Sunny's eyes out, including her damn eyelids, eyelashes, and eyebrows!" Jackie's gaze met mine; her face softened. "I worried about you so much! I have been here by your side since you were admitted. Barely eaten, hardly slept a wink, and that's the truth! I've prayed for you. Prayed for you every day, all day long. Prayed till my throat was raw!

"If you honestly want to know how I feel, I was terrified I might lose you—afraid little Ethan would be born without a father! To be quite candid, you've got me completely in your power. There isn't a pinch of my love that's not yours. I don't think I could live if I lost you!"

My face tightened. "Don't talk like that!"

"Now, for the first time, I love a man more than I know how to say. I feel you, Jason, in every drop of my blood! I *tremble* sometimes for your happiness."

"Your undressing of love is raw, gripping, powerful stuff!"

Jackie lowered her head. "You're making fun of me!"

"What? No!" I shot back, lightning quick, confused.

Jackie was silent for a moment; she leaned forward with eyes that watered. "Don't break my heart, Jason."

My body went stiff. "*Break your heart!*"

Sliding my arm round her waist, I stole a long, slow kiss. Then I gazed intently into her adorable misty eyes. "Jackie, you've gotta get past your self-esteem issues. You're not that chubby little bookworm from Potomac who nobody loved anymore. You're smart, talented, drop-dead gorgeous. We're as much in love as two people could truly be, and I'm never going to let *anything* part us again. I intend to share your every heartthrob, every sorrow, every joy—forever.

"As for Abe Goldstein, call him in the morning."

"Jason he's a super friend. We should at least—"

"Jackie, we'll call Abe, Liz, and all the others later. Tonight let's leave the world behind. How've you been holding up?"

"I'm just a very pregnant, gloriously happy bride-to-be who's greatly relieved her fiancé has finally come out of his coma."

My mind was racing. "We're engaged!"

Jackie held up her left hand. "Remember this lovely gold ring you placed on my finger barely more than a week ago? You're just experiencing a little temporary amnesia. Abe said it happens in cases like this. We were here in Saint Michaels on a weekend getaway. You fell while jogging the morning after you proposed."

"Didn't get down on one knee in front of a bunch of strangers, did I?"

"Frankie insisted! He overheard you proposing. Wouldn't have it any other way!"

"Frankie the waiter was there?"

"He was at the restaurant with his gorgeous ex-wife. Seated just one table away."

"Frankie—married!" I stammered in a disbelieving voice, my mouth falling open.

"They had two children."

I squeezed my eyes shut. "Please tell me he wasn't in drag!"

"His suit was Italian. His wife, French. Both were elegant.

"I saved the best news for last; he covered the check and insisted on helping me pick out a wedding dress. Even asked to be my maid of honor!"

"What—what'd you say?"

"I was speechless!"

"So am I!" I said, staring at Jackie in amusement.

I still couldn't believe it was all real. I sat opposite this attractive woman whose eyes were full of dreams and mysteries; I gazed at her in sheer silence. I felt bewildered. One instant I seemed to recognize her, the next, she seemed a complete stranger to me.

"Jackie—is it really you?" I said, excessively swallowing.

In a soft, throaty voice, Jackie said, "Turn around—don't look." Laughing it up, I complied. Then I heard a giggle in my left ear, and something as feathery as a butterfly's wing brushed my cheek on that side. I twisted to look, and quick as a flash, I heard an impish chuckle in the other ear while another butterfly stroke came on my right cheek. Then dainty beige panties were blown across my eyes. She flashed a sexy smile and uncovered her smooth, perfect breasts that were as sweet to look at as they were to touch.

I watched Jackie's playful performance, pretending just for kicks to be shocked. To me, she appeared incredibly fetching. I couldn't resist her. "Even pregnant, you're gorgeous as hell!"

"Flatterer!" Jackie said with a flushed appearance.

Lust stormed within my loins. The primitive torment tossed, swelled, boiled, and ran over. I took Jackie's naked body into my arms; she licked her lips. Then lowering her voice, she said, "All this can be yours. It's up to you!"

"You're pregnant! I'm in the hospital! You beautiful, shameless hussy—you're gonna kill us both." I grinned.

Jackie thrust out her chest, gave me a seductive, lingering touch. Sensuously parting her legs, she said, "You complaining?"

"No! I'm ready to die bravely."

We kissed, fondled, and embraced with torrid, breathless intensity. Her soft, warm, moist folds of love urgently enveloped my firm, hot, potent length of lustfulness. Jackie proceeded to use every art she knew and surprised me with a few spur-of-the-moment enchantments I'll never forget! I was gifted with lovemaking sizzling with primitive vigor. Fiery passion took hold of us both. We surrendered totally to its rapturous spell. It swept us out of our bodies. We dwelled once more where the enchanted live.

After being struck to the bone in an orgy of breathless delight, Jackie quickly surrendered to the spell of sleep in my arms. I lay there on this night of exhilarating splendor in a state of unabridged amazement. Through some incredible mystery, I'd apparently persuaded my *mystical emissary* to grant me a second chance at love. My heart was riding upon the wind, walking on moonbeams, ecstasy filling its core; it was dwelling in rapture raised to the nth degree.

I'd defied the power of death to keep Jackie from me. Now she was lying beside me once again, exquisite, radiant in her own internal light. One thing's for sure: there is no life until you've loved intensely, unlimitedly. Had our love been any more genuine, I might've gasped with wonder. I marveled not at the magic of the moment. I was lifted so far above marvel, joy, bliss that I had no standard by which to measure the experience.

The hours eased quickly by. An overpowering impulse seized me. I walked over to the closet. As I took my trousers from the wooden hanger, a tiny blue object fell to the floor. I picked up the pulsating pebble and strolled pensively toward the window. I touched the stone to my lips. A shudder ran through me; exquisite pleasure overwhelmed my senses. I froze, entered a mysterious, timeless, enchanted place.

Astonishingly, a floodgate opened and a waterfall of lost memories came rushing back into my mind. I wondered: *Could the incredible knowledge I just recalled possibly be true? Could my fantastic mystical voyage have actually been real?*

Tipping my head back and closing my eyes, I stood there awed, marveling at the wondrous journey I'd undertaken to arrive at this most treasured moment. Forming a steeple with my hands and pressing them to my lips, I glanced out the room's oversized window, looked up, spoke with an emotion-rich voice into the starry, postmidnight sky:

"Let the morning star of this new day shine upon a peaceful, thriving, loving world. A world where You, our Source—The Eternal Formless Figure in the Mist—are welcomed as You are in truth, not as people think You are or as people think You ought to be.

"My brethren portray You in king's robes, Mystical Mother-Father who brought forth the morning. Most are too blind to see You are a rushing brook, the wind in the trees, the sun and sand through which we run. Yet sometimes You are a magnificent tigress; we, a field of daffodils, and You romp, frolic through us. You spoke to each as You made us then walked with us silently out of the midnight black. You whispered, 'Go to the limits of your longing, yet let yourself not lose me in power, in wealth, in the nearby plane of enigma mortals call life.'

"According to the immortal plan begun when time was born, each soul has an important role to play in Creation. So for better or worse, we all will leave our mark on human history. The truth is God thinks by means of us, experiences life by means of us. We are the instruments through which the glorious Mother-Father pours Its life forth.

"The sacred rights of humankind are not to be searched for among antique documents or old musty books. They are written with a thunderbolt throughout the entire volume of our nature by the hand of God Itself, and they can never be erased by mortal power. That's why we have an inalienable right—a holy duty to God—to love ourselves and to live a happy, deeply satisfying life.

"As if that's not enough, it seems my amazing grandfather was right after all:

> "'*Sometimes truth is stranger than fiction. And that's a fact! I'm not being facetious!*'"